As a security contractor, government civilian and military officer, Myke Cole's career has run the gamut from Counterterrorism to Cyber Warfare to Federal Law Enforcement. He's done three tours in Iraq and was recalled to serve during the Deepwater Horizon oil spill. All that conflict can wear a guy out. Thank goodness for fantasy novels, comic books, late-night games of Dungeons and Dragons and lots of angst-fueled writing.

www.mykecole.com
Twitter: @MykeCole

Praise for the *Shadow Ops* series:

'A great book'

Patrick Rothfuss

'Hands down, the best military fantasy I've ever read'
Ann Aguirre, *USA Today* bestselling author of *Perdition*

'Blending military fiction with urban fantasy, this novel was an absolute blast to read – action-packed, tightly written and plotted, intense and utterly gripping'

Civilian Reader

'Propulsive . . . Highly entertaining . . . Reads like an intense game of Dungeons & Dragons'

Kirkus Reviews

'This action-filled adventure holds the reader's attention with occasional glimmers of hope that someday the oppressed magic-users might finally force those in power to respect them'

Publishers Weekly

'[Cole has] created a military urban fantasy for the twenty-first century, with all of the complexity and murky gray areas that entails. The action is sharp and vivid'

Tor.com

'It is a book that will have something for fantasy readers of every kind and pays homage brilliantly to Tolkien's legacy . . . Myke Cole is an absolute gift to urban fantasy and military fantasy sub-genres'

Fantasy Book Critic

'A nonsto

Fantasy Faction

By Myke Cole

Control Point
Fortress Frontier
Breach Zone

Reawakening Trilogy
Gemini Cell
Javelin Rain
Siege Line

MYKE COLE

SIEGE LINE

HEADLINE

First published in Great Britain in 2018 by
HEADLINE PUBLISHING GROUP

1

Cataloguing in Publication Data is available from the British Library

ISBN 978 1 4722 1194 1

Typeset in Zapf Elliptical by Avon DataSet Ltd,
Bidford-on-Avon, Warwickshire

Printed and bound in Great Britain by CPI Group (UK) Ltd, Croydon, CR0 4YY

Headline's policy is to use papers that are natural, renewable and recyclable
products and made from wood grown in well-managed forests and other
controlled sources. The logging and manufacturing processes are expected to
conform to the environmental regulations of the country of origin.

HEADLINE PUBLISHING GROUP
An Hachette UK Company
Carmelite House
50 Victoria Embankment
London EC4Y 0DZ

www.headline.co.uk
www.hachette.co.uk

For Wilma Pearl Mankiller,
who always fed the right wolf

The wolf that wins is the one you feed.

— NATIVE AMERICAN PROVERB

Author's Note

A glossary of military terms, acronyms and slang can be found at the back of this book.

Fort Resolution is a real place, and the Athabasca Chipewyan a real people. I've done my best to do both the place and the people justice, but in the end, I serve the needs of the story above all. Any errors are entirely my own.

Prologue
Snow Snake

Mankiller threw the spear.

Her grandpa had taught her to play snow snake when she was six, and thirty-six years later, the motion was second nature. Two shuffling steps, the arm whipping low, gently. She gave a little hiss of air as she released the shaft, not because she needed to, but because she always had.

The spear did look like a snake, a thin brown line skipping through the unbroken snow, sending up white puffs that revealed the thick ice of the frozen lake beneath. There was a soft thud as it struck the hay bale dead center, sending a spray of yellow across the white. Grampy always pumped a fist when he got a bull's-eye, but Mankiller stood frozen in her throw. Moving too quickly after letting the spear go could alter its course if you weren't careful.

Joe Yakecan snorted hard enough to set the fur edges of his hood waving. 'Weak. That'd been a caribou, he'd 'a jus' sniffed it and gone back to sleep.'

'Ain't a caribou,' Mankiller said, still not moving. ''S a hay bale.'

'Ya think?'

Mankiller didn't answer, trying to take in the moment

like Grampy told her. The sun reflecting off the smooth white surface of the snow. The sharp bite of the air against her nose. The spear pointing like a compass needle perfectly centered in the hay bale's side. *Save the good ones, Wilma*, Grampy always said. *Remember 'em for the times when the sun won't come up.*

Yakecan must have taken her silence for anger, because he added, 'I'm just kiddin', Sheriff. It's a good shot.'

'Great shot.' Mankiller finally turned to look at him, giving the tiny quirk of her hard line of a mouth that passed for a smile.

Yakecan looked like God had come down from heaven and stapled half a dozen animals together. He was as big as a grizzly, had a face like a Saint Bernard. His wide cheeks hung down to his neck, chins overlapping just enough to tell the world that this was a man who liked beer, fried chicken, and chocolate. He was as furry as a beaver, and it didn't help that he was always cold despite all that blubber. He covered himself in even more furs until he looked like a walrus.

Yakecan had been her deputy since Mankiller came to Fort Resolution after her tour in Afghanistan. She'd read his file from the Army, knew what he'd done in Iraq. Their first job together had been putting cuffs on Albert Haida after he beat up his wife. Haida was even bigger than Joe, and a mean drunk to boot. Haida had resisted, and turned out to be more than Mankiller had bargained for. She knew that he'd have hurt her, maybe even killed her, if it hadn't been for Yakecan. He might be as big as a grizzly, but Joe was as fast as a striking eagle. Haida was on his back, knocked senseless, before Mankiller knew Yakecan had even moved. When the Yellowknife cops came to take custody of Haida, they'd asked Mankiller how she'd got so banged up. Yakecan could have said Haida'd gotten the drop on her, that she'd needed him to save her. But he only stood there, smiling. *I've got you covered*, that smile said.

She never forgot it.

Yakecan smiled his usual smile now, open and easy, the kind of smile that made you feel rested. 'A great shot,' he conceded. 'Even harder jus' goin' over the open snow.'

'But you think you can do better.'

'Hell, I know I can.' Yakecan's smile got so big, his cheeks disappeared inside his hood. 'Watch thi—'

A howl split the air, long and mournful.

Yakecan's smile vanished. He glanced up at the bright sun, bent to retrieve the rifle where it lay propped against a small boulder of ice.

She put a hand on his elbow. 'C'mon, Joe. You know that . . .'

But Yakecan's eyes were scanning the horizon, the gun already at the low ready. 'All right, Wilma. Can't be too careful . . .'

He only called her by her first name when he was frightened.

'Joe, look at me.'

His eyes stopped scanning, met hers. She stared back. Her calming stare. 'Sergeant's Eyes,' her lieutenant had called them.

'Joe, they're howling in the middle of the day. You know what kind of wolves these are.'

As if on cue, another howl sounded, closer this time. Yakecan's eyes snapped away, and Mankiller followed his gaze to a low line of stunted trees, jagged gray limbs struggling through the thick snow.

A small shape, gray as the dead growth around it, detached itself from the trees, slunk along the icy ridge, its head turned toward them. Two dots burned in the center, brighter than the shining snow around them. Twin dancing fires, silver threaded with lines of thin gold. Wilma looked into the wolf's eyes for a moment, and then it turned its head away, trotted along the ridge.

Mankiller gave the animal a tentative wave, felt her heart swell. She swallowed the emotion, kept her hand on Yakecan's elbow until he finally sighed, letting the rifle barrel dip to the ground. She couldn't resist crossing herself with her other hand.

It was a moment before she could speak. 'Come on, Joe. It's your throw.'

Yakecan didn't move, tracking the wolf's progress. 'I don't like turnin' my back on 'em.'

'You know they ain't gonna hurt you,' Mankiller said. 'Might be your grandma under that fur.'

'Yeah,' Yakecan said, setting the rifle down. 'S'pose you're right. Might as well show you how the game is played, eh?' The smile was back, but there was no warmth in it now. 'Need the spear.' He nodded toward the brown line sticking out of the hay bale.

'That's right,' Mankiller said. 'So, go get it, Deputy.'

Yakecan's laugh was genuine. 'Aye, ma'am.'

He trotted toward the spear, froze as another sound echoed toward them.

Not a howl this time. A low, rhythmic thudding. Distant but growing closer.

'What's that?' he asked.

'Helicopter?' Mankiller asked, but she already knew she was right.

'Yeah. We expectin' anybody?'

Mankiller shook her head. 'Probably droppin' off hunters, or a research team.'

Yakecan looked doubtful. 'We'd have heard 'bout that.'

Mankiller grunted. 'Maybe they're jus' . . . passin' through.'

'We're in the middle of fuckin' nowhere, boss. Nobody jus' passes through.'

Mankiller grunted again. The rotors were much closer now, loud enough for the roaring of the turbines to be heard. 'Sounds like a pretty big helo.'

'Military,' Yakecan said.

'Why would they be flyin'—'

'They wouldn't. At least, they never have before.'

Mankiller nodded. 'Think we better get out of sight.'

Yakecan moved with his deceptive speed, snatching up spear and hay bale in a single smooth motion. Mankiller retrieved the rifle and led the way toward an icy gulch carved by the runoff of a day that passed for warm this far north. The melting snow had washed a sizeable pile of bracken down the slope, forming it into a makeshift lean-to when it refroze.

Yakecan fell in behind her instinctively, crouching his way down the slope, his tread surprisingly quiet despite the frozen crust over the snow. He held the hay bale easily in his huge arms, his breathing smooth and even. Ever since Afghanistan, Mankiller had always felt uncomfortable with her back exposed. On the few occasions she ate at Bullock's in Yellowknife, she always chose a chair with her back to the wall. Not when Yakecan was around. She kept her eyes front and scrambled under the frozen cover, felt Yakecan jostle her shoulder as he joined her.

The roar of the helo engine was even louder now, the dull *whup whup whup* of the rotors sounding like they were just over the ridge where she'd seen the wolf. Yakecan wedged his giant head up toward the icy cracks in the sticks overhead, his broad cheek pushing against her own with all the grace of a drunken bear.

'Move, you idiot,' she whispered.

He ignored her. 'I can't see it, boss. Sounds like it's right over us.'

'Calm down,' Mankiller said, grabbing a fistful of Yakecan's hood and pulling his head back. 'Let me look.'

The film of ice over the sticks refracted the light, a prismatic spray of color that danced at the edges of her vision, but Mankiller had been squinting practically since the day she was born. There was an art to it, a thing that every Dene mastered by the time they were a few years old, scrunching your eyes just enough to keep you from seeing stars, but not so much that you missed what you were after. Yakecan said it was bright like that in Iraq, only it was the sun shining off the sand instead of the snow.

The bright white outside first wavered, then bent, then finally resolved as she got her eyes just the right degree of closed. She swept her gaze up, over the hill, unerringly tracking the echo of the rotors to their source in the ice-blue sky.

A huge rotor churned above a gray oval, no bigger than a football from this distance. It looked a little like a much larger version of the American Black Hawks that had shuttled her from hilltop to hilltop in the Korengal Valley, jammed shoulder to shoulder with soldiers from Montreal or Kansas or Tbilisi or any other of a legion of places she'd never see.

But the Army helos were green or, if they were one of the newer ones, that weird digital camouflage pattern that was so easy to see, it might as well have been hot pink. This one was a silk gray that matched the tenor of the sky. The angles of the airframe were different, softer and more numerous, a deft series of geometrical tweaks that made her eye want to slide right off it. Army Black Hawks flew rough, huge wheels dragging at the air, the shuddering cabin making all inside sore, tired, and vaguely sick after just a few minutes in the air. This helo was as smooth as a bullet. No lights. No weapon pods. No markings of any kind.

She could feel Yakecan digging in his pockets, jostling her as he searched. 'Mighta left my field glasses in he—'

'Don't need 'em.' Mankiller cut him off, elbowing him back. Just as there was an art to squinting, there was an art to seeing too, and the two were closely related. She squeezed her eyes shut more, shrinking the light down further. Her peripheral vision vanished, but in the tunnel that remained, all was made clear.

It took her a moment to reacquire the helo, but once she did, it looked much as she'd expected. The huge bay doors were open, a gunner hidden behind the hardpoint affixed to the airframe. Mankiller could see the telltale lined cylinder of a minigun barrel, the long cable of the ammunition feed snaking inside.

'Is it military?' Yakecan asked.

'Looks like a Black Hawk, only four times the size,' Mankiller said. 'Loaded for bear. They have twenty-mil cannons on your ride in Iraq?'

'Yeah,' Yakecan said. 'Vulcan or some shit. That what's on there?'

'I count two. Guns out. Barrel's moving a bit; someone's harnessed up and watching. Good thing we got cover.'

'What, did a war break out in Canada?'

'Not as far as I know.'

'Well, shit. Is it American?'

'How the hell am I supposed to know?'

Yakecan sounded frustrated. 'Well, what flag's on the tailboom, boss?'

'No flag.'

'There's always a flag.'

'No flag. No number. No nothing.'

'That's some spy shit.'

The tenor of the rotors changed from a dull thudding to a higher-pitched whirring, the blades sounding almost frantic as they took on more load.

'It's comin' down,' Mankiller said.

Yakecan crowded up toward the gap in the sticks again. 'Why?'

''S a transport,' Mankiller said. 'Probably lettin' folks off.'

'Why the heck would they let folks off here?'

The helo sank lower and lower, so fast that Mankiller's stomach dropped a little, just as it would have had she been inside during so rapid a descent. It was a skilled pilot who could lower a bird that big that fast without crashing it, but it wasn't a pilot overly concerned with the comfort of their troops.

The pilot stopped the descent roughly fifty feet off the ground, jerking the airframe so hard that it practically bounced, making Mankiller wince. Ropes came flying out of the airframe, three to a side, thick black hawsers covered in some kind of fabric that she guessed would make them quiet as a whisper. A moment later, the first of the operators came down them. They were uniformly dressed in white, trousers bloused into combat boots, tactical vests and packs, carbines and pistols with enough mods and add-ons to make any holster-kisser drool. All were painted the exact color of the snow around them, slashed through with gray that mirrored the landscape. Even using her squinting trick, it was hard for Mankiller to focus on them.

Yakecan couldn't miss them now. 'What the . . .'

The men reached the end of the ropes, dropping into

the snow, guns coming up to the low ready, spreading out from the circle of the helo's rotor wash. She'd seen armed professionals execute the same maneuver every day in the war. These people knew their business. But the soldiers she knew had worn patches on their sleeves, flags of the nations that paid for all the expensive gear they carried. These operators were utterly unmarked, the gray-white surface of their parkas and tac vests marred only by the straps that held their ammunition and armor.

With a click, the belly of the airframe swung open, issuing a grinding roar almost as loud as the turbines spinning the rotors. Military transport helicopters usually offloaded from the ramp in the back, and Mankiller watched in shock as a giant metal cage lowered directly out from the bottom of the airframe, sinking slowly earthward on a thick metal cable. Somewhere in the cabin, there had to be a capstan, a winch, and one hell of a motor.

She looked at the helo's modified airframe, the gear on the operators moving out beneath it. The metal winch and cable. All customizations off aftermarket military hardware. Whoever outfitted this mission had an awful lot of money.

The cage thudded into the snow, the cable detaching and hauling skyward.

Yakecan didn't even bother speaking now. He stared, jaw open so wide, his chin disappeared below the parka's zipper.

The operators had turned. They were pointing their weapons inward now, at the cage.

She did her squinting trick, brought it into better focus.

It writhed.

For a moment, she had the crazy idea that it was filled with fat, gray snakes, giant pale worms, sliding and crawling over one another, but a moment later, her vision came into full focus and she saw they weren't worms.

They were people.

The cage was packed with people straining and clawing at the bars.

'Jesus.' Yakecan crossed himself. 'Are they naked?'

'Yeah,' Mankiller said. 'All of 'em.'

'They'll freeze. Ten minutes tops.'

'No,' Mankiller said. 'I don't think they will.'

The people in the cage were naked, but their skin was the color of old fish, the dirty gray of the snow on a well-used highway.

Their eyes burned. Like the wolf.

A shape appeared in the cabin door, leaning on the gun hardpoint. Now that Yakecan was looking at the cage and the ring of operators around it, he found the helo easily, eyes tracking up as the last of the cable winched in and disappeared inside the cabin. His eyes were wide enough already, but they looked like they were going to pop out of his head when they settled on what Mankiller was seeing.

'Is that a . . . a guy in a suit?'

'Yup,' Mankiller said.

'His head looks like a lightbulb.'

'He's got a white hood on, or a mask or somethin'. It's stretched over his face.'

'Wilma, what the hell is going on? This is the weirdest damn thing I've ever seen in my life.'

Mankiller nodded, put her hand out for the rifle. 'We're going back to town. We'll come back for the ATV later. I don't want to be throwin' up that much noise now. We'll walk.'

Yakecan looked grateful for the chance to put distance between himself and the spectacle outside their crude shelter. He immediately turned to scramble out from beneath the woven canopy of broken branches and ice, crouching as he made his way up the gulch's far side. 'You think they see us?' he whispered.

If they do, there ain't much we'll be able to do about it, Mankiller thought, but she said nothing. They hadn't brought snowshoes, relying instead on the ATV's broad tires. Now, hurrying on foot, they crunched and plunged through the crust on the surface of the snow with each step, making so much noise that it seemed to Mankiller they'd be heard even over the rotors. Her shoulders tensed with every step, waiting for a shot to ring out, to hear footsteps coming behind her.

But in the end, there was nothing, and before long, the rotors were fading in the distance and she and Yakecan entered a stand of stunted trees, following a winding logging trail that would see them back to Fort Resolution in an hour or so.

Mankiller plunged on in silence. There was a rhythm to labor, a drumbeat that reminded her of drum gatherings, or the beats they played at hand games. Following that beat let her lose herself in work, feeling only the steady pulsing of her feet crunching on the snow, rather than her aching legs, or the cold nipping at her nose.

But Yakecan had no ear for that rhythm. Fast and strong as he was, he didn't like hard work, and Mankiller could always tell when he was avoiding it. It was the same when he was frightened, or hurting, or almost anything else. He talked. He talked and talked and never stopped.

'Boss.' Yakecan sounded winded, the snow sucking at his boots, sapping his strength as much as it did hers. 'What the hell just happened?'

'I don't know.'

'Yeah, but . . .' Yakecan began. There was more to the

stuttering cadence of his speech. He wasn't just winded; he was hesitant, timid. He was deeply frightened.

Mankiller didn't blame him. So was she.

'Who were they? What do they want?'

'Nothing good,' Mankiller said. The light sputtered in the trees around them. The sun was going down, and it wouldn't be long before the temperature plunged. 'Come on.'

Chapter One
Public Servant

One Week Earlier

James Schweitzer fled into the darkness and the city of Des Moines roused itself to action.

Senator Don Hodges bounced on his shoulder, grunting with each jostling step. His suit was rumpled along with his elder-statesman dignity; only his hair remained perfect. Schweitzer's magically heightened sense of smell was nearly overwhelmed by the generously applied spray that held it in place.

'Put me down, damn it!' Hodges managed winded gasps between bumps. 'I can walk.'

'If you can walk, you can run,' Schweitzer said, 'and if you can run, you can run away.'

'I know I can't outrun you,' Hodges choked. 'I'm not stupid!'

'You're a politician,' Schweitzer replied. 'It's a job requirement.'

The explosions and gunfire in Hodges' office had drawn the attention of the police. Schweitzer could see the dancing colors of police car lights reflecting off the undersides of the thick clouds that hung low and close over the city. A living man wouldn't have noticed anything, but death and reanimation had made Schweitzer's senses more powerful. He knew how he would look to a passerby, a ragged corpse, missing an arm, running as fast as a speeding car, as silent as a stalking cat.

Or he would have been if it hadn't been for the man flopping on his shoulder. Hodges wheezed. 'Where are you taking me?'

'Somewhere we can talk.'

'We can talk right here.'

The lights may have been faint, but the sirens were loud enough to be heard by anyone. It sounded like every cop in the world was converging on the building Schweitzer had just fled.

'Nice try,' Schweitzer said. 'I don't think the cops would take too kindly to a zombie kidnapping a Senator. I'll put you down as soon as it's safe.'

'I'll call them off,' Hodges said.

'Do you think I'm stupid?' Schweitzer asked.

Hodges went silent for a moment, and Schweitzer could almost hear the gears turning in his head as he tried to figure a way out of this. But it was just a moment. The man thought fast. 'I just watched you take out my entire security detail in the blink of an eye. Surely, you can handle a few cops.'

'Surely, I can,' Schweitzer agreed, 'but you're forgetting that I'm one of the good guys here. I don't want to hurt other good guys.'

'Well, you're hurting me now.'

'I'd hardly call you one of the good guys, and I'm not hurting you. Not yet.'

Hodges went quiet again. Schweitzer's real gut had stopped churning the moment he died, but his spiritual gut more than made up for it, his anxiety's phantom limb. He hated threatening Hodges, even if it would secure his cooperation. Schweitzer's death and resurrection had made him into a horror-movie monster, but those changes were physical. His heart and soul were still his own, and he had fought like a lion to keep it that way. He wasn't a man who bullied others. Life in the SEALs had made him no stranger to the utility of violence, but that didn't mean he liked it. Stealth was key to his former role, but he had always preferred a stand-up fight, facing the enemy, showing the world who and what he was.

He thought of his wife, Sarah, and his son, Patrick, both gone now, one to the afterlife, the other to the care of his former enemy. He remembered how they'd looked at him as they'd fled through the woods from the Gemini Cell. Sarah, eyes forced wide so as not to betray her disgust; Patrick showing his naked fear of what his father had become.

Hodges might be his prisoner, but he hadn't taken the Senator to punish him. Eldredge had said that Hodges was the man who knew about the Cell and authorized its funding, which meant he was the man who could help Schweitzer shut it down. But that was nothing compared to the fact that threatening Hodges made Schweitzer feel like the monster he knew he looked like. His spiritual gut churned with the worry that if he acted that part often enough, it would eventually become a distinction in search of a difference.

Schweitzer raced for an unlit alley snaking its way between two office buildings, windows dark at this time of night. His augmented hearing brought him the sharp intakes of breath and mutters of every nearby security guard, street sweeper, or couple out for a late-night stroll. There were precious few of these in Des Moines. It was a city that truly died after dark.

He could smell the metallic tang of the Des Moines River, the soft stink of garbage and motor oil. He shouldered a

Dumpster aside, careful to keep Hodges' head clear, then burst out into the streetlights, speeding toward the railing that separated the asphalt from the dark water flowing beneath it.

Hodges, seeing what was about to happen, began to thrash. 'Wait! What are you . . .'

Schweitzer leapt the railing and yanked Hodges' body off his shoulder, locking the Senator close to him and arrowing him into as graceful a dive as he could manage. Despite his best effort, there was still quite a splash, and then all sound was swallowed by the river water enveloping them.

Hodges flailed, but he might as well have been a child, for all the good it did him against Schweitzer's magical strength. Schweitzer pinned him easily in place, his single arm as unyielding as an iron bar.

He kicked his legs, righting them and preparing to swim to the surface if Hodges panicked and swallowed water. But the Senator kept his cool, and Schweitzer could feel the muscles in Hodges' throat constricting as he pushed the air down out of his neck in an effort to keep his lungs inflated.

Schweitzer swallowed his surprise and took advantage of the reprieve. He kicked along, moving them underwater for about thirty seconds. Schweitzer could easily hear the rapid beating of the Senator's heart. When the oxygen starvation made the beats come slower, Schweitzer kicked off again, this time up to the surface.

'Don't screa . . .' Schweitzer was whispering in Hodges' ear, but he needn't have bothered. Hodges wasn't screaming, wasn't even gasping. He was taking short, shallow breaths, hyperventilating like a rabbit. That was good. They had taught Schweitzer to do that in training, a little trick that would help them stay down longer.

Schweitzer kicked off again, dragging them underwater until he heard the slowing of Hodges' heartbeat, then surfaced so he could take a breath. 'Just relax,' Schweitzer said. 'I'm not going to drown you.' But above the water, Schweitzer had a good scent of the blood in Hodges' carotid. He was frightened, to be sure. Excited, but not panicked. Not by a long shot. Hodges ignored him, taking one deep breath, then hyperventilating again.

Schweitzer could hear the whirring of helicopters, the screaming of sirens, but they were much fainter now, the response focusing on the Senator's office. Schweitzer moved down the river, away from the sounds.

At last, he dragged the Senator up onto the rocky shore under a bridge overpass, the tons of metal and concrete above them occasionally vibrating beneath a passing truck. Hodges lay on his back, gasping freely now, giving full rein to his lungs' desperate scramble for air. He coughed.

'You okay?' Schweitzer asked.

Hodges waved a hand weakly.

'I told you I wasn't going to drown you.'

'I figured . . . I figured if you wanted me dead, you would've done it back in my office.'

'I don't want you dead.'

Hodges propped himself up on his elbows, spat. 'What do you want?'

'What's with that breathing trick?'

'What?'

'You hyperventilated each time we surfaced.'

'I was panicking. You try being dragged under the water by a living corpse.'

Schweitzer shook his head. 'Don't fuck with me. They taught me that in BUD/S. Purges the CO_2 in your blood so you can hold your breath longer.'

Hodges opened his mouth to respond, then finally shrugged. 'You know what I did before I got elected?'

'I know you were in the CIA. I always figured you were an analyst.'

'Maybe I was, and maybe I wasn't. We all had to go through training before we went overseas.'

'What'd you do for them?' Schweitzer asked.

'How about you answer my question first?'

Anger flared. He was the stronger here. He had saved Hodges' life and now Hodges was in his control. He would decide who asked the questions. *No, that's how jinn think. You have to be smarter.* If he was going to get what he wanted from Hodges, they would have to work together.

'I need your help,' Schweitzer said.

Hodges looked genuinely shocked. 'What the hell could I possibly help you with?'

Schweitzer thought of Sarah stopping him in the forest as they fled the Cell what seemed a lifetime ago. Still alive, still his wife, him still clinging to the illusion that they were together, as they had been when he still breathed. *Wherever you are, they will come. It's the government. They don't give up. They don't run out of money. You have to stop this threat.*

Sarah was dead now, her body torn to bloody scraps, her spirit drifting in the soul storm. Alongside all the others he'd known and loved. His brother, Peter. His best friend, Steve. His mother. *So many dead.* But his son was still alive. Even now, Patrick was on his way west in the care of Dr Eldredge, the scientist who'd overseen Schweitzer's resurrection before going rogue himself.

Sarah was right. If he ever wanted a chance to be reunited with his son, if he ever wanted Patrick to have a life that consisted of something other than looking over his shoulder, he'd have to take the fight to the enemy.

He'd have to find a way to stop the Cell in its tracks.

Hodges took Schweitzer's silence for consideration. The burnt-sugar smell of his adrenaline increased. 'You *are* going to kill me.'

'That depends on you,' Schweitzer said. It was a lie and he knew it. Schweitzer wasn't above killing, but killing Hodges would solve nothing. If Hodges was going to help him, he'd have to be breathing to do it.

But it was too soon to play his whole hand. He crab-walked a step closer to Hodges. 'Tell me what you know about the program that created me.'

'I don't know a goddamn thing abou . . .'

Quick as a striking snake, Schweitzer seized Hodges by the throat and stood. He locked his hand precisely around the Senator's windpipe, knuckles digging up into the hypoglossal nerve. He would be able to breathe, but the pain would be extreme.

Hodges gave no sign of his discomfort other than a slight tipping of his head to ease the pressure. Schweitzer recognized the 'four by four' breathing technique he'd been taught in BUD/S. Four seconds in and four seconds out. Not a guarantee, but it would go a long way toward keeping Hodges from fainting or even wincing. Whatever he had done for the CIA, he was no analyst.

'I told you not to fuck with me.' Schweitzer put an animal growl into his voice; he hoped it was enough to convince Hodges that he wasn't human and therefore wasn't prone to human sympathy.

But Hodges didn't so much as blink.

Schweitzer snarled and lifted the Senator off his feet, letting his spinal column take his entire body weight. He couldn't hold him like this for long without injuring him. 'Just because I'm a good guy doesn't mean I won't hurt you until you tell me what I want to know.'

Hodges actually smiled. He gurgled around Schweitzer's vise grip, saliva bubbling out of the corners of his mouth. 'Look at you. You're exactly what you look like. A cartoon monster. Same on the inside as on the outside.'

A spike of hot rage mixed with sick shame. He remembered Sarah looking at him, fighting to keep the disgust off her face. Before he knew what he was doing, he'd shaken Hodges hard enough to rattle his teeth.

Hodges coughed, choked. His face had turned dark purple, his cheeks beginning to swell, but he kept smiling. 'You're not going to hurt me, Jim. I know that much.'

The rage bled out of him, and Schweitzer sagged. He could play the monster, but in the end, it was just play. He had been a monster to his targets and their lackeys when he'd still worked for the Cell. He had been a monster to his wife and son. *Why not be the monster? Why are you trying so hard to be human? You're not a human anymore.*

But when Schweitzer searched his dead heart, he knew the answer. Rightly or wrongly, he still wanted life. Not the parody of his current existence, a soul driving a dead machine, but *real* life. *I didn't have enough time*, he thought. *I was robbed.* The world owed him years, and all he knew was that he couldn't possibly collect if he acted the animal it was trying to make of him.

He jerked his fingers open, and Hodges slid down to his feet, hands going up to his throat, massaging the red blotches beginning to form there.

'You're right; I'm not going to hurt you.'

Hodges smirked. 'I know.'

'But you're a dead man anyway,' Schweitzer said. 'The Cell will come for you. You'd have been dead back in your office if I hadn't been there. Worse, you'd be walking around with something like me looking out through your eyes.'

'You're lying,' Hodges said, but Schweitzer could smell the terror in the chemical makeup of his bloodstream, could hear it in his quickening heart.

'You know I'm not. There's only one thing that can fight this force you supposedly know nothing about, Senator, and you're looking at it.'

'And that's what you want? To fight them?'

Schweitzer nodded.

'So . . . why save me?' Hodges asked. 'You're the only force that can fight them, go do it.'

'You also know that this program you know nothing about employs many creatures just like me,' Schweitzer said. 'I can't fight them all. Not myself. But you can shut the program down.'

Hodges sighed. For a moment, Schweitzer thought he would continue the I-Know-Nothing line, but he only shook his head. 'It's not that simple.'

'The Director is dead,' Schweitzer said. 'You know that? He's living dead, like me.'

Hodges head jerked up, the color bleeding from his face. 'How do you know that?'

Eldredge, Schweitzer thought. But he wasn't about to sell out his one ally, the man who even now was caring for his son. 'I have my sources.'

'If we're going to trust one another, then we have to trust one another.' Hodges spread his hands, smiling. At least he had a sense of humor.

'We'll get there. Did you know? About the Director?'

Hodges was silent, and Schweitzer could almost see him considering whether or not to lie to Schweitzer. At last, he settled on the truth. 'No, but now that I think of it, I'm not surprised.'

'You have to shut it down, Hodges. Give the order.'

The adrenaline content of Hodges' blood stayed level, as

did his heartbeat. He didn't move. He was telling the truth.

'You're crazy, Jim. Even if I could shut it down, think of the strategic edge it will give America's enemies. You think the Chinese don't have a similar program? The Russians? The Iranians? They do; they all do.'

Hot anger rose. 'I don't care. *This* program killed my wife and son, so *this* program goes down.' *Let him think Patrick is dead. Until I am certain he won't hurt him, I'm not revealing anything.*

'Patrick's dead?'

Schweitzer said nothing. Sometimes, silence was the most convincing answer of all.

'How?' Hodges looked genuinely stricken.

'None of your fucking business.' Schweitzer put some bitterness into his voice. 'Life on the run isn't easy on kids.'

'I'm sorry, Jim.' He was. His chemical scent confirmed it.

'You have to shut the program down. To save your own life if not anyone else's. They're not going to just let you go. They made a move on you, and you got away. They won't stop until they have you.'

'I told you it's not that simple.'

Schweitzer knew he was telling the truth. He'd been a captive in the Cell's facility for months. He knew that it was probably funded to the tune of billions, protected by administrative line items burrowed deep into military databases. It took years to decommission even a small military program.

It didn't matter. 'Nothing's ever simple with you fucking politicians. Solve the problem. Find a way.'

'Jesus, Jim. You were in the Navy your whole life. You know how these things are.'

'I also know that if someone high up enough wanted

something done, it got done. You're about as high up as they come. Make it happen.'

Hodges was quiet for a long time. 'I . . . Maybe there is a way. I'll need some help.' His face lit up; his hands twitched. He looked up at Schweitzer, grinned. 'Your help.'

Schweitzer didn't like that smile. 'What help?'

'I thought we were going to have to "get there" in the trust department. You aren't giving up all your secrets, I'm not giving up all of mine. Either way, we have to work together on this, so let's stop wasting time.' He turned to go.

Schweitzer put a hand on his shoulder, gently pulling him back. 'Not good enough. I need to know what you're planning here.'

Hodges sighed, but he didn't move. 'And I need to know how you can be so sure the Cell is gunning for me. Do you have any idea how many chits I'm going to have to call in to shut this operation down? And all based on your word.'

'Not my word, your experience. Did you miss the woman I tossed into your office? Did you miss the undead monster rampaging through the building?'

'There can be many explanations for both of those things without buying yours. Now, I'm willing to help, but that means you trust me and you help me. Make a decision, Jim. Or do whatever it is you're going to do with me and then fuck off to some hole and di . . . rot . . . Shit. You don't rot, do you?'

Schweitzer shook his head. 'I don't shit, either.'

Hodges laughed. 'Come on, Jim. I believe you. We have the same goal here. We can work out the rest after the job's done.'

'Fine,' Schweitzer said, 'but I will be watching you, and if you betray me . . .'

Hodges' smile melted into irritation. 'Save it, Jim. Do you honestly think I would ever let a magical being as important as you go? I know what you mean to the future of this government's study of magic. Our interests coincide here. You have to believe that.'

Schweitzer didn't believe that, not in the slightest, but he didn't see what other choice he had. He couldn't fight the Cell on his own, and Patrick would never be safe until he beat them. Hodges was his one chance.

Schweitzer took it.

Chapter Two
Head Man in Charge

The Director could hardly remember a time when his heart still beat. He hadn't been dead that long, not nearly as long as Nandhimitra, the spirit he'd been paired with when he'd reawakened after the explosion to find he was no longer alone in his own body.

Over the months, the Director learned enough to guess that Nandhimitra had been in the soul storm over two thousand years. The spirits of the dead projected an image of how they envisioned themselves, and Nandhimitra appeared to the Director as a heavily muscled giant with an elephant's head. It was the icon of some ancient civilization. The Director didn't care to find out which one. Nandhimitra had been like all the ancient souls the Cell used, feral and blood-starved, mad for the warmth of human flesh and the heartbeat they could never have themselves.

Nandhimitra said that in life, he had been a great warrior. The spirits always were. But the Director had been a better one, the best who'd ever lived. Which was why Nandhimitra was gone, leaving him in sole possession of his corpse. The first one in the history of the program to exorcise the jinn from his own dead body. Behind the stretched fabric of his white hood, his eyes burned solid silver, the beautiful argent of a soul wholly his own.

The Director had spent the entirety of his new existence in the presence of those whose eyes burned gold, a metal-colored stamp of weakness. Gold eyes meant a soul could not compete with the predatory energy of the spirit paired with it, allowing itself to be pushed out because it lacked the strength to remain.

Even Gruenen, the South African mercenary, hadn't been able to hang on to himself when he was paired with Schweitzer's wife Sarah. In the end, she'd won control of his body long enough to use his own magic to defeat him. He couldn't be called a Silver Operator. Not truly.

Every single operator they'd created went Gold. Every single one, save himself.

Not just you, one other. He pushed the thought away. It made him angry, and anger was seldom useful.

But the thought wouldn't be denied. He had been the greatest in afterlife as he had been in life. Until Schweitzer had fled to a Virginia farm, dug in his heels, and won. It didn't surprise him; he and Schweitzer were cut from the same cloth. If anyone were to equal his signature achievement, it would be Schweitzer.

In life, he'd had a name not much different from Schweitzer's, a common pair of syllables as fallible as his flesh. Part of his reward for winning the struggle for his own corpse had been to dispense with his name. He liked his title better. It matched his intention and his ability both. He was the Director.

Even after he'd passed every test that could be thrown at him, moved through crucible beyond crucible to stand shoulder to shoulder with the greatest warriors of his age, even wearing their coveted symbols, bathed in the glow of their enduring brotherhood, he had wondered, *Am I the best among them?* He had read of warriors who had transcended their humanity, their greatness making them into icons, gods. Alexander. Hannibal. Frederick. Eugene. Sherman. The question begat a suspicion nursed in the deepest corner of his mind. He pondered it as he fell asleep each night, the hard terrain digging unnoticed into his back and shoulders. Was he great? Truly great?

And it was now, in this new unlife, that he found the answer he'd sought.

He became dimly aware of a staccato clicking. Mark's chattering teeth, interrupting his reverie. His augmented eyes showed the deep red glow of her body heat faded to a pale pink as her core temperature cooled dangerously in the refrigerated room. She would have stood there without complaint, her precious heat bleeding out until she succumbed, rather than disturb him. Mark was a mighty warrior, but she was still a human, imprisoned in a fragile cage that would fail her at a moment's notice. 'Ah, Mark. My apologies; I've been neglecting you.'

Mark wasn't her name, of course. Calling all males by female names, and vice versa, was just one of the hundreds of rules that ensured the Cell stayed beneath public notice, layers upon layers that succeeded where grand gestures failed.

She tried to answer, stuttered out a reply too jumbled by her gray-blue lips to be understood. Mark certainly deserved to die for letting Eldredge past her and into the Director's freezing office. It had led to the discovery of the Director's identity and Eldredge's eventual flight. He'd certainly killed humans for less, but he also knew that that was what she wanted more than anything, and the exquisite punishment of forcing her to continue drawing breath was too beautiful to be passed up.

And besides, losing Eldredge and Dadou Alva, his most powerful Sorcerer, had made him cautious. Humans might be weak, but they weren't an inexhaustible resource, especially not the strongest ones he needed to help him run his organization.

He placed a gloved hand on her shoulder and gently steered her through the huge steel door and out into the warm air of the office outside. He pushed Mark into her chair behind the reflective surface of her ebony desk. She slumped gratefully into it, shivering and rubbing her hands together, steam rising from her broad shoulders. The Director listened to her heartbeat, watched the steady red glow of her body heat rise, and knew she would be fine. Within moments, her hands and ankles were bright red and swollen. She must be in considerable pain, not that she would ever show it.

'I'm s . . . s . . . sorry, s . . . sir,' she finally managed.

'No, no, Mark. It's I who should apologize. I was lost in thought.'

She looked at him in a tangle of surprise and adoration. Snot streamed from her nose, marring her perfect makeup. Her face was as blocky and hard as the rest of her. 'No excuse, sir,' she said. 'I didn't want to disturb you.'

'If it means you're going to freeze to death,' the Director chided her, 'I want to be disturbed.'

'If I die' – she smiled – 'you'll make good on our deal?'

'Not if you kill yourself or by inaction allow yourself to be killed,' the Director reminded her. 'I'll have no suicides in my ranks. We're professionals.'

'I'm almost forty, sir.' The petulance in her face made her look decades shy of that. 'My body isn't getting any more suitable.'

'It's not your body I'm worried about, Mark. When I judge your spiritual strength to be sufficient, I'll take your life myself and personally supervise putting a jinn into your corpse, but you don't want to be a ravenous, mindless

Gold, do you? It's one hell of a fight to wrest one's own body away from a jinn. I should know.'

'You were the first, sir.'

'That's right,' the Director said with a sudden heat, 'not Jim.'

He could smell the adrenaline dumping into her warming bloodstream, could hear the acceleration of her heart. He was frightening her. 'Yes, sir.'

'It's a tough fight, but I think you're up to it. Do you?'

'I'll damn well try, sir.' The truth was that she would never be able to stand against a jinn, that she was weak and desperate, that she would go Gold the moment the Summoner bound the spirit into her. It didn't matter; he needed a living hand to manage his affairs now that Eldredge was gone, and if he was to have hers, he must feed her desperate notions of one day joining the ranks of the undead.

'Be patient, Mark. I promise I won't forget you.' He let pass unremarked the fact that she had almost frozen solid precisely because he did forget her. She straightened, shivered.

'Are you well enough to see to some things for me? Or should I call someone else from the pool?' he asked, pitching his voice just flat enough to make it a threat.

'No, sir. I can handle it.' That was good. She might be a little slower than normal, but it was important to keep one's people used to enduring hardship in the name of the cause. Also to remind them who was boss.

'Good. I want to review the incentives. Can you have them gathered in the central holding cell?'

'Review them, sir? Personally?'

'That's right.' He wasn't surprised at her incredulity. He could count the number of times he'd left his refrigerated office over the past few years on a single hand. But all that was before Schweitzer had escaped, then Eldredge. Before Dadou had been killed. 'I think this organization could benefit from a little more of a personal touch from leadership.'

'Yes, sir.' Mark stood, swayed. The prolonged cold had shunted too much blood to her heart and lungs, desperately trying to keep them warm at the expense of the brain. He gave her even odds of fainting and made no move to catch her. His magically enhanced ears could hear her jaw creak as she gritted her teeth. She took an unsteady step, kept her feet. *Well done*. He would keep her.

Her walk grew stronger with each step as her body temperature increased and her heart pumped faster. The Director followed her to his personal elevator. He understood the temptation to lean against the wall inside, but Mark resisted it, showing him how strong she was. How worthy of the gift she so desperately wanted and could never have.

The elevator opened onto the cell level, the long central corridor studded with the freeze and burn nozzles that could turn the space into either an inferno or a blizzard at the touch of a button. Video cameras relayed the length of it to the same control center that Eldredge had used to make good his escape. There were only two guards down here, more a formality than anything else. The Director doubted that any two men, no matter how they were equipped, would stand a chance against an escaped Gold. Faced with the choice of either stationing an army in the cramped hallway or relying on the automated freeze and burn nozzles, the Director had gone with the latter.

The two guards down here were among the few to have seen him before, and while he could still smell the adrenaline spike of their fear, they didn't show it as they stood to attention. He had long since taken to making sure every inch of his skin was covered. The suit, the hood, the gloves and shoes, all were ancient and rotting, and that was fine. Mystery was an important part of fear and control, and so long as he kept the basic shape of a man, kept his appearances minimal, and did not speak, humans would spin whatever stories they liked, telling themselves he was a dangerous eccentric rather than a monster. Mark's slavish devotion was only one of a range of reactions humans might have when they discovered that their master was a corpse.

He followed Mark in silence, making his way beneath slots that hid access hatches that could seal the corridor at a moment's notice. Cell doors lined the walls, each one more than two feet thick, with a small pane of transparent palladium that granted a fishbowl view of the cell beyond.

The incentives had individual cells that ringed a large central pen. The doors here were of normal thickness, with reinforced glass instead of transparent palladium. Mark pressed a button next to the door and louvered steel panels opened to give a better view of the interior. At the same time, the internal doors popped open and a few of the incentives emerged, blinking, into the central chamber.

Their orange prison jumpsuits were clean, and apart from a few days' growth of beard, they looked fit enough. The Director listened to the sounds of the guards' breathing, judged that they were far enough away not to be able to hear the crooning hiss of his voice. 'Only three?' He twitched a pinky toward the reinforced glass.

'Five, sir,' Mark said. 'Two aren't coming out, for some reason.'

The Director listened, pinpointed their heartbeats, confirmed the count was accurate. 'We need seven.'

'Why, sir?'

'We deployed everything we had for Schweitzer. I need all the Gold Operators rounded up and brought back immediately.'

'Understood, sir. But we don't have another two. That will take time.'

'Surely, someone on my staff has committed an unpardonable offense.'

'It's a disciplined shop, sir. As per your orders.'

'Get me volunteers, then. Tell them it's a chance to cover themselves in glory. You know how to make people do what you want, Mark.'

Her smile at the compliment was so small as to be imperceptible, but the Director missed nothing. 'Yes, sir. I'll figure it out.'

The incentives, and any volunteers who joined them, would likely not survive, but the Director didn't need them to. He only needed their warm blood and beating hearts to tempt the Golds into the cage he'd use to bring them back.

'I want the op run tonight. All the Golds back here and ready for another mission. Get them restrained or frozen so the technicians can effect any needed repairs.'

'You have a plan, sir? Someone to replace Dadou?'

'I'd like to pursue your lead.'

Now her smile was obvious. 'It's thin, sir.'

The Director said nothing. Let her think that it was thin, that his own sources hadn't corroborated the intelligence. 'Still. We should investigate it.'

'Just some folk tales, sir.'

'Just some? How many, specifically?'

'Eight, sir.'

'Do you think it curious,' the Director asked, 'that there are eight existing folk tales, all dating from the same time period, and all confined to the same local region?'

'I do, sir. That's why I brought it to your attention. Still, I'd like to have more to go on before deploying.'

'Fort Resolution has a population of under five hundred. The entire region has fewer than 7,500 souls. I would be shocked to find two documented folk tales that matched up, let alone eight. Why do you think so many people would be so eagerly telling the same story?'

'Not a lot to do in the Northwest Territory.' Mark shrugged.

'*Not a lot to do in the Northwest Territory* means kids having sex in the backseats of cars. It means drinking and firearms accidents. If there are eight matching folk tales, it is because people are very excited about them indeed.'

'Sir, if we're going on a rumor here, do you think it's smart to depart with so many of the Gold assets?'

Her questions were growing irritating. 'I think I know what I'm doing,' he said. 'Don't you?'

Mark's head snapped forward, taking in the silent stares of the incentives beyond, their hands waving for her attention. They wanted a lawyer. They wanted to know why they were being held there. They wanted out. 'Yes, sir. Sorry, sir.'

'Good. How soon can you have the Golds back here?'

'A day, sir? Maybe two? You never know with them.'

The Director knew better than anyone. 'Back in their pens by midnight. Show me what you're made of.'

Mark stiffened. It was an impossible task, and he could feel both her terror and her excitement at the challenge. 'I'll tr . . . Yes, sir.'

'Good. I'm going back to my office. I'll eagerly await your report.'

'Sir.'

She knew better than to accompany him back to the

elevator. He returned to his office and shut the door. His laptop had gone into sleep mode, leaving the room in inky blackness, the frigid air wrapping around him. It wasn't entirely true that the magically resurrected dead did not rot. Better to say that they rotted very slowly, and he could both see and feel the thin layer of bacteria at work on his dead flesh, their movements slowing and finally stopping under the barrage of the cold.

No room could ever be said to be fully dark, and so long as there was even a shred of light, the Director could find his way. He could just make out the figures of the Golds he'd come to think of as his bodyguard. They had claimed to be brothers when Jawid had drawn them together from the void. Three souls bound so tightly by love and obligation that to bring one was to bring them all. It had taken the Director a month to find suitable bodies for all three, and he never regretted it for an instant. Eldredge had dispatched one of them, and the other two now stood patiently in the darkness, golden crowns and pectorals flashing to the Director's magically augmented eyes. Since Dadou's death, he no longer had a Summoner capable of providing the direct translation he'd always used in the past, but he'd taken the precaution of teaching himself a few Proto-Uto-Aztecan words. He used them now. *Go, soon.*

Xolotl spoke. At least, that's what it called itself. The Director had his doubts. Its remaining brother called himself Quetzalcoatl, which seemed the height of hubris. It didn't matter. They worked his will, and that was enough. *Living, soon?*

They wanted the same thing he wanted, a living body to inhabit. The warmth of live flesh enclosing them, the thudding of a beating heart to count the passing seconds. They believed he could give that to them. He had come so close with Dadou. That was why they obeyed him. That was why they stood patiently in the darkness, resisting their urge to tear Mark to pieces, to bathe in her blood. That was why they were loyal. And the Director knew that the very instant they ceased to believe this, they would be just like any other Gold – wild, vicious.

Yes, he replied. Their shared vocabulary was maybe twenty-five words, but successful marriages had gotten by on less. Besides, less time spent talking was more time spent working on making good on their demands.

He opened the laptop and pulled up the file titled OP_ FROZEN_KEEP. He rolled his spiritual eyes. Military types and their hyper-macho names for operations. Even when he'd been in the military himself, he'd thought them ridiculous. Mark had been hip-deep in that culture since she'd enlisted straight out of high school, and it showed.

Mark had pivoted off an article in the *Journal of Ethnography*, a cataloging of Athabascan folk tales titled 'Magical Death'. It was interesting in its own right, but she was right to think it wasn't solid enough to commit so many of his Gold resources. That decision was driven by another report, this one from his source in the Canadian Security Intelligence Service.

NW_DILIGENCE got eyes on target on 05 JAN before being driven back by extreme winter conditions. Inability to make contact and concern about suspicions of subject's granddaughter, who is Sheriff at Fort Resolution, forced call for extract at 1738Z on the following day. NW_ DILIGENCE acquired three images (attached) of target's 'pet' wolf described by NW_DILIGENCE_FWD_103. FWD_103 described animal as a 'cousin', lending credence to NW_DILIGENCE's assertion that target is reincarnation of 'Lived-With-The-Wolves', a local werewolf legend.

Images are grainy, and first two are unremarkable but provided for context. Third image needs color enhancement as wolf is facing camera, but is cause for medium confidence assessment attached. Canadian Security Intelligence Service has provided subsequent analysis and clarified that there are no indicators of Necromancy. Mapping and Charting Establishment confirms that the photo has not been digitally manipulated.

If the report was to be believed, and the Director had never had reason to doubt DILIGENCE's reporting before, then a powerful Summoner was living somewhere in the Canadian wilderness. The Director didn't know where in that wilderness he was, but he *did* know where the Summoner's granddaughter was, and that was as good a place to start as any.

The Director brought up the third attached photo and looked over it again. The Canadian Mapping and Charting Establishment had enhanced and colored it to the extent it could, but the picture had still been taken through a blizzard at its peak, and while several overlays were used, the majority of the resolution came through long-wavelength infrared. The resulting image was grainy and broken, a vague black shape standing out against a snowy hillside. Far below, the hamlet of Fort Resolution glowed like a star to the LWIR sensor.

The image was date- and time-stamped, with Military Grid Reference System coordinates punched in next to a description of the location – S. SLAVE REGION. NW TERRITORY. The flat expanse was so featureless that anything that wasn't a tree or a rock would stand out.

The Director could tell the shape was a wolf, but only just. Its neck was bent, long tongue lolling out to lick the snow. It had a patch of tangled fur on its shoulders that made it look hunchbacked.

But the Director only cared about its eyes, which were staring directly into the camera lens, as if it had known it was being photographed.

They were balls of flame, the color enhancement showing them as gold as Aspen leaves in fall.

Chapter Three

In from the Cold

'There's a rest area off the highway about a half-mile that way.' Hodges pointed. 'Should only take us ten minutes to walk.'

'What do we need a rest area for?' Schweitzer asked.

Hodges quirked a smile. 'To rest.'

Schweitzer turned his leering skull face toward Hodges. 'Do I look like the kind of guy who appreciates a good joke?'

Hodges shrugged. 'Thought maybe all that being dead might lighten you up.'

Schweitzer said nothing.

Hodges sighed. 'Look, Jim. I need to do a few things before I can help you. The first is getting us out of here quietly. The second is making contact with some people. Please help me to do that. If we're going to work together, then let's start the work. Otherwise, get rid of me, or kill me, or do whatever the hell it is you plan to do.'

Schweitzer paused, considering, then finally reached out for Hodges' waist. The Senator spun away from him, but even down an arm, Schweitzer was more than twice as fast, and within a moment, he had Hodges bundled back over his shoulder. 'Where are we going?'

Hodges sighed, head dangling almost level with the gray skin of Schweitzer's ass. 'There.' He pointed.

Schweitzer leapt, and Hodges tensed as they sailed up and into the darkness. 'Why take ten minutes,' Schweitzer said, 'when you can take five?'

They thudded down, Schweitzer crouching not to absorb the impact to himself, but to take some of the pressure off his cargo. A long, grassy rise ended at a giant disk of light centered around a trio of gas pumps jutting up from a stretch of broken asphalt. There was a single car idling near the stub of a building.

'Why are we here?' Schweitzer asked as he eased the Senator to the ground.

'Pay phone.'

'They still make those?'

'It's the only one left in the state. I pulled some strings to make sure it was kept in place. There's a little old lady that lives nearby, refused to get a smartphone. Best human-interest story of my career.'

'Why don't you have a smartphone?'

'I do,' Hodges said. 'It's back in my office. You want to head back over there to pick it up? Maybe you can talk your way through the police cordon.'

'What if someone recognizes you?' Schweitzer asked.

Hodges was already stripping off his suit jacket and unknotting his tie. 'So much of what people see is expectations and context. In a suit, I'm a Senator. In my under-shirt and slacks? I'm just another white guy who got drunk, yelled at his wife, and got thrown out of the house.' He started up the hill.

Schweitzer caught his elbow. 'Hodges . . .'

The Senator shook off his hand. 'Jim, this isn't my first rodeo. You have to trust me.'

Schweitzer let him go, and in moments, Hodges had entered the circle of light, leaning casually on one of the giant poles supporting the overhead lights, grabbing the receiver, his back turned from the small building and its giant glass window. If the clerk inside noticed him, they gave no sign.

Hodges punched a number into the stainless steel face, then returned to his slouch, phone cradled between his neck and shoulder. He spoke softly, his breathing smooth and even. Nothing looked out of the ordinary. Training. Schweitzer recognized a professional when he saw one.

Schweitzer dialed his hearing down through the lower frequencies, filtering out the hiss of the wind and the rasp of the waving grass, to focus in on Hodges' soft voice. The Senator didn't stay long on the phone. Schweitzer only had time to catch the final words before Hodges hung up and trotted out of the light and back down to where Schweitzer awaited him. '. . . four one four zero three three. I say again, four one four zero three three. Sunoco on Garage and South Fourteenth Street. Immediate.'

Hodges reached Schweitzer's side, his face lit. His breath was coming fast, from excitement, not exertion.

'What the hell was that?' Schweitzer asked.

'A little code I use with my staff for emergencies. You never know who's listening.'

'That's secret-squirrel even for me.'

'I worked at the CIA. I chair the Senate Select Committee on Intelligence. You learn a thing or two about tradecraft.'

'So, what do we do now?'

'We wait.'

They didn't have to wait long. Within minutes, a small green sedan pulled onto the asphalt just outside the circle thrown by the sodium lights over the gas pumps. The driver got out, went around to the back of the vehicle, deep in the shadows. It was too dark to see anything but the driver's vague shape – male, pudgy, and balding – but Schweitzer's augmented eyes could see him as clearly as if it were a bright day. He was unzipping his pants, groaning loudly, making a great show of pissing in the bushes, without the actual pissing.

Hodges was already up and moving toward him, and Schweitzer followed until the Senator turned to him. 'Stay here.'

'What are you . . .'

'Jim, we've come this far. I'm not just going to ditch you. I wouldn't destroy you and there's nothing to be gained by leaving you. Just trust me. That's one of my people.'

'I'm coming with you.'

'Jim, you'll scare him half to death. Stay here.'

If you're going to trust him, then you're going to trust him. If Hodges was planning to spring a trap, he was going to need more than this dumpy guy in khakis and a polo and a car too small to carry anything threatening.

Hodges emerged and the man gave up the pretense of urinating. Schweitzer dialed his hearing back in to listen. 'Sir, how's it going?'

Hodges ignored him and went around to the vehicle's trunk. 'Pop it, Noah.'

The man used the remote to comply, and Hodges began to rummage inside, emerging a moment later with a suit on a hanger and a hooded sweatshirt. He turned toward Schweitzer, then spun back to Noah. 'Do you have your lucky hat?'

'I always have my lucky hat, sir. You know that.'

'Give it to me.'

'Sir?'

'Give it to me.'

'Sir, it's my lucky hat.' Steel came into Noah's voice.

'Do I look like I'm joking here, Noah?' Hodges matched it.

Noah sputtered, gestured, caved. A moment later, he was reaching across the driver's seat, then handed Hodges a dirty white ball cap, the brim so curved it was practically a threadbare tube.

'Thank you. Now get in the car, and don't turn around no matter what you do.' Hodges took the cap and raced back to Schweitzer, tossing the pile of clothing at his feet.

'Put it on.'

'A suit?'

'It's my spare. I always keep one in the trunk of the campaign car. Hoodie too, in case I need to hide my identity. The cap will hold the hood out further, create a shadow. Keep your head down so he can't see your eyes.'

Schweitzer began tugging on the suit. 'This isn't going to work.'

'With anyone else, I'd agree, but Noah's one of my people. He's been paid to not ask questions for over fifteen years now. He'll keep his mouth shut long enough to get us where we need to go.'

'And where is that?'

'Washington.'

'The state?'

'The capital. You wanted someone who can help us; that's where she is.'

Schweitzer forced one of his thick thighs into the trouser leg, felt the fabric strain. 'This is too small.'

'So, rip a seam. It doesn't have to look good, just cover you.'

'Si . . .' Schweitzer stopped himself. He wasn't a living man anymore; he didn't owe a Senator, particularly not this Senator, any particular deference. Yet the old habit was still comforting. *It means there's still something of the human left in you, something of the man you used to be.* 'If he's one of your people, can't I just go up there and you can tell him to shut up?'

Hodges rolled his eyes. 'Jim. Have you looked in a

mirror lately? He may be one of my guys, but he's still a guy. He's not going to understand . . . this.' Hodges indicated Schweitzer with a sweep of his arm. 'People need comfortable lies, Jim. He'll know there's something wrong, but so long as it isn't staring him in the face, he'll take what I give him. Now get dressed. I'll give you a wave when everything's ready.'

Hodges sprinted back to the car as Schweitzer finished struggling into the suit. He did wind up splitting seams in the trousers, on the back of the thighs and through the crotch, but nothing that would be obvious once he was sitting in the car. His missing arm made the shirt and jacket a challenge to get on, but it also meant there was plenty of room. The hat barely fit on his broad skull, so misshapen and notched from the punishment it had endured over the past few days that he might as well have been trying to put it on a cauliflower. He wrapped the hoodie on over the rest, making sure the fabric was draped far out over the cap's brim, leaving his face in shadow.

Schweitzer's augmented hearing could make out Hodges speaking to Noah as clearly as if they were standing right next to him. 'Keep your eyes front,' Hodges said.

He could hear the creaking of the leather seat as Noah began to turn to look at his boss and checked himself. 'Sure thing, but can you please explain to me what the hell is going on?'

'Someone is going to be joining us,' Hodges said as he stuck his hand out the open window and waved. Schweitzer jogged up the hill, smoothly opened the back-seat door, and slid in. Noah started and began to turn toward him, but Hodges stopped him with a hand on his shoulder. 'I am very concerned about my guest's privacy, Noah,' Hodges said, a warning in his voice. 'How long have you worked for me?'

'Fifteen years, sir. Give or take.' Noah's voice told Schweitzer that his mouth was dry, and Schweitzer could smell the terror in the chemical makeup in his blood.

Hodges' voice went gentle. 'Have I ever given you a reason not to trust me?'

'No, sir,' Noah answered without hesitation. 'Not once.'

'Then trust me now. Eyes front, and drive.'

'Where are we going?'

'The airport. We're flying to DC.'

Noah began punching up the dashboard phone. 'Sir, if you'd just told me, I would have called . . .'

'I'll call Justine.' Hodges was already raising his phone to his ear. A moment later, Schweitzer heard the click of the connection. 'Justine, it's Don. How soon can you have Eric on the flight line? Any copilot is fine. We're heading there now.'

Schweitzer focused his hearing on Noah, ready to spring if the man stopped the car, or turned around, or risked a glance in the rearview mirror. It meant he couldn't hear the other side of the Senator's conversation, but he figured the greater danger was in the front seat.

'That's fine,' Hodges went on. 'We're heading there right now. Oh, one more thing? Just the pilots. No crew. And, Justine? No crew means no questions. We'll take care of ourselves on and off the plane. Just have the pilots close the cockpit door and keep it closed until we're off. Yes. Yes, that's right. I know you do. Justine, the last thing I want is to do interviews right now. The press are going to go nuts as it is, and I don't want people knowing there was an attempt on my life. It's going to be a nightmare if folks know it was my office. I want out of town until the press on this dies down. What? I don't know. Say I was already there. There the whole time. Then say I was in the air. Just say they were going after another target that happened to be in the building. Okay, do that. I will. Thanks. Bye.'

The car had pulled off the road and onto the busier street, and Schweitzer sank down into his seat. In a few minutes, Noah pulled off onto a dark access road, and Schweitzer could make out the airport's control tower in the distance. Noah drove in silence, navigating them through a switchback that took them off the deserted road and onto an even narrower two-lane bit of cracked blacktop that ended at a low metal gate beside a guard shack. Even in the darkness, Schweitzer could read the sign: RESTRICTED – AIR OPERATIONS AREA. ONLY AUTHORIZED PERSONNEL DISPLAYING VALID SECURITY BADGES ARE ALLOWED BEYOND THIS POINT. OFFENDERS SUBJECT TO ARREST AND PROSECUTION.

A guard seated in the shack snoozed by the light of a computer screen and started awake as Noah waved a badge in front of a reader and the gate rolled back. Schweitzer could hear the low whine of jet engines sucking down air as they spun up.

The car pulled inside, the gate rolling slowly closed behind them, and at last came to a stop fifty feet from a small jet. Schweitzer recognized it, a C-37, a twelve-passenger shuttle popular with government and business executives. Back when he'd still drawn breath, he'd sat on board one of these planes in plain clothes, looking for all the world like a businessman instead of a SEAL, bound for Bogota and the kind of mission where uniforms were frowned upon.

A red-haired woman, looking young enough to be Hodges' daughter, stood waiting to greet them in sweatpants and a hoodie that matched Schweitzer's own, her face still puffy from sleep.

Noah rolled down the window and Schweitzer lowered his chin toward his neck, shrinking deeper into the shadows. 'They're getting prepped now,' the woman said. 'What's going on?'

'Nothing is going on,' Hodges said. 'I am flying to DC to be out of here before the press storm breaks. You are going back to bed once we're in the air.'

The woman snorted. 'Fat chance of that. We'll have to make a statement tomorrow morning. Explain all this.'

'This is why I pay you the big bucks, Justine. You figure out a way to explain this. I'll figure out how to save the nation from ruin.'

Schweitzer could hear the muscles in her face stretch into a smile. 'Who's this?' Schweitzer belatedly reminded himself to move the muscles in his chest, simulate the rising and falling motion of a living, breathing man.

'This' – Hodges' voice was a warning – 'is someone who's accompanying me to DC.'

'He won't even let me look at him,' said Noah. 'Don't bother.'

'Sir,' Justine began, 'if you're in some kind of trouble, I'd appreciate a heads-up, because this is the kind of shit that can—'

'I am in some kind of trouble,' Hodges said, 'but it's not the kind you can help me with. We're going straight to Langley once we touch down.'

Justine paused. 'Sir, are you sure that—'

Hodges cut her off again. 'Justine, have I ever, in all the years we've worked together, asked you to keep your mouth shut and let me handle something?'

Now Schweitzer could hear her jaw working. 'Is this the first time, sir?'

'I'm afraid so.'

Justine sighed. 'So, just let you get on the plane and figure it out from there.'

'You are the most resourceful person I have ever met.'

Hodges' voice was genuine. 'The only reason I'm not working for you is because you don't want it as badly as I do.'

Justine was silent, and for a moment, Schweitzer had a creeping sensation that she would snake a hand out and snatch back his hood, but she only sighed and drummed her fingertips on the window. 'Have a safe flight, sir.'

Schweitzer let his head rise a fraction of an inch, just enough to make out Hodges' warm smile. The man had a politician's gift for seeming like he actually gave a damn. 'I'll be watching the news for your statement.'

Justine wheeled and walked toward the low metal Quonset hut that was the flight line's only structure, and Hodges leaned forward and put a hand on Noah's shoulder. 'Thanks, Noah. Just drive straight home and get some sleep.'

'I don't like this, sir,' Noah said.

'You work in politics.' Hodges clapped him on the shoulder. 'Who said anything about liking it?'

He stepped out of the car, shut the door lightly behind him, and beckoned for Schweitzer to follow. Schweitzer did, single hand thrust into the suit's pants pocket, head down so low that he navigated by following the sound of Hodges' footsteps.

The Senator's instructions had been followed to the letter. The airplane cabin was empty, the cockpit door sealed. The interior was much as Schweitzer expected. Deep-cushioned reclining leather chairs circled a wooden table polished so brightly it shone. It was set with a service that was probably worth more than a car, and divided by a long groove that Schweitzer knew concealed a video monitor. The money on display was staggering and what Schweitzer had come to expect from the ostentation taxpayers afforded America's ruling class.

Hodges ignored it all, heading straight to the cockpit door and shouting through it. 'I'm on board. Go ahead and get us to Reagan. Stay in the cockpit until you know we've deplaned, then head on home.'

The pilot answered over the aircraft PA. 'Got it, sir. We'll be on the ground at Reagan in two hours and twenty minutes.'

Hodges turned to Schweitzer and held a finger to his lips, then settled himself at the head of the table and began punching buttons on a desktop phone. Schweitzer stood, unaffected as the plane began to taxi, his balance so perfect that he may as well have been a statue, and Hodges paused in his dialing to gesture Schweitzer into a chair. Schweitzer stared at him, and he shrugged. 'You're making me nervous.'

Schweitzer took a seat as the plane tipped skyward and the phone call went through. The voice on the other end sounded tired. 'NCS Watch.'

The National Clandestine Service. Hodges was calling the CIA.

'Senator Don Hodges, blue blue one one niner white.'

'Standby. I confirm you at blue blue one one niner white. Go ahead, sir.'

'SAD Watchfloor, please.'

The CIA's Special Activities Division was its paramilitary branch. Many of Schweitzer's brothers in the teams went to work for SAD when they got out of the navy.

There was a buzzing click and another bored voice answered. 'Watch.'

'Senator Don Hodges. I need you to connect me with the boss, please.'

A momentary pause and intake of breath as the watchstander registered the request and verified the identity of the caller passed from the main switchboard.

'I'd say you'd be waking her up if she ever slept, sir, but either way, she'll be ornery getting a call this late.'

'Don't I know it. Put me through.'

Another buzzing click, and then steady beeping as the call connected.

The voice that answered was alert but clearly shrugging off the traces of sleep. There was the slightest hint of an accent that Schweitzer immediately identified as Persian. 'Don, praise God. I've been watching what happened in Des Moines.'

'I'm fine.'

'What the hell happened?'

'I'll tell you when I'm on the ground. We're coming into Reagan. Can you have a driver meet me on the tarmac?'

'Of course. You want to go to the Hay-Adams?'

'No, I want to go to your office, and I want you to meet me there.'

'Jesus, Don. Can you give me anything?'

'Only that I'm in trouble and I need your help.'

If the urgency in his tone riled her, Schweitzer couldn't hear it in her voice. 'Okay. When do you land?'

'In about two hours. Come alone, and send me a driver who knows how to mind his own business.'

'Roger that,' she said. 'This better be good.'

'It is the best thing ever,' Hodges said. 'See you in two hours.'

He broke the connection and steepled his fingers, looking at Schweitzer over the top of them. 'That was—'

'The Director of the CIA's Special Activities Division,' Schweitzer answered. 'You remember I used to be a SEAL, right? SAD's our retirement plan.'

Hodges looked pained and leaned forward, whispering, 'Will you shut up? I don't want the pilots to hear your voice.'

Schweitzer tuned his augmented hearing for a moment, listened to the sound waves attenuate as they traveled toward the cockpit door. 'They can't.'

Hodges hesitated. 'You can tell? How?'

Schweitzer leaned forward, raising his chin until he could see the silver fires of his eyes reflected in Hodges' own. 'Magic.'

Hodges sighed. 'Jala and I were at the Farm together. She's good at keeping secrets.'

'What's she going to do?'

'Jim, do you think I would pack you onto my personal aircraft and fly you to Washington, to a private meeting with the Director of SAD because I intended to betray you?'

Schweitzer remembered his wife's words as they fled through the forest, the Gemini Cell hot on their heels. Her eyes had been hard to match her voice. She wasn't frightened of him, even after what he'd become. *No, Jim. We are in this together. If you want to help me, that's fine. I accept your help, but I won't accept a leash and I don't report to you. We're not going anywhere until we come up with a plan.*

Oh, God, Sarah, Schweitzer thought. *I miss you.*

Schweitzer wrestled with a sudden surge of loneliness. He wanted someone he could trust, someone he *knew*. Pete or Steve. His brother or his brother.

'No,' Schweitzer said, 'but that doesn't mean this is a good plan. I don't work for you, Hodges. You need to keep me in the loop.'

'Jim, you have to understand that some secrets can be kept too well. Spies make their livings not trusting people. She's going to have to see you to believe you.'

'And then she'll help us shut the Cell down? After seeing me?'

'I certainly hope so.'

'What if you're wrong?'

'Then we're probably screwed, but then again, with the Cell gunning for both of us, we were probably screwed anyway, right?' He patted the overstuffed armrest. 'Try to enjoy the flight, Jim. I waved off a flight attendant, but you can help yourself to . . .' He began to gesture to a mini-fridge built into the bulkhead, then glanced at Schweitzer's dead face. The words died. 'Oh . . . sorry.'

Schweitzer didn't answer. Instead, he pushed his consciousness outward, reaching for Sarah, for some hint of her lingering in the void beyond. He was getting better at navigating it with practice, feeling the boundaries between the world he occupied and the one that awaited him when his physical body was destroyed.

But no matter how good he was, he wasn't good enough to catch more than the maddening scent of Sarah's rose-water perfume, the trail that he'd once tried to follow and found led nowhere. He remembered watching her bathe herself in the stream, her healthy body beyond him, his cold arms unable to hold her. He remembered her telling him to leave, to bring the Cell down. *Save my son, you sonofabitch! What the hell is wrong with you?* My son, not our son.

He had lost so many close to him, and as far as he understood, all of them would be here. His best friend, Steve; his brother, Peter; his mother. Steve had been like kin to him, but even if he'd thought Schweitzer was dead, he'd still slept with his wife, and for that reason, Schweitzer had no wish to speak with him, though he missed him so badly, it hurt.

Peter was another matter. Schweitzer remembered his brother's strong jaw, his hard eyes. He'd blazed the trail into the SEALs that Schweitzer had followed, and the day Peter had pinned the trident on him and punched it into his chest had been one of the greatest in his life. *Proud of you, bro.*

He thought briefly of reaching for Peter, but as close as he was with him, he had no trail to follow. At least with Sarah, there was the scent of her perfume. With Peter, there was only his memory and the churning chaos of the soul storm.

He swallowed the agony. Sarah had charged him with saving her son. That much he could do, and bringing down the Cell was the only way to do it.

It was pointless, but still he hovered in the void. Was the soul storm twisting her as it had Ninip? Was she half-mad now? Ravenous with the red hunger that drove the Golds? He turned his thoughts to the last time they'd made love, to the light making her a thing of hammered silver. There had been life and there had been love, and they were all he wanted now.

They landed at a smaller airstrip beside the commercial airport, running past a giant Coast Guard airplane hangar with an unlimbered F-16 parked outside. An armored sedan crouched so close to where the airplane taxied to a stop that the unfolding staircase almost hit the driver's door. The windows were tinted too dark for normal eyes to penetrate, but Schweitzer could make out a driver and passenger, both in body armor, with pistols gently lifting their jacket seams. Hodges arrowed straight for the back as if it were his family car, and Schweitzer followed his lead.

He'd only been to CIA headquarters twice, but he remembered the trips clearly, the long ride up the George Washington Memorial Parkway through the wooded back-yards of McLean, the houses of America's aristocracy standing sentinel over the hub of the nation's secrets. He'd always felt a faint pang of jealousy at the wealth, but a part of him had thought it would be his someday, after retirement and a lucrative career in defense contracting, the usual path for a SEAL. Now he was jealous again, but for the trappings of family that whirred past. A child's plastic tricycle lying on its side; a patio table and chairs under an umbrella, set with plastic flatware for four.

The CIA's off-ramp was marked by a brown and white sign, and the exit delivered them up to a checkpoint, where the guard waved them through after a glance at the driver's badge. They'd insisted on checking every passenger's ID the last time Schweitzer had been there, but clearly the Director of SAD had more pull.

The car wound its way up through a parking lot several times the size of a football field, nearly empty at this late hour. At last it rolled to a stop, the driver and passenger getting out and walking up a narrow concrete path without so much as a backward glance. They were G-men down to their thin ties and cheap suits, so stereotypical that Schweitzer felt his flat line of a mouth attempt to twist into a smile. Hodges and Schweitzer followed their escorts along the path, past the building's entrance and around the side. Schweitzer shot Hodges a questioning glance, but the Senator only walked confidently on.

A moment later, their destination became clear: the broad geodesic dome of the CIA's outdoor auditorium, silent and dark save for the soft glow of running lights tracing the sides of the stone steps.

Beside it stood a bronze statue of a boy in a frock coat, his long hair tied in a queue, and his wrists bound with rope, a noose looped over his neck. NATHAN HALE, the plaque read. I ONLY REGRET THAT I HAVE BUT ONE LIFE TO GIVE FOR MY COUNTRY.

Schweitzer froze as the message hit home. He *had* more than one life to give for his country.

Hodges paused at his elbow, following Schweitzer's gaze to the plaque. 'He'd have been jealous of you, Jim.' He clapped Schweitzer on the shoulder and jogged through the auditorium's entrance, between their escort, who had taken up guard positions to either side.

The auditorium was as vast as it was empty. Panels split the walls and ceiling into scatterings of triangles. Listening to the sound of his footsteps on the carpeted aisle, Schweitzer could tell those panels were designed to reflect sound within, ensuring that everyone in the giant chamber could hear every word, and that those outside could not. Like the exterior, it was lit only by the running lights along the aisles, casting a soft glow just powerful enough to show a woman among the rows of seats, hands resting on the back of one, waiting for them.

Her long black hair was loose around her strong shoulders, the lean muscle of her body visible even through the conservative cut of her suit. Her face was narrow, her eyes wide and expressionless. *Sniper's eyes*, Schweitzer thought, *looking for an angle of attack.*

'Jala Ghaznavi,' Hodges said. 'It's good to see you.'

Where Hodges' voice dripped with genuine pleasure, Ghaznavi's response was flat. 'It's good to see you, too, Don. I'm glad to find you weren't hurt.'

Hodges shrugged. 'I'm not so easy to kill. We've worked together long enough for you to know that.'

'We've also worked together long enough for me to know that you're slicker than goose shit, Don. You're a politician, for the love of God.'

'I know I haven't always shot straight with you, Jala, and I'm sorry for that. I promise you, I've got my hat in my hand this time.'

Ghaznavi looked irritated. She jerked her chin at Schweitzer. 'Who's this?'

'This is James Schweitzer.'

Ghaznavi looked thoughtful for a moment. 'That name is familiar.'

'It should be. He's the SEAL who was murdered in that hit in Hampton Roads.'

'That would make him dead, Hodges.'

'He is.'

'Necromancy makes robots out of corpses, Don. The only thing they're good for is soaking up bullets and scaring the shit out of uncooperative assets.'

'This is different. Schweitzer is reanimated. He's still Schweitzer, only superpowered.'

Ghaznavi sighed. 'Don, for the love of our history together, please show me some damned respect. If this kind of magic existed, I'd know about it.'

'The program that created him was buried deep, Jala. Deeper than even you can dive.'

'Bullshit.'

Schweitzer was getting pretty tired of being talked about as if he wasn't in the room. He raised his hand and opened his mouth to speak but closed it again as Hodges' hand settled on his shoulder. 'Have you heard of the Gemini Cell, Jala?'

'Rumors.' Ghaznavi crossed her arms. 'That's this super-secret project that gave us this walking corpse?'

'The same,' Hodges answered.

The Senator paused for dramatic effect, but Ghaznavi only cocked her head. 'Is he missing an arm?'

'Doesn't slow him down even a little.'

Ghaznavi pursed her lips and stepped out into the aisle. 'So, this RUMINT on the Gemini Cell is true. A super-secret program dedicated to black magic. Do you have any idea how stupid that sounds, even to me?'

Hodges shrugged. 'It's real.'

'Now I know you're fucking lying to me. Every rumor I've ever heard said the President ordered it shut down.'

'He did,' Hodges said, looking at his feet, his shoulders sagging.

The realization dawned on Schweitzer and Ghaznavi at

the same moment. Schweitzer was able to keep the reaction off his face, but Ghaznavi snapped her fingers, her eyes widening.

'But you didn't,' she said. 'You kept it going. You kept it secret. Oh, my God, Don. You slick bastard. It was your program. Why the hell would you do that?'

Hodges turned his hands in lame circles. For the first time, his voice lacked the honeyed tones of the politician, and Schweitzer could hear the raw passion of the man. 'Because the shutdown order was stupid. It was an overreaction to a security breach that resulted in no actual compromise. Because the Gemini Cell was the most powerful weapon this nation ever developed.'

Ghaznavi cocked an eyebrow. 'More powerful than the nuke?'

'Magic is the new nuke,' Hodges said. 'One we can use without destroying the whole fucking world.'

'So, why are you telling me this?' she asked.

Hodges looked at the floor for a long time, and Schweitzer could smell the terror and stress on him, could hear his heart pounding. 'Because I was wrong. Because now it's out of control.'

Ghaznavi laughed. 'And you can't go to the President, can you? You can't do this out in the open. You disobeyed a direct order. He'd fry you, and so would the public. You want to save your own skin.'

'The Cell is a loose nuke, Jala. I want to save the country's skin.'

'Oh, come on, Don. If you wanted to save the country's skin, you'd hang yourself and drag this whole thing into the light. People don't come to me because they want things done nobly. You asked for an audience with the Spider Queen, and you got one. Whatever you want done, you want it done on the down-low.'

'I want you to help me shut it down, Jala. It's going to take an army, and SAD is the only army I know that can fight a war without anyone knowing. I have nowhere else to go.'

'That's nice, Don. What's in it for me?'

'Does there have to be something in it for you?' Hodges' voice shook.

'You know damn well there does,' Ghaznavi answered, 'and it better be fucking good. I was in the middle of dynamite TV when you called and ruined my night.'

'You can have it. Help me shut it down, and I'll put the program at your disposal. All its secrets, all its capabilities. You can direct it. You can make it work for SAD. I still control the line items. Black funding sources, completely invisible. It's a lot of money, Jala. It can buy a lot of toys.'

'You're asking me to keep a secret from the President.' Ghaznavi came toward him.

'You keep secrets from him all the time,' Hodges answered. 'You can do this in your sleep. I can choke off the money, make sure it comes to SAD. But someone has to do the wet work. Someone has to clean up this mess. I need your operators, Jala. I need your tanks and your planes and your guns. All of it.'

Ghaznavi clucked her tongue against the roof of her mouth, her gaze finally shifting to Schweitzer. 'So,' she sighed, 'this mummy standing next to you is a walking corpse. That's what I'm going to see when I have him unwrapped?'

'I'll save you the trouble,' Hodges said, sweeping his hand over Schweitzer's hood and pushing it down. Ghaznavi stared straight into Schweitzer's burning silver eyes. Her face betrayed no reaction, and he smelled no change in the chemical cocktail of her blood. He heard her heart rate increase slightly, but that was all.

She shrugged. 'I've seen Necromantic toys before.'

'This isn't a Necromantic toy.' Hodges' frustration was palpable. 'Look at his eyes, for Christ's sake.'

She stared right into them, unimpressed. 'Does it talk?'

Schweitzer had had enough. 'I'm right here,' he said, 'and I talk just fine.'

She sucked in her breath, her heart jumping, but outwardly, she showed nothing. 'Maybe he's some kind of advanced robot.'

'I'm not a robot,' Schweitzer said.

'That's exactly what an advanced robot would say.' She smiled up at him, her face lit with curiosity and something that looked suspiciously like delight. Not fear. Not disgust. After all this time, it felt like an embrace.

'I'm not . . .' Schweitzer began.

'Shut up.' She grinned, reaching one perfectly manicured hand into her pocket and producing a small pocketknife. She snapped the blade out with a practiced flick of her wrist. She placed a hand on Schweitzer's shoulder, the warm pulse of her pumping blood against the cold surface of his skin. He found himself leaning into the touch in spite of himself. A human being, alive and well and touching him, not to hurt him, just to touch him. It made him feel real.

She used the knife point to slide the hoodie's zipper down a few inches, pop the button off the shirt beneath.

'I don't heal,' Schweitzer said. 'If you damage me, I'll need . . .'

'Shut up,' she repeated, smiling like a sun in splendor now, digging a small furrow into Schweitzer's gray flesh, following it with her fingertips, probing, feeling.

'Jala,' Hodges said. 'This is ridiculous. You know I'm not lying.'

She sighed, her eyes never leaving the incision. 'Do you want my help or not?'

Hodges put his hands on his hips and shook his head, and Schweitzer watched her work, reveling in the warmth of her hand and the child's delight in her eyes.

After a moment, she closed the knife with a click. 'Well, you're not a robot.'

'I told you,' Schweitzer said.

'Shut up,' she said a third time, but at last she could not keep the awe off her face. 'So, you're really brought back from the dead. Not a zombie, not a walking corpse. A real . . . person.'

Schweitzer nodded, wishing he could grin back at her beyond the rictus parody he always wore. 'If it'll get you to stop cutting me, yes.'

She giggled. Schweitzer guessed she was in her late forties. She sounded like she was twelve. 'My father told me that in heaven, we'd all live in hollowed-out pearls on saffron sands, shaded by golden trees. That true?'

Schweitzer shook his head, suppressing the pang of sadness as she withdrew her hand, taking the warmth of life with it. 'No, ma'am. If your father was talking about heaven, then I wasn't a good enough guy to get there.'

'Where'd you wind up?' she asked.

'I wasn't there for long,' Schweitzer said, 'but I'm pretty sure it was hell.'

Her smile vanished. 'My dad called hell a "dark storm".'

'That is . . . that is pretty much exactly right.'

Her pensiveness yielded to sympathy. 'I'm sorry, Petty Officer Schweitzer. This must be . . . trying for you.'

Schweitzer said nothing. There was nothing to say.

'Did you see God?' she asked.

Her sympathy shook him far more than her curiosity had. It was a moment before he could answer. It took everything he had to keep the emotion out of his voice as he replied. 'I don't know that there is a God, but if there is, he has a lot to answer for.'

She nodded. 'Tell me how you came to be with my friend Donald Hodges.'

Hodges opened his mouth to speak and she raised a hand, her eyes never leaving Schweitzer's. 'Shut up, Don. I want to hear his side of it.'

Schweitzer told her. The only thing he omitted was the meeting with Eldredge and entrusting Patrick to his care. Until he was absolutely sure he could trust them, let them think his son was dead. Hodges tried to interrupt several times, Ghaznavi raising a hand and Schweitzer talking over him before he finally gave up.

'For a SEAL,' Hodges breathed, 'you're the least circumspect motherfucker I've ever met.'

The delight was back in Ghaznavi's eyes. 'So, you're the Javelin Rain incident. It wasn't a nuke. I was wondering why my Measures and Signals guys came up with nothing.'

'Yes,' Hodges said. He sounded defeated. 'That's right.'

'Okay,' she said, shaking her head. 'Color me amazed, but I believe you. So, how bad is this?'

'It's pretty bad,' Hodges said. 'The Cell is completely rogue, and they're here in the US.'

'Where?' Ghaznavi asked Schweitzer.

'Somewhere near Alexandria,' Schweitzer said. 'I remember seeing the tower in Old Town when I got out.'

'They're in Colchester,' Hodges said, 'under a cover facility.'

'Non-official cover?' she asked.

Hodges nodded. 'A company called Entertech.'

'Entertech?' She grinned again. 'You clever fucker. I can't believe it.'

Hodges sighed. 'I put a lot of work into this. It's flawless.'

'Except for the rogue part.'

'We're going to fix that, right?'

'I think so, yes,' she said, 'but I'm going to need a lot more detail. We're talking about an assault on a fixed position on American soil, just a few miles outside the capital. Do you have any idea how hard it will be to keep something like that dark?'

'You can do it.'

'I'm going to need everything you've got on the facility. Blueprints, personnel rosters, real estate plats for the property. Physical plant and durable-goods orders. Anything we can use.'

Hodges puffed out his cheeks and shook his head. 'I don't have any of that.'

Ghaznavi finally looked away from Schweitzer. 'What?'

'I've got nothing.'

'How is that possible? You said this was your program.'

'I authorized funding and strategic direction. The actual ops were run by the program's Director.'

'Who is dead,' Schweitzer added. 'Like me.'

Hodges looked up sharply, met Schweitzer's eyes, his face darkening. Schweitzer held his gaze. This couldn't be about secrets now. It had to be about solving problems.

At last, Hodges looked away and nodded.

'Fuck,' Ghaznavi said. 'That's bad.'

'Yes,' Hodges sighed. 'Yes, it is.'

'Didn't you have anyone else on the inside?'

'My lead scientist, Dr Eldredge. He bolted when he found out that the Director was dead. I have no idea where he is.'

Schweitzer had an idea, but he kept it to himself. To reveal Eldredge's location was to reveal Patrick's.

'Absolutely nothing? No lines on their comms? Ops frequencies? Perimeter patrol patterns?' Ghaznavi asked.

'I've got the layout of the cover facility, but that's only

the uppermost level. The real action is below it.'

'We'll have to go in blind,' she said. 'I don't like it.'

'A secret underground facility in the middle of a highly populated area and likely defended by a small army of superpowered undead?' Hodges cocked an eyebow. 'What's not to like?'

'I'll go with the team,' Schweitzer said.

Ghaznavi and Hodges both stared at him. Schweitzer shrugged. 'I believe your exact words were that I wasn't a "walking corpse". I was a "real . . . person". Like you.'

'Perfect memory is one of your magic superpowers?' she asked, smiling.

'Nope. Mom made me do drills in kindergarten, thought it'd help me get ahead in school.'

'Did it?' she asked.

'No, ma'am,' Schweitzer said, 'but it made arguments with my wife pretty heated.'

She laughed, but Schweitzer made sure his tone was anything but light. 'My point is this: I'm a person, dead or alive. That means you don't get to throw me around, no matter who the hell you are. I want in on the team, and you need me on it.'

'Why?' she asked.

'Because I can't die,' Schweitzer said. 'Because I can bend cold iron with the one hand left to me. Because I can put a bullet through a dime at three hundred yards. Because I can hear a pin drop through a wall. Because I can smell if someone is lying. Because I am the only person out of all of us who has spent significant time in the Gemini Cell facility.'

'You were a prisoner in the Gemini Cell facility,' Hodges said. 'All you saw was the inside of a holding tank.'

'I said I could smell lies. I didn't say I was any good at telling them.'

'Surely, you got some sense of the lay of the land,' Ghaznavi said. 'Didn't you move through the facility at all?'

Schweitzer nodded. 'A bit, and I remember some of it.'

'But not enough to build a plan, damn it,' she said. 'Aren't you supposed to be some kind of magic-powered supersoldier?'

'When they were handing out superpowers,' Schweitzer replied, 'I took "run faster than a car". I didn't have enough points left to get "mental maps". Anyway, I've been inside, which is more than I can say for either of you.'

'I've been inside,' Hodges said.

'You go, then,' Schweitzer said. 'I'm sure the team will be well served by an aging mortal who hasn't run an ass-in op in over twenty years.'

Hodges looked at his feet again. 'Yeah. You're right.'

'He is,' Ghaznavi said. 'Okay, Jim. You're on the team.'

'How fast can we get moving?' Hodges asked.

'Moving with a sense of urgency isn't the same as rushing. We've got some work to do. And the first item of business,' she said, turning to Schweitzer, 'is you.'

Chapter Four
Technology Is a Beautiful Thing

Darkness blanketed the CIA campus. The low head-quarters building was lit just enough to keep Schweitzer from seeing the stars without engaging his magically powered vision, and he didn't bother. Walking beside Hodges and Ghaznavi, he felt almost human. Sensory limitations were a part of that, and even if it was just for a few minutes, he wanted to preserve the illusion.

They went in through a back entrance, crossing a rubber mat emblazoned with the CIA's crest, eagle's head and compass rose. Bronze plaques adorned the wall, marching toward a row of stainless steel turnstiles that abutted a desk manned by a bored-looking guard. He didn't bother to glance up as Ghaznavi badged through the turnstile, finally stirring as she opened a small gate, allowing Hodges and Schweitzer to enter. She held up her badge and he stiffened, waving her through. They turned right, meandering down a hallway with carpeted walls that undulated back on itself, waving back and forth as if it had been designed to deliberately confuse them. Schweitzer could hear the sound waves bending with each step, felt himself instinctively dialing out his hearing, pushing harder and harder to hear the guard desk, the low hum of computers in the hallway beyond.

The corridor emptied out into a junction. A metal door concealed a trash chute beside an elevator open and waiting for them. Ghaznavi didn't speak until the doors were shut and it was humming upward. 'I don't understand why you want to come.'

For a moment, Schweitzer thought she had addressed the question to Hodges, but when he glanced up, the SAD Director was looking at him.

'What do you mean?' he asked.

'On the raid on the Cell,' she said. 'You fought like a mad dog to get out of there.'

Schweitzer shrugged. Ghaznavi's gaze was piercing; she had the interrogator's gift of making it seem as if she saw into your heart, that it was useless to lie to her. Fortunately for Schweitzer, he had the SEAL training to counter it. As far as Ghaznavi was concerned, Patrick was dead, and he wasn't going to disabuse her of the notion. 'They pissed me off.'

'Bullshit,' she said almost before Schweitzer had finished. 'I didn't get where I am in this organization by being gullible.'

'You also probably didn't get there by being pushy,' Schweitzer said. 'For now, all you need to know is that I want in on this mission.'

'You're dead,' she said. 'Why should you give a damn about what living people do?'

Schweitzer was stunned by the question and, worse, his inability to come up with a response. As the elevator doors chimed open, he turned to her, putting heat in his voice. 'Revenge isn't about the living. It's about the dead. They killed my wife and son. I'm not going to buy a house or save for retirement now.' He gestured to the gray ruin of his body. 'Making things right is all I have left.'

Ghaznavi stared at him for another moment before

dropping her gaze, giving a satisfied grunt. She stepped out of the elevator, and Hodges and Schweitzer followed her down another corridor to a plain door with an enormous dial-faced lock over the handle. A green magnet reading OPEN was stuck to the surface beside a long oak tag card crowded with signatures. She slapped her badge against a black card reader beside the handle, and the door opened with a click.

The room inside was formal to a fault. The walls were covered with dark wooden panels, contrasting sharply with a sterile, unmanned secretarial desk. Furled flags stood in the corner below a dark flat-screen monitor. Two doors led off the suite, and Ghaznavi took the rightmost, entering into a larger room dominated by an L-shaped cherry wood desk covered with mementos of a storied career in government: mugs, miniature flags, plaques and commemorative plates, a model airplane, white with a blue stripe, tail markings conspicuously absent. The walls were nearly covered with certificates and degrees, photos of a young-looking Ghaznavi smiling with hard-eyed insurgents and teams of American operators. A huge triple-paneled print of Harriet Tubman dominated the room. She was leading the way down a rough-hewn tunnel, a group of terrified runaway slaves trailing behind her. Her eyes were resolutely forward, a candle held aloft to cut through the darkness. Below it was a wooden plaque, engraved letters stained gold. YOU SHALL KNOW THE TRUTH, it read, AND THE TRUTH SHALL SET YOU FREE.

Ghaznavi made herself comfortable in a swivel chair, putting her feet on the desk and her hands behind her head. She slipped her heel out of one shoe, letting it dangle from a toe and jerking it in the direction of a small, round table surrounded by four chairs in the opposite corner.

Hodges pulled up a chair, and Schweitzer joined him. He had no need to sit, but it was a gesture in the direction of humanity, and he made it a rule never to pass those up.

'You ready to start planning?' Ghaznavi asked.

'No,' Hodges admitted, reaching into a bowl of nuts in the table's center. 'Where do we even start?'

'We start with a team,' she said. 'We keep it small, we keep it to the best, and we need a lynchpin, a quarterback.'

'I thought that was you,' Schweitzer said.

'I'm the boss.' Ghaznavi pushed a button on a phone on her desk, spoke over the ringtones sounding through the speaker. 'I have people for that.'

A voice answered; Schweitzer recognized it as the same one Hodges had spoken to on the plane. 'Watch.'

'Andy, it's Jala. I need Reeves.'

A moment's intake of breath, long enough for Schweitzer to know that Ghaznavi didn't make a habit out of calling the SAD watch floor. 'Yes, ma'am. He's home; did you want me to . . .'

'Yup. Tell him he has twenty minutes to get his ass to my office.'

'Ma'am, Mr Reeves lives thirty minutes away.'

'Tell him to speed.'

'Yes, ma'am. Out.'

The line went dead and Ghaznavi stared at Schweitzer, only the slow rise and fall of her shoulders indicating she was alive.

'Rude to stare,' Schweitzer said.

'I'll have to check the manual,' Ghaznavi answered, 'but I'm pretty sure when you meet a sentient walking corpse brought in by a United States Senator and escaped from a program so secret that even I didn't know about it, you get a pass.'

She glanced over at Hodges and cocked an eyebrow.

'*Khodaye*, Don. You look like you're about to pass out.'

'I'm fine,' Hodges assured her, but Schweitzer could hear the rapid beating of his heart, could smell the proteins building up in his blood. The Senator's cheeks were pale, a light sheen of sweat showing beneath his immaculate hair. Too much stress. Too little sleep.

'There's bourbon in the cabinet behind you,' she said. 'How about you pour us both a drink?'

Hodges looked grateful, stood, and turned to the cabinet.

'What am I, chopped liver?' Schweitzer asked.

Hodges froze. 'You're . . . dead liver.'

Ghaznavi uncrossed her arms, set her feet on the floor, and leaned forward. 'Do you even eat and drink, Jim?'

'Of course,' Schweitzer said, though the truth was that he wasn't sure. He hadn't tried since his death.

'I can smell the chemical composition of your blood,' Schweitzer said. 'I can hear your heart beating. You think I can't taste liquor?'

Hodges shrugged. 'Rocks or neat?'

'A single cube, please,' Schweitzer said, 'and better make it a double.'

Hodges poured and set the glasses down on the table. Ghaznavi joined them, lifted hers. 'To secrets,' she said. 'The darker, the better.'

Schweitzer lifted his glass, the feel of the crystal in his hand evoking a cascade of memory. The condensation on the surface. The chill of the ice cubes clattering against the rim, the dull sloshing of the liquid. Sarah had once bought him a bottle of Virginia Gentleman back when they'd still been dating. They'd sat in the bed of his truck and watched the boardwalk on Virginia Beach, the crowds moving by, smiling and laughing, shining in the darkness as if lit from within. Sarah had swiped a couple of her mother's good crystal glasses and her ice bucket. He remembered the smoky burn of the liquid as it traveled down his throat, the fire it lit in his belly.

'Bottoms up,' he said, and tossed it back. His stretched features forced him to tilt his head back to keep the liquor from dribbling out of his mouth. It orbited the back of his throat before he forced his muscles to swallow, an old reflex rusty from lack of use. His dead taste buds reported the flavor in glorious detail he'd never known in life. But it was just that, a report, like his feeling of pain or fatigue, a thing distant, told by a third party.

He managed to keep the disappointment off his face. He might be dead, but he was a person, drinking with other people. He nodded to Ghaznavi. 'Delicious, thanks.'

'You're welcome,' she said. 'My dad always used to give me shit about drinking. To this day, he looks down on me for it. Old fool doesn't know what he's missing.'

'Now what?' Hodges asked.

'Now we drink' – Ghaznavi raised her glass – 'and we wait.'

They drank, and they waited, and the companionable silence was the most wonderful thing Schweitzer had known in a long, long time.

At last, a buzzer sounded. Ghaznavi returned to her desk and pushed a button on her phone. 'Come!' she shouted to the door before taking her seat in the swivel chair again.

Schweitzer heard the dull thud of a footstep followed by a long, metal scrape, and a man limped into the room. His bright red hair was still sleep-tousled, longish, fading into his thick beard. He wore a dirty, faded ball cap with a subdued American flag, a flannel button-down shirt, and sweatpants that hung to his ankles. One foot wore a hiking boot, the kind of high-performance model operators always used instead of standard-issue. The other foot was missing. In its place was a long, J-shaped carbon-fiber blade.

Schweitzer followed the outline of the prosthesis up the sweatpants and saw it terminated at the man's knee.

The man's eyes were still sleep-fogged but narrowed, flicking around the room, noting danger areas in the corners, looking at the occupants' hands rather than their faces. Schweitzer could tell he was an operator, possessed of the same casual deadliness Schweitzer had worked so hard to cultivate. This must be Reeves.

'Came as quick as I could, ma'am.'

Ghaznavi smiled at him. 'You're late.'

'I know you said to speed, but I figured even if I tinned my way out of being pulled over, it would slow me down. Did forty-five the whole way.'

'Sound judgment. This is why I hired you. I'm sure you know Senator Hodges.'

'Heard of him, that's for sure.' Reeves inclined his head. 'Good to meet you, sir. I'm Ernest Reeves.'

Hodges nodded, waving a hand over the lees of his scotch.

Reeves' eyes strayed to Schweitzer, who was still staring at his prosthetic leg. Did he still run ops like this? How had he driven here?

Reeves noted Schweitzer's gaze and folded his arms across his chest. 'Anyone ever tell you it's rude to stare?'

The rush of embarrassment made Schweitzer feel more human, and he was grateful for that. He raised his head, his burning silver eyes gleaming from the shadows gathered beneath his cap. 'I'll have to check the manual, but I'm pretty sure when you've been killed and brought back from the dead, you get a pass.'

Ghaznavi snorted laughter, waving at Schweitzer. 'Reeves, this is Jim Schweitzer.'

Reeves frowned. 'The SEAL? Didn't he get his ID burned?'

'That's right,' she said.

'And they whacked him.'

'Also right,' Hodges said.

Reeves' eyes narrowed, then widened, but only for a moment. They didn't waste time on Schweitzer's face, darting repeatedly to his hand, shoulders, and legs. Reeves was a professional. He knew he was in the presence of something he didn't understand, but he stayed focused on the threat. Time enough for explanations later.

He followed Schweitzer's gaze to his leg. 'I guess dying didn't teach you manners.'

'No . . . sorry,' Schweitzer said. 'I just . . . I never met an operator who overcame something like that and stayed in the fight. Respect.'

Reeves seemed mollified. 'CIA's not the Army. You get a little more latitude. I don't let it slow me down, anyway. Are you really dead?'

Schweitzer eased his hood back. 'Yeah. Guess we've both overcome obstacles.'

Reeves had his game face on now, showed no reaction other than a slight tightening in his hands. 'Please tell me this gives you superpowers.'

Schweitzer nodded. 'Just like Superman, only without the pesky breathing.'

Reeves turned to Ghaznavi. 'I assume this is why I'm here, ma'am? There has to be a read-on for this.'

Ghaznavi waved the thought away. 'I'll get with the security officer and have a code word assigned. For now, just keep your mouth shut. Well, except for your team.'

'There's a team?' Reeves asked.

'I need you to assemble one. I was thinking a squad. Or two fire teams. Either way, you're the lead, and he's your second.'

'He is?' Reeves jerked his chin at Schweitzer.

'Well, it certainly isn't me,' Hodges said.

'No offense,' Reeves said to Schweitzer. 'Never worked with a dead guy before.'

'None taken,' Schweitzer said. 'I've never been dead before.'

'So, what is this, ma'am?' Reeves turned back to Ghaznavi. 'Magic?'

'That is exactly what it is,' Ghaznavi said.

'Yup,' Hodges said as Reeves' eyes moved to him.

'Sorry you had to find out like this,' Schweitzer said. 'Kind of sudden.'

'So, you're not a robot, or like some super-fancy special effect?' Reeves asked.

'No,' Schweitzer said, 'and please don't cut me open to check. Your boss already tried that, and it doesn't heal.'

'Ma'am, I have to ask,' Reeves said to Ghaznavi. 'Is this some kind of practical joke? Am I being filmed?'

'Come on.' Ghaznavi thumped her fist on her desk. 'Does that sound like the kind of thing I would do?'

'Respectfully, ma'am?' Reeves smiled. 'Absolutely.'

Ghaznavi glanced quickly to Hodges, who smiled, then back to Reeves. 'It's not a practical joke. That is Jim Schweitzer, and he has been raised from the dead as part of an op that harnesses magic, which, as you have already deduced, is totally real.'

''Kay.' Reeves chewed the inside of his cheek. 'He reliable?'

'More reliable than a lot of living people,' Schweitzer answered for her. 'At least I know what side I'm on.'

'What side is that?' asked Reeves.

'Same one as when I was in the Navy,' Schweitzer answered.

That seemed to satisfy Reeves, who nodded. 'What's the op?'

'The unit that . . . created Schweitzer has gone rogue,' Ghaznavi said. 'They tried to push a button on Senator Hodges. Schweitzer saved him. We've got to shut the operation down immediately.'

Reeves continued working on the inside of his cheek, sucking in the corner of his moustache in the process. 'I take it they won't be cooperative.'

'Nope.'

'Where are they?' Reeves asked.

'Colchester.'

Reeves finally looked shocked. 'Colchester, *Virginia*?'

'About a half-hour drive from this very office, not counting for traffic.'

'That's . . .'

'About fifteen hundred people,' Ghaznavi said. 'Goes up to around ten thousand if you count the commuting communities surrounding it, which you should.'

Hodges cocked an eyebrow and Ghaznavi shrugged. 'In my line of work, you want to know your home turf.'

'You mind if I sit down, ma'am?' Reeves asked, already pulling up a chair.

'Want a drink?' Hodges asked, then filled a glass with ice before Reeves even answered.

Reeves cradled his head in his hands for a moment, then rubbed the back of his neck before looking up. 'How quiet does this need to be?'

'Dead silent,' Ghaznavi said. 'Not a word in the press. We can't even have urban legends developing. Not a blade of grass stirred on a neighbor's lawn.'

Reeves sighed. 'You're willing to throw some money at this?'

'You'll have an open funding line. Keep receipts and be specific in your justifications.'

Reeves gratefully accepted the glass from Hodges and

sipped at it thoughtfully. 'How many enemy are we talking about?'

'No idea.'

'Not even a ballpark?'

'Nope, and because I know you're going to ask, we've got no map, either. Just an eyewitness description of the facility.'

'Who's the eyewitness?'

Schweitzer raised his remaining hand. 'My memory's pretty good.'

Reeves looked doubtful. 'Ma'am, this is impossible. Even with an open line. If I had three years to plan and . . .'

'You've got three days. By now, they know that Hodges survived. They'll be in the wind or worse before long. We can't risk leaving this.'

'Christ. I hate going in blind,' Reeves said.

'You're going in?' Schweitzer asked. 'I thought you were the ops planner.'

'I lead from the front,' Reeves said. 'You got a problem with that?'

'No,' Schweitzer said. 'Not at all, I'm just . . .' *Idiot. Just stop talking.* But a part of him thrilled at the exquisitely human experience of putting his foot in his mouth. Reeves stared into his eyes, unfazed by the obvious magic in the burning silver.

'I'm sorry,' Schweitzer said. 'I didn't mean to underestimate you.'

Reeves tapped his prosthetic. 'This is a carbon-fiber high-tension running blade. I probably move faster than you.'

'You've never seen him run.' Hodges laughed. 'It's pretty impressive.'

Reeves kept his eyes on Schweitzer. 'You just shamble along behind me there, zombie. Besides' – he gestured at

Schweitzer's missing arm – 'I'm not the only gimp in the room.'

'We'll fix that,' Ghaznavi said, 'but before we pick a munition, we need to figure out the terrain.'

Schweitzer wasn't sure what he'd expected, an ops center with a holographic display maybe, anything other than the plain, run-down-looking conference room that lay beyond a hidden panel behind Ghaznavi's desk. A single bathroom was its only other exit ('You don't expect me to use the regular restrooms like a plebe, do you?' Ghaznavi asked him when she saw him glance at it), and the only unusual feature was a large central table surfaced with dry-erase board and cluttered with colored markers.

Ghaznavi seated herself behind a battered laptop and started typing. Reeves folded his arms across his chest and stared openly at Schweitzer. After a moment, Schweitzer returned it. 'What?'

'You stared at me.'

'You going to ask me on a date?'

Reeves stroked his beard. 'What's it like, being dead?'

'People keep asking me this.'

'Well, it's the kind of thing people want to know. What's it like?'

'It sucks. Stay alive for as long as you can.'

Reeves laughed. 'No, I mean. Is there a God? Did you meet him?'

'I already asked him all this,' Ghaznavi said, not looking up from her laptop.

'What'd he say?'

'He already told you. Being dead sucks.'

Reeves grunted, then opened his mouth to ask another question. The words died as Ghaznavi spun the laptop to face him, showing an overhead map of Colchester, Virginia. It was overlaid with satellite imagery, a neck of land jutting out into the blue-gray Potomac river, mostly blanketed with trees and uninhabited marshland but threaded through with worrying lines of roads indicating the presence of subdivisions, houses cheek by jowl. People.

Reeves was apparently thinking the same thing, because he sucked in his breath and began chewing on the inside of his cheek again. He sighed, snatched up a marker, and began copying the map outlines onto the table's surface.

'We've got one thing going for us,' Hodges said, picking up a marker himself and marking a star on Reeves' growing map. 'The facility itself is in an office park off 242. It backs up to the wildlife refuge, and you've got the regional park right across the street.'

Reeves stared at the Senator. 'Respectfully, sir, Gunston Hall is right there. That?' He tapped the laptop screen. 'That is a church. That park is going to attract more people than you think. These houses here can't be more than a klick away. To call this particular battlespace "unforgiving" would be charitable.'

'Solutions, not problems,' Ghaznavi said. 'Toxic spill? Some kind of animal-disease outbreak in the wildlife refuge? We could call a quarantine and clear out the whole area.'

Reeves shook his head. 'Needs to be boring. News is going to be all over this as it is. Nothing unknown. Something people have seen before. How about Legionnaires' disease? There's been like two reported outbreaks of that in the past year. If it's bad enough, we could call a quarantine. Say it's in the water.'

Ghaznavi nodded. 'That'd work.'

'You're going to have to get some talking heads on the air. Private-sector people saying the government is overreacting.'

Ghaznavi was typing now, making notes in a corner of the screen. 'I'll contact the media team.'

'How current is this imagery?' Reeves pointed to Ghaznavi's laptop.

'It's open-source, so probably not very.'

'I'm going to need up-to-the-second.'

'Okay.'

'And I'll need drone overflights. Saturation coverage. I need to see everything moving on the ground in a five-mile radius.'

'Done.'

'Nighttime too. Forward-looking infrared cameras.' He looked up at Hodges. 'You said this is a cover facility, right? Office?'

'That's right.' Hodges nodded.

'Okay, then it should be deserted at night. Heat signatures might help us suss out what we're going up against. If we're lucky, we might even get rotations.'

'I wouldn't rely on that,' Schweitzer said.

'Why not?'

'Because the guards might not give off any body heat.'

Reeves was quiet for a moment. 'You're not the only dead guy?'

'Not by a long shot.'

Reeves stood up, sighed. 'This just keeps getting better.'

Schweitzer shrugged. 'The only easy day was yesterday.'

Reeves smiled at that. 'I guess you better give me a rundown on your capabilities.'

'He can't die,' Hodges answered, 'but he can be destroyed if you chop him up fine enough. Super speed, super strength, super senses. Like a comic book superhero.'

Reeves grunted. 'There's a part of me who still feels like I'm being tricked here.'

'No trick,' Schweitzer said. 'Everything he said is true.'

'How'd you lose the arm?' Reeves asked.

'Tried to block a hatchet with it. Hatchet won.'

'Can you shoot one-handed?'

'Better than you with two.'

'I was thinking of fitting him with a prosthetic,' Ghaznavi said.

'Flamethrower,' Schweitzer said. 'The only way to beat things like me is to burn them or tear them apart.'

Ghaznavi shook her head. 'I don't think we can do that.'

'How about a chainsaw or a buzz saw?' Schweitzer asked. 'I fought a . . . thing like me when I was on the run. It had one.'

'That, we should be able to do.'

'Really?' Schweitzer asked. 'Cool.'

Reeves smiled, tapped his prosthetic leg. 'Technology is a beautiful thing, man.'

'What else do you need?' Ghaznavi asked.

'Frank Cort, and I need both of us fully up to speed. What was this program, how does this . . . Magic, is it magic?'

'It's magic,' Schweitzer said.

'Jesus. Magic. How does it work? I need to know as much about the layout as possible. How many bad guys? I mean, normal bad guys. Ones that can be killed. How many are . . . like you? How are they equipped?'

'You need a targeting package,' Schweitzer said.

Reeves cocked an eyebrow. 'I forget you were a SEAL.'

'Then you also probably forgot that even dying doesn't change that,' Schweitzer said. He stood, snatched up a marker, and moved to a clear portion of the table. 'I'll draw what I remember. You all need to catch some rack time? I don't need to sleep, but I . . .' He remembered Sarah, bent at the waist, panting from racing to keep up with him as they fled through the Virginia woods. *Patrick and I aren't like you. We can't keep going like this.*

Ghaznavi looked from Hodges to Reeves. 'I think I speak for all of us when I say that after the surprise meeting you has given me, I'm not going to sleep for a week.'

'All right,' Schweitzer said. 'Let's get to work.'

Chapter Five

Double Back

To die was to triumph over fear. Even after all this time, the Director marveled at how much fear had held him back. Death had liberated him from every limitation, unchained him from appetite, given him strength beyond his wildest dreams. He wished he'd started down this path much sooner. All that time wasted for what? Fear of the unknown, fear of a little pain, fear of fear itself, the rising panic as the body failed and darkness gathered.

Stupid. Fear gained him nothing. He was frightened of what might happen to the Cell, of how things would change now that he'd made his attempt on Hodges. He was frightened of his body being destroyed, of being returned to the void. But such fear had power over him only if it stirred him to inaction. He was loath to leave the Cell, but he needed to find that Summoner. He toggled the commlink in his laptop and brought up Mark.

'Sir?'

'Where are we on the helo prep?' They were bound from Virginia to Indiana for a refueling stop. Even with its extended fuel tanks, the Director's helicopter could make only around four hundred miles before having to take on fuel, which it did at the series of dumps the Cell had placed all over the country. After that, it would be on to Lake Geneva, then Minneapolis, Minot, and out over Canada, bound for the ass end of the Northwest Territories.

Finding one old man in that vast wilderness would be harder than finding a needle in a haystack, but if that man could do even a fraction of what the intel suggested he could, it would be worth the effort.

'Another hour or so, sir, and we'll be ready to go.'

'Outstanding. And the Golds?'

'It's going to take a little longer to get them fully mission-capable, sir. There are two whose enthusiasm aggravated some previous tears.' Xolotl and Quetzalcoatl, at least, were pristine. With them alone, he could probably take on a city.

'Is it something that can be repaired en route? I'm anxious to get underway.'

'I'll ask the lead engineer, sir.' The Director could hear the irritation in Mark's voice. Not at him, but at herself for not anticipating the question.

'Very well, let's go ahead and—'

There was a beep on Mark's end of the line. 'Stand by, sir,' she said, and toggled channels.

She had switched channels to pick up the other call. Without asking for his permission. He could feel the rage swelling from somewhere deep within him, knew it wasn't productive, that nothing could be gained from letting it anger him. But his professional sangfroid was a toy boat on a storm-tossed sea, and within an instant, he was overwhelmed with fury. People like Mark were only useful insofar as they knew their place. If she thought that . . .

Mark toggled back. 'Sir' – she was breathless – 'I think you're going to want to hear this.'

He bit back the hard words, fury yielding to curiosity. 'Who is it?'

'It's Diligence, sir.' A code name, the same one given to each of his asset handlers around the world. Only the two letters preceding it differentiated their identity.

His rage evaporated as quickly as it had come. 'Put her through.'

The line clicked.

'Sir.' The woman's voice on the other end was no longer Mark's, but the Director recognized it. 'Got something that couldn't wait.'

'Ah, Diligence,' the Director said. 'I have no doubt your news is of the utmost importance.'

'Sir, one of my assets just gave me a really disturbing report out of SAD. It sounds like they're scrambling a team of hard operators to hit Entertech.'

'To hit Entertech? Or to hit the Cell? Do they know about us?'

'Asset didn't say, sir.' Diligence was careful not to identify the asset even by gender. Worth every penny, and Diligence had cost a lot of pennies.

'When do they roll out?'

'Unclear, but I think soon, maybe a day at most. Asset says they're going with no targeting package. That makes me think they're not aiming to hit Entertech, sir. Plenty of stuff to scrape off the Internet there to flesh out the target.'

'Concur. Who's driving the op?'

'Looks like it's Ghaznavi herself, sir.'

'The Director of SAD? Personally?'

'That's what the asset says, sir.'

'That's . . . unusual.'

Diligence didn't respond.

'Has this asset been reliable in the past? Responsive to tasking?'

'I wouldn't be bothering you if they weren't, sir.'

How the hell could they have found out about the Cell?
'Was it Eldredge?'

'If it was, sir, he got in without anyone noticing, and my asset hasn't seen or heard about him. It's possible, I guess.'

'It can't be Schweitzer.' *Could it?* 'I want your opinion here,' he added, knowing she wouldn't give it unless it was specifically requested.

'It has to be, sir.'

'You didn't hear them specifically mention Schweitzer, though? How the hell could they keep *that* a secret?'

'It's SAD, sir. Keeping secrets is what they do. My asset tells me they've had a VIP visit and that everything has been in tight lockdown since. They were able to get some sketch on the op but nothing on the reasons behind it. My money is that Schweitzer found his way there.'

'Is Hodges still in the wind? Did they find a body?'

'I've got nothing on that, sir, but that's also not my territory. You want to call—'

'I know who to call.' The Director cut her off, and immediately regretted the snarl in his voice. There was never anything to be gained by showing any emotion in front of a subordinate.

'Sorry, sir. Didn't mean to presume.'

'Is it possible your asset got burned? They're being run back against you?'

'Sir, I could be flattering myself here, but not a chance in hell.' The Director liked her confidence. That kind of surety was unusual in the living. It marked the elite from the rank and file.

'All right, we have to assume the team is coming for the whole Cell. They're going in fast and they're going in blind. They're hoping that surprise will make up for ignorance. Risky.'

'That's Ghaznavi's style, sir. Served her well for years.'

'Well, they will get a surprise, just not in the way they think. Bury your asset and stand by for instructions.'

'Yes, sir. You know how to reach me.' The commlink went dead.

The Director toggled the channel back over to Mark. 'Leave off the preparations. I need you to get all our ready units scrambled.'

'Understood, sir,' Mark said. 'May I ask what we're scrambling for?'

'Welcoming party,' the Director said. 'We're going to have visitors.'

Chapter Six
Surprise

'What do you think?' Ghaznavi asked.

Schweitzer tested the shoulder. He could feel electricity humming down the wires snaking from the dead muscle of the stump into the actuators of the mechanical arm. He tensed his muscles and the arm moved, just as his old one had.

'It's . . . like magic.'

Ghaznavi laughed. 'You ever read Clarke? Science fiction writer.'

Schweitzer shook his head. 'I was more into elves than spaceships.'

'You don't know what you're missing. He said that any sufficiently advanced technology is indistinguishable from magic. It's just wires, Jim, carrying the signal from your muscles and converting it into motion.'

The carbon-graphite appendage was completely silent, sliding against black metal joints as Schweitzer brought the forearm up to his face, admired the fork that framed the shining silver disk of the buzz-saw blade.

'Too shiny,' he said. 'It'll give away our position.'

Reeves looked up, stroked his beard. 'Shit, rookie move. Sorry.'

Schweitzer rotated the mechanical arm, gave the buzz

saw an experimental spin. 'We can paint it black.'

'You sure you wouldn't rather just have a gun?'

Schweitzer shook his head. 'If it's alive, I can close with it and do my job. If it's not alive, a gun won't make a difference.'

'So, what am I supposed to do if we run into something like you?'

'We *will* run into something, something*s*, like me. Pack a machete. Make sure someone on the team has a flame-thrower.'

Ghaznavi stood aside to make room for a technician who began slopping black paint over the buzz saw's shining metal surface. 'I can't fucking believe this. Where the hell am I going to get a flamethrower? We haven't used them since World War II.'

'We're going to be in a tight space without a map,' Reeves said. 'I don't like deploying area-effect weapons in close quarters. Too big a chance of zapping your own people.'

'This is different,' Schweitzer said. 'The only way to beat us is to utterly destroy the body. Shred it or burn it.'

Reeves looked up at Ghaznavi. 'My mission, ma'am, my call.'

'That's the call you want to make?' she asked. 'Schweitzer's the only one in this room who's had contact with the enemy.'

'Experience can lead and it can mislead,' Reeves answered. 'No explosives except for breaching charges, and no flamethrowers.'

Ghaznavi raised her hands. 'You're the ground boss.'

'Respectfully' – Schweitzer was used to the informality of working in the teams, but he wasn't sure about the relative rank here; he guessed that, this being their first time dealing with the undead, neither did they – 'that's the wrong call, man.'

'Your objection is noted, but you're not in charge and this isn't a vote. You're the superman you say you are, you won't miss a flamethrower,' Reeves said. 'You want in on this, and I say I'm fine with it. You'll be a serious asset and I'm glad to have you on board, but my ops run by my orders. That's just how it's going to be.'

'I'm a superman down an arm and going up against a whole lot of other supermen. Whatever, man. I'm in. Hope you've got a good team.'

'The best,' Reeves said.

'He's right,' Ghaznavi agreed. 'They are.'

'This is a little different from what you've seen before,' Schweitzer said.

'No doubt,' Reeves answered. 'We pride ourselves on adaptability.'

Schweitzer chuckled internally. 'Fair enough. I was the same way.'

'You still are,' Hodges offered. He'd been standing against the ready-room wall, arms folded, staying out of the way as the technicians worked and Reeves planned. 'New territory for all of us.'

Schweitzer raised the prosthetic, gave the buzz saw another spin. 'At least I've got a future working in a lumberyard after all this is over.'

The door opened and another man walked in. He could have been Reeves' younger brother. Same woodsman's civilian clothing. Same beard and rumpled hair. Same killer's eyes. He was already in the process of suiting up, body armor and a tactical vest over his black compression shirt. A stylized ancient Greek helmet was emblazoned on his shoulder patch, with the words MOLON LABE beneath. Schweitzer had worn a similar patch on scores of ops. The words were Greek, a quote from Herodotus, relating the words of Leonidas when the Persian king Xerxes had demanded the surrender of the three hundred Spartans at Thermopylae. *Proud Xerxes wants not your lands, but only your arms*, the Persian king's herald had said. *Molon labe*, Leonidas had replied. *Come and take them.*

'You rang,' the man drawled, setting his carbine on the table as he cinched down the covers on his magazine pouches. He wiggled his eyebrows at Reeves. ''Sup, bro. What's the plan?'

Reeves jerked his chin toward Ghaznavi, and the man looked up at her. 'Whoa! Sorry, ma'am. I didn't know you were here.'

'No worries,' Ghaznavi said. 'Frank Cort, this is Senator Don Hodges.'

'Sir.' Cort tugged on the brim of his threadbare ball cap. His eyes settled on Schweitzer and he started.

'And this is Jim Schweitzer,' Ghaznavi continued.

'Sch . . . the SEAL?'

'Nice to meet you,' Schweitzer said.

'But you're dead.'

'Yes, I am.'

Cort looked up at Reeves, eyes narrowing. 'If you're fucking with me, bro, this isn't funny. I'm on recall status right now, and my wife isn't exactly—'

'I'm not fucking with you. That is Jim Schweitzer sitting right there, and he is dead.'

Cort looked back at him, stammered.

'I know it's a lot to take in,' Schweitzer said.

'You've got a buzz saw for an arm.'

'We just installed it,' Ghaznavi said. 'Pretty cool, huh?'

'I lost the real arm on my last op,' Schweitzer offered.

'You do ops? Doesn't dying . . . I mean, are you still in the Navy?'

Schweitzer shrugged.

'Focus, man,' Reeves said. 'We're going to jump in a few hours and I need your head in the fight.'

'This is . . .' Cort shuddered.

'Lock it up,' Reeves said. 'I'm doing a single element and a single team. I need my best and I need them reliable. Magic is real and the dead walk the earth. Mission doesn't change.'

Cort sobered, swallowed. 'Okay.'

'*Okay* okay?' Reeves asked. 'I need you with me here, Frank.'

'Yeah, man. I'm good.'

'Outstanding,' Reeves said. 'Okay, get yourself set up and we'll go over the plan.'

'Targeting package?' Cort asked.

'There isn't one,' Schweitzer said, standing.

'We're going in blind?' Cort asked.

'It's kind of an emergency,' Ghaznavi offered, smiling weakly.

'Where are we dropping?' Cort asked. 'Can you tell me that, at least?'

'No drop. We're driving in under cover. I was thinking a medical truck. Do we still have one painted up?' Reeves asked.

'Yeah, I think so,' Cort said. 'So, this is domestic?'

'Colchester,' Reeves said.

'Virginia? As in right down the fucking road?' Cort asked.

'He said the same thing,' Schweitzer said, jerking his thumb at Reeves.

'Jesus Christ. Can I sit down?' Cort asked.

'He said that, too,' Schweitzer added.

Cort blinked at him, and Schweitzer could see the man struggling with the shock of meeting him. Like Reeves,

Cort was relying on his training to stay focused, but he was clearly shaken.

Schweitzer extended his buzz-saw arm, realized what he was doing, brought it back, and offered his hand instead. 'Well, sorry about the shock, Ernest. Call me Jim.'

'He's Frank,' Reeves said. 'I'm Ernest.'

Schweitzer stretched the smear of his gray lips in what passed for a smile. 'And I'm very funny.'

'Not really,' Reeves said. 'If we're going to work together, you need to be able to tell us apart.'

Schweitzer shrugged. 'All you living people look alike to me.'

There were eight of them, and while Schweitzer couldn't be sure if the names they gave were real, they matched their genders, at least. Reeves and Cort were the only full names he got. It was first-names-only for the junior members of the team, the single nod SAD made to secrecy among the ranks. Trifling. Such half measures hadn't protected Schweitzer when he'd still been alive.

The toughest-looking were the two women, Sharon and Kristine, with scarred faces and hard eyes. Sharon's black hair was shot through with premature gray, swept back into a stub of a ponytail. Kristine had dispensed with hair altogether. From the patchy look of the stubble sprouting beneath the scrape marks, she didn't put a lot of effort into shaving it cleanly. Sharon spun a small knife point-down on the reinforced palm of her glove. Kristine cleaned the barrel of a disassembled 9mm pistol that already looked spotless enough to eat off.

The next four were men, two Johns and two Mikes. The names were unlikely enough that Schweitzer wondered if they were real before deciding it didn't matter.

Reeves and Cort were the least impressive of the lot, which said something for the hard-bitten look of them. The urban-woodsmen outfits were set aside, and they all looked like operators now, black compression shirts, thigh rigs and chest harnesses bristling with ordnance.

They stood around the table, eyes locked on Schweitzer. Reeves had decided that it was best not to risk the team's reaction to Schweitzer. 'They're professionals,' he'd said, 'but everybody has their limits.'

Schweitzer had once again covered every inch of skin with a black bodysuit, STF armor, and a riot policeman's helmet with a tinted facemask that Ghaznavi said they normally used to transport prisoners. The buzz saw was draped with black cloth, and a sharp look from Reeves silenced any questions. Still, the team shot nervous glances at the hulking black figure with the cloth draped over his arm. Schweitzer did his best to make his chest gently rise and fall, to shift in his seat, even once raised a hand to scratch at his neck despite the glove and armor. Human motions made by living hands. *Nothing to see here, folks. Move along.*

'This,' Ghaznavi said, 'is James. He will be accompanying you on the run. This target is almost completely dark, and what little light we have comes from him. Please give him your full attention.'

'Hey,' Schweitzer said. Eyes widened at the dull rasp of his voice. Schweitzer could smell the adrenaline rising in their blood, could see the tension in their hands. They knew something was wrong with him. They were para-military fighters in the government's most secret army, used to operating in the dark without asking questions, but that didn't erase human curiosity or unease.

'I was a prisoner in the facility for . . . well, I'm not sure for how long, exactly. A few months, I'd guess. I don't have a photographic memory and I never made a map, but I can tell you a few things.'

Kristine drew out the machete at her waist, tested its edge. 'Can we start with these? How come we're carrying 'em?'

'I thought we were going to Colchester,' Sharon said.

'We are,' Reeves said.

Sharon snapped her knife shut and drew out her machete in a single, fluid motion. 'Did a jungle grow up there overnight?'

'It's not for plants,' Schweitzer said.

'What's it for, then?' one of the Mikes asked.

'It's for monsters.'

'Monsters,' Sharon said flatly.

Kristine pointed her machete at Reeves. 'Now I know I am most definitely being fucked with.'

'You're not being fucked with,' Ghaznavi said. 'I give you my word.'

That shut them up. Whatever rankless familiarity existed among the team clearly didn't extend to Ghaznavi.

'Monsters,' Sharon said.

'Yes.' Schweitzer nodded. 'They will look like people, but they aren't. They are ten times stronger, ten times faster, and ten times more vicious than anyone you've ever faced.'

'What're they packing?' Sharon asked.

'They'll come at you barehanded. Some will have claws . . . and they'll bite.'

All eyes turned to Reeves, who shrugged. 'Whaddya want me to say? This is new to me, too.'

'There'll be humans with them, pipe hitters like you. They'll be loaded for bear and most of them will have come out of JSOC or at least SOF units.'

'Do we have any numbers, or positions, or patrol routes?' Kristine asked.

Schweitzer shook his head.

'Shit,' said the same Mike. At least, Schweitzer thought it was the same Mike.

'So, we're going up against an unspecified number of enemy of an unknown disposition and with unknown armaments, backed up by an unspecified number of super-powered vampire . . . monster thingies, and no map of the ground?' Sharon sounded angry.

'If we do it right, we don't have to fight the monster thingies at all,' Schweitzer said. 'They're kept in refrigerated cells. Those cells are operated from a central control hub that's close to the surface. We get in there, we make sure the monsters stay in their cages. Then the only thing we have to worry about is the people.'

'And you know the layout here? Where this control hub is located?' Sharon asked.

'Yes,' Schweitzer answered. 'We go in fast and quiet. We take the control hub, we lock the facility down, then we can clear it at our leisure.'

'This is bullshit,' Kristine said, slapping her machete against the armor plating in her palm. 'I'm assuming you don't have any schematics on the control mechanism? Is there an override? We're going in completely blind. We're going to get our asses handed to us.'

'This is the mission, Kristine,' Cort said. 'You didn't sign up to drink piña coladas on a beach. You agreed to do what you have to do when you have to do it.'

'This isn't a mission,' Kristine shot back. 'This is running into a brick wall with a blindfold on.'

'Tell me something, all of you,' Ghaznavi said. 'Do you think that I would be willing to risk a boots-on-the-ground operation not only inside the country but practically inside the Beltway if the need was not dire? Do you think I would send someone else if there were someone else to send? You are this nation's beating black heart. You are the ones who wash the dirty laundry. If I had more to give you, I would give it to you, but I don't.'

'Why are the monster thingies kept in refrigerated cells?' Sharon asked.

'They're dead,' Schweitzer answered. 'Keeps them from rotting.'

'So . . . zombie monsters.' Sharon smiled. 'I feel like I'm dreaming.'

'You're not dreaming,' Ghaznavi said. 'This isn't the first time you've faced something new and unpleasant. You'll have total surprise. James will lead you to the control hub and you'll get the facility secured. From there on in, it'll be a shoot house.'

'Shithouse, more like it,' Kristine muttered.

'Anyone wants out, say the word,' Ghaznavi said. 'I'll find replacements. No strikes against you; you have my word on that. But I am promising you that if you stick, you will be participating in one of the most important ops this agency has undertaken in the nation's history.'

Schweitzer smelled adrenaline again, but judging from the flush of their cheeks and the light in their eyes, it wasn't from fear this time.

'Anybody out?' Reeves asked.

Silence.

'All right,' Reeves said. 'Let's get underway. We can talk more in the truck.'

The truck was white, painted with the logo of the Centers for Disease Control. An orange light bar was mounted across the top. The operators were crammed inside, four to a bench, Reeves and Schweitzer closest to the exit. Empty weapon racks were bolted to the walls over their heads. The actual weapons were packed into hard black plastic cases on the floor. All of the operators wore fluorescent yellow hazmat suits, bulky enough to conceal their tac vests and go-bags, ammunition and trauma kits, grenades, zip ties, and lock cutters. CDD – BIOHAZARD RESPONSE TEAM was stenciled across the back of each one.

The operators' heartbeats were steady, only a slight elevation in the adrenaline content of their blood indicating their excitement over the coming op. They looked locked-on. Schweitzer hoped it was enough.

'Lay it out for us one more time,' Reeves said.

Schweitzer gestured at the crude map sketched out on the tablet computer. 'Straight through the lobby, T intersection. Left wing leads through to the control room. The walls will be studded with freeze and burn nozzles. The cold jets pump liquid nitrogen. The others pump . . . fire, I guess. Not sure about the ignition mechanism. You can tell the difference between them by sight. Burners have pilot lights. Freezers will have frost on them.'

'What are they for?' Sharon asked, her eyes narrowing.

'The monsters,' Schweitzer said. 'They're precious, so they want to freeze them if they get loose. If that fails, they go to the burn. Those nozzles can turn a hallway into an icebox or a volcano at the touch of a button.'

'How the fuck are we supposed to get through that?' Sharon asked.

'Because they're not expecting us,' Schweitzer said. 'And by the time they figure out we're there, we'll have our fingers on those buttons.'

'These monsters are as bad as you say?' Sharon asked.

'Worse,' Schweitzer admitted, 'but they'll be locked in their cells, and once we have the control room, that's where they'll stay.'

'What if you're wrong?' Reeves asked.

Schweitzer didn't answer.

'Jesus fucking Christ.' Sharon shook her head.

'Lock it up,' Reeves said. 'We've been through worse.'

'We've been through better,' Kristine added.

'Two minutes,' Ghaznavi's voice came over the commlink in each of their ears. Schweitzer felt the truck shudder as it downshifted. His augmented ears could hear other vehicles in the distance, the soft clicking of their flashing lights. Emergency vehicles cordoning off the area, making sure that no civilians wandered onto the raid site. Schweitzer could only imagine the superhuman effort that Senator Hodges was even now expending to manage the rest of the op, massaging the news and media, making sure the story of a possible biohazard was making its way into the local rumor mill, with agents telling tales at nearby watering holes.

The team stood, moving to stack on the doors, then abruptly realizing they were supposed to be infectious-disease responders, not killers. They milled around uncertainly, looking askance at Reeves. 'Act natural,' he offered. Cort looked up, incredulous, and Schweitzer could hear him clearing his throat to speak when the truck shuddered to a halt and the doors swung open, letting the lights from the parking lot flood in.

The team picked up the weapons cases and jumped down to the asphalt. They were in a broad parking lot bathed in harsh white sodium light wavering as insects battered themselves against the glowing tubes. A few cars were parked, silent and dark, between stubs of white lines.

A squat, featureless black building stood at the parking lot's far end, the smooth, reflective surface broken only by a pair of double glass doors. ENTERTECH/PHASE III, INC., frosted letters painted across the glass, SERVING THOSE WHO SERVE. A stainless steel mail slot was punched into the doorframe at foot level and a small half dome of a camera was mounted at the top. Otherwise, there was nothing.

Schweitzer could see Reeves arching an eyebrow through the clear plastic of his suit's faceplate. 'You . . . uh . . . notice anything?'

Schweitzer dialed his augmented hearing out, scanned through the infrared spectrum. Nothing. 'Clear,' he said.

Cort nodded and slapped a dot to the side of the camera. It was the size of an eraser's head, adhesive on one side. It stuck fast. Cort stepped back, keeping his eyes on the door the entire time, unzipped his suit and reached inside to his tac vest. Schweitzer heard the click of a button, and blue electricity sparked across the surface of the camera. There was a quiet fizzle and pop, and smoke wafted up into the night sky.

'Guns up,' Reeves said, and the team knelt as a single man, unlocking the plastic cases and lifting the weapons out, stacking on the doors. Schweitzer pulled the cover off his buzz saw and stood opposite them. There were a few sharp intakes of breath, but that was the sum of their reaction to this latest strangeness.

Reeves nudged the door; it was locked. 'Sharon, come up,' he said, but Schweitzer stopped her with a wave of his hand.

She froze, looked askance at Reeves. Schweitzer didn't wait for his answer but instead moved up, putting his hand at the precise location of the locking bar. What he was about to do would dazzle the team members who didn't know what he was, but that couldn't be avoided. They would be finding out soon enough anyway.

He pushed on the seam between the doors, adding pressure slowly, until the doors gently groaned and the locking bar strained. He could hear the fibers of the metal trembling, a reverberating song like a high-tension cable in the wind, and at long last, they parted with a soft snap. Schweitzer heard more sharp breaths, but the team again stayed focused as he flowed into the room beyond.

The words they'd seen on the door were written larger here, in blocks of stainless steel moving diagonally up the wall behind an L-shaped desk made of the same reflective black material as the rest of the building. A monitor glowed gently atop the otherwise bare surface. No guards, no administrative personnel.

'Two cameras,' Schweitzer whispered, gesturing to the vaulted corners of the ceiling.

Cort knelt, reaching inside his unzipped suit and producing what appeared to be a small pistol. He aimed it at the cameras in turn, and Schweitzer could see a pencil-thin beam of ultraviolet light visible only to him. The cameras sparked and went out in turn.

'Suits,' Reeves said, unzipping his own. The team followed suit, leaving the bulky hazmat suits on the floor and stepping out of them in their ops gear, weapons trained on the only exit to the room, two featureless double-doors behind the desk.

'White, white. Blue,' Reeves said into the commlink. 'We're on deck and ready.'

'Blue, this is white,' Ghaznavi's voice came back. 'Go on your mark. Everything looks good from up here.'

Schweitzer scanned the room once more, straining his abilities to push beyond the walls and doors. No heat signatures whatsoever. 'It's clear,' he said, 'but we're going to get jumped.'

'Why do you say that?' Reeves didn't sound surprised.

'I broke out of here at roughly the same time of night,' Schweitzer said. 'There was a lady behind the front desk. The lights were on. There were people around. It shouldn't be this deserted.'

'Yeah,' Cort said, scanning the corners. 'This whole thing stinks.'

'Stack up.' Reeves jerked his chin at the doors. The team, whatever their misgivings, moved to comply.

'Straight through there.' Schweitzer gestured at the door. 'T-shaped corridor I drew for you. Cell blocks are down one floor. Admin offices to your right. Helo hangar is to your left.'

Reeves leaned forward, nudged the door with the side of his hand, it gave gently. He whispered into the comm-link. 'Unlocked.'

He pulled a long, narrow wand from his tac vest, flicked his wrist. The wand telescoped out, a mirror unfurling from its end. Reeves crouched, slid the mirror under the door.

'No heat signatures,' Schweitzer whispered.

Reeves nodded. 'It's clear. Buttonhook by element. Gold left, silver right. On my mark.'

Schweitzer heard the round break before it impacted. A short cough of primer igniting, the tiny roar as metal pierced the sound barrier, the acrid whiff of propellant, and then the wet thud as it pierced bone and brain. One of the operators dropped like a sack of stones, and the rest scattered.

'Contact rear!' Reeves shouted, the need for stealth long past. Schweitzer whirled. The space behind them was empty, but he could hear a dull rattling in the ceiling above. He scanned the infrared and saw the dissipating patch of heat where the propellant gas had vented from the muzzle; it spread and thinned outside a louvered air intake in the ceiling.

'They're overhead!' Schweitzer shouted, setting the saw spinning.

The team's weapons went up, but they were far too

disciplined to fire without a clear target. Cort and two others scrambled behind the desk. Concealment, not cover, but it was better than nothing. The remaining operators eyed the door, but the corridor behind it was an unbending six feet, every step of which would silhouette the team, making them easy targets. A fatal funnel.

'Everybody out!' Schweitzer shouted, gesturing at the front doors. The enemy would get a shot at them as they passed, but it was far better than sending the team scrambling deeper into the facility through a tight space where burst fire would scythe them down in seconds.

The team lacked Schweitzer's superhuman reflexes, but they were still the best of their kind. They didn't hesitate. They fired three-round bursts into the ceiling, intended to scatter an enemy, forcing them to keep their heads down while the team made their escape. The team fired and moved slowly, carefully. There was no risk they would stumble, and their weapons spit rounds precisely where they aimed. Schweitzer could tell from the sound of their hearts and the smell of the chemicals in their blood that they were rattled, but to anyone else, it would appear the team was unhurriedly moving to the exit, firing accurately the whole while. When he'd been a living SEAL with a beating heart, Schweitzer had been the same.

The metallic rattling reached a crescendo and the drop ceiling shuddered, followed by frantic scratching. Schweitzer scanned the ceiling. A Gold wouldn't be sniping, but there were still no heat signatures. There was someone up there, hosed down with Freon or lying in a refrigerated compartment. The scratching was farther back, just over the doors leading to the parking lot. A living, breathing enemy wouldn't make those sounds.

Schweitzer waved frantically back toward the passage behind the desk. Fatal funnel or no, they needed to go through it, and fast. 'Go back in! Go back in!' he shouted.

And now the team did hesitate. Because it wasn't sound tactical advice. Heading back into the tight space would guarantee at least one death, probably more. They froze, some of them coming off their sights to glance at the ceiling by the main entrance, looking for what caused Schweitzer to change his mind.

The shooter in the ceiling fired again, and another operator spun and dropped. Another one of the Mikes. Not even sixty seconds and the team was down by two.

And then the ceiling exploded, showering them all in white dust.

Three figures dropped twelve feet onto the hard concrete floor. The drop would have broken the leg of any normal person, but they only crouched, absorbing the shock and rising slowly. Their skin was gray, shot through with plunging metal cables and clumsy purple scars. Their faces were leering skulls that rivaled Schweitzer's own. Their long gray tongues hung to their waists, one flung carelessly over a thick shoulder. Bone claws sprouted from their fingertips. They leaned forward, their golden eyes burning with anticipation.

'Back! Go now! As fast as you can!' Schweitzer shouted, sprinting toward the Golds.

'What ab—' Cort said into the commlink.

'You can't fight them! Just get the hell out of here!'

Schweitzer reached the first of the three. In life, it had been a short man, thick in the neck and shoulders. Bone spines ran in a single line from its chin, over its head, and down its back. The Gold's eyes flicked to Schweitzer, then over his shoulder to the team, drawn by the thumping of their hearts. It jerked left, then dove right with superhuman speed. Schweitzer swung his buzz-saw arm, felt the blade catch in the back of the thing's thigh as it shot past. It would have felled someone who could feel pain, but of course, pain was nothing to a Gold.

The team, to their credit, didn't panic. They set up a walking retreat, moving and covering one another, leapfrogging back to the hall. It was by the numbers, the tactically sound decision in the face of a normal enemy.

But against Gold Operators, it was much too slow.

The first Gold reached the desk where Cort and one of the Johns were retreating, just as the shooter in the ceiling fired again. The bullet drilled the other John retreating back to the door. The Gold reached the John beside Cort and delivered an uppercut that sent his head sailing toward the ceiling with a wet pop. Four down.

The team's sangfroid began to crumble. They fired on burst, backing pell-mell into the fatal funnel, still facing the enemy. Schweitzer felt rounds whir past his head. They weren't being careful in their aim anymore. A few of the bullets found the Golds, who ignored them beyond righting themselves as the impact staggered them backward. They fell on the decapitated operator's sinking corpse, raising their hands as the hot blood rained down, tipping their chins upward like children dancing in a storm.

'Runrunrunrunrun!' Schweitzer shouted to the team. It was too late for a tactical retreat. The delight in savaging the corpse wouldn't stop the Golds for long.

And now the team did break and run, turning their backs on the enemy and bolting through the corridor, turning sharply left and moving out of sight.

The Golds didn't bother with Schweitzer. His heart was still, his body as cool as their own. The dead only cared for the living. They knelt, bowed over the steadily diminishing remains of the operator, as if in prayer. Even after sharing his corpse with one of them, feeling its urges as his own, Schweitzer couldn't understand them. They didn't need to eat, weren't driven by any hunger he knew, yet still they tore the flesh to bloody ribbons, chewed it with relish.

He remembered how clever Ninip had been when it thought guile would gratify its lust for blood, or would corrupt Schweitzer so that Ninip could cast him out, claiming his body for itself. But like all Golds, Ninip's cunning could be marshaled only in service to its appetite. Golds might look like people, but they were animals, more self-determining than rabid dogs, but only just.

Schweitzer brought the buzz saw up over his head. The Golds didn't so much as turn as he brought it down, cleaving the first of them almost in two, the spinning blade passing with little resistance through its skull, catching briefly on the ribcage, before he drove it all the way to its waist. The Gold tried to turn, but its split spine couldn't hold it upright, and it flopped over on its side.

The other two rose, howling in rage at the interruption. The first showed more presence of mind, leaping for Schweitzer's mechanical arm instead of his throat. The second punched him hard enough to make his bones vibrate, tearing him free from the grasp of the first and sending him smashing through the entryway doors to land on his shoulders out in the parking lot.

'*Khodaye!*' Ghaznavi's voice buzzed in Schweitzer's ear. 'Status? Do you need extract?'

'Negative,' Reeves said before Schweitzer could answer. 'We've got four down, but we're still in the fight.'

'You are not still in the fucking fight.' Schweitzer leapt to his feet. 'Did you miss them kicking our ass for the past—'

'We're positioned now,' Reeves cut him off. 'We can still do this.'

Schweitzer looked past the broken glass hanging in the metal doorframes. The remaining two Golds had turned from Schweitzer and raced for the corridor, following the heartbeats of Reeves' remaining people. As they left, two ropes dropped from the ceiling. Two figures slid down them and into view.

Schweitzer could hear their beating hearts, but their STF armor smoked with cold, the gel inside each cell supercooled. Their heat signatures were invisible, as gray as the skin of the dead Golds. The people under the armor must be freezing, but a good operator could do their job no matter what the conditions.

He didn't doubt the operators roping down to the lobby floor were freezing, cold enough to keep them out of even his magically augmented visual spectrum, and he also knew that it wouldn't slow them down at all.

Good thing he was behind them.

They scanned the room, getting on their gun sights. It was more than long enough for Schweitzer to cover the distance between them. He swept the buzz saw up and the blade caught the operator under the armpit. Shear-thickening fluid was designed to harden when impacted by terrific velocity on a small point – the striking of a bullet. Compared to a bullet, the serrated edge of the buzz-saw blade moved at a leisurely pace. Against it, the armor was only so much liquid. The operator screamed as the saw bit into him, the scream turning to a gurgling choke as the blade moved through his ribs and into his lungs. He collapsed, drowning in his own blood.

Schweitzer turned on his companion, flicking the mechanical arm to one side, hearing the wet splatter of the blood sheeting off. The enemy turned, sighted his carbine, and fired. Not panicked but hurried, and the shot broke high, the round catching Schweitzer's helmet and tearing it off. A few inches lower and it would have punched a neat hole in the metal plate that made up his face. As it was, it snapped his head back, sent him staggering a few steps.

The enemy operator took one look at the flickering silver of Schweitzer's eyes and didn't bother to fire again. He turned and ran, bursting through the broken entry doors and out into the parking lot. Schweitzer thought to go after him, realized he couldn't spare the time if he was going to help Reeves and his team. He ran for the corridor behind the desk.

'One squirter,' he said into his commlink. 'Main entrance, coming out into the parking lot.'

'We've got him,' Ghaznavi said. Shots rang out from outside.

'Reeves!' Schweitzer called into the commlink. 'Where are you? I . . .'

He rounded the corner, came to a skidding halt. One of the Golds was down, a sizeable chunk of its thigh sloughing off from a machete cut. The other was riddled with bullets, just finding its feet after what looked like an entire extended magazine of 5.56mm ammunition had been emptied into its face. Its head was a loose pulp, the gold flames lopsided, flickering at odd angles.

Schweitzer resisted the temptation to assess the situation. The Golds were so fast that any hesitation would give them enough time to kill another one of the team. Schweitzer threw himself into pulp-head, arms wrapping around its waist. It slammed face-first into the wall hard enough to crack the cinder block, spraying dust. The Gold roared through its pulped mouth, swung an arm back, trying to use the momentum to turn itself around. Schweitzer pressed forward, holding it in place. He brought his knee up into its spine, then again and again.

The Gold managed to get an elbow into Schweitzer's ribs, but the blow lacked leverage, and Schweitzer barely felt it. Another knee to the spine, another, and Schweitzer finally felt the cracking he'd been hoping for as the Gold's spine shivered and broke. He delivered two more knee shots, one to the short ribs on either side of the shattered spine, felt them give way. The Gold's torso sagged and Schweitzer let it go, praying that he had damaged it enough to put it out of the fight.

He let the Gold slump against the wall, spun to face the other. It had only been a moment, but that was more than enough time for a Gold to kill a human, no matter how well trained, even with a cut in its thigh . . .

The remaining Gold lay on the ground in four neat pieces. The head lay on its side. One arm had been severed at the shoulder and kicked away to the wall. The second had been cut off at the elbow, lay next to the body. Reeves stood astride it, a machete in each hand, the flat black surface of the blades dripping with glycerol. Deep notches scarred the edges, bent and blued where they had struck the metal cabling inside the Gold's body.

Reeves took a shuffling step on his prosthetic leg. 'Everybody okay?'

'No,' Cort said, 'but nobody else is dead, if that's what you're asking.'

'I'll take it,' Reeves said. 'Look, I'm sorry, but we have to bug out. I thought we could hang in, but this is too close for comfort. They were waiting for us. Who the fuck knows what other surprises they've got planned?'

'You're the boss,' Cort said. The rest of the team murmured assent.

'But no fucking Quick Reaction Force. No extraction. We walk out of here with our heads up,' Reeves said.

The faces around him lit with pride and determination.

Schweitzer heard the operators grunt with satisfaction. 'Fuckin' A, chief,' Cort said.

Reeves finally looked up at Schweitzer. 'Didn't I tell you it was rude to stare?'

'Sorry,' Schweitzer said. 'I just . . .'

'Never seen a gimp in a fight?'

'I've never seen a living person beat a Gold before. Not in a stand-up fight. I didn't think it was possible.'

'Keep watching.' Reeves smiled. 'I'm full of surprises.'

Reeves turned to the team. 'Get up and guns up. We're clear back out of here, but I'm not taking any chances. I'll take point. Frank, anchor.'

'On it, boss,' Cort said.

'No,' Schweitzer said, pointing deeper into the facility. 'We have to go that way.'

'We're compromised,' Reeves said. 'The control room isn't going to help us now. Those things are out of their cells.'

'That's not it,' Schweitzer said. 'There's more contacts by the front door where we came in. At least two alive, and at least another three like these.' He gestured to the crippled Golds on the floor. 'Look, man. You did great here, but you can't keep it up. Not against this many.'

He met the eyes of the team around him, saw the question written on their faces: *How can you possibly know this?*

'I can hear them,' Schweitzer said. 'Heartbeats and a . . . scrabbling. The Golds don't move like people do. Call the QRF.'

Reeves shook his head, stamped his metal foot against the floor. 'We fight our way out. I'm not risking any more lives.'

'Don't risk your own. You killed a Gold straight up. There's nothing more for you to prove. The mission is scrubbed, so cut your losses and go.'

Reeves held Schweitzer's gaze for a long moment. A soft whispering reached them, echoing out from the building's vestibule. More ropes dropping. Scratching followed, like a cat walking on metal with its claws out. 'We don't have a lot of time,' Schweitzer said.

Reeves cursed, toggled his commlink. 'White, white. Blue. QRF for extract. We're sheltering in place.'

Schweitzer shook his head. 'We may have to fall back.'

Reeves nodded, the determination that was as close to fear as a SEAL came showing in his eyes. He looked at Schweitzer but spoke into the commlink. 'We'll try to hold to the first deck, but we may have to go deeper.' He pulled out a small metal canister, thumbed the end, and tossed it into a shadowed corner. 'I've marked our last position. Keep in mind the enemy may move the beacon.'

'Blue, white,' Ghaznavi said. 'We're spinning up the QRF. Going to be a minute.'

Reeves nodded to the team. 'Frank, get a munition on this entryway. Sharon, you and Kristine on the other egress. Schweitzer, stick with me.'

Schweitzer heard a click, a metal thud, and the rapid clacking of bone claws. 'They're coming right now,' he said.

'Frank! Put a siren on it!' Reeves shouted, dropping to one knee and letting the machetes dangle from his wrists by their lanyards. He raised his carbine and thumbed the selector switch to the airburst rounds. 'So much for keeping quiet.'

Cort knelt, pulling a slender black wedge from a pouch on his tac vest, setting it in the entryway, trailing a wire back to a detonator in his hand. 'Not braced,' he said. 'The casing is going to go flying.'

'Yeah,' Reeves said, as the first of the Golds turned the corner.

It bristled with short bone spines, thin and curving, looking like the corpse of some giant porcupine. They covered its hands and feet, clacking on the concrete floor, breaking its grip so that it skidded on the smooth surface as it turned the corner, sliding into the far wall. The spines whispered against the cinderblock as the Gold turned, mewling with eagerness, started toward them.

'Boss!' Sharon shouted from the other entrance. 'Multiple contacts inbound to my position.'

'Figure it out!' Reeves shouted back. 'We're tied up here.'

Another Gold appeared behind the porcupine, and another. Schweitzer was focused on the nearer threat, registering the new arrivals only as man-shaped flashes of gray. Cort was uncoiling the wire, crouching back as far as he could. 'Now would be a good time, Frank!' Schweitzer called, spinning up his buzz saw.

'Fuck,' Cort breathed. 'Cover up!'

The black wedge exploded, spraying a cloud of metal balls into the corridor. Schweitzer could see the sparks as they ricocheted off the walls, leaving tiny gray-white pockmarks in the cinderblock. With no support, the wedge spun as it detonated, the plastic black case launching into the air, slamming Reeves' chest hard enough to activate the cell on his STF armor. The suddenly hardened plate saved his life, but the blow picked him up and launched him across the room, sliding on his shoulders until he slammed into the far wall beside Sharon.

The mouth of the wedge turned as it exploded, the metal balls spraying mostly against one side of the corridor, leaving the newly arrived Golds completely unscathed. The Porcupine was cut to ribbons, scraps of gray flesh and splinters of bone raining across its fellows as they charged forward.

Schweitzer resisted the almost-overwhelming urge to race to Reeves' side, to help Sharon face whatever was coming from behind. They were hard operators. They would find a way. Ops worked because team members trusted one another to get their jobs done.

And Schweitzer's job was clear.

Schweitzer raced into the smoke-filled corridor, so fast that a few of the ricocheting balls bounced off him, their force so attenuated that they didn't activate the cells on his STF armor.

He chopped down with the buzz saw, felt the smoke around him stirring as the Gold in front of him leapt backward into a somersault, legs whipping up so quickly that its feet ripped past mere inches from his face. Cold and dead, the Gold left no heat signature, and Schweitzer squinted through the clearing smoke to catch a glimpse of the creature completing the flip and landing on its feet again, crouching deep, hands spread wide. Schweitzer didn't see the second Gold and didn't wait to. He had this one moment while his enemy regained its balance. He wasn't going to miss it. He crossed the distance so quickly that he could feel the smoke whipping over his shoulders in what must have looked like miniature jet contrails to the operators in the room behind him. He swept the buzz saw down, forcing the Gold to raise an arm to block before it had balanced itself from its flip. It toppled sideways, and Schweitzer only had to change the angle of the blade to send it past the Gold's guard and deep into its shoulder. He put his good hand against his carbon-fiber forearm and pushed it through until it sparked against the floor. The creature fell in two pieces.

Gunshots from behind him. The rest of the team was handling whatever had been coming through the opposite door.

Schweitzer was scanning for the next threat when it hit him. Burning gold eyes and gray flesh flashed in his vision, and then arms were wrapped around his waist, carrying him into the corridor wall. Schweitzer elbowed the Gold in the back. It shuddered but held on. He elbowed it again, this time bringing a knee up into its sternum, hammer and anvil. He felt ribs crack, and the Gold let go, allowed Schweitzer to kick it back into the corridor, where it stumbled into more gray shapes rounding the corner.

Schweitzer didn't bother to count the new arrivals. He knew there were too many.

'Reeves!' Schweitzer backed up as fast as he could without falling. 'We've got to get out of here!'

'We're clear back here!' Reeves shouted back. 'I think.'

Schweitzer finally turned. Smoke boiled out of the rear corridor, filling the room. He could make out the heat signatures of Reeves, Cort, Sharon, and Kristine stacked on the doorway. Schweitzer couldn't see any Golds, but then again, with the smoke, he couldn't really see anything.

Thudding of bare feet behind him. There was no time and no choice.

'Go!' he said, deliberately slowing to let the operators into the corridor first. He didn't know what was ahead of them, but he knew what was behind them. In this case, the devil he knew was *not* better than the one he didn't.

Reeves didn't hesitate. He shoved Kristine into the corridor, then tapped Sharon to follow, motioned to Cort. Getting his people out first. A good leader.

Then the smoke swirled aside long enough for Schweitzer to see the shiny metal nubs on the walls. Some were scorched from whatever explosive the team had used to clear the corridor, but Schweitzer could still smell the liquid nitrogen, see the tiny blue flicker of pilot lights.

'Reeves, no! Don't . . .'

Kristine was already pelting down the corridor, running heedlessly, all too aware of what was coming behind Schweitzer. The cloud of liquid nitrogen hit her broadside, first bulling the smoke away, and then turning it into dazzling filaments, curling in on themselves and sawing toward the floor like threads of cotton candy blown on a strong wind. She didn't scream, merely slowed, then stopped mid-stride, one arm raising to shield her face.

Sharon skidded on her heels, threw herself backward, arms pinwheeling. The freezing vapor billowed out, and Cort and Reeves spun away from either side of the corridor, back into the room that had suddenly become a trap, freezing death before them, rending death behind.

The Golds' feet thudded behind him, and Schweitzer could hear the whisper of air as the first of them leapt, trying to clear Schweitzer's dead body to get at the living ones behind him.

Schweitzer grabbed Sharon. She shouted, throwing an elbow into his side, unable to tell if the arm around her belonged to friend or foe. But she was already off-balance and falling backward, the billowing cold of the liquid nitrogen still spraying, filling the corridor with pale white gas and twisting filaments of frozen smoke. Kristine was still in there, arm raised, knee up in mid-stride. Her armor, her vest, her weapon and magazines, her skin and hair, all were a stark, brittle blue-white.

Schweitzer yanked Sharon down to the floor, rolling aside and covering her with his body. The Gold overshot them, hurtling headlong into the cloud of freezing gas, shrieking in frustration as it went. Schweitzer could hear the dull tinkling like shattering glass, Kristine's remains breaking apart as the monster slammed into her. He could hear the scrabbling of its claws as it spun around, got back to its feet, the high creaking as the cloud of spraying coolant began to overcome the suppleness of its dead flesh, pushing the temperature down below what even the glycerol in the monster's veins could handle.

It might move fast enough to get out before it froze, but Schweitzer couldn't worry about that now. He rose to meet the next Gold he knew was surely coming.

Reeves' carbine barked, three shots in quick succession. Schweitzer saw the vaguely gray shape of a Gold stumble. Its knee was ripped and ragged, the joint separated, no longer able to support the Gold's weight. Reeves had put three rounds in a row dead center into the creature's knee-cap, a target less than two inches square. The man was good.

Sharon kicked away from Schweitzer, her eyes locked on his face, dinner-plate wide. Reeves and Cort already knew what was behind the mask. Not Sharon.

'I know,' Schweitzer said, leaping to his feet. 'But trust me, I'm on your side.'

He reached the Gold in a few steps and swung the buzz saw back and forth, taking first the head, then a good portion of the shoulders, then the top of the thing's chest. By the time the fourth stroke swept back to split its ribcage, it had stopped fighting and Schweitzer gratefully glimpsed the corridor behind it, empty for now.

He whirled. Reeves, Cort, and Sharon were already on their feet, stepping back a few paces to avoid the spreading liquid nitrogen cloud.

The Gold that had leapt over him had managed to crawl nearly all the way back out of the corridor before freezing solid. It was on its hands and knees, one clawed hand extended, mouth pulled back in a hungry snarl. Glycerol icicles hung from cuts in its hands, gouged by the fragments of what had once been Kristine.

At last, the coolant supply spent itself, or maybe their

enemies assumed they were all finished and it was no longer necessary. The spray stopped, leaving the cloud of freezing gas to settle into a dirty rime on the corridor's walls and floor.

Schweitzer could see that the frozen corridor let out into another T intersection. This time, he led the way, dancing nimbly around the frozen Gold and the shattered fragments of the frozen human, and emerged crouched, saw spun up and ready. Empty. No Golds. No heat signatures.

To the right, a code-locked door opened onto what Schweitzer knew was an access corridor to what Schweitzer assumed were offices, judging by the lack of freeze and burn nozzles on the sections of wall he could see through a narrow window cut into the door. The control room was somewhere back there. Useless to them now that the Golds were already out.

To the left was a larger set of double doors, even bigger than the building's entrance. Behind them, Schweitzer could see a long, narrow hallway. It went on for about thirty feet before suddenly widening out into a huge space blocked by an enormous plastic curtain, clear but thick enough that Schweitzer couldn't see through it.

'Clear!' he shouted back to Reeves. 'Come on!'

Reeves, Cort, and Sharon cleared the corridor and came shivering out into the T intersection as Schweitzer raced to the double doors and wrenched one off its hinges.

'Maybe try the handle first?' Cort winced at the scream of the metal and the clanging as Schweitzer tossed the door aside.

'I promise you, it was locked,' Schweitzer said, moving through.

The team followed as Schweitzer ran the length of the hallway and pushed through the plastic. There was a faint pattering of bare feet behind them, more Golds, but not close. Yet.

'Status?' Ghaznavi's voice buzzed in his ear. 'Ernest, what the hell is going on down there?'

'Working on an exit. QRF is welcome any fucking time,' Reeves answered as Schweitzer swept the plastic aside, bringing his spinning saw blade up.

A broad concrete pad stretched before him. Six helicopters crouched on it, two giant Chinooks and two Little Birds, all limbered, rotors tightly bound and wheels chocked. A modified Black Hawk was also limbered, draped under camouflage netting.

A solitary Little Bird stood ready to go, toward the bay's wide mouth, open to the sky and washed with the colors of the setting sun. Schweitzer could hear a heartbeat, sketch the vague outline of a heat signature, a man crouching inside the cabin.

'One contact inside!' He pointed at the helo.

Schweitzer heard a curse, and a man leaned out of the helo's cockpit, leveling a pistol. He was dressed in jeans and a button-down work shirt, a baseball cap with a curved brim. Not all that different from how Cort and Reeves had looked when they'd first answered Ghaznavi's call. The Cell and SAD probably dipped in the same pool and had recruited them from the Army's Special Operations Aviation Regiment as soon as they'd gotten out.

The pistol cracked, the round punching a neat hole in Schweitzer's saw blade, missing the motor housing by inches. The guy was a good shot and knew precisely what he was up against, else he would have put the bullet in Schweitzer's forehead instead of his saw. Schweitzer heard gunshots as the SAD operators returned fire, but the man with the pistol was already disappearing back into the helo cabin. Schweitzer heard a rising whine as the helo's air intakes began to spin up.

'They're going to take off,' Schweitzer said into the commlink. 'That thing's our ticket out. Can anybody fly—'

'I can,' Sharon answered. 'I'm qualled on that platform.'

'Good. Keep him alive if you can,' Schweitzer said. 'Intel.'

He launched himself at the helo cabin and was rewarded with three rounds slamming into the chest cells of his STF armor. The cells did their job and the bullets didn't penetrate, but impact sent him skidding on his back and away from the fight.

Schweitzer could hear the scrabbling of claws and slapping of bare feet. More Golds behind them and closing. Sharon and Reeves were up on their sights, walking slowly toward the helo, ready to put a bullet in anything that moved. Cort was looking at Schweitzer, eyes fixed on the smoking dents in his armor.

'Dude! I'm already dead,' Schweitzer shouted at him, propping himself up on his elbows. 'Get in the fucking fight!'

Cort looked embarrassed, got back on his sights, and moved to the helo.

Schweitzer leapt to his feet, but Reeves was already shouting, 'Drop your weapon!' The command was followed by three short pops.

'He's down,' Reeves said over the commlink.

'Not out of the woods,' Schweitzer said into the commlink. 'Multiple contacts inbound.'

'Living or dead?' asked Reeves.

Schweitzer positioned himself between the hangar entrance and the helo, the air intakes whining louder as the rotors slowly spun up. 'Dead. Here in a minute.'

'Shit,' Reeves said. Schweitzer could hear the clicking

of switches and the popping of buttons in the background as Sharon worked the helo's controls.

'No time for flight checks,' she said. 'Get on the bird, Schweitzer.'

'No time for that, either,' Schweitzer said, spinning up his buzz saw as the first Gold tore the plastic sheeting aside and burst into the room. It paused for a half second, taking in Schweitzer before focusing on the heartbeats coming from inside the helo.

Schweitzer could hear those hearts too, their rapid beating the only indicator of the team's stress that managed to penetrate their professional exterior. The rhythm was overlaid by something else, a dull whining and a churning roar, louder than the helo rotors. It was followed by a clinking sound, like links of chain being dragged over a bed of nails.

Or rounds sliding through a magazine well. 'Get the fuck out of the way!' Sharon yelled.

Schweitzer dove aside as the helo's .50-cal cannon's electrical motor engaged and the barrels spun out two thousand rounds a minute into the hangar's entrance. Schweitzer felt the bullet contrails skim past the soles of his boots, and then he was rolling to safety. The Gold was caught mid-stride, shredded by the metal storm that swept left and right as Sharon swiveled the gun's three rotating barrels. Schweitzer heard metal whining off concrete as the bullets ricocheted off the walls and floor, turning the corridor into a blender on puree. There might have been other Golds behind the first one, or there might have not. It didn't matter. Nothing in that space bigger than a mouse could have escaped.

The sound of the rotors shifted as Sharon pulled on the collective, forcing the blades to take weight and pull the helo skyward. The cannon kept up a steady stream of fire, spinning barrels arcing gracefully downward as it rose. Sharon wasn't taking any chances, and Schweitzer knew she wouldn't land for him. He gathered the magical strength in his legs and leapt, shooting into the air higher and faster than the most gifted basketball player in history.

But he was competing with an engine climbing at over two thousand feet per minute. He watched the helo skid receding in his vision, the ground rising hungrily beneath him. He waggled his fingertips, straining his shoulder, trying to eke out the last inch of his grip. He felt his fingers brush metal. And snag. His knuckles stretched, the joints separating. A human's hand would have lost its grip, the ligaments separating, the tension overwhelming the bone to rip it into fragments. Schweitzer felt his fingers hook, bite, and hold. He held on as the helo roared out through the open bay and into the sky.

Schweitzer spared a look down at the small building, growing smaller by the moment, and the parking lot outside. Three vans were parked there, surrounded by SAD operators in their tactical gear. No effort was being made at concealment now. They were quickly prepping to extract whatever was left of the team. Farther out, a team in orange hazmat suits were standing up barricades beside military Humvees.

'Jesus,' Schweitzer said into the commlink. 'You could have fucking warned me. You nearly ground me up just as fine as the bad guys.'

'I told you to get on the bird,' Sharon replied. 'I'm not in the habit of repeating myself.'

And then she was toggling the radio channel, getting comms with Ghaznavi's control helo, waving off the extraction. What was left of the team was out, and Schweitzer looked down on the silent building concealing the warren of tunnels that made up the Gemini Cell facility beneath.

They wouldn't be going in blind again. They would cordon it off, spin their story to the press, and try to figure out what to do next.

Reeves read his mind. 'Now what?'

'Now,' Schweitzer said, 'we rope it off and come up with a plan.'

'What plan?' Cort asked. 'There's just one of you and dozens of those other things.'

Schweitzer didn't answer. The helo shot out over the blackness of the woods behind the building, making slow, lazy loops, gun trained on the building, until SAD controllers on the ground guided it home.

Chapter Seven

Sense of Urgency

The Director stood in the open helo bay. He hadn't ordered the overhead bay doors closed and saw no reason to bother. The horses were out of the barn already.

The SAD team had stolen his standby helicopter and used its GAU-19 to shred the access corridor. Huge furrows were dug in the walls and floor, the ceiling blackened from the ricochets skidding off the surface, heating the paint until it bubbled. The remains of three of his Gold Operators were spattered through the wreckage, so finely minced that it was difficult to tell the flesh from the rubble.

Still, they'd managed to kill five of the SAD operators. That was something. The Director had ordered the four corpses that could be recovered put in the cold storage and prepped for Summoning. Magical Operators used the capabilities of the body they inhabited had in life, which was why they were built almost exclusively from the corpses of special operations personnel. The SAD troopers had done a lot of damage; the least they could do now was be of some use. Of course, he would need to recruit a new Summoner first, but now that the facility was locked down, he could turn his attention to finding one.

The Director looked up at the lightening sky, listened to thrumming motors outside. They were assembling quite an army out there. He could pick out the baritone grumble of vans and sedans, the deeper coughing of heavier vehicles. Strykers, certainly, and something on treads but lighter than a tank. He could hear the thudding of boots and the crackle of radio static. There were a lot of them, in a tight cordon that reached all the way around the facility. He dialed his magically augmented hearing farther out, could detect only a single helo, probably a Black Hawk, making a slow rotation of the building's perimeter. They didn't have the airspace closed yet, not securely.

The Director didn't fault himself for inadvertently providing the SAD team with their means of escape. It was his backup helo, and one should always have an emergency escape vehicle. His real mistake had been overconfidence. He was so certain that with the advantage of surprise and with so many Golds fighting on their home turf, even the mighty James Schweitzer couldn't have turned the tide. And Schweitzer hadn't, in the end. That had been the work of the AH-6's GAU-19 and the fatal funnel it made of the hangar access corridor.

But the airspace was clear enough for now. He could get out if he moved quickly, but it wouldn't take Jala Ghaznavi long to muster whatever resources she'd need to make the skies a lot more hostile. Once he was bottled up here, all chance at reaching the Summoner in the Northwest Territory would be lost. He'd taken his shot, done what damage he could.

Time to go.

The Director walked to the wall and punched a five-digit code into the keypad, then turned and waited as the hangar floor slid silently open, yawning wide to reveal an elevator pad large enough to carry three helicopters side by side. The Director stepped onto it, clasped his hands behind him, and waited as the elevator made its slow, quiet descent into the dark.

When it finally settled to a stop, the Director stepped off into a second hangar, a maintenance bay lined with repair equipment, bullets, hydraulic fluid, tools, and paint. The cabinets seemed to go on forever. The Director's 'away' helo stood beneath another set of bay doors, these covered by a layer of dirt and grass and opening out of the hillside behind the building. The helo was enormous, nearly twice the size of the dual-rotor Chinooks that the Director had flown in when he'd been alive. It was patterned off an old Soviet helicopter, the Mi-26. He'd seen it when the Army had leased one to haul stranded tanks off an Afghan mountainside.

The Cell's engineers had made some modifications. Rotor and engine muffling, radar dampening. It had been painted to camouflage it against the sky. Much of the airframe had been replaced with composite materials to cut down on the radar cross section. All joints were baffled, the engines silenced to the fullest extent possible. You could never make a machine so large and loud invisible, but the Director had come as close as he possibly could.

The rest of the modifications were for cargo. An enormous metal cage dominated most of the lower deck, leaving just enough room for a single man to walk outside it while staying out of reach of the wide, reinforced metal bars. A massive winch was installed in the bay's top, the thick metal cable anchoring to the thicker metal cage. Chains hung into the cage's interior, each ending in a hook. Each hook was slathered with still-steaming blood dripping from hunks of fresh meat speared through the barbed tips.

'Incentivize the cargo bay,' the Director said into his commlink. 'Spin up and let's roll out immediately.'

'Aye, sir,' came his crew chief's response. The air intakes whined and the rotors slowly began to churn. With a groan, the bay doors began to slide open, dirt and grass showering the deck as the pale dawn light flooded in. A man jogged to the helo from a corner of the room, leading another man in cuffs. An attempted rape, the Director had been told, and the prisoner had chosen to 'participate' in the program rather than face court-martial. The Director made sure that all of his employees understood that there was no leaving the Gemini Cell, even to go to prison. He couldn't risk idiots running their mouths on the outside.

The prisoner went cooperatively enough until he saw the cage, the meat, and the hooks, then began to scream and pull. His escort had a good hold of him, but their progress toward the helo slowed, and the Director knew that every second counted now. He wasn't going to risk giving Ghaznavi the time she needed to close the airspace.

In an instant, the Director had reached the prisoner, seizing his elbow. His grip tightened and the Director felt the bones beneath the soft skin crunch. Amazing, how delicate the living were! He could hardly believe he had ever been like this. The prisoner screamed louder but stopped pulling. The escort released him and fell back, hands coming up in wordless plea.

'Allow me,' the Director said, and whisked the prisoner up the ramp. The man struggled again, heedless of the pain from his broken elbow, but it was the fluttering of a butterfly in a steel vise. There was absolutely no danger of his breaking free. The Director lifted him by his cuffs and slung him over a hook in a single motion, as effortlessly as hanging up an empty plastic bag. The man's toes dangled off the bay floor. 'Come on!' he shouted at the Director's back as he went back down the ramp again. 'Jesus Christ, this wasn't what I . . .'

The Director ignored him, stepping away from the ramp and readying himself. The rotors chopping the air over his head stirred the lapels of his threadbare black jacket. He regretted the need to use incentives, but it couldn't be helped. If he was going to get the Golds into that cage, he had to give them a reason. The smell of fresh blood and the heat of the warm meat would help, but nothing could top a beating heart for getting a Gold to do what you wanted. 'Load up,' he said into the commlink.

There was a loud hiss of air and a reinforced door in the hangar wall slid open. The Director could hear the clanging of other doors opening in the corridor beyond. There was a moment of silence broken only by the whipping of the rotors and the screams of the prisoner inside the cage, drowned out to the living but certainly audible to him.

Then the scrabbling of claws, the slapping of bare feet on concrete.

The first of the Golds to burst into the hangar was what the Director affectionately called 'salvage'. It was cobbled together from the dismembered parts of its body, an unfinished attempt to cut it to pieces to the point where the corpse could no longer hold the soul bound inside. The severed arms, legs, and head were attached by a series of metal cables ranging in thickness from fishing line to sturdy rope. It wasn't a natural join, and the thing's head lolled slightly as it bounded toward the helo and the heartbeats inside.

The Golds were little more than wild dogs, and like wild dogs, they hardly ever did what you wanted. The salvaged Gold made for the helo cockpit instead of the ramp leading up to the cage, no doubt lured by the greater number of heartbeats inside. The stream of Golds coming behind it followed suit. They exhibited limited pack behavior, but only insofar as it led them to what they thought was greater slaughter.

The Director leapt to intercept the Gold, backhanding it across the face so hard that he worried he'd overstress the cables and decapitate it. The thing's head stayed on and it took the path of least resistance, bounding up the ramp toward the shrieking prisoner. A single heartbeat readily available was better than a hard fight.

And it would be a hard fight, the Director knew. He was faster than the fastest of them, stronger than the strongest of them. Time and time again, he had repeated this process, corralling the Golds, extending his will over them by sheer force. None had ever so much as challenged him. He was confident that he could defeat any of the monsters, any three undead things, maybe even any five at once.

Save one. The only one he hadn't faced. *Schweitzer.*

But that day was coming; he knew it.

He nodded in satisfaction as the rest of the Golds bounded up the ramp and the prisoner's screams abruptly ceased. Behind the stream of Golds came Xolotl and Quetzalcoatl, walking as calmly as if they were out for a Sunday stroll. Their gold crowns and pectorals flashed as they stopped, waiting for the Director. The gold and jewels were stupid gewgaws, vestiges of the vanity of the living. Had Xolotl and Quetzalcoatl been Silver, like him, they would no doubt realize that.

But they were, no matter how relatively intelligent, still Golds. He gestured to the cage.

Quetzalcoatl shook its head, pumped air through its desiccated throat. *No. With you.*

He sympathized. He wouldn't want to be shut up in a cage with the rest of the Golds either, but the fact remained that while his living crew had all seen Golds before, they hadn't seen these particular ones, not with their command over their appetites and their beaten gold and their jewels. It would be . . . unsettling.

He tried to find a way to explain it to them, but his limited grasp of the language wouldn't allow it. At last, he settled on saying, *They living*, and miming a man trembling in fear.

Xolotl shrugged. *You king.*

Yes, he supposed he was. The crew wouldn't ask questions if he made it clear that questions were frowned upon. He briefly considered pressing the issue, then decided there was little to be gained from it. His living servants would be more understanding than his dead ones.

The pair followed him as he jogged his way to the cockpit, hauling himself in.

The helo was big enough for the pilots to be seated on a separate deck above him. The cramped space below was his mobile office. Of course, the Director didn't need any of the trappings of an office, but he did need to make certain concessions to his human staff if he wanted them to be cooperative. He didn't refrigerate the helo interior, but neither did he heat it, and his people were bundled into thick winter clothing around the battered folding table. For now, they were sweating, but they knew how cold it would get once they were airborne. The airframe shook as the living crew secured the cage door, took up their positions, raised the ramp.

Mark was seated at the head, her eyes as adoring as ever. 'This is unexpected, sir.'

'I do try to keep people on their toes,' the Director said as Xolotl and Quetzalcoatl climbed aboard behind him.

He stopped the collective intake of breath with a gesture.

'These are my bodyguards. You may refer to them as X and Q. They will be with me on this trip, and they are to be treated as if they are invisible. I hope I make myself clear.'

'Crystal, sir,' Mark stuttered. He wondered how she would feel to know she had been in a room with them at least half a dozen times, her weak human eyes unable to penetrate the darkness the few feet to where they stood. No one else said a word, their accelerated heartbeats the only evidence of their shock. That would do, he supposed.

'So,' he said, 'you were saying this was unexpected. What precisely was it that you did not expect?'

'Well, it's just that we repulsed the SAD team,' Mark said.

'We did, and that is why I feel comfortable resuming pursuit of our original objective.'

'Sir, you can't honestly think that SAD will stand down. They'll just pour more peo—'

'I am perfectly aware of what SAD will do,' the Director cut her off. 'That is why our original objective has taken on renewed importance.'

'Sir?'

'We are, to put it mildly, found out,' the Director said. 'I have complete faith in our facility's ability to hold out against even the might of SAD for a time, but not forever. Sooner or later, we are through here. We need a new Summoner, and the only one I know of is in the Northwest Territory. In defeating their team, we have bought ourselves some time. In fact, having them busy with our presence here might even ensure they never pursue us at all.'

'Sir, I know you have confidence in the leads, but they're still just folktales,' she said. 'Staking everything on that is . . . risky.'

The Director put his fists on the table, leaned over them. The people around the table drew back, all save Mark, who leaned even closer, as if mere proximity could bring her the gift of death and reanimation she so desperately sought. 'Do you think that I would be willing to take such a risk if I wasn't acting on some more-specific intelligence that maybe you are not privy to?'

She looked down. 'No, sir.'

He leaned closer, until the fabric of his hood nearly brushed her ear. 'If you're so uncomfortable, perhaps you have a better idea? A plan that doesn't involve holing up here until the full might of the United States government is brought to bear on our position?'

Mark bit her lip. 'No, sir.'

'I thought so; let's make the best of it, shall we?' the Director asked. He opened the laptop on the table and began tapping out a general order to all personnel inside the facility. Help was on the way, he wrote. Until then, they were to hold their ground to the last round and the last breath.

The airframe shook as the helo lifted off, rising up through the bay doors and out into the gold-orange streaks of the dawn sky.

Chapter Eight
To the North

By the time they checked out of the medical tent and reported to Ghaznavi, the facility was already surrounded. The SAD operators gave no sign they even noticed, but Schweitzer was astounded by the scope and completeness of the combat cordon.

And that's what it was, a combat cordon, but a combat cordon expertly designed to look like a medical quarantine zone. Sawhorses and plastic pylons marched off in orderly rows, long loops of fluorescent yellow tape reading CDC: QUARANTINE – DO NOT CROSS strung between them. People in hazmat suits patrolled the edges. Schweitzer could smell the propellant through the fabric, knew that the suits concealed submachine guns and pistols, the seals loose enough to permit quick access. In the distance, he could make out a second blinking line of pylons and more fluorescent tape. This was only one line of many.

They'd covered Schweitzer with a fire blanket and a roll of camouflage netting they'd found stowed in the back of the helo. It looked ridiculous, but it was enough to keep the people manning the perimeter from seeing what Schweitzer really was. They stared at the strange figure hulking alongside Reeves, but they were SAD, used to not asking questions.

'Impressive,' Schweitzer said to Reeves. 'When you button a place down, you really . . .'

One look at Reeves' face and the words died in Schweitzer's mouth. The operator's mouth was set, his shoulders tight. Schweitzer could see the barely contained grief and shock, the superhuman effort it took to maintain his composure. *They lost brothers and sisters in there,* Schweitzer thought, *and you want to crack jokes about the perimeter.* The thought was followed by another, that he had been dead so long that dying was losing its gravity. Another thread of his humanity slowly fraying. *No. You are still James Schweitzer. You will never let that go.*

'I'm sorry,' he said, 'I—'

'Don't,' Cort cut him off. 'It's the job. That's all it is.'

Schweitzer thought of mentioning that his own brother had been a SEAL, gunned down on an op. Schweitzer had even lost his own life to his profession. But the look in Reeves' eyes stilled his tongue. Reeves kept up the stare until Schweitzer nodded and turned away.

'What the fuck are you?' Sharon asked, her grief nearly drowned in barely concealed rage.

'One of the good guys.'

'What the hell makes you different from those things we—'

'Secure that,' Reeves barked. 'He's one of the good guys. Getting in his shit isn't going to bring anyone back to life.'

Sharon snapped her eyes forward and gritted her teeth. Schweitzer opened his mouth to say something and thought better of it. He could only make things worse.

A National Guard Black Hawk helicopter made loops of the site, guns conspicuously visible through the open bay doors. In the few minutes since it had arrived, Schweitzer had heard it warn off at least two news helicopters.

Schweitzer could hear more rotors beating in the distance, too fast and carrying too much weight to be civilian news helos. Probably more military airframes to make sure the cordon covered the air as well as the ground.

They found Ghaznavi and Hodges in the command trailer, a white double-wide with the CDC logo painted on the side. It was as good a comms center as Schweitzer had ever seen. Banks of computers were staffed with watch-standers, foreheads creased in concentration and faces slick and white in the glow of the monitors. One wall of the trailer was entirely covered with a bank of screens, each showing a different news channel, and a computer plotter overlaid with the positions of SAD assets, civilian homes, facilities of public interest – churches, schools, water and power stations.

Ghaznavi and Hodges had their eyes glued to a newscast. A plastic-looking woman was talking in worried tones about a sudden outbreak of Legionnaires' disease that had already claimed two lives. Hodges sighed in apparent relief. 'Guess all those gunshots didn't sink us after all.'

'Jury's still out on that,' Ghaznavi said. 'It's early days.'

'Sorry, boss,' Reeves said.

She turned to him, eyes narrowing. 'Sorry for what?'

'Everything got fucked up.'

'The macho-operator act curries exactly zero favor with me, Reeves. You know that. You went in blind. You got jumped by an enemy with supernatural ability. You were surrounded and pinned down and it all unfolded before I could get the QRF into position. You and the rest of your team have nothing to be sorry for.'

'Thank you, ma'am,' Reeves said. 'Still, it's my responsibility—'

'It's now your responsibility to stay frosty and be ready

to get back in there on a moment's notice. Later, it'll be your responsibility to help me through the grieving process. We lost good people today.'

'Yes, ma'am.' Reeves looked at his feet.

Schweitzer thought of the cordon outside and felt some satisfaction. They had lost operators, yes, but in the space of a few short days, he'd gone from fleeing the Cell to surrounding it. *Now who's on the run?*

'All right, cordon's up,' Ghaznavi said. 'Press seems to be buying what we're selling for now. Force Protection is absolutely swearing to me that the battlespace is completely clear of civilians. Looks like we have this contained.'

'Just give us a few hours to regroup and give me another team, a bigger one,' Reeves said. 'Let me get back in there, ma'am. I can—'

'Absolutely not,' Ghaznavi cut him off. 'You're out of your fucking mind if you think I'm letting you go back in there blind.' For the first time since Schweitzer had met her, Ghaznavi looked shaken. 'I rushed it,' she whispered, eyes still on the screens. 'I got excited and I rushed it. I haven't done that since I was in my twenties.'

'It's understandable, Jala,' Hodges said. 'It's not every day you come face to face with stuff like . . . this.' He gestured at Schweitzer.

'Thanks,' Schweitzer said.

'Still on me,' Ghaznavi said. 'I'm not losing any more people. We keep it contained and we don't send another team in until—'

'Until what?' Reeves asked.

'Until we know what we're going up against. Until my Measures and Signals people can get some kind of idea of the layout of the structure. We can use infrared thermography to give us some kind of a map, and I need to figure out a way to understand how big the garrison is.'

'Respectfully, ma'am, what's the plan? How are we going to do that?' Reeves asked.

'I don't know, okay?' Ghaznavi answered. 'I just know that I'm not sending you back down there and that's final. Now, everybody out of here except for Schweitzer.'

'Ma'am, I—' Reeves began.

'Did I stutter?' Ghaznavi asked him. There was a pause as they locked eyes, and finally Reeves dipped his head. 'Aye aye, ma'am.' He shuffled back out of the trailer, the rest of the team behind him. Cort looked sidelong at Schweitzer, but Schweitzer ignored him. Being the only undead guy around had some privileges.

No sooner had they left than one of the watchstanders held out a phone. 'Ma'am. It's the air boss.'

Ghaznavi rolled her eyes. 'Is it a fucking emergency?'

The watchstander wasn't cowed. 'He says you're going to want to talk to him.'

'Excuse me,' Ghaznavi said to Hodges, picked up the receiver. 'This better be good.'

The color drained from her face before Schweitzer could dial his hearing in to eavesdrop on the conversation. Ghaznavi listened for another moment before asking, 'You're sure?

'Okay. Keep me posted.' She handed the receiver back to the watchstander. 'I need to sit down.' She slumped into a chair, put her head in her hands.

'What is it?' Hodges asked.

'West access point says they saw a transport helo westbound before we closed the air cordon. Said it looked like an old Russian Hind, only bigger.'

'Does SAD fly old Russian Hinds?' Hodges asked.

Ghaznavi shook her head.

'Fuck,' Hodges said. 'Do we know which way it went?'

'Don, I have the best air boss in the business. If that helo can be found and intercepted, he will find and intercept it.'

'Will he be able to find and intercept it?' Hodges' voice had taken on a panicked warble.

'No,' Schweitzer answered for her. 'Sky's a big place.'

'Fuck,' Hodges whispered. 'Word of this reaches the President, and who knows what the fuck he'll do? We're lucky it's stayed quiet thus far.'

'It might be time to bring the President in on this,' Ghaznavi said.

Hodges' mouth gaped. 'What? Are you kidding me? Why would you do that?'

'Don't you remember what we learned down on the farm? Never be the senior person with a secret,' Ghaznavi said.

'You run SAD, Jala.' Hodges' voice was an even timbre between anger and fear. 'You keep secrets for a living.'

'You're right,' she said, raising her voice. 'I do keep secrets for a living, and that means I know that when you can't keep a secret any longer, you'd best be the one to blow the whistle.'

'Jala,' Hodges began.

'Reeves is the best,' Ghaznavi spoke over him. 'I know his record before he got out of JSOC, and he has been my man on the ground for pretty much every mission I've personally overseen since I took over. He accomplishes the mission, always. Nothing stops him. And he just got his ass handed to him, Don. He got kicked around like a schoolkid. And they squirted. They *got out*. There is a helo somewhere out there carrying god knows what and headed god knows where.'

'That's not a reason to go telling tales out of school,' Hodges said.

'Don, I am telling you that after what I just saw, I am not convinced that we're going to be able to keep this contained. We need to be planning for the possibility that the bad guys are going to break out of there.'

'Jala, I don't think you understand what'll happen if you invite executive scrutiny,' Hodges said.

'You're right, I don't. But I do have an idea of what'll happen if I don't invite executive scrutiny and he finds out anyway,' Ghaznavi said. 'It's an option we have to consider.'

'Damn it,' Hodges said, punching his fist into his palm, pacing.

'This is bigger than my job or yours, Don. We have to do this one right.' Ghaznavi's voice was placating but flinty enough for Schweitzer to understand that she would go to the mat on this issue.

Hodges stood, hands on his hips, and glared at her. Schweitzer felt the tension mount as the time stretched out.

'What's in the Yukon?' Schweitzer asked.

Whatever Hodges and Ghaznavi had expected him to say, that wasn't it. 'What?' Hodges asked.

'You guys look at the plotter in that helo we stole?' Schweitzer asked. 'It had a waypoint set for the Great Slave Lake. Isn't that in the Yukon?'

'That's the Northwest Territories,' Hodges said. 'It was in the helo plotter?'

Schweitzer nodded. 'Someone had the route set. Wanted to save time on flight checks, I guess. Why would they set a waypoint there?'

'I have no idea,' Hodges said.

'Could be a red herring,' Ghaznavi said.

'I don't think so,' Schweitzer said. 'They were waiting for us. They were ready. They knew they had overwhelming force. They weren't expecting us to make it out. They sure as hell weren't expecting us to steal a helo.'

'Get the team back in here,' Ghaznavi said.

Schweitzer nodded and opened the door. He turned back to Hodges and Ghaznavi, smiling as much as his rigid face would permit. The team stood clustered around the trailer's small metal staircase, doing their best to look as if they hadn't been trying to listen in.

'She wants you to come back in,' Schweitzer said.

Reeves had the decency to look ashamed as he led the team back inside. 'You knew we were out there?'

'The whole time,' Schweitzer said. 'Heard your heartbeats.'

'Schweitzer said there was a waypoint in the helo you stole,' Hodges said. 'Heading to the Northwest Territories. Anybody catch that?'

The team looked shamefaced again. 'I was kind of busy flying the bird,' Sharon said.

'You sure?' Reeves asked Schweitzer.

'Positive.'

'So, they were going to the ass end of Canada,' Reeves said.

'Why the fuck would they be heading to Canada?' Cort asked.

'Cache? Citadel?' Sharon asked.

'Guesswork,' Ghaznavi answered. 'We can leave it to the analysts. In the meantime, we'll get answers directly from the source.'

'What source?' Schweitzer asked.

'Northwest Territories are in Canada, right? We ask the Canadians.' She walked to a conference-call phone squatting between two of the computers. 'Any reason I shouldn't do this, Don?'

Hodges shook his head.

'Okay,' Ghaznavi said, and hit a button.

'Watch,' a voice answered.

'Jake, it's Jala again. Doesn't anyone else answer the phone over there?'

'What can I say, ma'am? I love my job.'

'Can you put me through to the CSIS watch floor?'

'I can indeed.' There was a click and another voice answered. Schweitzer heard the rising vowel shift of a Canadian accent. 'Canada, how can I help you?'

'This is Jala Ghaznavi of SAD. I need to speak with General MacDonald.'

'Thanks for calling, ma'am. General MacDonald isn't available.'

'If he's asleep, I need you to wake him up. This is an emergency.'

'Okay, ma'am. Can you tell me what this is regarding?'

'It's under . . . What the fuck's the code?' She looked down at the table, and a watchstander scribbled something on a sticky note, sliding it into her field of vision. 'Crystal,' Ghaznavi said. 'It's about a possible Crystal evolution in the Northwest Territories.'

Schweitzer could hear the breathing on the other end of the phone quicken. Keys tapped. 'I just want to confirm here, ma'am. You want to speak to General MacDonald regarding a Crystal occurrence in the Northwest Territories.'

'Near the Great Slave Lake,' Schweitzer added, drawing a dagger glance from Ghaznavi.

'That's right,' she said.

'Hold, please.' Another click. Silence.

'They're probably looking up the code word themselves,' Hodges said.

'No,' Schweitzer said. 'Her heart rate increased. I could hear it. She knew what it meant.'

A moment later, the phone clicked again. The voice that answered had a slight French accent. 'Joint Task Force. Desmarais.'

'Des . . . Colonel Desmarais?' Ghaznavi asked.

'Yes, this is Director Ghaznavi?'

'Please, call me Jala. I think there's been a mistake. I was trying to reach General . . .'

'No mistake, Jala,' Desmarais said. 'I just need to confirm. You have evidence of a Crystal evolution near the Great Slave Lake? Because if you do, I'm about to get on a helicopter to wherever you are.'

'That's what I'm saying.'

'Okay,' Desmarais said. 'Where are you? My aide is telling me you're not in your office.'

If Colonel Desmarais' knowledge of her comings and goings rattled her, Ghaznavi didn't show it. She glanced up at Hodges, who nodded. 'I'm in Colchester.'

'England?'

'Virginia.'

That stopped Desmarais in his tracks for a moment. 'Okay, no helicopter. I guess I'll drive. Can you send an address to my aide?'

'No, I need this quiet. Go to my watch floor; I'll have a duty driver bring you in.'

'Okay. I'm heading over there now.'

'Keep it quiet,' Ghaznavi said.

Desmarais snorted. 'Quiet is what we do. See you in an hour or so.'

Desmarais hadn't been kidding about keeping quiet. When he stepped out of the Centers for Disease Control van Ghaznavi had sent for him, Schweitzer was amazed. Most spies and Special Ops types made only a perfunctory effort at disguise, like the careless woodsman look that

Reeves sported. That veneer relied on the casual observer being too busy or too unconcerned to spot the obvious lean muscle and hard eyes, not to mention the tactical applications of the brim that shaded the shooter's eye from the sun, the extra pockets on the cargo pants for magazines, the hiking boots that could see you through a forced march over broken terrain.

Desmarais had gone full CIA, right down to the fake belly under his stained sweatshirt and the fake butt filling out his dad jeans. Schweitzer could smell the makeup adhesive that held a scattering of beard to his clean-shaven face, could see the lift under his left shoe, forcing him to walk with a slight limp.

A young woman came behind him. Her costume was more perfunctory but still convincing, a white lab coat and fluorescent orange pelican case marked MEDICINS SANS FRONTIERS.

Schweitzer slumped in his folding chair, shrugging the blanket over his shoulders, making sure the saw arm was concealed. The hood drooped over his brow, keeping him well covered. The weave of the fabric was tight but not so tight that Schweitzer's magically augmented vision couldn't make the colonel out as he strode into the room, extending his hand to Ghaznavi. 'Director, thanks for agreeing to meet with me.'

She smiled. 'I told you to call me Jala; please sit down. Have you met Senator Don Hodges?'

'I haven't had the pleasure,' Colonel Desmarais said, 'but your reputation precedes you, sir.'

Hodges smiled. 'Oh, don't believe everything you hear.'

'This is my aide, Nicole. She's read on,' Colonel Desmarais said.

'Read on to what?' Hodges asked.

Desmarais smiled. 'I have to say I wasn't expecting a

Senator to be here. It's . . . unusual.'

'I have a personal interest in this particular evolution,' Hodges said.

Desmarais looked around, giving Schweitzer a good look at his eyes. They hit the corners, probing for danger areas. When he looked at the watchstanders, at Ghaznavi and Hodges, he looked at their hands, not their faces. He was an operator, or had at least been trained as one; that much was obvious. His eyes settled on Schweitzer and lingered for a moment. Schweitzer made sure to lift and lower his chest slightly, mimicking breathing. 'And would you mind telling me what this evolution is, exactly?' Desmarais asked. 'An outbreak of Legionnaires' disease that's got you quarantining an office park an hour's drive from your office? That's also . . . unusual.'

'Colonel.' Ghaznavi tapped the table. 'I appreciate your curiosity, but you weren't even the guy I called, so you'll forgive me if I ask you to lay your cards on the table first.'

Desmarais smiled. 'Jala, I'm not Israel or Russia here. I'm Canada. We're practically the same country.'

'There's no such thing as a friendly service,' she said, 'even among allies. Especially among allies.'

Desmarais' smile faded into a pensive look. 'Can you at least tell me why you think there's an arcane development near the Great Slave Lake?'

'We found a waypoint in a computer GPS system associated with an arcane target. We think it was deliberately set, and we want to understand why.'

'Can you tell me more about this target?' Desmarais asked.

'Can you tell me more about what the fuck is going on?' Ghaznavi asked. 'Why my call was immediately routed from CSIS to your task force and why you're here instead of talking to me on the phone? And why you're not General MacDonald?'

Desmarais exchanged a glance with Nicole, who snapped open the case and removed some papers.

'I'm sorry' – Ghaznavi cocked an eyebrow – 'is your laptop broken? Are you actually handing me printed paper? Are you going to ride back to HQ on a stego-saurus?'

'You can't hack paper,' Desmarais said.

Ghaznavi scanned the pages, Hodges leaning over her shoulder. 'What's the TL;DR here?'

'We've been tracking some rumors for a long time about arcane developments in the Northwest Territories, and the most interesting ones are specific to the Great Slave Lake region. It was interesting enough for CSIS to put some collection on the target and it backed the rumors up . . . to a degree. Let's just say we're interested.'

'Interested enough to circumvent CSIS and put JTF2 directly on it?'

'The rumors go back decades. There's a lot of them.'

'How many?' Ghaznavi asked.

Desmarais looked over at Nicole.

'Documented?' Nicole said. 'Three thousand six hundred and eighty-two.'

Hodges cocked an eyebrow. 'Is that . . . a lot of rumors? Because it sounds like a lot of rumors.'

Desmarais shrugged. 'You have to keep in mind that this is folklore going back decades.'

'And the content of these tales?'

'Are publicly available. I've included some of the better ethnographic articles in that packet. It centers around the reincarnation of "Lived-With-The-Wolves", an Athabascan hero. The Athabasca Chipewyan are a First Nations people who live in the region.'

'Dene,' Ghaznavi said. 'That's what they prefer to be called.'

Desmarais nodded. 'You know something about Canada's native history.'

Ghaznavi waved the compliment away. 'I know they're not Eskimos. That's about the extent of it.'

'Well, the point is that Lived-With-The-Wolves is supposedly constantly reborn in one person or another, and is supposedly able to do the usual stuff, heal the sick, tell the future, turn into a wolf, et cetera. Nothing that ever got us to pay attention.'

'But you're paying attention now,' Ghaznavi said.

Desmarais nodded. 'Around the time I was getting out of academy, the folk tales changed, specifically around what it was that Lived-With-The-Wolves could do. The healing stories and the clairvoyance petered out and the rumors took on a remarkable consistency.'

Desmarais gestured at the packet.

'This is the Internet era,' Ghaznavi said. 'Reading ink on paper is an admission of old age.'

'Just tell us, Colonel,' Hodges said.

'The stories are all the same, that Lived-With-The-Wolves brings back the spirits of the dead and unites them with the bodies of animals so that their loved ones live on inside them. The Royal Canadian Mounted Police first got wise to the stories when they were busting a drug ring out in Whitehorse, but the consistency was startling enough that they alerted CSIS, and they brought us in once they were convinced that the source was arcane. JTF2 is handling anything magic now—'

'I know,' Ghaznavi said.

'Right, well. That's a really unusual and really specific story to suddenly penetrate the folklore. So, we put people on the ground to find out what we could.'

'And what did you find?' Hodges asked.

'So far? Nothing,' Colonel Desmarais said.

'Nothing? It's your country!' Ghaznavi said.

'Not out in the Northwest Territories,' Colonel Desmarais said. 'It is in the cities, if you can even call them that, like Yellowknife. They're mostly set up to handle tourist trade from outdoorsy types coming to see the aurora borealis, but once you get outside that? "Remote" doesn't even begin to describe it. You've got less than fifty thousand people living in over a million square kilometers. Finding one man is like finding a needle in a haystack.'

'You're sure it's a man?' Ghaznavi asked.

'Sure as we can be from the stories. We've got a couple of people on the ground out there, but to be honest, the JTF has been lax about recruiting from the Dene people.'

'They have to be Dene?' Hodges asked.

Desmarais nodded. 'They're around forty percent of the population. You don't score points in what we do by sticking out. Anyway, Lived-With-The-Wolves is a Dene figure, and he's not working his magic for white folks or Inuit up that way. So, yeah. We need Dene to run the op.'

'And you don't have any.' Ghaznavi looked irritated.

'Cut him some slack, Jala,' Hodges said. 'We had the same problem with Arabs and Persians right after 9/11.'

She sighed. 'Yeah. Manpower is always the biggest hurdle in this business. All right, what do you have?'

'This.' Desmarais flipped through the package to a glossy eight-by-eleven photograph of a grainy gray figure hunching across a shoulder of rock pushing out of the snow.

'This is a wolf,' Ghaznavi said, looking unimpressed.

'No.' Schweitzer finally spoke, his augmented vision picking out the details in the photograph from across the room, even through the weave of the hood that covered his face. 'Look at its eyes.'

Desmarais stiffened at the rasping sound of Schweitzer's voice, and Schweitzer could hear the quickening of his heart, but to his credit, he didn't move.

Ghaznavi and Hodges bent over the photograph. A moment later, Hodges cursed and Ghaznavi sucked in her breath.

Desmarais grunted in satisfaction. 'I take that to mean that you know something about this.'

'Colonel Desmarais,' Hodges said, 'you've got to get us on the ground wherever this photo was taken. I think I know what's happening here.'

Desmarais clucked his tongue. 'I can do that,' he said, 'provided that it's a joint operation, and provided you tell me what the hell is going on.'

'You've noticed the eyes, I take it,' Schweitzer said.

Hodges and Ghaznavi looked sharply up at him. 'Jim, please,' Hodges said.

'No.' Schweitzer raised his good hand, letting the blanket fall away from him, revealing the torn STF armor. He brushed the hood off his head, lifted his metal chin, and watched Desmarais' eyes narrow as he took in Schweitzer's face. 'I don't work for you,' Schweitzer said. 'I work *with* you, and I am choosing to reveal myself now, because secrets aren't going to win here. Truth is.'

'Jesus Christ,' Desmarais whispered. 'Is this some kind of a joke?'

'Look at the eyes, Colonel,' Schweitzer said. 'Tell me what you see.'

Desmarais took a long time to answer. 'Our . . . our imagery people are still puzzling over it,' Desmarais said, 'but so far, the verdict is that they're made of fire.'

'Like mine,' Schweitzer said.

Desmarais picked up the photo, his eyes never leaving Schweitzer's. He glanced down at the photo and then back up. 'No,' he said slowly. 'These are a darker color.'

'They're gold,' Schweitzer said. 'Mine are silver.'

'What does that mean?' Colonel Desmarais asked. 'Is it a different color for people and animals?'

'I'm not sure myself,' Schweitzer answered, 'but I think it has more to do with self-control. When you're in control of yourself, when you retain your humanity, the color is different.'

'Retain?' Desmarais asked. 'The gold-eyed lost it? Wait, does this mean there are other people like this? How many? Where?'

'We don't have exact numbers,' Ghaznavi said, 'but quite a few. Some are in that building out there.' She pointed in the direction of the Entertech cover facility. 'We're worried that some of them might be on their way to the Great Slave Lake.'

Desmarais finally looked away from Schweitzer and met Ghaznavi's eyes. 'To find Lived-With-The-Wolves?'

'The target we're working,' Schweitzer said, 'it's looking for a host. There's a certain arcane transfer that has to occur to get it into one. I killed one of his people capable of facilitating that transfer. It's possible she was his only one. If I am guessing correctly, your Lived-With-The-Wolves has the same ability. The proof is that wolf.'

'Are you dead?' Desmarais asked. 'I've heard of some . . . people with the ability to raise the dead, but never . . . thinking and talking like you do.'

'Yes, I'm dead. And I still think and talk. My name is James Schweitzer; you may have heard of me.'

'The SEAL? Yes, we've heard of you. We heard you were . . .' Desmarais smiled.

'Well, you're right. I was. I came back.'

'Through magic, a kind we've never seen before,' Desmarais said.

'You have seen it before,' Schweitzer said, tapping the photograph. 'You just didn't know what you were looking at.'

'So, is Lived-With-The-Wolves a man?' Desmarais asked.

'Jim, you don't have to—' Ghaznavi said, then quieted at a gesture from Schweitzer. 'Jesus Christ, Jim. You don't know what the fuck you're doing.'

'On the contrary,' Schweitzer said. 'When I was alive, I dealt with secret-squirrel crap all the time. I know exactly what I'm doing.' He turned back to Desmarais. 'Yes, Lived-With-The-Wolves is probably a man. You said the stories say he's putting the spirits of loved ones into the bodies of animals?'

'That's what they say. We don't have any hard evidence, though. We haven't captured any of these animals yet.'

'If their eyes are gold,' Schweitzer said, 'then they will probably be just that, animals.'

'So, is that wolf dead?' Desmarais asked. 'Like you?'

Schweitzer looked at the photograph. His augmented vision brought the picture into sharper focus, picked out details the living people around him would surely miss: brightness of the animal's coat, the wet gleaming around the muzzle that indicated saliva, a tiny cut on the hock that was still scabbing over. 'No,' Schweitzer said in amazement. 'It's alive.'

'I'm confused,' Desmarais said.

'So am I,' Ghaznavi added.

'Does it work for both living and dead creatures?' Desmarais asked. 'The magic?'

'I've never seen it work on someone alive, but I heard talk that it did. Our target certainly believes it does, and it is definitely not a coincidence that there's a wolf with burning gold eyes in the exact area indicated by the waypoint in the helo plotter. Either the Director is there or he's going there, and that means we have to go there and fast.'

'Who's the Director?' Desmarais asked.

Ghaznavi ignored him, staring at Schweitzer. 'Yeah. You're right. We'll need to put together a team.'

'Reeves is still spun up and wanting to make good on what just went down,' Schweitzer said. 'I don't exactly need prepping. Let's go.'

'Wait a minute.' Desmarais thumped his fist on the table. 'I know you think of Canada as a client state, but you're not going anywhere, certainly not anywhere in the sovereign territory of Canada, without the knowledge and consent of my government.'

'Oh, come on, Colonel,' Ghaznavi said, 'you're not telling your government about this any more than I am mine. This isn't my first rodeo, and you're going to help us and take us to wherever we can find . . . this.' She tapped the photograph.

'No, I am not,' Desmarais said. 'I am—'

'We are going to work together on this,' Ghaznavi interrupted him, 'together and inside your borders, and nobody is telling anyone about it outside of SAD and JTF2, and that's final.'

Desmarais' jaw clenched, the most emotion Schweitzer had seen him display since he came in. 'What makes you so sure?'

'Because' – she stabbed a finger at Schweitzer – 'there's only one living-dead guy here with burning eyes who can think and talk. And he, like everything else good and right and wonderful in the wide circle of the world, is American.'

'That was a hell of a thing, decloaking like that,' Ghaznavi said as Schweitzer hovered over the team. True to his prediction, Reeves took the news like rain in a desert and was currently hunched over his laptop, writing up a new loadout plan for extreme cold weather.

'There's roads out there,' Reeves said. 'Yellowknife's a big city.'

'Define big,' Hodges said.

'A little under twenty thousand,' Reeves said.

'On what planet does that qualify as "big"?' Ghaznavi asked. 'That's less than a tenth the size of Arlington.'

Reeves said nothing, squinting into the laptop's glare.

'Jala has a point.' Hodges turned the conversation back to Schweitzer. 'That was one hell of a risk you just took, Jim. Not just for yourself but for the nation.'

'I lost patience with the dance of a thousand veils you had going on,' Schweitzer said. 'We need to be out there yesterday, and we all know that Desmarais wasn't going to budge unless you put your cards on the table.'

'As long as we're using your metaphor,' Hodges said, 'you don't open with your whole stake, Jim. You ante up and raise slowly. You reel them in.'

'Yeah, except you have no stake,' Schweitzer said. 'You have one chip. Me. And you either play me or you don't. Sorry for skipping the foreplay, but thanks to my "decloaking", as you put it, we probably saved a day.'

'We have rules regarding this stuff,' Hodges began.

'You'll forgive me if I don't buy that particular line,' Schweitzer said. 'Do the rules say that you can just reach out to the government of Canada on your own accord and set up an op? You're committing the United States to a foreign policy position. Doesn't the President or the Secretary of State get to weigh in?'

Ghaznavi snorted, 'POTUS? SECSTATE? They're just public servants.'

'Who the hell are you, then?' Schweitzer asked.

Ghaznavi and Hodges exchanged a knowing glance.

'We're the people who run things while the public servants make speeches and cut ribbons. Been that way since people decided they were willing to give up some power to tough customers in exchange for being kept safe.'

Reeves kept his face neutral, eyes on the laptop screen. 'You sure you're supposed to be having this conversation in front of me? Sounds top secret.'

'Have you met Schweitzer?' Hodges asked. 'He doesn't believe in secrets.'

Reeves puffed out his cheeks. 'Welp, I think I've got it. Nearest armory that can fill this order is in Maryland, and it's probably smart if we go in wearing Canadian gear and under their cover. You want me to socialize that with the good colonel or—'

'I'll handle it,' Hodges said. 'Just print me out the loadout sheet and I'll see what his people can fill.'

'God knows what concessions he'll want for that,' Ghaznavi added.

'We're wasting time,' Schweitzer said.

'What's the rush?' Ghaznavi asked. 'For all you know, the Director isn't even going there.'

'He's going there,' Schweitzer said. 'Or he's already there.'

'You know that?' Hodges asked. 'Is it from the magic?'

'No.' Schweitzer shook his head. 'This time, it's just a gut feeling.'

'Do you even have a gut?' Reeves asked.

Hodges stared at him.

'What?' Reeves asked. 'Might've rotted away.'

There was a knock at the door, and Ghaznavi opened it. Desmarais entered, Nicole beside him, carrying a blue three-ring binder. 'I want to get in the air,' Desmarais said. 'Since the op's in our backyard, I think it's best if your people load out with our gear. I've got the sheets here.' He gestured to the binder. 'I hope this is all okay.'

Reeves cocked an eyebrow at Hodges. 'I think we could be persuaded.'

'Good.' If Desmarais noticed Reeves' tone, he didn't show it. 'I've got a fixed-wing at Reagan ready to go. We can be in Yellowknife in roughly ten hours.'

'We'll load out there?' Reeves closed the laptop and stood up.

Desmarais nodded. 'Canadian Forces Northern Area HQ is in Yellowknife. I've already arranged for everything to be ready when we arrive.' Desmarais looked at Schweitzer. 'I'm just concerned that—'

'No offense taken,' Schweitzer said. 'I'll make sure I'm covered up.'

'Thanks,' Desmarais said. 'I want to keep the footprint as small as possible. Three operators, Schweitzer, and—'

'And me,' Ghaznavi said. 'Senator Hodges will be staying here.'

'Like hell I wi—' Hodges began.

'Colonel, will you please excuse us for just a moment?' Ghaznavi smiled.

Desmarais nodded and left, Nicole trailing him.

'I'll excuse you too,' Reeves said. 'Need to go round up Frank and Sharon.' He followed after Desmarais, looking grateful to be out of the room before the fireworks started.

'I'm sorry, Don,' Ghaznavi said. 'We're all going and you're staying here. That's how this goes.'

'Why?' Hodges asked.

'Because I need this facility kept hemmed in, and I need to make sure it's done in a way that keeps the public from ever knowing about it. You're the right man for that job.'

'I'm a Senator,' Hodges said. 'I've got a lot of other jobs.'

'More important than this one?' she asked.

Hodges stammered for a moment before sighing, 'No.'

'Good. I'll keep you posted and vice versa. Constant comms. Both ways, I promise.'

Hodges nodded. He squinted at the image of the facility squatting dark and silent in the feed projected on one of the trailer's screens. 'Those fuckers. They would have taken my body if I'd let them.'

'If *I'd* let them,' Schweitzer said.

'They're going down,' Hodges said. 'I swear.'

Ghaznavi laughed. 'What the hell are you going to do? You're a Senator, not an operator.'

'Yeah,' Hodges sighed, 'I am. You're the ground-pounding shadow warrior. You go on the secret mission. I'll make sure it smells sweet back at home.'

She stared at him.

'I'm agreeing with you,' Hodges said. 'Accept it before I change my mind.'

She nodded and tapped Schweitzer on the shoulder. 'What do you think of all this?'

'You suddenly care what I think?' Schweitzer asked.

'Of course I care what you think,' she said. 'You're the only one with firsthand experience in all of this.'

Schweitzer thought for a moment. 'I feel like we can trust Desmarais, if that's what you're asking. And that picture isn't photoshopped.'

'You know that from your magic super vision?'

'That helps, but it's not the thing here. Being alive is . . . noisy. Being dead helps you to focus in ways you couldn't before. You can pick out details. I don't think that photo was doctored.'

'I'll have it analyzed just in case,' Hodges said. 'I still remember my way around CIA. Photo unit in the same spot?'

Ghaznavi nodded to Hodges, turned back to Schweitzer.

'All right. Let's get this row on the shoad. How do you like cold weather?'

Schweitzer opened the trailer door and stepped out into the dark. 'I'm more worried about you. I've got antifreeze for blood.'

'I've got coffee for blood,' Ghaznavi said. 'We'll see who cries uncle first.'

Chapter Nine

Resolution

Mankiller and Yakecan hiked the remaining miles to Fort Resolution in silence. Mankiller kept running through what she had just seen in her mind: the helicopter, the cage full of gray-skinned, flame-eyed people, the hard-bitten men with guns. It couldn't be real. She had to have been hallucinating. But she heard Yakecan puffing alongside her. If it was a hallucination, then it was one they both shared. The life of a small-town sheriff had its dangers, but she couldn't remember the last time she'd felt this frightened.

Bob Earl was pointing his rifle at her as she stepped out of the tree line and onto the frozen track that was Fort Resolution's only real road.

'Early Bird', as she called him, had been failing to surprise her for her entire life, and she wished she could say she was surprised now. 'Jesus, Sheriff,' Early Bird slurred, his purple nose peeking out over his scarf like a Christmas ornament, so swollen she wondered how his tiny, close-set eyes could peer around it. 'I almost shot you.'

'Jesus fuck.' Yakecan shook his head, started forward. Mankiller was faster. She reached Early Bird in two steps and yanked the barrel of his .375 Ruger Alaskan down.

'What the hell did I tell you?' she asked.

'What're you yellin' at me for?' Early tugged on his rifle, immediately saw the futility of the act, and let the weapon drop. 'You were makin' the trees shake. Thought maybe it was a deeb . . . bar.'

'A what?'

'It's drunk for a deer or a bear,' Yakecan offered.

'I speak fluent drunk, thanks,' Mankiller said, ripping the rifle out of Early's hands and working the action, sending the rounds tumbling into the snow.

Early went scrambling after them. 'Aw, Sheriff! Those are Partition Golds! You know how much those cost to . . .'

'I know how much they'd cost me if you went and put one in my gut, you damned idiot. You count yourself lucky I ain't puttin' cuffs on you right now.'

'All right, Sheriff, all right.' Early patted the air. 'No need to get so angry.'

The words made Mankiller even angrier. At least three different retorts rose to her lips, all dismissed in an instant. At last, she settled on shaking Early Bird's rifle at him. 'I'm keepin' this!' She spun on her heel and stormed off toward the station, Yakecan hurrying behind.

Sally Valpy was wrestling a log into the bed of her pickup, her parka studded with its perennial covering of splinters and woodchips. 'Hey, Sheriff! ?édlánet'é. Where ya . . .'

'Not now, Sally.' Mankiller brushed past the older woman, ignoring the look of openmouthed surprise.

'Sorry,' Yakecan said. 'She's in a hurry.'

'I can see that!' Sally called after them, accusation ringing in her voice.

Mankiller's stomach twisted at her tone. She took her duty to the people of Fort Resolution seriously, and she didn't like being rude. The old wood carver only wanted to say hello. Mankiller would bring her a fruitcake later. Sally was batshit crazy about fruitcake.

Mankiller put on speed, concentrating on the burning in her thighs, the soft crunch of her boots over the snow-pack, the bobbing gray shape of the station growing in the distance. She wanted only to concentrate on walking as fast as she could, but she soon heard Yakecan huffing along behind her. 'Boss, where are we goin'?'

She whirled on him, ready to curse him for an idiot, to tell him he could damn well *see* where they were going when the station was right in front of his eyes. But Yakecan's moon face was pale with fear, his eyes wide. He wore the dumbfounded half smile that meant he knew he was out of his depth, that he needed *orders*. That smile grew, his cheeks continuing to rise until they were obscured by the fur trim of his hood.

Yakecan made Mankiller mad every time he opened his fool mouth, but the man had a way that made it hard to *stay* mad, and no mistake. Mankiller found herself smiling back. 'Gonna try to raise Yellowknife, talk to Superintendent White.'

'What's he gonna do?'

'I dunno,' Mankiller said. 'Call the RCMP, maybe. Maybe call the Army.'

'The Army?'

'Military helo just offloaded a squad of hard operators, didn't it? Not more'n a few klicks out. They could be on their way here. That ain't right, and we can't handle it, the two of us. We need help.'

'Maybe they're not coming here.'

'That don't matter!' Mankiller swallowed her frustration. 'We need help on this.'

'White's a dick.'

'I know it, but he's the guy we have to call, so let's go call him.'

They trudged on, and the station rose out of the frost-choked air. It was little more than a double-wide trailer, the back opening into a low concrete pillbox that served as the cells. They were storage, more often than not. Mankiller preferred to let the drunks of Fort Resolution sleep it off in their beds unless they absolutely had to be taught a lesson. Given that there was little to do in Fort Resolution other than drink, it proved to be an essential policy.

'Boss . . .' Yakecan's breathing was labored as he struggled to keep up.

'Yeah?'

'The . . . that cage. Can we talk about what was in it?'

Mankiller felt a shiver settle in her spine, work its way up to the back of her skull. 'You and I saw the same thing, Joe.'

'You . . . uh . . . you gonna tell Superintendent White about that?'

'I dunno,' she said. 'Probably not.'

'Yeah,' Yakecan said. 'I don't think he'd understand. Looked like magic to me . . . like maybe the same magic your grandpa's got.'

'You don't know what it looks like, Joe, and neither do I,' Mankiller said. 'And we need to slow down and be thinkin' on it until we *do* know. Just keep it to yourself for now, okay? Hard enough to explain this as it is.'

Oliver Calmut met them on the porch. He was in his long johns, his feet just kicked into his boots to come outside. His pointed elbows shivered as he hugged himself. 'Sheriff, been tryin' to call you.'

'Jesus, Ollie, put some pants on.' Sometimes, the informality of her leadership style had drawbacks.

Calmut swatted at his stringy black and gray hair and

ignored her, holding the door wide. Mankiller and Yakecan kicked the snow off their boots in what passed for the station's foyer, a closet-sized mud room on the opposite side of the Plexiglas-shielded booth where Calmut sat beside the station's only radio. 'Was worried about you,' Calmut said, making his way around to his seat. 'Couldn't raise you for a radio check.'

Calmut's snowsuit lay crumpled on the floor beside his rolling chair. Mankiller couldn't blame him for taking it off. It was at least ninety degrees inside. 'Jesus, Ollie. Didn't I tell you to get the heat fixed?'

'I called Freddie,' he said.

'And?'

'And he's busy.'

'Busy with what?'

Calmut shrugged. 'Anyway, Sally Valpy was around lookin' for you. She got into it with Denise Unka over some trees Sally was takin' for her carvin'. Sally says Denise threatened to set her shed on fire.'

'Denise's been threatenin' to burn Sally out since I was a kid.' Mankiller shrugged out of her parka. 'Can you open a window?'

'Been openin' 'em,' Calmut said, turning to crack the window beside his desk. 'It's good for about five minutes, then it's freezin'.'

'Anyway, I saw Sally on the way here. I'll deal with that in a bit.'

'Fine by me,' Calmut said. 'Only, you need to answer your radio. You had me worried.'

'We mighta been outta radio range,' Yakecan said, already sweating. 'We were playin' snow snake up on the pond.'

Calmut looked at Yakecan accusingly.

'We can take a break, Ollie,' Yakecan said. 'Anyway, why didn't you call us on our phones?'

'Tried,' Calmut said. 'Both of yous. No love.'

Yakecan glanced down at his smartphone. 'I should have signal out there.'

'I shouldn't,' Mankiller said. 'Satphone?'

'Well, that's for emergencies,' Calmut said, 'but I was gettin' to that when you showed up.'

'All right, well, we're here now.'

'Yup, so I can call Sally and—'

'No,' Mankiller said. 'I need you to call Superintendent White in Yellowknife.'

Calmut looked up at her, his basset hound eyes incredulous. 'Why are we callin' him?'

'We saw somethin' up on the pond,' Yakecan said, paused, looked to Mankiller for permission. She shrugged and he went on. 'Guys with guns and a helicopter.'

'Like hunters?' Calmut asked.

'Like soldiers,' Mankiller said.

'Canada's bein' invaded?' Calmut's wattles shook.

'Hell if I know. Raise up White and maybe he can tell us.'

'Yeah . . .' Calmut made no move to pick up the phone. 'He's a dick, boss.'

Yakecan snorted laughter, and Mankiller bit back her impatience. 'Just call him, Ollie.'

Calmut shook his head, sighed, reached for the phone. 'He's gonna make a snide remark, and I'm gonna hang up on him.'

'If he makes a snide remark, it'll be to me,' Mankiller said. 'You just talk to Darla and get him on the phone.'

Ollie held the receiver to his ear, a slow smile dawning across his face. 'Somebody up there likes me.'

Mankiller sighed. 'You didn't even dial yet, Ollie.'

'Can't.' Calmut set the phone gingerly in its cradle, grinning so hard that his eyes nearly vanished in a chasm of laugh lines. 'No tone.'

'Whaddya mean, no tone?' Yakecan asked.

'Phone's dead.' Ollie tapped the hook switch. 'Got nothin'.'

Mankiller snatched the receiver out of his hand, held it to her ear. The silence made the plastic seem heavier, as if she held a dead thing, the corpse of her connection to the outside world. Ollie was staring up at her, eyes wide. 'Easy there, Sheriff, you don't gotta—'

'Hand me the radio, Ollie,' Mankiller interrupted. She knew she was being rude, but the urgency rising in her gut wouldn't be denied.

Calmut recognized her agitation, knew from long experience that there was nothing for it but to do as she said. He handed her the radio. She thumbed the switch, heard the familiar static. 'Joe, it's Wilma for a radio check, over.'

Static from the radio. Otherwise, silence.

Yakecan laughed. 'C'mon, boss, I'm standing right here.'

'That's my damn point,' Mankiller growled. She thumbed the radio switch again, spoke into it. 'If you're standing right here, how come it ain't workin'?'

Yakecan's smile slowly melted. He pulled his radio off his belt, thumbed the switch, checked the volume knob. 'Looks okay . . .'

''Cause it is okay,' Mankiller said, pulling out her smartphone. 'Check your phone.'

Yakecan did, shook his head. 'No signal.'

The shiver in Mankiller's spine settled in her stomach, the same vague illness she felt when she went outside the wire on convoy duty in Afghanistan. 'Comms are cut. Someone don' want us talkin' to nobody.'

'Come on,' Calmut said. 'I'm sure it's just—'

'All three comms modes down at the same time?' Mankiller said. 'It's not a coincidence.'

Calmut's expression was a mix of bemusement and fear. 'You think it's those fellas you saw up on the pond with the guns and the helicopter?'

Mankiller turned to Yakecan. 'Get yourself an 870 out of the locker. Load up with slugs.'

Yakecan nodded, still vaguely smiling, as if he hoped this whole thing would turn out to be a joke. 'Sure, boss,' he said. 'You don't want me to grab one for you?'

Mankiller looked down at Early Bird's Alaskan propped against the wall where she'd set it when she'd taken off her coat. 'Get me a box of .375. Early Bird was kind enough to lend me his rifle, and I don't see why we shouldn't put it to use.'

Yakecan paused. 'Think we're gonna be usin' 'em?'

Mankiller shrugged. 'Hope not.' She turned to Calmut. 'Ollie, you keep tryin' to raise Yellowknife. I don't think it's a technical problem, but get Freddie over here as quick as possible. If he says he's busy, tell him I said to get unbusy and quick. If there's a way to get comms back, get 'em back.'

'Okay, Sheriff.' Calmut had gone pale.

'We're goin' over to the municipal building, talk to Mayor Kettle,' Mankiller said.

'We are?' Yakecan asked, emerging from the arms locker with an 870 in one hand and a box of cartridges in the other. 'You don' wanna—'

'Joe, a helo full of operators just touched down in our backyard and our comms are cut. Now, maybe I'm bein' paranoid, and that's fine. I'll be all embarrassed and say sorry later. For now, we need to treat this like a bona fide emergency, and that means we go guns up and talk to the Mayor.'

'If you're right,' Yakecan asked, tossing Mankiller the ammunition and shrugging his parka back on, 'what're we supposed to do? We can't fight all those guys, not to mention . . . the other stuff.'

'No, we can't,' Mankiller said, zipping her parka back up and then loading the rifle, careful to keep the muzzle pointing at the floor, 'but that don' mean we wanna be caught flat-footed, neither.'

She pulled open the door, shivered as the frigid air blew in. 'Ollie, you clear on everything?'

Calmut was busy pulling his snowsuit back on. 'I'm good, Sheriff.'

'Ollie, grab a pistol and keep it with you.'

Calmut looked up, shocked, but smart enough to nod. 'Sure thing, Sheriff. I'll load up a Glock and stick it in my waistband. Real gangster-style.' He grinned, showing the gaps in his teeth.

'Load up .357,' Mankiller said. 'I got a Taurus revolver back there.'

Calmut's grin evaporated. 'That's a lot of gun, Sheriff.'

'If you need it and don't have it' – Mankiller shrugged – 'you're never gonna need it again.' She stepped out into the cold, the snowpack crunching under her boots. She didn't look back, but Yakecan's huffing breath told her he was following.

The municipal building was only slightly larger than the station and included the rest of the hamlet's services from the court clerk to the fire department to the mayor's office. It was distinguished from the squat, brightly colored houses only by its size, fresh coat of paint, and the three disk-shaped plaques displaying the seal of the Deninu Kue First Nation, the Akaitcho Territory Government, and the commemoration of Treaty 8.

Mankiller's steps quickened as her feet found the firmer ground of the parking lot beneath the snow, the big double window of the mayor's office bobbing in her vision.

'Sheriff!' Sally was quiet most times, but she could get a good screech going when she was angry, and she was definitely angry.

Mankiller stiffened, considered ignoring her and making the final dash for the front door. But years downrange had trained her ears, and she instantly calculated Sally's distance and trajectory from her voice and the sound of her footsteps crunching in the snow. There was no way Mankiller would make the door without giving Sally a chance to snatch at her collar, which she didn't doubt the older woman would do. She sighed, turned.

'Damn it, Sheriff!' Sally shouted, her cheeks shaking. 'We voted you in to do a job! You work for the people of this—'

'Sally, we've got—'

'Don't you interrupt me! I remember you when you was jus' a kid 'n' you went runnin' into—'

'Sally!' Mankiller yelled.

'C'mon, Sally.' Yakecan put a placating hand on the old wood carver's elbow. 'You don' wanna be scrapping with the law. Ollie told us what's goin' on with you and Denise. I promise that we're going to—'

Sally shook his hand off. 'This is serious, damn it! Now, I know we've gotten into it before, but this time she—'

'Sally.' Mankiller wasn't yelling this time, but the tone in her voice cut through the conversation. Sally trailed off and looked at Mankiller's eyes, which were ranging over her shoulder, looking at something behind her. 'You still got that Winchester? You shot a bear with it once, right?'

Over Sally's shoulder, Mankiller spotted two men moving at a crouch between houses. Their white and gray snow-suits blended with the landscape as well as clothing could, and they held similarly colored weapons at the low ready.

'More 'n once.' Sally nodded.

'It loaded?' Mankiller asked as Yakecan followed her gaze to the two men just before they weaved between buildings and disappeared from view.

'Always.' Sally finally turned, but the men were gone. She took a step in that direction.

Quick as a striking snake, Mankiller reached out and touched her shoulder, gently enough not to hurt her but firmly enough to keep her from taking another step. 'Your house is in the other direction, Sally. Go get your rifle and stay inside.'

'Sheriff, I . . .' Sally turned back to her.

'Do it,' Mankiller said, and her tone shut Sally up. The old woodcarver nodded once and took off running.

'You see anyone on your way, you tell 'em to do the same,' Mankiller called after her.

Mankiller made sure a round was in the chamber of the Ruger and brought the gun up to the low ready. It was longer and heavier than the C7 she'd carried in Afghanistan, but the sweet spot on her shoulder welcomed it like an old friend. 'You ready?' she whispered to Yakecan.

'Guess we ain't goin' to the mayor,' Yakecan said, checking the chamber on his 870.

'Mayor'll find out on his own soon enough,' Mankiller said, and set off. It had been years since she'd carried a long gun against a human opponent. The Ruger was familiar enough from years of hunting, but even ground-stalking big game like bears lacked the same kind of throat-closing tension. The Army had trained her to recognize it, to learn to live with it. Eventually, it had become an old friend. Like riding a bicycle, she never truly forgot it, and she found herself visually partitioning turns around house corners into pie slices, taking them a sideways-scrabbling step at a time, ready to pull the trigger the moment anyone appeared in her sights. She leaned from her waist, advancing at a slow walk, her rock-solid gait keeping her hands as steady as possible. Running around might look good in the movies, but even a gun with as much kick as Early Bird's Alaskan would be useless if she didn't hit what she aimed at.

Yakecan dropped back behind her, covering her as she moved, then advancing as soon as she stopped and brought her weapon up. The leapfrogging dance was second nature to anyone who'd been downrange, and Yakecan had done it day in, day out with the other soldiers in his squad in tougher conditions than these. 'Moving,' 'covering,' they whispered to one another as they went, handing off roles as smoothly as if they were telepathically linked.

They moved past the propane storage dump and the generator park, its chain-link perimeter blue with frost. This was as close as the hamlet of under five hundred square kilometers got to a bad neighborhood. They passed Bob Crosshill's purple-sided double-wide. The trapper was home, and Mankiller could see him peeking from behind the curtain, motioning his wife away from the window with one meaty hand. Mankiller spared him a glance, hefted her rifle, and mouthed, *Get your gun*.

She moved on, rolling out onto the snow-covered track that wound its way to Highway 6, the one connection between the hamlet and civilization. She scanned the ground for footprints, wasn't surprised by their absence. The wind off the lake obscured tracks here even in the height of summer. If there was so much as a dusting of snowfall, it was hopeless.

Who were these armed interlopers? What did they want? What the hell were they doing all the way out here? She pushed the questions out of her mind. Whoever they were, they were armed and in her town. They'd answer for that, no matter who the hell they were. She'd settle the score here and then go find her grandfather. He'd know what to do. He always did.

She paused, scanning the horizon. Nothing but the low tops of the houses, silver stovepipes belching warm white smoke into the air. Word must have spread. The hamlet was dead silent, the streets deserted. Of course, in Fort Resolution, that was hardly notable.

Yakecan sidled up alongside, whispered, 'Where you think they went?'

Mankiller shook her head, looked again. She had just seen them come around . . .

Gunshots. Yelling.

Mankiller took off running, heard Yakecan's sigh as he realized he'd have to beat feet to keep up with her.

'Shoot you in your fuckin' ass!' she heard Sally bellow.

Mankiller put on speed. Somehow, the bastards had circled around and come from behind her, past Sally's house. If she hadn't told the old wood carver to go home and load up, they'd probably be at the municipal building by now.

'Come around my house, you fuckers!' Another shot.

Mankiller had been careless. That, or these guys were very good. She hoped it was the former.

She raced past the Loon, the hamlet's one bar, and rolled the corner, getting up on her sights as she came. The world shrank to the Alaskan's front sight post, everything in the background receding into a blur that identified itself only as target and not-target.

The blur that was Sally was bent over on her porch, blurry arm clamped to her blurry stomach, sinking to her knees.

Two white blurs were pointing black blurs up at her. The enemy.

Mankiller stopped, lined up center mass, let her finger take the slack out of the Alaskan's trigger. 'Police! Drop your weapons, right now!'

Yakecan was shouting beside her, but his voice was only a low buzz. Mankiller had dropped into the zone, what some of her battle buddies had called 'bullet time', back in the craggy hell that was the Korengal Valley. The world went gray, her vision tightening even further, until even the target vanished, and the sight post was all, glowing like a diamond.

Time slowed. The enemy didn't answer, he merely turned, and the black blur that was his weapon rose. He looked to Mankiller like a marionette spinning in a jar of molasses, languid and clumsy, taking forever.

The trigger was already tight against the spring. She nudged it a millimeter back, not anticipating, letting it do what triggers did in their own good time.

This trigger's own good time turned out to be instant. *Bang.*

The Alaskan punched her shoulder and Mankiller was working the bolt before the smoke even cleared, not knowing if she'd hit her target, not knowing what the other bad guy was doing. It didn't matter. If she was going to win, she had to push through.

The spent brass spun away and the next round slid home. Mankiller's focus never wavered from the front sight post, never allowed the rest of the world to clarify around her. Instead, she swung the muzzle to where she'd seen the other gray-white blur of the enemy, heard Yakecan's 870 boom twice in rapid succession.

More smoke, a shout. Boots crunching on snow. She took a shuffling step to her right. Her last shot would have told an enemy where she stood. Movement, no matter how small, would reduce the chances of a lucky shot fired into smoke hitting her. She stayed on her sights, staring into the cloud of spent propellant, as if by her will she could make it clear.

The moment stretched out, an eternity to Mankiller, her gut churning as she stared into the swirling gray that might be pierced any second by a bullet speeding straight between her eyes.

But when the smoke finally broke apart, the blurry gray-white shape of the remaining enemy was receding, boots pounding on the frost-covered ground. Mankiller lined up her shot, tensed her finger. The blur whipped around the vinyl-sided corner of Denise Unka's single-story ranch and vanished.

Mankiller exhaled, brought her weapon down to the low ready, moving her finger off the trigger and indexing it above the guard. The world came into focus as her eyes moved away from the sights. Her head swam for a moment, and then line and color crowded her senses, all the sharper and more wonderful for its brief absence. A slight pain throbbed in the side of her neck from where the muscle had cramped.

She kept her eyes on the corner of Denise's house. Ready for the enemy to come back. 'You okay?' she asked Yakecan.

Yakecan panted. 'I think I hit him.'

'You think?' Mankiller permitted herself a glance all around them. Apart from Sally groaning on her front porch, there was no one.

'Take overwatch,' Mankiller said.

'Where you goin'?' Yakecan came back up on his sights, backing up as Mankiller trotted toward Sally's house.

'Sally's gutshot. Need to make sure she won't bleed out.'

'What the fuck, Sheriff? What're we gonna do?'

'First thing, we get Sally back to the station.'

'Not the health center?'

'Hell, no. You're goin' to the center and tell Nurse McNeely to come to the station, but first she's gotta go home and grab a rifle.'

'The station ain't a hospital, boss. We don't have—'

Mankiller whirled on Yakecan, anger curdling in the back of her throat. 'Stop fuckin' arguin' with me, Joe. How many bad guys you see rope out of that helo? Six? Seven? I bet there's twenty on there at least. You think after we gunned down one of their people and sent the other packin', they're jus' gonna cut their losses and go home? We got more enemy inbound. Station's the easiest place to turtle 'til we can figure out how to get comms with the outside.'

Yakecan nodded. 'Yeah. Sorry, Sheriff.'

Mankiller dismissed the apology with a shake of her head and sprinted the rest of the way to Sally's side. 'Hey, lady. You doin' okay?'

'They fuckin' shot me!' Sally shrieked. She was slumped against the wall of her house, hands soaked with blood, clamped over her abdomen. Her face was nearly as white as the snow that blanketed her stoop.

'Yeah.' Mankiller tried to keep cheerful. Morale could make the difference between hanging on and slipping into the black. 'They sure did. Lemme take a look?'

Sally moved her hands to reveal a ragged hole in her abdomen. Mankiller leaned in close on the pretense of examining the wound, but got what she really wanted, the odor. Sally's gut smelled like an open sewer. The bullet had surely perforated her bowels. If she didn't bleed out or die of shock, the peritonitis would probably take her.

'Am I gonna die?' Sally asked as Mankiller forced the sour look from her face and smiled.

'Stop being such a baby,' Mankiller said. 'You got Kerlix or gauze or whatever?'

'Clean towel,' Sally moaned.

'That'll have to do. Joe! Get in there and grab a clean towel or a shirt or something.'

Yakecan nodded and raced into the house.

Mankiller stood. 'Sit tight, Sally. I want you to hold your jacket over the hole. Push as hard as you can.'

She went to the side of the man she'd shot. The .375 round had caught him just above his body armor, shattering his sternum. The bone had sent the bullet careering out of his shoulder. Bone fragments must have pierced his heart.

He was definitely military. The snowsuit, mask, goggles, armor, and tac vest were all top-of-the-line. He carried an MP5 submachine gun loaded with 9mm rounds. Perfect for close-quarters combat, the weapon of choice among commandos. She rifled through his pockets, looking for a wallet, an ID badge, anything that might help her understand who he was or why he was here.

The man didn't have a scrap of paper on him. No dog tags, either. Mankiller would have liked to have stripped the body to check for tattoos, but it would have to wait. Even if the enemy didn't return, Sally wouldn't last.

'Got a clean T-shirt!' Yakecan shouted triumphantly from the door, holding a ball of white cloth over his head.

'Good for you! Don't jus' stand there! Stick it in the damn hole!' Mankiller stood and trotted back over to them.

'Sorry, Sally,' Yakecan was saying as he pried her hands away from the wound.

'This is goin' to hurt like hell, but it's the only way I can keep you safe enough to get you back to the station, okay?' Mankiller asked.

Sally gave no response. Her eyes were focused but staring over Mankiller's shoulder at nothing. Her breathing was coming in shallow, rapid gasps. Sweat stood out on her forehead despite the cold.

Mankiller snatched the shirt from Yakecan and stuffed it into the hole in Sally's gut, packing it in as tightly as she could manage, praying she didn't do any further damage to the organs inside. The shirt was instantly soaked with blood, and the smell was powerful enough to make Yakecan wrinkle his nose, but Sally showed no more reaction than a slight groan. They were losing her.

'Sally? Listen to me. We're getting you someplace safe. I need you to stay awake. Can you do that?'

Sally nodded weakly.

Mankiller looped one of Sally's arms around her shoulders. Yakecan grabbed the other without having to be asked. Sally got her legs under her, stumbled weakly, but her feet were moving at least, and that meant there was some hope.

'What about the body?' Yakecan jerked his head toward the enemy Mankiller had shot.

'We'll come back.'

'No, I mean, his gear. If more bad guys are coming, shouldn't we?'

'He's got a go-bag and an MP5. We got bigger and better guns in the station. Priority one is stabilizin' Sally. Priority two is gettin' comms up. We need help and we need it right now.'

Sally was small and light in full health. Wounded, she seemed even lighter. She barely slowed Mankiller and Yakecan as they raced back to the station, weapons dangling in their slings, each bump against their hips reminding them of how vulnerable they were should the enemy return.

The enemy didn't return. Instead, it was Bob Crosshill, finally scaring up the guts to quit his house and see what the fuss was all about. He held his fowling gun, a double-barreled antique that was only slightly better suited for scaring criminals than it was for shooting birds. 'Jesus, Sheriff. What the hell happened?'

'Bobby, go back to that dead bad guy and strip his gear, then you come meet me at the station and tell everyone you meet along the way. You got me?'

'I . . .' Crosshill's mouth worked, his eyes wide, fixed on Sally's wound.

'Everybody, with guns, at the station, Bobby. You got me?'

'Yeah, Sheriff.' Crosshill finally looked up at her. 'I got you.'

'Go,' Mankiller said, and Crosshill took off running.

Calmut met them coming up the steps. 'Jesus. Sally! You okay?'

Sally gave no answer, chin bumping her chest, eyes finally shut.

'Comms?' Mankiller asked, shouldering him out of the way.

'Freddie's over at the municipal building, but he said nothin's wrong.'

'Nothin's wrong? What the hell does that mean?'

'Nothin's wrong with the antennae or the systems. Mast's up, good signal. Comms shouldn't be down.'

Which meant they were being jammed. Mankiller felt a sick terror in her gut. Fort Resolution wasn't an incidental target. Whoever these people were, they were here on purpose.

'Why the hell aren't you takin' her to the health center?' Calmut asked.

'Ollie, I need you to shut the fuck up and do what I tell

you,' Mankiller said. 'Go get the nurse and bring her here. Armed, please. I want the whole town here with guns, yesterday.'

'Yeah, but—'

'Ollie, get it fuckin' done right now. I am not playin' with you.'

'Okay, Sheriff, I'm goin'.' Calmut ran as fast as his skinny legs would carry him. Mankiller noted the .357 bumping in its holster against his hip with some satisfaction. At least he had listened to her in that one thing.

They shouldered their way into the station, the heat hitting them like a wall. Mankiller could feel her pores opening under the heavy parka.

They pushed back into the station's main room and kicked the pelican case of medical supplies off the gray cot that sat outside the cell door. They lay Sally on her back on the narrow stretch of fabric stretched tight between aluminum rods, more stretcher than bed. Her skin had gone gray, her eyelids and lips the sick purple of a fresh bruise. She was breathing, but only just, and Mankiller didn't bother to try and wake her. Sally needed care beyond what Mankiller would be able to give her now. She needed to be medevaced to Yellowknife and soon.

'We don' get comms up, we're gonna lose her,' Yakecan said.

'Thank you, Captain Obvious,' Mankiller said through gritted teeth.

'What now?' Yakecan asked.

'Now we go grab the mayor and then the rest of the town, get 'em back here.'

'You so sure more bad guys are comin'?'

'If they aren't, I'll be happy as hell to look stupid.'

Yakecan nodded, checked the action on his 870, looked

back up. 'That was good shootin', Sheriff. You did that guy right.'

'Yeah,' Mankiller said, embarrassed. That guy wasn't the first man she'd ever shot, but he was probably the closest to her when the round had left the muzzle. She was surprised at how little she felt after the act. Not sad, not frightened, not elated. It was a speed bump, little more than the stirring of air, a thing to be contemplated and dealt with further down the line. She looked up at Yakecan, noted the drifting, dreamy look on his face. There was no bemused smile, no trace of anger. He was scared bad.

'Joe. How you doin'?'

'I'm okay, Sheriff. This is jus' . . . I didn't expect this.'

'Nobody did.'

'Whaddya think they want?'

'Don't care. Whatever they want, I want the opposite and badly.'

'Yeah. What about . . . What about the things . . .'

'Shut up, Joe.' Mankiller had been deliberately avoiding thinking about that wriggling mass of flesh they'd seen in the cage. 'We'll deal with that when we have to. Not before.'

'Okay, boss, but I was jus' thinkin' maybe it's like what your grandpa does—'

'I thought of that too, okay? If'n it is, we know what we gotta do to take 'em out.'

'I jus' . . . I didn't think it worked with people.'

'Joe, will you shut up and come on?'

'Okay,' Yakecan said, and hurried after her.

They made it out into the hall before the sight out the window brought them up short.

A man had emerged from the door of the municipal building, walking deliberately toward the station.

He was naked.

'Is that . . .' Yakecan began, coming up on his sights.

The man began to pick up speed toward them. His skin was a darker gray than Sally's, save for his arms, which were red to the elbow. Gore dripped from his mouth, from bone claws that emerged from his fingertips. His tongue, black as a new tire, was too long and thick, hanging from the corner of his mouth. His eyes burned gold, fixed steadily on the station window, as if he knew Mankiller was inside.

Tires crunched on the snow outside the door. Mankiller heard an engine coughing.

She raced to the door, threw it open, bringing the Alaskan up and sighting in on the naked man walking toward them.

'Hey, Sheriff.' Crosshill's voice. 'I brought a whole mess of guns and all my traps, I wasn't sure if . . . Jesus, what're you—'

'Get inside right now, Bobby!' Mankiller's world had already blurred away, the front sight on her rifle drawing into focus. She wished this was Afghanistan, that she could simply pull the trigger and put a round through the dark gray blur hovering in her sights. She already knew what it was, knew what that meant. But it wasn't shaped like a wolf, it was shaped like a man, and she wasn't a soldier now, she was a cop, and that meant there were protocols that had to be followed. 'Police! Get down on the ground!' she shouted. 'Put your hands behind your head!'

The thing shrieked, a cry that sounded almost gleeful, somewhere between the piercing scream of an eagle and the bark of an angry dog. It launched itself at her so quickly that the frozen ground churned beneath its bare feet, sending up a spray of frost behind it.

'Bobby, look out!' Mankiller shouted, slapping the

trigger back. The Alaskan jerked, the shot breaking high, but she saw the blur spasm as the round caught its shoulder. The .375 round was powerful enough to drop a bear at two hundred yards, but it only served to knock the creature to one side. It hardly slowed, but it missed the door, crashing into the bannister of the low staircase hard enough to shatter it, bone claws slicing through the railing and splintering the steps beneath.

It was down for a mere instant, then leapt to its feet, sweeping a clawed hand toward her.

Mankiller leapt aside, her shoulder striking the hood of Bob's car before she tumbled to the ground, the Alaskan's butt smacking her in the face hard enough to split her lip. She heard the doorframe crack as the thing's hand smashed through it.

She could see Bob in her peripheral vision, backing away, off-balance. She scrambled backward on her hands and heels, trying to give herself enough distance to line up another shot.

Not that another shot would help. The monster was already recovering, finding its balance, turning toward her.

Up close, Mankiller got a good view of the burning eyes, so like the wolves and bears her grandfather made. The soul of an ancestor brought into a human corpse? She shuddered as it crouched, spread its bloodstained hands, and roared. *It's trying to spook me. It enjoys it.*

She wouldn't give it the satisfaction. She picked up the Alaskan and sighted in, knowing full well that as fast as that thing was, it would reach her before she could pull the trigger.

She heard the station window bang open, saw Yakecan leaning out, bringing the 870 up, sighting in.

The shotgun slug could punch a hole nearly an inch across through a buck's heart, cutting through all the surrounding bone and muscle like it was hot margarine. Mankiller's eyes widened and she threw herself to the side. 'Joe! Don't shoo . . .'

The 870 roared and the creature's head exploded like a rotten cantaloupe, raining fragments of metal and jellied gray matter down on her. She felt the ground churn a few inches to her left as the spent slug buried itself.

'Fuck!' Mankiller scrambled to her feet, struggling to get the tumbling Alaskan back into her grip. 'Damnit, Joe! You 'bout fuckin' shot me!'

The monster lifted its pulped head sagging on its thick neck. It opened its mouth to roar again, but the slug-adjusted orifice could muster nothing more than a choked gurgle. Its gold eyes still burned from now-lopsided sockets. It reached out with one red hand, grasping the truck's bumper, bent low.

Bang. Bob, shooting at the thing from the truck's far side. From the sound of the blast, it was a weak round, 9mm. Even if he could hit it, it wouldn't do anything.

'Bobby, get out of here!' Mankiller said, dashing away from the truck.

The creature grunted, strained, lifted. The truck groaned as its front end rose. Mankiller could see the wheels hanging over empty air, and then the monster gave a final push and the truck toppled end over end, the bumper shearing away, the cab crushed beneath its own weight.

Mankiller threw herself aside as the truck tumbled. The bed's tarp went flying, and something struck her in the leg. She went down hard, fumbling the rifle again, got her arms up over her head.

It was raining guns. Pistols, boxes of ammunition, huge steel crescents. As they thumped to the ground, Mankiller winced at how close they'd come to staving in her skull. *Bear traps. The damned idiot brought bear traps.*

The creature was already following the tumbling truck, ignoring Bob and Joe, making straight for her.

'Shit! Boss! I'm comin'!' Yakecan was shouting. It wouldn't matter. He couldn't stop this thing. No one could.

Mankiller felt the throbbing in her leg. Whatever had struck her hadn't torn her pants, and she didn't see any blood. She got up to one knee and aimed the Alaskan again. The creature gurgled, picking up speed.

Boots pounding on frost. Yakecan beside the thing, pointed the 870 at its ribs, fired point-blank.

The shot threw the monster onto its side, but it simply rolled back to its feet, came on after her. At last, terror seized her. She dropped the Alaskan, scrambling back on her hands and heels once again, panic driving now, all the fight in her utterly absorbed by the need to run. 'Stop it, Joe!' she shouted. 'Stop it!'

It reached out, seized her ankle, the claws sinking into the thick fabric of her snow pants.

'I got it, boss!' Yakecan said, held the 870 over the back of its knee, fired.

The leg sheared off, spinning into the air and tumbling away, trailing a thread of metal cable and spewing gray fluid. Was it a robot of some kind? A cyborg?

The thing turned, snarling, flailed at Yakecan. Its newly shortened limb robbed it of most of its leverage, but it still mustered enough force to backhand Yakecan into the ruins of the station steps, the 870 tumbling from his hands. Its grip on Mankiller's ankle tightened. She could feel bones grinding beneath her skin.

She reached back to grab at the ground, as if good purchase would be enough to break its hold. Her rational mind told her it was useless, that the thing had dead strength, so powerful that she would have a better chance ripping her foot off her leg than breaking free.

Her fingers scrabbled, searched, closed on the cold steel crescent of trap jaws, the sharp edges of its teeth gliding beneath her gloves. She ripped it up and brought it down, meaning to club the monster in the head and succeeding only in pounding her own shin. Her howl of agony was cut short by the length of chain that followed, smacking her in the back of her head hard enough to dim her sight.

The thing yanked on her leg, hauling itself up her body. She had thought it would rip off her foot, but she could see now that it planned worse. It was climbing her, making its way to her chest.

Her heart.

She spit, screamed, pushed. It was useless. She was going to die.

The thought gave her clarity, an odd measure of peace. She felt some of the panic recede and her focus return. If this was to be her end, then she would make it a worthy one. She brought the bear trap up between them, forced the jaws open with all her might. The effort made her grunt, and she felt the muscles in her back burning painfully, her spine singing out as ligaments tore. The trap bucked and pulled, the spring plate rattling against the frame. The traps normally took two people to set, and there was no way she could get the spring plate in place now. She held it with all the power she could muster, then slammed it down on the thing's pulped head, releasing the jaws.

They snapped shut halfway down the monster's face, crushing what remained. The flames of its eyes vanished, swallowed in the vortex of its collapsing skull. It shuddered, slumped, the head drooping to Mankiller's abdomen as it adjusted to the weight of the added steel. It let go of her ankle, raising a hand to its head, slapping weakly at the jaws.

Crosshill appeared behind it, his wood axe in his hands, rising over his head.

'Jesus, fuck, Bobby! Be care—' Mankiller scrambled away as he brought the axe down between the thing's shoulder blades. It jerked, and Crosshill yanked the axe back up again. The next stroke severed its arm at the shoulder. The next split it halfway across its waist. The next took off the head, drawing sparks from the chain and sending the trap flying.

Crosshill struck again and again, breaking the monster into smaller and smaller pieces, until at last he stood, leaning on the handle, panting. 'Holy . . . fuckin' . . . shit. Joe, you all rig—'

'The fuck is wrong with you?!' Mankiller scrambled to her feet. 'I got Joe shootin' at me and you choppin' at me. You *tryin'* to kill me?!'

Crosshill blinked, look down at the ruined mess of the creature beneath him. 'I just saved your life, Sheriff.'

'It was a near thing. A damn near thing.'

'Well, I'm fuckin' sorry.' Crosshill stabbed an angry finger at her. 'Next time, I'll just let it bite your damn fool head off.'

'Jesus.' Mankiller was shaking with rage. Just a few hours before, she had been playing snow snake with Yakecan up by the . . . Yakecan.

She ran to his side. He was sitting up, rubbing his head, the 870 butt resting on his cheek. 'Jesus H. Christ . . .'

'You okay, Joe?' Mankiller held up a hand. 'Look at my finger. Tell me if—'

Yakecan pushed her arm down. 'I'm okay, Sheriff. Just got the wind knocked out of me. Help me up, wouldja?'

Mankiller reached down, but Yakecan was already pushing himself to his feet. He dusted himself off, stooped to retrieve the 870, then stood, staring in silence at the scattered fragments left by Crosshill's axe. 'Hands is all red,' he finally said.

'Yeah,' Mankiller agreed. 'He was comin' from Municipal.'

'So, guess that means we ain't gettin' the mayor.'

'Guess so,' Mankiller said.

'What the hell is going on, Sheriff?' Crosshill asked.

'Not sure, but I got an idea. Know some things.'

'What things?' Crosshill's voice was straddling the line of panic.

'I know we're under siege, and there's a lot more of these' – she gestured to the remains of the dead thing on the ground – 'inbound.'

'So, what do we do?' Crosshill asked.

Mankiller looked at him like he was simple. 'It's a siege, ain't it? We dig in and hold on.'

Chapter Ten
The Right Call

The Director stared down the hillside at the plumes of smoke curling from the forest of silver smokestacks dotting the scattered hamlet of Fort Resolution.

A sparse forest. This was every bit as isolated as the most distant backwaters nestled in the ridges of Afghanistan. If not for the slim stretch of poorly maintained country road connecting it to the transportation network, it would be little more than a camp.

Xolotl and Quetzalcoatl flanked him silently, their gray bodies adorned with only their gold and jewels. The Director briefly considered asking them to dress. The constant reminder of their unlife made the living members of the Cell nervous, but even if he had the language, he doubted they would comply.

He turned to Mark instead. 'This is . . . rustic.'

'Population's less than a thousand, sir.' Mark's voice was muffled by her hood. She was dressed as the rest of the Director's living servants: white parka and snowsuit, tactical gear. 'Most of them still make their living as hunters and fur trappers, just like the old days. It's like the Middle Ages out here.'

'If they are so backwards,' the Director mused, 'how is it they managed to kill one of my men?' He gestured.

'The sheriff is an Army veteran, sir. Six years in.'

'Special Operations?'

'No, sir.'

'A Ranger, then.'

'No, sir.'

'What did she do for the Army?'

'Just one tour, sir. Explosives Ordnance Disposal.'

'You mean to tell me that one of my operators, a man who completed a twenty-year distinguished career with the most elite special forces unit in the United States *before* he started running ops for us was caught out and killed by a woman who spent six years defusing bombs?'

'She got a Medal of Bravery, sir. That's a pretty big deal in the Canadian Army.'

'No doubt she got it for her expertise in documenting the disposal of ordnance,' the Director said. This was why you could never rely on humans to get things done. The Golds were the only truly effective tool in his box.

As if she sensed his thoughts: 'She took out a Gold, too, sir.'

'No.' The Director turned his gaze to the wreckage outside the police station. 'It took three of them to do that, and they were lucky.'

'Yes, sir.' The Director could tell from Mark's tone that she didn't agree, but there was no need to correct her just now.

'I do not believe that releasing the Gold was the wisest choice,' he said.

'Ops made the call, sir,' she said. 'Once he saw we had a man down, he didn't want to leave anything to chance.'

'Such as?'

'Such as them calling for help or being inspired by the victory.'

'How would they call for help?' The Director turned to

look at her. 'We have jammed cell and satellite comms. We have cut the landlines. They don't even have VHF.'

'Maybe one of them has a crystal radio set, sir.'

The Director swallowed his frustration. This mission had to be a success. He had considered the alternative to finding the Summoner and securing his cooperation. It would be easy to hide himself and the remaining Golds in the vast wilderness, and the bitter cold would do nearly as good a job as the refrigerated cells back in the facility. But the humans wouldn't be able to survive long out here, and without the infrastructure of the Cell, he'd lack money, equipment, and transportation to do anything more than hide. No, he needed a living body and soon. 'Tell me, Mark. Why are we here?'

'To find the Summoner, sir. The sheriff's grandfather.'

'That's right. Tell me, do you think that releasing a Gold into the hamlet is a good means to that particular end?'

Her adrenaline spiked. She knew where this conversation was leading. 'I thought . . . They killed one of ours. I thought a show of force was required. Maybe they'd give up resistance once they saw what the Golds could do.'

'The Golds' – the Director finally turned his head toward her, shuffling infinitesimally closer – 'are not discriminating about who they kill, Mark, you know this. The one you sent entered and exited the municipal building. Tell me, do you think it left anyone in there alive?'

'No, sir. Probably not.'

'Probably not,' the Director repeated. 'So, the entire town government, any one of whom may have had information on our Summoner's whereabouts, are now lost to us.'

'You said the sheriff is the one who matters, sir. You said she would help us find him.'

'Are you making excuses? Are you not taking

responsibility for an error in judgment? Is that what my ears are hearing?'

Mark's adrenaline skyrocketed. Her voice shook. 'No, sir. Of course not. It was entirely my fault. A bad decision, and one that won't be repeated.'

'Yes.' The Director looked back to the town. 'It was. You are fortunate that the sheriff and her allies were able to destroy it, loath as I am to lose such a powerful asset.'

'Yes, sir. I'm hoping the encounter broke their spirits in spite of the victory. Seeing a Gold can be unsettling. Now we can go in to parlay for the information.'

'I find it startling that I understand the minds of living humans better than you, despite the difference in our condition,' the Director said.

'Sir?'

'Sheriff Plante . . .'

'Mankiller, sir.'

'Mankiller is a nickname. Her last name is Plante. Also, do not interrupt me.' Mark stiffened at the reproof, keeping her eyes forward.

The Director paused to let his disapproval sink in, then began speaking again. 'Sheriff Plante is an Afghanistan veteran, an Army sergeant. Not easily intimidated. She was, for many years, willing to don a flimsy blast suit and handle unexploded ordnance. Tell me, when faced with the presence of undead monsters, do you think she will balk? Or do you think she will be galvanized to fight?'

Mark's silence was answer enough.

The Director nodded. 'Well, I've always said, if you want something done, you have to do it yourself.'

'Sir?' Mark turned to him.

'I'm going down there. I'll do the negotiating personally.'

'Sir, I can't allow that,' Mark said quickly. 'If anything were to happen to you—'

'I'm sorry, the funniest thing just happened. I thought I heard you say that you couldn't allow me to do something I intended to do. That is odd, isn't it? That I would hear something like that? Surely, I'm mistaken.'

Mark's eyes were wild now. If she agreed with him, she was telling the Director he had made a mistake. If she disagreed, she was admitting that she believed she could forbid him to go. The Director could almost hear the wheels turning in her head. At last, she settled on her safest course. 'Yes, sir. That is odd.'

'Odd, indeed,' the Director mused. 'Position two sniper teams to cover me, please.'

'I'll come with you, sir,' Mark offered.

'I think it will be better,' the Director said, 'if we don't have such a soft target in range of the enemy, or a beating heart to distract the Golds, don't you?' He gestured to Xolotl and Quetzalcoatl, who inclined their heads as one to consider Mark.

She stammered, desperately searching for a counter-argument. At last, she sighed. 'Yes, sir.'

'The snipers, please.'

'At least let me get you in some armor, sir. Or give you a gun.'

He turned back to her. Her concern was touching, or would have been if he were a weak, fragile human. Armor and weapons were for the living man he had once been. They hadn't done that man a lot of good. They would only slow him down now.

The Director said nothing, only stared at her as her resolve crumbled and she raised a hand to her commlink and began calling in the orders.

'Excellent,' the Director said. 'You're in charge until I get back. I'll keep the comms channel open.'

Xolotl and Quetzalcoatl glided smoothly behind him,

but the Director could feel the tension in them. They were wound like springs, unsettled by the nearness of so much life.

The hamlet was tiny, little more than a trailer park nestled up against the frozen surface of the lake. The houses were barely more than ice-encrusted double-wides surrounded by beaten-up pickup trucks and snowmobiles. He could make out a few multi-level businesses, the spire of a chapel. Word of his coming must have spread. The streets were deserted, the only sounds the gusting wind and a distant hammering.

He made his way toward the station. The part of him that remembered his warrior training was horrified by how exposed he was. Alone, in the open. Anyone behind any window could be sighting in on him. His augmented senses might detect them, but there was no guarantee of that, and even if he managed to avoid an attack, he couldn't speak for Xolotl and Quetzalcoatl. They were meant to be a deterrent or, if need be, a last resort. He didn't want to use them if he could avoid it, and he certainly didn't want them damaged.

He turned the corner past a run-down shack sporting a weathered sign showing a water bird, its single purple eye fixed on him. Its beak was drawn back in a grim-looking smile. THE LOON, it read above an unlit neon beer advertisement. The blinds were drawn, the door padlocked from the outside. Tracks showed that the owner had left in a hurry.

The Director scanned the ground. It was sporadic permafrost out here, hard enough that it didn't take impressions well, but wind kept the tops of the snowdrifts blowing, and he could make out a few crisscrossing tire tracks striped with footprints. People, all moving quickly toward a single point. The sheriff must have summoned everyone to the station. She was likely turning it into a blockhouse. Smart woman. Tough, too, but not tough enough. She was human, and no matter how strong a heart beat in a human breast, it was still just that, a heart. A thing of meat and blood. Delicate and easily stopped.

At last, the station came into view. It was little more than a trailer, a Frankenstein structure that looked like several shacks cobbled together. Four pickup trucks had been drawn up to form an L-shaped barricade around the shattered remains of a short wooden staircase leading to the front door. Sandbags were piled haphazardly beneath them, packed with ice and snow to fill in the gaps. There was some evidence of a halfhearted attempt to add dirt to the construction, but it had been short-lived. If they were going to dig up this ground, they'd need a jackhammer. The Director didn't doubt that, with time, they'd get one. This had to be ended quickly.

He heard soft voices, the dull scrape of a shovel. Heartbeats, fast and hard. People working. Xolotl and Quetzalcoatl fanned out and moved up alongside him.

He stopped a good distance from the truck barricade. Nothing to be gained by bringing the Golds that close. Anyone who cared to look could see them well enough for them to make their point. None challenged him. If the Sheriff had put out pickets, then they were looking in the wrong direction. That was good.

'Hello,' he ventured. He smiled inwardly, realizing it was the same hoarse whisper he used every day. No one could hear him at this distance. When was the last time he had actually raised his voice?

He gathered air into his dead lungs and pushed it up through his throat, working the muscles there to project the sound. Yelling was like riding a bike. You never really forgot how to do it, even after dying.

'Hello!' he tried again. The higher volume made his voice into an angry bark. It sounded impressive, even to him.

The voices and the scraping stopped. He heard the racking of a shotgun slide and the barrel appeared over one of the truck's beds. The man behind it was older, his pinched face exhausted. His eyes were rheumy, but his aim seemed good, and the Director could tell from the solid *thunk* of the shotgun's bolt that it was loaded with slugs.

'Don't shoot!' the Director called. 'Well . . . I suppose you can if you like, but it won't do you any good.'

'Who the fuck are you?' the man asked.

'Well, that's not a very nice way to welcome visitors. You may call me the Director. I am the one who has placed your town under siege.' He could feel Xolotl and Quetzalcoatl tensing beside him, put out a hand to stay them.

'Lemme see your face.' The man's voice was frightened but determined. The Director didn't bother trying to scent the chemical cocktail of his bloodstream. It would surely tell him the same thing.

'What I look like isn't important. I was wondering if I could speak to Wilma Plante. She's the sheriff here, if I understand correctly.'

'Why'd she wanna talk to you?'

The Director gestured to the Golds beside him. 'It's my understanding that you fought one of these earlier today?'

Silence, but the man's look told the Director that he had at least seen it.

'You know what they can do. You should also know that I am the only thing holding them back. I have dozens more just outside town. Now, I have put up with a lot of hostility from you when I've been nothing but civil, but if you don't get the sheriff right now, I will release them.'

'We did for the one you sent before.'

'You did! It was very impressive. It was also very lucky. If you like, we can see how you handle these two. And if, by some miracle, you manage to defeat them, we'll up the ante to six. Now, are you going to get the sheriff for me, or am I going to unleash these fellows?'

'Now, you listen to . . .'

'That's enough, Ollie.' A woman's voice, gruff and commanding. She stood at the top of the broken staircase, almost entirely shrouded in her parka and snowsuit. Her hands wore only thin leather gloves that left the fingers free. They looked tiny in the midst of the winter swaddling. Her face was reduced to a small circle by the fur-lined hood, but what he could see was as hard as iron. Her eyes were dark slits, alert and calm. The Director had seen those eyes before, in the faces of the pipe hitters who shared the hard ground he trod in his days as a living warrior. The hardest of the hard, the elite of the elite. Seeing those eyes, he felt a brief spasm, not of fear, for he would never fear a human, but of acknowledgement of the task before him. That it would not be easy. That was fine. He remembered the mantra of his time as a living warrior: the only easy day was yesterday.

A man appeared at her side, nearly twice her size and so swaddled in cold-weather gear that he looked like a walrus walking upright. The Director heard the heartbeats of everyone slow as the woman appeared, her command presence calming them all.

'What do you want?' she asked. Her voice was low, just loud enough to carry.

'You're Wilma Plante?' the Director asked.

She didn't answer, only held her .375 bolt action rifle at

the low ready. It was made for hunting bear, and he didn't doubt it would do some damage, even if it lacked the power to truly harm him.

'I was hoping for the chance to speak to your grandfather, Sheriff. He's a little tough to find, and I'm generally good at finding people.'

'My grandpa's dead,' the woman said.

'Oh, come now,' the Director said. 'We both know that's not true. I'll thank you not to lie to me, Sheriff. It's impossible to have a productive discussion unless both parties negotiate in good faith.'

'Nobody's negotiatin' nothin',' she said. 'More likely I'm gonna put a bullet in you, you don' get movin'.'

'Oh, don't be silly,' the Director said, gesturing to the Golds. 'We both know that's not going to help against us.'

The sheriff smiled, raised a hand. The walrus beside her put a jar into it.

'Yeah, figured,' she said. 'You seem to know a lot about me. You know what I did in the Army?'

'Explosives ordnance disposal,' he said. 'Sadly, I don't have any bombs I need defused.'

'Didn't just defuse 'em,' she said.

The Director listened to her heartbeat, not liking how slow it was beating. Her blood sugar smelled flat, normal. He couldn't remember the last time a human had been so . . . unimpressed. Was she high? No, he would have smelled the chemicals on her. Alcohol stank worse than gasoline. Marijuana was even more pungent. She took the jar slowly, holding it gingerly out before her. 'You know what this is?'

The Director scented the air, caught the tarry smell of acetone, the burned rubber stink of peroxide. It was home-brewed triacetone triperoxide, TATP, the favored explosive of insurgents and criminals. The sheriff raised her arm to a throwing position, steady as a surgeon, taking elaborate care not to jostle the jar at all.

'You're not setting a very good example for the citizenry of Fort Resolution,' the Director said. 'If their own sheriff is making homemade explosives, why shouldn't everyone?'

'Desperate times.' The Sheriff smiled. 'Now fuck off back to wherever you came from or I'll put this right between your feet.'

The Director felt a wild thrill course up his spiritual spine. He couldn't remember the last time he'd faced a human so fearless, so intractable. 'TATP is notoriously unstable. Odds are you'll blow your arm off and the space between my feet will be just fine.'

She shrugged. 'Got another arm.'

Would she actually do it? The Director felt the same rippling thrill as he realized that he truly believed she would. She stared at him, unblinking.

Kill, Quetzalcoatl said. Neither of them could know what TATP would do, but they knew when they were being threatened.

No, the Director said. *Soon*.

Because she had him. If he was right, he would lose the best chance he had to locate her grandfather. If he was wrong, he would be blown to pieces, his soul returned to the storm, and everything he'd fought for lost in an instant. Either way, he had to back down.

'You are only buying time,' he said. 'We are not leaving, and we are not letting anyone go. All I want is a little information, and I promise no more harm will come to any of you.'

'You never met Dene people before,' she said. 'We pay debts, we never leave a friend out in the cold, and we never, ever, ever roll over on family.'

Her obstinacy was as irritating as it was repetitious. He

was tiring of this. 'You have no idea what you're up against,' he said. 'You've seen what just one of us can do. I have an army.'

'I fought armies before.' She shrugged. 'Got a whole bathtub full of this stuff. Out here in the territories, everyone's got a gun. Got bear traps and dynamite and ice hooks. Hell, we even got a flamethrower we use for tough ice. You send whatever you want. Jus' don' expect us to talk all nice like now. Next time you come, it's on.'

The Director stood in stunned silence, unable to think of how to have the last word, to end the conversation in a way that would not give a boost to the enemy's morale. The sheriff spoke into the silence. 'Unless, of course, you want to surrender now.'

The Director heard a snort of laughter from somewhere behind the barricade of trucks.

Humans, laughing at him.

Kill, Xolotl said. *Kill now.*

No! The Director raised a fist. *Soon. Soon, soon!*

He turned back to the humans and stammered out his next words. 'By the time I am done with this place, no one will be able to tell anyone ever lived here.'

The sheriff's smile slowly withered. 'Fuck off back home, son. Last chance before we see jus' how unstable this stuff is.'

The Director spun, waving the Golds back. They went reluctantly, and he could feel their sullen stares boring into his back as they returned the way they came.

He was well past the Loon before he was able to process what had happened. She would dig in and fight. She was willing to die and, by her example, inspire her people to do the same. The precariousness of his position sent a tremor through him. If he couldn't locate the Summoner, if he couldn't bring this woman to heel, then what were his options? How long could he keep his presence here concealed before the Canadian government found him? How long before the Americans followed suit? He pushed the thought away. *The only easy day was yesterday.* He had fought against longer odds before death had given him power beyond imagining. He had always won. He had triumphed over death itself. He would find the Summoner. He would take him. The Summoner would transfer the Director's soul into a living body. And once he did, nothing in the world, and nothing beyond it, could stop him.

He moved faster, the Golds hurrying to keep up as they moved up the rising ground back to the bivouac. He thought of the sheriff's slow heartbeat, her very blood smelling unimpressed. It didn't matter; she was *human*. Even if she were the strongest human who ever lived, she was still bound by the network of nerves and chemicals that the Director had known when he still drew breath. Even as one of the most elite warriors the world had ever known, he had still felt fear, still felt despair. Death was the only thing that could put someone beyond that, and the sheriff was not dead. Not yet.

He could break her. He just had to ratchet up the pressure. He would find her limit and push past it. Then he would cradle her head gently in his hands and she would tell him what he wanted to know.

He had promised her that no one would be able to tell that anyone had ever lived here. Idle threats were the end of credibility. He had to make good on it.

Best get started.

He heard the crunching of packed snow and realized with a start that his sniper cover had fallen in beside him, were escorting him back to the camp. They had gotten right up next to him, close enough to put a knife in his back. He hadn't noticed. Situational awareness returned to him in an instant, and he cycled quickly through all of his senses. Full range of hearing, from the worms in the earth below him to the birds above. He could see the heat signatures of the people in the camp as clearly as if they were aflame. He could filter the smell of the spruce sap from the lichen on the rocks beneath the frost. All of his senses were as sharp as ever.

He had been distracted, so rattled that he had lost the bubble. It was an unforgivable lapse of focus, the kind he had scarcely made even before his death.

For a moment, rage nearly blotted out his senses. TATP or no TATP, he would go back there now. Right fucking now. He would lock his hands around her fat throat and squeeze until the hard look in her eyes widened into terror, until he saw that she knew her death was coming, knew that it was by his hand that it was delivered.

He stopped walking, the snipers and the Golds stopping with him, guns at the low ready. He took a spiritual breath, steadied himself. He stayed still for a full minute, until he was certain he had regained his focus, sure that he was thinking straight again. Blind rage would not serve him here. A show of force was needed, but a controlled show of force. Something more than the single Gold Mark had so ill-advisedly sent.

He began moving again, picking out Mark's shape from her heat signature, the broad span of her shoulders, the slight twist in her leg where a broken knee had healed off-center.

'Who would you say are our most effective assets in the Gold Teams?' he asked before she had finished drawing breath to welcome him. Mark's knowledge of the program's logistics and operational assets were encyclopedic. One of the many reasons she was of so much use to him alive.

'Twenty-two is in the best repair, sir. Seventeen has effected some interesting bone plates that could provide limited protection from small-arms fire.'

'How is their temperament?'

She shrugged. 'They're Golds, sir. I'd describe their temperament as "blender".'

'Fair enough. Have them readied.'

'What's the op, sir?'

'We're going to send a message to our friends down the hill. They need a bit more convincing before they cooperate.'

'That may be a bit more convincing than you wanted, sir.'

'I just want them as a last resort. I'm going to hit that station from the opposite side of town. Personally, with my bodyguard.'

He could hear the sharp intake of breath as she began to protest, the sudden contraction of the muscles in her throat as she remembered what had become of her last attempt. She froze, stammered, finally formed coherent words. 'Yes, sir.'

'I also need you to assemble a squad and move them up-country. No Golds; beating hearts only. Press west along the lakeshore. There's a town out that way, no?'

'Enterprise, sir. But that's over a day's walk. Closer to two.'

'Well, then make sure they pack for an overnight stay. I want them to drum out every trapper, miner, and drifter in their path. Question them about Lived-With-The-Wolves. See if they can find where the old man is living.'

'Sir, we only have a platoon; losing a squad is going to leave us light.'

'Oh, we'll muddle along fine, I'm sure. I'm afraid my negotiations with this woman may become . . . protracted, and I want to make sure we're not leaving any stones unturned.'

He could tell she wanted to argue by the tension in her jaw, and he gave her a moment to, eager to see if she could summon the nerve. But in the end, she only swallowed and looked at him, dipping her chin deferentially. *And that, my dear, is why you are not cut out to be reborn.*

He turned back to the Golds. *Kill now,* he said. *No kill woman talk.* He mimed the woman hefting the jar of TATP. *Kill woman talk, no live, yes?* If they killed the sheriff, they would never be put in living bodies.

Quetzalcoatl and Xolotl exchanged a glance, spoke quietly in their own language, then turned back to him. *Yes.* They nodded. He would have to hope they understood.

'You're going back in now, sir?' Mark asked.

'I am, and I'm going to give these two fine fellows some scraps as a reward for their obedience.'

'I'll post the snipers again.'

'Do as you like,' the Director said. 'I've got a feeling our dear sheriff is going to have her hands full.'

The Director set off at a trot, leading the Golds across the hillside. He would approach the barricade from the opposite side. It wouldn't surprise him if she had pickets posted who would spot his approach, but he had gotten nearly up to the barricade the last time before he was spotted.

He knew the plan was risky. Just because the Golds appeared to understand him didn't mean they actually did, or that they could restrain their predatory lust once the killing started. He didn't doubt he could beat them into compliance, but that didn't mean one of them wouldn't be able to take out a potential intel source before he did. It was a risk he'd have to take.

Fort Resolution was so small that they were able to

circle to the town's opposite side in just a few minutes, descending the hill at a crouch.

Some of the houses had open doors and windows, signs of a hurried exit. That was good. Frightened townsfolk might put pressure on the sheriff to come to terms.

He passed the town's municipal building. The Gold Mark had sent had shattered the glass double doors in front. He could see the frozen trunk of a dead man in the wreckage, hand trailing in the glass fragments. There might have been some lucky survivors, but judging from the smell of frozen blood in the air, he doubted it.

At last, trucks and ATVs began to appear, parked to either side of the track to the station, forcing the Director and his bodyguard into a narrow chute.

The Director slowed as he approached the corner of the municipal building. Once he rounded it, he would be in view of the station and any shooters the sheriff may have positioned to cover this approach. He looked around but could see no heat signatures around him. He dialed his hearing in, listening for breathing or shifting feet. There was only the soft crunching of the snow as they moved along.

Crunch. Crunch. Crunch.

Click.

The Director grabbed the Golds' elbows and launched himself to the side as the shrieking of a metal spring sounded beneath the snow. Xolotl came easily, but Quetzalcoatl jerked in his grip, pinned to the spot. The Director held on for a moment, realized that Quetzalcoatl was stuck fast. He let go and slammed into the side of one of the trucks, turning to face Quetzalcoatl, who had fallen on its side.

Its foot was stuck in a massive bear trap, rusty jaws sunk deep into the ruin of its leg. The giant metal semicircles were so big, they had closed halfway up the creature's shin, shattering the bone and driving so deep that they nearly met. The Director could already tell that Quetzalcoatl's pristine state was finished, its leg held together by little more than a few strands of bone and gristle.

He looked around at the cars again, realized that the vehicles weren't parked randomly. It was an effort to narrow the approach to the station, to funnel a prospective attacker into a narrow front that would force them to walk over a line of traps. He looked at the pit where the trap had been buried, saw the smooth white snow beside it. Enough for another two traps side by side before the tire of a parked truck closed off the rest of the way.

'You clever bitch,' the Director whispered. He let go of Xolotl and turned to Quetzalcoatl, which was trying to push itself up to its feet, failing. He pushed it back down into the snow. Any movement would damage the leg further.

Quetzalcoatl said something angrily, and the Director felt Xolotl's hand on his shoulder, shrugged it off. *Help*, he managed in the harsh phonemes of their language. Xolotl stiffened, released him, but stayed close by.

The Director ran his finger over the jaws, looking for a seam he could use to pry them apart. He knew right away that it was useless. The trap's torsion had been tuned to its absolute maximum, and the teeth had been hastily filed down to create as smooth a cutting plane as possible. Trappers aimed to fix their prey in place with as little damage as possible. This trap had been adjusted to amputate a foot. The hunter's tool was now a weapon of war.

The Director glanced over his shoulder at Xolotl. *Cut.*

Xolotl leaned in close, nodded. The leg was almost completely severed. The techs might be able to reattach and reinforce it, but it would be easier just to give the creature a prosthetic if they wanted to return it to service.

Xolotl said something to Quetzalcoatl, who sat up and took a closer look at the trap before uttering something that was clearly a curse. The Gold grabbed the broken leg as close to the jaws as it could and twisted the two halves apart. Even with its strength, it took some doing, but after a moment, it was able to tear the leg off below the knee and toss the ruined limb into the snow. Quetzalcoatl flipped onto its stomach and rose on its one good knee, then it crawled forward a few feet. It would be able to move slowly, at least. *Go*, it said.

Burning rage threatened to overwhelm the Director. Not only had that woman been unafraid of him, she had outsmarted him, managed to do real damage to the operational capacity of one of his assets. This was becoming personal.

No. You are a professional. Nothing is personal. You just need to focus. He was intending to rattle her, to attack her morale, and the opposite was happening. He looked down at Quetzalcoatl attempting to crawl forward, reached out and grabbed its shoulder, hauling it back.

It sat up, snarling at him. *Kill*, it said. *Kill, kill, kill, now.*

No, he said. *Soon.*

He held up a hand when Xolotl stepped forward. The truck nearest to them was an old seventies model with a narrow chrome bumper, and the Director sheared it off with a quick jerk of his hands. He probed one end in the snow until the traps leapt up with a loud clang of metal, sending sparks flying. He dropped the bumper, listening to the echoes of the scraping metal attenuate throughout the town. He had most certainly been heard, but that was all right. He looked up at Xolotl and nodded; the Gold considered, nodded back.

He looked down at Quetzalcoatl, wondering if he should scrub the mission. At last, he decided against it. The Gold would look even more horrifying crawling toward the enemy, and he could only imagine how furious it must be. Tricked and injured by humans. If that had happened to him and he'd been denied vengeance, he'd go mad. Even if he only had Xolotl with him, it would be more than enough to flush the defenders out. He had underestimated Sheriff Plante's resourcefulness, but a clever human was still a human.

The first round sparked off Xolotl's crown the moment they turned the corner. The track to the station was an open lane of fire. The Director could see at least three humans sheltering behind the engine block of one of the barricade trucks, muzzles flashing. Another round kicked up a spray of snow at his feet. The speed of the impact and size of the snow plume told him this was high-powered ammunition. The kind you'd use to bring down bear or elk. It couldn't stop them, but it could do serious damage.

They would need to close the distance in a hurry. Xolotl didn't need any urging; it glanced down at the crown knocked off its head and resting in the snow, and launched itself forward. The Director followed, zigzagging to the opposite side of the track. There were a few trucks scattered across the wide plaza in front of the municipal building. It looked almost haphazard, but the Director was wise to the sheriff's tricks now, could see that the vehicles formed islands the defenders could use for cover, that would force an attacker to slow down as they negotiated them.

A living attacker, anyway. The Director vaulted lightly over the first vehicle. Xolotl merely dropped its shoulder and smashed into a truck's passenger door, knocking the vehicle out of its way in a scream of metal and shattering glass.

There was a low boom, and the Director felt the tiny pellets of a shotgun shell tear through his shoulder. He tensed his legs to compensate for the force of the blast, kept himself upright. He could feel the cold air infiltrating through a hole in his hood where one of the metal balls had pierced his neck. More damage to a body that couldn't be healed. He cursed inwardly. Someone would pay for that. He caught a glance of the walrus who had stood at the sheriff's shoulder earlier. He was racking the slide of a smoking police shotgun. The Director pivoted in his direction, placing a hand on the hood of the first truck in the barricade and leaping over it. There were two men and a woman on the other side. They ducked as the Director sailed over their heads, their fear stink so strong that he could smell it easily even through their thick winter clothes.

One of them, an older woman with her hair in a tangled gray bun, held what looked like a pressure washer, long hose connecting to a silver tank on her back. The Director could smell the gasoline, the gelling agents, the pressurized CO_2, and was already turning even as he completed his arc and began to descend. This must be the flamethrower the sheriff had spoken of. He had hoped to ignore the defenders at the barricade and make a push to reach the sheriff immediately, but he couldn't leave this weapon in his backfield.

As if in answer, the woman leveled the tube and spat a gout of flame at him. He dodged it easily, but the spattering droplets still landed on his shoulder, the viscous liquid adhering, setting the cloth ablaze. The man beside her, a fat goliath with a purple nose, levelled a huge revolver at the Director, one of the .357 high-powered jobs you could use to hunt big game, and fired. The Director dove forward, dodging under a round big and powerful enough to take his head off.

He caught the man about his waist and drove him into the truck's side hard enough to sink him into the metal a solid six inches, shattering his spine. The man coughed blood and collapsed, and the Director turned, rabbit punching the woman. It was a weak blow for him, but still it snapped her head to the side, spitting teeth. She pirouetted slowly, unconscious, her finger fixed on the trigger, spraying liquid fire in a dazzling arc that set the next truck alight and turned two of the defenders into howling human torches.

The Director stripped off his burning jacket. The shirt beneath was scorched and ragged, showing his gray-white skin through the rents, but at least it wasn't burning. How long had it been since he'd seen his own skin? Months at least, maybe even a year. He had no need to look at himself. The jellied gasoline had blackened his shoulder but spared his bicep and the tattoo he'd gotten when he'd first graduated from SEAL Qualification Training in Kodiak. It showed an eagle perched on a trident before an anchor, a flintlock clutched in one talon. He was surprised at the spike of emotion the sight of it stirred in him, how glad he was it had not been harmed. He was beyond it now, beyond all awards and honors, metal gewgaws to give him an air of invincibility. He *was* invincible, and no symbol would ever change that.

The burning truck suddenly sprang into the air, slamming against the building's side before landing on its back. Xolotl plowed past it, making toward the unconscious flamethrower woman. It reached her, howling, hammering her with its fists like some mad gorilla, gold eyes blazing. Within moments, her head was a compact mush, her blood mixing with the slowly spreading pool of jellied gasoline.

There was a crack, and a round whined off the barricade's edge. More defenders, farther back, drawing a bead on him. The Director turned, snatched at Xolotl's arm. They needed to get into the building before the sheriff could flee. They had killed at least four and shattered the barricade as if it had been made of spun glass. That was a fine start.

Xolotl snarled, snatching its arm away, burying its face in the ruins of the woman's head, its own crowned again, this time with gore. He knew better than to try to force the issue. The creature was furious at the injury done to its brother, at the humans who had dared to knock the crown from its head. There was nothing for it but to let it slake its lust until it calmed enough to reenter the fight. Besides, it wouldn't do for the defenders to be seeing infighting.

He heard a crackling of flame, the gentle flexion of metal under pressure, smelled the sudden shift from oxygen to CO_2. The burning truck. He launched himself backward as the burning vehicle detonated, had just enough time to see the fireball expand, shifting from red to orange to white, black edges enveloping Xolotl, before he turned facedown and sprawled in the snow, a wave of heat sweeping over his back. Screams, the pattering of falling debris. Something soft and thick thumped against his head and bounced off.

And then it was over. The post-blast quiet was stark, the gunfire and shouts replaced by the gentle crackling of flames and the gusting wind. The Director turned, propped himself up on one elbow.

The blast had bowled the truck back through the barricade, sending two more vehicles tumbling on their sides. They had, mercifully, not ignited. The building's side burned brightly, and he could hear the shouts of the defenders now as they raced to put it out.

Xolotl was a smoking ruin just beyond the mostly vaporized corpse of the woman with the flamethrower. Its arm lay a few feet distant, burning brightly. The Director patted his hands over his body, snuffing out a half dozen small flames kindled on the remains of his charred shirt. He tested his feet, found he could stand.

Farther down the track, Quetzalcoatl still crawled along, too far away and moving too slowly to be of any use.

Damn it. In just a few moments, he'd lost his two best Golds, one destroyed, one rendered combat-ineffective. His own body had been damaged. Was it worth it? He judged the fire slowly consuming the building's side and decided it was. With their defenses smashed, the defenders would already be in a panic. He turned to circle the building. He'd find a window and leap in while they were distracted fighting the fire.

He heard the cough of a two-stroke engine, the roar of an accelerator rolled all the way open. Snow spraying. The Director raced past the window to the building's corner. A snowmobile was in full flight, the walrus clinging to the handle bars, expertly muscling it through the cars drawn up on the building's opposite side. The walrus dumped the clutch, threw his bulk against the handlebars to keep the bucking nose down, wiped his goggles clear of spraying snow.

The Director paused. He should let the man go. He had pickets posted around the town's edge for just such contingencies. They should be able to find and put a stop to a fat lump of a man on a snowmobile loud enough to be heard across the Bering Strait.

The walrus ripped a thick piece of purple plastic from under his parka and began shouting into it. The Director could hear the vibrations of the VHF signal distorting his voice through the engine's roar. It didn't matter; the signal was jammed for at least fifteen hundred meters around the hamlet, and one of the Director's snipers would have put a round through him long before he breached that range.

Stupid but brave. He had balls, this walrus. Maybe it was a lesson he took from the sheriff. The Director remembered the man, steady as a rock, sending a shotgun blast into his side as he leapt over the barricade of trucks. He was the first human to have harmed the Director since he died.

Before the Director knew what he was doing, he was racing after the snowmobile, magical strength lengthening his strides.

He told himself it was because the man might have the information he needed, that the sight of him taking down a man fleeing on a snowmobile with the throttle wide open would illustrate the futility of resistance. He told himself if he couldn't be permitted a little fun in his new state, then what was the point? But he knew that it was all sizzle. The steak was this: this was a man who had shot him and lived. The first human to mark his body since he had stopped breathing. Like the sheriff, this walrus had looked at him and not been afraid. This was vengeance, plain and simple.

His training screamed at him to go back. This wasn't the warrior's way. He was a professional who never let his heart rule his head. But that wasn't right, was it? The warrior's way was a *living* way, and it had ceased to own him the moment his heart ceased to beat. The Director's way was a *new* way, one all his own, one he invented day by day, learning as he went.

If, by some miracle, the walrus made it through, he

could summon help. The Canadian police, the Army. The Director would be able to handle them someday but not now. Leave the man to the pickets or chase him, it was a bad choice either way. But no choice was as bad as indecision. He was already moving; he wanted to kill the man, so that was what he would do.

To his credit, the walrus didn't waste a lot of time on the radio. Once he was certain he wasn't getting through, he jammed the receiver back in the pocket of his parka and focused on keeping the throttle open wide. The machine fishtailed briefly on the packed crust. The Director could hear the rattling of the chain drive as it opened up distance. He put on speed, pushing his legs farther, leaning forward as he moved faster. The snow-mobile still widened the gap, shrinking in his vision. The magic that animated the Director's corpse made him faster than a cheetah sprinting after prey, but even a sprinting cheetah was slower than the whirring chain, the slamming pistons driving it so quickly that the Director could hear it buzzing like a swarm of hornets, could feel the spraying snow drifting past his face.

'Squirter outbound from the southwest,' he said into the commlink. One of death's many blessings was never being out of breath. 'Target is on a snowmobile, making one hundred knots.'

'Acknowledged,' came the reply. 'I don't see—'

'You should hear him! Christ, he's got the throttle wide open!' The Director was surprised at his own words. Showing anger to his people wouldn't do. But he watched the shrinking of the machine and felt the gap opening by degrees, the responsibility shifting from him to the spotter and shooter somewhere in the woods overlooking this sorry excuse for a town. If there was any hope of stopping the walrus, it would depend on the power, focus, and determination of his snipers, a pair of fragile bags of meat. The thought made him furious.

'I have eyes on, ready,' the shooter said.

'Range, one zero zero zero meters. Elevation, three. Minute of angle – no. Come down 1 MOA,' the spotter said.

The snowmobile flew past the last remaining buildings and skidded out onto the road along the frozen lake shore, then switched back abruptly, diving through unplowed banks of high snow. The walrus leaned on the handlebars, loading the springs hard, and the Director grinned as the snowmobile's back end broke loose, fishtailing, engine roaring as it rose above the snow. It took a few seconds to regain traction, but in those seconds, the Director closed the gap, stretching his legs until he felt the femoral head scrape against the dead tissue lining the socket of his pelvis. A living man would have been left disabled, howling in agony. The Director just kept running, watching the distance shrink.

'Come down,' the spotter was saying. The Director had forgotten about the sniper team. He didn't need them now. He would have the walrus tackled into the snow in a matter of moments. The thought of the sniper team stealing his triumph at the last instant sent a fresh surge of fury through him. 'Stop!' he shouted into the commlink. 'Cease fire!'

But the spotter was already speaking. 'Send it.'

No. It was his kill. The walrus had shot *him*. The walrus had fled from *him*. The walrus had opened a lead on *him*. His vision went red, the bone spines rising from his back, head, and hands for the first time in years. He gave the rage free rein and lunged.

His legs pumped and pushed; his feet left the ground. The snowmobile drew closer. He could smell the oil sealant on the walrus's parka, see the wind rustling the tips of the faux fox hair bordering the hood. He could hear the pounding of the walrus's heart.

Bang.

The gun's report echoed, giving the Director's augmented hearing a host of data denied the living ear. The shot was a thousand yards out to the northwest, firing a 7.62mm NATO round. The wind had put English on the bullet, and the Director could tell from the whistling trajectory that the shooter had compensated. Gravity was acting on the long shot, dropping the round toward the walrus's head as he . . .

The Director felt the round punch through his hip, spinning him in the air. He put out a hand to stop himself, felt his palm dig in, only to have the inertia of his body rip it free, sending him tumbling again in a spray of snow. He gave in to it this time, knowing there was nothing for it but to let the inertia spend itself. He endured the indignity of the roll, the snow packing down his shirt collar, stuffing his nose and mouth. At last, he stopped, his head banging off a rock, legs sticking straight up out of the snow.

He threw himself onto his feet, eyes roving. The sniper team were the only ones close enough to see, and they would have been utterly focused on the target. Even now, they would be just coming off their scopes. That was good. He couldn't lead people who had seen him humiliated.

And humiliated he was. He could hear the angry-hornet buzz of the snowmobile's engine whining in the distance, interspersed with the occasional throaty cough as it plowed up a steep bank of new snow.

You moved too fast. You got too excited and you fouled their shot. You should have just hung back and let them take him out.

It was what a professional would have done, but he had

been too angry, too caught up in taking vengeance to do it right. It was unforgivable. In his time as a SEAL, he had trained endlessly on this very point, ensuring his human mind stayed dominant over his monkey mind. But he had also trained never to dwell on the past. What was done was done, and beating himself up over it would solve nothing.

As if he had read the Director's thoughts, the shooter's whisper sounded over the commlink. 'Doubtful.'

The spotter answered, voice trembling slightly. 'Shot blocked.'

'Bravo element is eyes off,' the spotter said. The Director could hear the fear in his voice, could tell that he knew what had blocked the shot, who he had just put a bullet through. 'We have no shot, I say again, no shot.'

The Director tested his hip and leg. The round had penetrated a few inches left of his navel and rebounded off the bone, chewing a long furrow through the flesh to exit out his buttock, almost at the small of his back. The leg worked fine.

'Orders, sir,' the spotter said. He wanted to know if they should send pursuit. The part of the Director who was still the professional knew that would be best, to send the helo up, get eyes on from the air before trying to engage in extremely difficult, unknown terrain.

'Hold what you've got,' the Director said. 'I'll get him myself.'

He wheeled and plunged into the thick snow, forging through the rough trail broken by the snowmobile's skis. Once again, he told himself his reasoning was practical. He couldn't draw limited assets away from the hamlet or he would risk losing the sheriff, but he knew the truth. The walrus was his. *His.*

The sniper shot had frightened the man; the Director

could smell his elevated blood sugar even from there. Better, it had driven him off the snowpack, forcing the snowmobile to chew through snow-covered brush, bouncing on uneven terrain as the walrus sought to move away from the sniper team. That he had been able to determine their position and was able to move in the right direction spoke to some degree of training. The thought made the Director feel better; if he was being bested by a trained warrior, it took the sting out of it somewhat.

And he was being bested. Because, as he started running again, the same deep snow that slowed the vehicle's chain drive slowed his own steps. The distance between the Director and the machine didn't widen, but it held, and he squinted through the funnel of churning snow at the walrus's back, taunting him with its nearness.

He felt something catch, snap free inside his hip. His step shortened, staggered. He cursed. Maybe the round had done more damage than he thought. He pumped his legs faster, pushed himself harder. He felt the wobble in his hip, stumbled again. The snowmobile coughed over an ice-encrusted log, landing in a clatter of breaking branches before the tread dug in and sent it leaping forward.

There was no denying it. The gap was widening.

The walrus reached back into his parka now, brought the radio receiver out. The Director listened for the jammer's hum, but it was attenuated enough at this distance that it drowned in the engine's roar. If the walrus wasn't clear yet, he soon would be.

The Director howled, long and loud, an animal shout of rage and frustration. It was crude and more akin to the Golds than he liked, but he was past caring now. The walrus stiffened at the sound, glancing over his shoulder, the radio paused halfway to his mouth.

And then the Director suddenly had hope.

Through the spraying snow, he caught a tiny glimmer, no more than a spark, so brief that most would have thought it a trick of the light, a flash reflected off the snow. But the Director's eyes were too sharp, his need to kill this man too keen. He saw the spark for what it was: frozen water, wide enough to catch the sun's rays and send them scattering.

He dove to the left, the joint of his damaged hip grinding. For a moment, he felt the joint separate, worried he might fall. He clapped a hand to his hip, pushed down with all his strength, felt the bone sliding beneath the skin. It held, if only just, and he was off and running again.

The walrus was only now turning to look in front of him, and the Director could hear his shouted curse as he sighted the frozen water, metal thudding against rubber as he slammed against the handlebars, desperately trying to turn the vehicle.

The tread dug in, spraying snow, the engine air intakes roaring. The snowmobile slewed drunkenly to one side, threatening to topple over, one ski waving madly in the air, half the tread spinning madly, biting nothing. For a moment, the Director thought he had him, but the walrus stood on the footrests, leaning his considerable weight into the high side. The center of gravity shifted, and the machine *thunk*ed back down onto both skis in a burst of white powder.

The Director howled again, charged. The walrus turned, slammed the handlebars once more. The snowmobile coughed and shuddered, the nose pushing out toward the water, the tail moving toward the Director, trying to open the lead again.

But it was too late now. The Director was too close, and the machine had shed too much speed. With a cry of triumph, the Director launched himself at the walrus a second time. He extended his hands, felt his jaw unhinge, gray tongue swelling and extending, eagerly anticipating the hot rush of the man's blood.

But the walrus still had a surprise left. He threw his body in the opposite direction, hauling the handlebars after him. The snowmobile tipped up, dragged earthward by the walrus's heavy bulk, turning the vehicle into a metal shield. The Director had time for a howl of surprise before he smashed into the vehicle's undercarriage.

The whirling tread chewed through the cloth of his hood, ripping it away. It made short work of the cheek beneath, and the Director could feel the flesh grind away, flap open, his swollen tongue sliding out of the gap to dangle down by his shoulder. He screamed, the anger in full command now. He tore his head back, threw his shoulder down, and slammed the snowmobile's fairing, splintering the plastic.

The machine shuddered, tumbled, rolling over and over, dragging the walrus with it, jerking him like a rag doll. The Director leapt free, landed in a crouch, watching the snowmobile carry the walrus down toward the frozen water. The Director would have thought he would shake free, but the walrus hung on, the heavy machine pummeling him with each toss. The Director rose and followed at a walk, conscious of his unstable hip joint, not wanting to make it worse. He would let the machine do its work first. It was still his kill, since he'd set it in motion. If he was lucky, the walrus would still have some life in him, and the Director would take his time in ending it, ensuring the man understood the cost of all the trouble he'd given him.

But the snowmobile spun on its side, then skidded out over the bank of the frozen lake. It hung precariously for a moment, tempting the Director to run for it, before disappearing down the bank. The Director heard the cracking splash that could only be the ice giving way and the water beneath welling up to receive machine and man both.

He paused, listening. The frustration of losing the walrus was fading now that the man had clearly paid for his defiance. The Director had done more damage to himself than he had wanted, but that was sometimes the case in battles. He dialed his hearing down, heard nothing more than the shifting ice, the bubbling water, and the slowing of the Walrus's heart, sounding fainter as he sank beneath the surface. The radio crackled as it shorted, then went silent.

The water couldn't be warmer than thirty degrees. Even someone as well insulated as the walrus wouldn't last more than ten minutes. The heart beat slower, fainter, followed by the rustling whisper of the ice riming over, already filling in to cover the hole punctured by the snowmobile.

The Director raised a hand, probed his wounded face, felt the exposed bone of his jaw, the row of teeth above. It would be horrifying to see. That was good, he supposed.

He felt hungover, shaken, the way he'd felt when he was alive, the post-combat comedown shakes of subsiding adrenaline, the vague illness of his whole body having been tuned to the single task of taking a life. He hadn't felt it since he died, until now. That was good; he could accept his wounds because they came from a fellow warrior, no matter what his appearance.

Water under the bridge. The threat was neutralized. The danger passed.

Still probing his flayed cheek, the Director turned and slowly stalked back to his camp.

Chapter Eleven
Walking Dead

Once Mankiller was sure the monster was gone, she turned her attention to the fire. The station still had four fire extinguishers in good repair and fully charged, and she and Calmut were soon dousing the building's side in white foam. They were lucky there was little more than a gentle breeze, and the flames already had an uphill battle against the ice riming the station's siding.

She got back on her sights the moment she was certain the fire was out, squinting through the billowing vapor at the remains of the barricade. She was skilled at spotting the shifts in shadow that spelled movement, even in poor visibility. There was nothing. The barricade was still and silent. And that was not a good thing. Because there had been four people out there: Denise, Early Bird, Gunther, and Alba Rodriguez, who had been a crabber in Alaska before she picked up her sea bag and walked east on a lark.

Another minute on the sights and Mankiller finally vaulted out the window, dropped the three feet to the packed snow.

'What're you doin'?' Calmut called down to her.

'Shut up and cover me,' Mankiller said, keeping her

weapon at the low ready as she made her way to what remained of the barricade.

The line of trucks was little more than burned wrecks now, the remains of their paint blistering, the snow around them long since turned to gray slush. The gas tanks had already exploded, so they wouldn't have to worry about that, and the flames had died down to the point where even a strong wind wouldn't blow them against the station. She could waste precious chemicals putting them out, but there was no point.

The defenders hadn't fared so well.

Denise was little more than a black smear on the snow. One of the monsters had flattened her head, and it looked like the flamethrower had exploded on her back, cooking what was left. Gunther had run halfway around the station before he succumbed to the fire. Early Bird was collapsed beside the truck, recognizable only by his bulk. There was more left of him, but he was burned just as badly as Denise. Mankiller cursed inwardly. Her last words to Early had been unkind, and she still held the rifle she'd confiscated from him. He had it coming, but seeing his corpse didn't make it any easier. Even if he had been drunk, had been on the verge of shooting her, she wished like hell that she'd thrown an arm over his shoulder and told him just how much she loved seeing him around the town, sober or no. Early had helped her dress a deer she'd shot last summer, spending a whole day and getting his parka bloody up to the elbows, for no other reason than wishing to be neighborly. He was a drunk, but so were a lot of folks. Joe liked a drink now and then. So did she.

Alba had been blown clear by the blast, was lying in a heap on the barricade's far side. Mankiller had seen plenty of dead bodies in her day. It was hard to look at dead folks, especially ones you'd come to know. In a way, them being all burned up was a blessing. A burned body looked so little like the person she had known that it made it easier to get the detachment she needed to cope.

Denise, Early, and Gunther were lost causes, but she had to do due diligence with Alba. The girl was surely dead, but Mankiller needed to at least check her pulse. Even from this distance, she could tell she'd have to look at Alba's face, whole, eyes sightlessly staring. The sight of that face would do damage, the kind that lasted. *That's your job. To suck up that damage so other folks don't have to.*

Mankiller swallowed and made her way to Alba's side, knelt, turned the girl over.

Alba hitched a gasping breath, her eyelids fluttering before snapping shut. Mankiller cursed, stripped off her glove, shoving two fingers against Alba's neck. No pulse. 'Ollie! Throw me the defib right now!'

She heard Calmut scrambling inside the open window, and then the red plastic box came sailing through the air to land in the snow just a foot from Mankiller's knee. Mankiller popped it open, stripping Alba's chest and getting the leads attached. She pushed the activation button, staring at the screen, waiting for the red charging light to turn green. ANALYZING, the screen read. PLEASE WAIT.

'Keep me covered, Ollie!' Mankiller shouted, her eyes still locked on the screen.

'I got you, Sheriff!' he called back.

ATTACH PADS, the screen read. CHARGING.

'They're already fuckin' attached, you stupid sonofabitch!' Mankiller shouted at the machine. It couldn't have taken more than five seconds for the light to turn green, but to Mankiller, it felt like five years. She could imagine Alba's brain, slowly starved of oxygen, dying a little more with each passing moment.

'Clear!' she shouted as soon as the light turned green.

There was no one to hear, but following protocol helped some sense of normalcy return to a world inhabited by the kind of monsters who had done this to Alba. Alba's chest jerked, her back arched, elbows hammering into the ice.

ANALYZING, the screen read. PLEASE WAIT.

'C'mon!' Mankiller shouted.

'Sheriff!' Calmut shouted from the window. 'Look out!'

Mankiller threw herself to the side just as something gray launched itself at her. She rolled, came up with her rifle braced against her shoulder.

It was another of the monsters. This one was lean and long-limbed, dragging itself forward by its hands. It was missing part of its leg, sheared off halfway down the shin, likely a victim of Crosshill's bear traps. She recognized it as one of the two who had come with the one who had called himself the Director. Its gold crown was gone, but the jewelled pectoral was still strapped across its narrow chest.

It hammered one fist down on the defibrillator, drove the long claws on its other hand into Alba's throat. Hot blood sprayed, and it thrust its face into the stream, gray tongue rolling out of its mouth.

Calmut's gun barked, and the snow next to Mankiller's foot jumped.

'Damnit, Ollie! Don' you fuckin' shoot me!' Mankiller shouted as she sighted in on the monster and pulled the trigger. Even the Alaskan's big-bore round did little more than snap the thing's head back, sending it sprawling.

It righted quickly, flopping over onto its stomach and scrambling for Mankiller even as she was standing and racing for the window. 'Ollie! Hatchet!'

Calmut was one step ahead of her, jumping down from the window with Freddie's sledgehammer, the big two-hander he used to drive the wood maul. Calmut might have been old and skinny, but he swung that hammer like a carnival strongman, cracking the thing so hard that its head deformed, rebounding off the frozen ground even as Calmut was raising the hammer for another blow. It tried to rise, but the hammer came down again, and this time, its head was squashed as flat as Denise's.

Mankiller abandoned the idea of going after the hatchet and pulled her long knife instead, kneeling on the monster's back and sawing at its shoulder. She ducked to the side as Ollie brought the hammer down on its spine, shattering it in a sickening crunch. 'Don' knock me with that thing, either!'

The monster snapped its arm up, sending Mankiller flying as if she had been nothing more than a straw doll, the knife spinning from her hand. She slid on her back, rifle bouncing in its sling, the barrel smacking her in the eye something fierce. She scrambled to her feet, raising the rifle, desperately trying to sight in through the tears in her battered eye.

She needn't have bothered. Calmut had gotten two more whacks in since she'd been thrown. The monster was little more than a twitching sack of shattered bones, but Calmut just kept raising the hammer and letting it fall, again and again and again. His eyes were wide and his teeth bared. He made little grunts with each stroke of the hammer, sounds like an animal would make.

Mankiller slowly lowered her rifle, went to Calmut's side. If the defibrillator had revived Alba, it had been short-lived. She lay pooled in her own blood, her throat laid open to the spine, eyes staring sightlessly upward.

Calmut kept hammering.

'Ollie.' Mankiller touched his elbow. ''S all right. You got it. It's done.'

Calmut's eyes returned to their normal size, but he still

took two more whacks before he finally let the heavy steel head slump in the snow and leaned on the handle, panting.

'You okay?' In all their years working together, she'd never seen him like this.

'Yeah.' Calmut cuffed a tear away from his eye. 'I jus' . . . I fuckin' hate these things.'

'Yeah,' Mankiller said. 'Me too.'

'Alba's gone,' Calmut said.

'I know it. I'll get a detail together so we can get 'em all buried.'

'Defib's gone too.'

'Well, hopefully, we won' need it. There's another one in the chapel, but I don' wanna stray too far from here unless we gotta, okay?'

'Sure.' Calmut was already turning, heading back to the open window, where a crowd of citizens had gathered, crouching with their guns, doing their best to look brave. It wasn't much of an army, especially when you considered what they were up against.

'That gold?' Calmut nudged the pectoral with the toe of his boot. There was precious little left of it after the flurry of axe blows.

'Leave it,' Mankiller said. 'We can worry 'bout gettin' rich after all this is over.'

'They comin' at us again?' Calmut asked.

Mankiller nodded. 'Jus' don't know how soon.'

Calmut looked back at the folks in the window. 'Sorry bunch, ain't they?'

'Let's jus' hope Joe got through.'

'That one . . . guy was after him pretty quick, boss. I dunno that I like his chances.'

'Joe's harder'n he looks,' she said. 'If anyone can make it, he can.'

They returned to the window and helped the burial

party down. Sally's sister Angela came first, her jowls shaking. She'd been Sally's staunch ally in hating Denise, and Mankiller wondered what she'd think, seeing her bitter enemy so poorly served. She didn't envy her the hurt she would probably feel. Somehow, the death of an enemy was almost always worse than that of a friend. Maybe it was because you realized you would never have a chance to make things right.

But no sooner had Angela's boots hit the snow than she turned and scrambled back up the building's scorched sides.

Mankiller and Calmut both whirled, guns coming up.

A lone figure was shuffling down the track, dragging himself along like a horror-movie zombie.

'Guess they're comin' already,' Calmut said as he sighted in.

'No.' Mankiller pushed the barrel of his gun down. 'They're faster than that.'

She started forward at a walk and, after three steps, burst into a run.

Because it was Joe Yakecan coming down that road. His clothes had been soaked and frozen solid. Red icicles hung from his lips, a gory winter beard. He shuffled and shivered, arms hugging tight about his chest.

'Joe!' Mankiller shouted. 'Joe, I'm comin'!'

Yakecan nodded and stopped walking, swayed on his feet.

Mankiller ran with everything she had, but she was still three steps shy of Yakecan when he fell.

Chapter Twelve
Fight Through

Yellowknife was a passable city, but Schweitzer was still amazed by the remoteness. It nestled into a scrub of semi-tundra, stunted trees, and half-frozen bogs. The lake itself was beyond beautiful, a long blue-gray scroll of placid water dusted with frost. The vista was broken by shifting chunks of green-tinted ice catching the thin light and scattering it into a spray of color that made the living members of the team squint.

The Canadian Forces Northern Area HQ was a huge, modern structure, the glass front evoking the squat frame of the Entertech office building that covered the Gemini Cell facility. It looked weirdly out of place in the pristine wilderness. Barbed wire rolled out to abut a robust flight line big enough to take heavy transport planes. RCAF – 440 TRANSPORT SQUADRON, read a sign posted to the fence.

They'd debated how best to mask Schweitzer and finally settled on what would draw the least attention. They put him in a snowsuit and parka with a large, fur-lined hood, his head covered by a neoprene facemask that left only his burning eyes exposed. These were covered by a pair of ski goggles with a reflective plastic lens. The only catch was his buzz saw of a hand, covered by the parka, leaving his right sleeve empty. It looked strange but not nearly as strange as it would have had the broad disk been left exposed.

'This would go easier if we had more support,' Schweitzer said as they bundled him into all that gear. 'The American and Canadian governments have a lot of resources they can throw at this.'

'Hell, no,' Ghaznavi said.

'You're only protecting Senator Hodges,' Schweitzer said. 'Sometimes, you have to put the mission before the man.'

'It's not just about Hodges,' Ghaznavi said.

'The hell it's not,' Schweitzer answered. 'I don't—'

'She's right, Jim,' Desmarais cut him off. 'This is something best handled by the dark side. Big government always places appearance over operational efficiency, and this is far too important to fuck up. We don't need to be voting on this one. We need to move quickly and decisively. That is the polar opposite of what big government does. It's why organizations like SAD and JTF2 were created.'

Schweitzer nodded. Desmarais had a point. 'I'm just saying that you don't have the benefit of the experience of the fight we just went through in Colchester. If it gets . . . overwhelming out there, we're going to wish we had more resources to draw on.'

Desmarais hefted his smartphone. 'All those resources are still available to us just as soon as we call for them. All I'm advocating for is to put that call off for as long as possible.'

'Just trust us, Jim,' Ghaznavi said. 'We may not be magically powered supersoldiers, but we've both been doing this kind of thing for a long, long time.'

They were met on the flight line by a lone woman in military fatigues. She saluted Desmarais, not so much as glancing at anyone else. 'Welcome to Yellowknife, sir.'

Desmarais acknowledged her with a nod. 'I'd like to get loaded and moving as quickly as possible, thanks.'

She nodded. 'Everything's been prepared. Please follow me.'

She led them to a long, low Quonset hut abutting the flight line. A pair of black SUVs were parked beside it, the windows tinted. Schweitzer was surprised to see that the flight line was completely deserted. No aircrew, no mechanics, no fuelers. Desmarais had likely ordered it cleared, just as he had probably ordered the woman not to acknowledge anyone else but him. Schweitzer's respect for the man grew.

Inside, three operators waited, ready to roll. Two were dark-haired women with wide faces and almond eyes. The third was a man so pale that he would probably be invisible in the snow. The woman who'd greeted them didn't follow them in, simply closed the door behind them, leaving them in the room's slightly warmer air and harsh fluorescent light. It looked like a dozen other ops ready rooms Schweitzer had been in, bare save for a cheap folding table in the center, piled high with gray hiking duffels stuffed with gear. A manifest was printed and taped to each one.

One of the women got to her feet, extended a hand to Desmarais. 'Nice to meet you, sir. I'm Master Corporal Nalren, detailed to the 427. Thanks for your trust in me.'

Desmarais took her hand in both of his, shaking it firmly. 'Everyone I've spoken to says you're the best there is, Master Corporal. I'm honored to have you on board.'

'Thanks, sir. I'd like you to meet Corporal Fitzgerald and Leading Seaman Montclair.'

Desmarais shook the other woman's hand. 'So, you're our bluewater rep?'

'Brownwater, sir,' Montclair answered. 'Riverine ops my whole career. Got my boat packed in that duffel over there.'

'Well, I hope we don't need it. And both of you speak Denesuline?'

'Yes, sir,' Nalren said. 'Do you anticipate our needing it?'

'I'm not sure. The package we're securing is an old man out in the sticks. If he just moved there to seek his solitude, he'll probably speak English. But on the odd chance he's old-school, I want to make sure we can talk to him.'

The three Canadians exchanged glances, turned confused faces back to Desmarais. 'Anyway,' Desmarais said, 'I'd like you to meet Jala Ghaznavi and her team.'

Ghaznavi shook Nalren's hand, then introduced the rest of the team, save Schweitzer.

'This is Jack,' Desmarais said, gesturing to him. 'He's got a special role on this mission.'

'Just Jack,' Montclair said. 'No rank. No last name.'

'That's right,' Desmarais said.

'Uh-huh.' Nalren arched an eyebrow. 'Look, sir, I appreciate the need for secrecy here, but in the end, you brought me on to run an op. It's gonna be really hard to do that if I don't know all the players on my team.'

'Trust me,' Desmarais said. 'If there was anything I needed you to know about Jack here, I would tell it to you. All I need you to do is bring him along. He'll volunteer information when the situation warrants it.'

'You're not hot under all that?' Montclair asked. 'Gonna take us a while to load out.'

Schweitzer shook his head and Ghaznavi smiled. 'He doesn't talk unless he has to.'

Nalren turned back to Desmarais. 'I know it's a little unusual,' he said. 'Your patience and flexibility are greatly appreciated.'

Nalren shrugged and turned to Ghaznavi. 'So, you're running the op?'

'I'm the executive,' Ghaznavi said. 'Reeves runs the show. He just has to call me "ma'am".'

Nalren smiled and gestured to the gear. 'Well, let's go over everything and get everyone billeted out. Six of us makes two sticks. I guess we should divide on national lines, eh? And I guess you three are our HQ element?'

'Actually,' Desmarais said, 'Jack will be rolling with the American stick.'

'We're travelling light,' Fitzgerald said. 'Twin Otter's only rated to four thousand pounds, and we're going to take up sixteen hundred of that with just passengers. I tried to keep it to just ess—'

'Try eighteen hundred,' Desmarais interrupted. 'Maybe even two thousand.'

'Sir?' Fitzgerald asked.

'Jack weighs a bit more than most folks.' Desmarais smiled. 'He's a big eater.'

'Don't look that big,' Nalren mused.

'He mostly eats metal,' Ghaznavi said.

Fitzgerald shook his head. 'I'll have to ditch some gear.'

'Why such a light plane?' Reeves asked. 'I know we want to keep this quiet, but surely you can spare something with a little more lift?'

'Not out here,' Nalren said, smiling. 'You think this is the middle of nowhere, wait'll you see the south shore. We could drive, but there's so little road traffic that they'd spot us a mile out. Only real way to approach quietly is by seaplane.'

'Won't that make extraction tough?' Reeves asked.

'This is Canada,' Nalren said. 'Tough is how we like it.'

The flight from Yellowknife to the Great Slave Lake's opposite shore took under an hour in a shaking DHC-6, the twin propellers spinning threateningly close to the fuselage. The huge pontoons were fitted with wheels that enabled them to make their bumpy ascent from the Yellowknife flight line, but they would come down in the water. The plane was painted white and blue, with the words VIKING AIR stenciled on the side, but otherwise bore no markings. The windows were tinted, but Schweitzer's magically augmented vision enabled him to see the lake stretching out beneath him. He watched the huge ice floes, some the size of buses, gently drifting in the huge expanse of water below. It wouldn't be easy to land this crate in that.

As if she sensed his unease, Nalren tapped Schweitzer on the shoulder, gestured to the pilots in the cockpit. 'Don't sweat it, Jack,' she said. 'Those guys are out of the 427. They could land this in a teacup if they had to.'

Schweitzer nodded, hoping they wouldn't have to.

The flight was taken up mostly with the final targeting brief, going over the ops plan as the thin light failed into one of the most glorious sunsets Schweitzer had ever seen. 'It's getting on winter,' Nalren said. 'You ever see the aurora?'

Schweitzer shook his head. Ghaznavi looked like she would tell the Master Corporal to stop interrogating Schweitzer, but she only watched, uncomfortable.

'Well, maybe you'll get lucky. It's quite a sight.'

Schweitzer nodded. He didn't tell her that Sarah had always wanted to see the aurora, that he had gone so far as to price out a lodge in Alaska where they would have a pretty good chance. It would have been expensive, and he'd been saving for it when the pistol had been jammed under his chin. He wished now that he hadn't waited, had charged the trip to his credit card and worried about paying it off later. He'd always thought there'd be time.

'Okay.' Desmarais leaned over his ruggedized laptop, screen facing out. 'Here's what our sources tell us – Lived-With-The-Wolves is supposedly one Charles Plante, an Athabasca Chipewyan First Nation trapper who lives somewhere southwest of Fort Resolution. We don't know exactly where, but we have to secure him.' The screen flashed a black-and-white mug shot of an old man, his skin so wrinkled that it nearly absorbed his features.

'If we don't know where he is, then how are we going to secure him?' Nalren asked.

'His granddaughter is Wilma "Mankiller" Plante, the sheriff of Fort Resolution. She's an Army veteran, been a cop her whole life after she got out. Straight shooter, good lady. We think she'll be cooperative.'

'Mankiller?' Reeves asked.

'Wilma Mankiller was a famous Cherokee chief. Guess the family liked her legacy.'

'I don't want to tell you guys how to do your job, and I know we're guests here, sir . . .' Reeves began.

Nalren turned to stare at him, and Ghaznavi leaned over and punched him in the arm. 'What?' Reeves looked pained.

'Just make your point,' Desmarais said. 'I know you're guests, but it's one team, one fight.'

'Well' – Reeves recovered his composure – 'it's just that we're coming out here loaded for bear. We're ready to hit the ground guns up. You say this sheriff is a lifelong public servant and willing to cooperate. So, why aren't we picking up a phone and calling her instead of showing up on her doorstep ready for a fight?'

'Fort Resolution is even more remote than Yellowknife,' Desmarais answered. 'To call it the edge of civilization would be charitable. Less than five hundred people live in that town; most of them make their living in traditional trades like trapping or fishing. These people are practically off the grid already. They're not easy to get in touch with at the best of times.'

'Surely, they've got something,' Reeves said. 'Satphones? VHF? Something? They're not in tents out there, are they? I mean, if the town's got a sheriff, it's gotta be at least partly civilized.'

'They've got all those comms channels,' Desmarais answered, 'and none of them work.'

'So, shouldn't you be sending an engineer to—' Reeves began.

'You're not following me, Mr Reeves,' Desmarais interrupted him. 'No comms channels are responding. They're completely dark.'

'Could a storm do that?' Ghaznavi asked.

'A bad one, maybe,' Desmarais replied, 'but we've been in touch with Environment Canada. There's no storm, and there hasn't been one in the past month. We've tasked satellites to get us some overhead imagery, but it's going to take a while.'

'The Director,' Ghaznavi said. 'He beat us there.'

'Maybe,' Desmarais said, 'probably. We have to assume the worst.'

'So, call in the Canadian Army,' Reeves said, 'the RCMP, surround the place.'

Desmarais shook his head. 'This has to be small, and it has to be quiet.'

'Why?' Reeves asked. 'Since we're speaking plainly.'

'For the same reasons it has to be small and quiet for you. You didn't have the Army hit that facility in Colchester. We're not dropping the Army on Fort Resolution.'

Reeves went silent.

'We keep this quiet. We get the town secured and we convince Sheriff Plante to take us to her grandfather. Once we know we have him secure, we can take the fight to the Director. All right.' He brought up a map of the town. 'We know the country, so it's our stick on point. I want you to—'

The plane shook. Schweitzer heard the distinctive pop of chaff firing, saw the red-yellow flashes just off the plane's wing.

'Taking fire!' the pilot shouted back to them. 'Strap in!'

Desmarais shut the laptop and slid into his seat, slinging the buckle across his chest until it clicked. The rest of the team followed suit.

'Any idea where—' Ghaznavi began, but stopped at a gesture from Desmarais.

'They'll get us down,' he said. 'We can figure the rest out then.'

'This might be a little uncomfortable,' the pilot shouted, and the plane lurched, the nose dropping at a sickening angle, the frame groaning in protest. The engines roared, whined. The floor slid and the team sagged in their harnesses.

There was another boom, and the plane shook again. Schweitzer heard a dull pattering of some kind of crew-served gun. Whoever was firing on them definitely had them dialed in, and Schweitzer didn't like their chances of making it down in one piece. The Twin Otter was a propeller-driven cargo plane, not designed for evasive maneuvers against a determined foe. It would come down to the skill of the pilots. He hoped Nalren was right about them.

Schweitzer had landed in fixed-wing aircraft under fire before. He would never forget his first trip into the 'VIP' strip at Baghdad's airport. The plane then had been a C-130, a massive tub of a transport plane at least four times as large as the Twin Otter. They'd ordered the windows covered, so there was no way to see the angle of descent, but Schweitzer had felt it, a churning sickness in his living stomach as the pilot had thrown the plane into a corkscrewing dive, so tight and fast and Schweitzer thought for sure that he'd overcommitted, that he couldn't possibly pull such a large and heavy plane up in time, that at any minute, he would hear the bang of the nose impacting the tarmac, and then he would know no more. When the bang came, Schweitzer jumped, but he wasn't dead. The horizon had suddenly righted, and the plane was taxiing on its landing gear, safe behind the flight line's barricade walls.

The Canadian pilots performed the same corkscrewing dive, the same speed, the same insane angle. Schweitzer watched out the window now, seeing the lake and the sky swap places again and again. The chaff fired again, the yellow sparks spiraling up and out of view.

The plane shook once more and Schweitzer saw flames shooting out from somewhere just behind his window. Smoke filled the cabin as the horizon finally righted and the pilots got the pontoons under them. 'Going to be bumpy!' one shouted.

The plane hit the water like a meteor. Schweitzer could see the waves splashing up, sheeting down the windows. A chunk of gray ice the size of a bus sped by, missing the wingtip by inches. The team lurched in their harnesses, a few smacking their heads on the ceiling despite the straps. Schweitzer heard the engines roar as the pilots desperately tried to shed speed. The plane shuddered again, and Schweitzer could tell by the crunching sound that they had struck ice. That meant that whoever was firing on them had lost their sight picture, but that didn't mean they wouldn't regain it. This wasn't Baghdad and they didn't have barricade walls to cover them here.

Schweitzer slapped the release on his harness and stood, crossing to the plane's door. The plane was still racing along, shaking, lurching from side to side. The team stared at him wide-eyed. He should have been thrown from his feet, rattled like a marble in the aisle between the seats. But Schweitzer's magical strength tensed the right muscles at precisely the right moment, locking and unlocking in perfect synchronicity with the pitching craft. He moved like a man walking a boat's gently rocking deck, crossing to the door, yanking the handle down.

'What the hell are you doing!?' Ghaznavi shouted to him.

'Setting up a firing position,' he answered. 'Did you think they'd just stop shooting at us because we landed?'

The wind ripped the door open the moment the latch released, banging it against the side of the fuselage. He could see the gray water rushing by, churned to white froth by the plane's pontoon. Slush and chunks of ice the size of baseballs slammed against it, chipping paint and spinning off into the boiling lake. The shore was a good way off but growing closer each second. Whatever braking the pilots had managed, Schweitzer didn't think it was going to be enough.

They confirmed his suspicions a moment later. 'We're going to have to beach!'

'Sit down!' Nalren called to him. 'Jack, you gotta strap in!'

Schweitzer squinted at the leaping shore. He could see gray figures moving among the rocks. It was possible they were locals running to help. It was also possible they were the shooters running to intercept. Schweitzer knew which one he would be betting on.

'Gun!' He turned to Nalren, motioning to the holster strapped to her thigh.

She stared at him, uncomprehending. There was no way he would make a shot from this kind of bouncing platform. It was insane to try.

'Give it to me, damn it!' he shouted, and Nalren released her death grip from the harness, slumping against the broad nylon strap. She reached down and thumbed the holster's release, looked at him again, eyebrow arched.

'I'll catch it. Trust me.'

She yanked the pistol out and tossed it in one movement. It was a crazy throw, her arm shaking like everything else in the plane. The weapon flew sideways, and the rest of the team shouted at the sight of a loaded gun sailing through the air. Schweitzer let go of the doorframe and leaned, snagging it out of the air as easily as if it had been thrown straight to him. In an instant, he had it nestled in his hand, a wooden-handled .45 FN, the old Belgian pattern, unchanged since World War Two. He knelt in the doorway, shrugging off the parka, freeing his buzz-saw arm. He brought it across his chest, braced the pistol against his elbow, wedged himself into the doorframe.

The figures were still moving along the shore. Even his augmented eyes couldn't pick out their clothing at this distance, not through the mix of lake fog, spraying water, and the constant staccato interruption of the towering bergs of ice as they whipped past. He could see only the silhouettes, long streaks held at their waists. Guns, big ones. Hunters might have guns. Heck, out here in the sticks, everyone probably had them. *Make the call. Wait much longer and they'll get another shot on you.*

He squinted at the guns, long, thick. Heavy-looking. It was possible that some gun nut was out hunting with a .50 cal BMG, but he wouldn't count on it. He sighted in, fired.

In life, Schweitzer was renowned for his ability to make impossible shots. On the last op he'd run before he'd died, he'd taken down a crewman on the pitching deck of a freighter in complete darkness, two hundred yards out.

Death only made him better. His senses were his to command, all distractions set aside, dead muscles responding exactly as instructed. He had become a machine, in complete control over every aspect of his physical form. It was as if time had slowed, making all things plain. He could see the distance the figures would travel at their current pace, could feel the bullet's trajectory as it left the gun, calculate the stirring of the wind.

The gun popped, but there was no recoil. His hands were far too strong. The gun moved no more than it would have in a block of cement. One of the figures stumbled, his weapon flying from his hands, and disappeared behind the rocks. The other stopped running, crouching for cover. There were more figures coming now, farther down the shoreline, but Schweitzer knew he'd bought them some time.

He turned back to the team and saw that every eye was fixed on him, wide and disbelieving. 'Bought us maybe a minute, so make sure you clear the craft the moment we get . . .'

'Impact!' the pilots shouted.

For a moment they were flying again, the nose rising and the white-gray of the sky showing through the windows. Then, the pontoons struck ground, first groaning, then screaming, and finally shearing off entirely, sending the fuselage rumbling onto the rocky shore. Schweitzer felt the plane try to roll, the engine housing and wing keeping it upright, dragging it in a lazy circle, the propeller blades snapping off. One slammed into the fuselage, driving through the metal, leaving a piece of quivering steel in the cabin. The nose caught, crumpled. Schweitzer could hear the roar of flames as the electrical systems caught fire, burning brightly despite the water pouring into the cabin. The team was hammered between their harnesses and their seats, but Schweitzer needed only a firm grip on the doorframe to keep himself from being thrown.

The plane's shrieks began to subside back to groans as it sketched another lazy circle, finally shuddering to a stop. The smoke in the cabin was nearly blinding now.

Schweitzer looked down at the sloshing water. It was mostly free of ice here, with shoulders of rock forcing their way through the surface, the waves white around the edges. Schweitzer couldn't be sure that it was shallow enough to stand up in, but there was only one way to find out. He would have liked more time to make an informed decision, but he knew the first rule of an ambush: if you were not moving, you were right where the enemy wanted you. *Get off the X.*

'Everybody out!' Schweitzer shouted, and jumped.

The freezing water embraced him, so cold that he could feel the temperature of the glycerol in his veins plummet instantly. The water was up to his chest by the time his boots hit the rocky bottom, a steep slope that forced him to jog a few steps to stay upright. He kept the pistol above the water and trained on the shore but didn't shake the cover off the buzz saw. He didn't need it yet, and there was no need to freak the Canadians out any more than they already were.

He could see the plane out of the corner of his eye, aground but still partially submerged. The fuselage was bent around a spine of ice-encrusted rock, the waves slapping it mercilessly. It wouldn't take long to break it apart. Nalren appeared at the open door, her carbine at the low ready; she glanced dubiously at the water, up at Schweitzer, back down.

Schweitzer knew what she was thinking. The team wouldn't last more than a few minutes in this water. He had to keep the fire off of them so they could get to dry land. One of the enemy was already up from behind the rocks, moving their way closer. More were coming behind. All carried weapons, which was good. It meant they weren't Golds. This close, Schweitzer could make out the military parkas, the tactical harness. Not locals, then. He'd made the right call in deciding to fire.

Nalren was shouting to Fitzgerald, motioning to the water as the first of the enemy reached the rocks and sighted in. Schweitzer saw the dull green of a warhead, the flanges covering the shooter's face.

'RPG!' Schweitzer shouted, fired.

The FN fired a .45 cal round, heavy and thick, but it was still less than a half-inch in diameter. The distance was at least one hundred yards, skirting the edge of the weapon's effective range. He could see the shooter getting his sights, could see the RPG steady as he prepared to pull the trigger. There was no time for the slow, steady pull that Schweitzer preferred. He slapped the trigger, felt the weapon jerk in response.

The bullet cut through the frothing waves, and Schweitzer smiled inwardly, knowing it would strike its target the moment it left the muzzle. Right on the piezoelectric trigger.

Schweitzer didn't see the weapon explode, incinerating the shooter with it, but he heard the dull *whump* as he turned back to the airplane, shouted to Nalren, 'Forget the boat! There's no time! Get in the damn water!'

He turned back to the shore as the first splash sounded behind him, heard the sharp intake of breath as Nalren felt the shock of the cold. To the uninitiated, a sudden submersion in freezing water could make the muscles seize, turning a person into a brick at the very moment that they most needed to be moving. The SEALs trained for this, spending hour after hour in the freezing waters off Kodiak, skirting the edges of hypothermia. He wasn't sure how the Canadians trained. They were one of the few special operations corps he'd never run a joint op with, but he prayed they were up to the same standard. He heard Nalren begin sloshing her way toward shore, her weapon held high over her head, not bothering to sight in at this distance.

The enemy didn't have to worry about water. The first of them had reached the rocks lining the shore, and Schweitzer could hear the echoing report of their ranging shots, plinking against the rock outcropping as they estimated elevation and windage. They were good, very good. The team didn't have more than a few seconds before those rounds started drilling home.

Schweitzer squatted, the freezing water rising up to his neck, and pushed off, easily clearing the water and landing on a ridge of rock breaking the surface. 'Get to shore!' he shouted to Nalren, took a running jump to the next peak of stone rearing high enough to clear the crashing waves. He fired as he went, not bothering to aim, seeking only to draw the enemy's attention, to let them know a threat was approaching fast.

And he was approaching fast. The magic that animated Schweitzer gave him the balance of a mountain goat, the strength of a Thoroughbred. He leapt from rock to rock, his feet touching down on slick stone barely bigger than his boot sole.

There was a report, and he felt the stirring air as a round shrieked past his head. Good, they were shooting at him. As he closed the distance, he could finally make out the enemy's faces, could begin to smell the stink of adrenaline in their blood, the sweet tang of the rising sugar as it dawned on them what they were facing. These were Cell operators. They knew what the undead could do.

At last, he came down on a broken boulder close enough to make the leap to the shore. He put as much power into the jump as he could, sailing up and over the cluster of enemy, shaking the cover off his buzz saw, tensing the muscles that set the blade spinning. He came down in the middle of them, four men with carbines, a fifth with a .50 caliber sniper rifle that would be all but useless at this close range. Schweitzer shot him anyway, simply because he was closest, snapping his head back and spraying his brains out the back of his hood onto his comrade. Schweitzer followed with a sweep of the buzz saw that sheared off the top of the next man's skull before he could even raise his weapon.

Schweitzer felt a hammerblow on his back, the cells in his armor activating to repel a high-powered round. It drove him forward a step, and he let the momentum carry him into one of the other operators. The man had given in to his fear, was backpedaling madly, firing from the hip, in no danger of hitting anyone. Schweitzer cut him down anyway, because men who had lost their courage could find it again, and besides, if he'd wanted to live, he shouldn't have shot down Schweitzer's plane.

Schweitzer pivoted around the strike, letting the momentum turn him even as the enemy body collapsed. He got back on his sights, letting his focus shift to the front sight post. The world beyond became a gray-white blur, two darker blotches sketching the outline of the enemy. The man who'd shot him was advancing, fearless, sighted in now. His carbine barked, and Schweitzer felt the cells around his shoulder hammered, the arm suddenly heavy under the hardened liquid. But Schweitzer also had his sights dialed in, and with his unnatural steadiness, accuracy was a foregone conclusion. The enemy dropped with a hole through his right eye, and the other's nerve finally broke. The man turned and ran, heedless, carbine swinging in its sling.

Schweitzer sighted him, had him dead to rights. Shooting a man in the back might be considered craven in Hollywood, but on a battlefield, it was standard procedure. An enemy who ran might be moving to a better position, or he might be bringing word to another force. In all his years with the SEALs, Schweitzer had trained to put the round on the target without any regard to which way it was facing.

But now he hesitated. Death had been Schweitzer's existence for so long now that he remembered less and less of what it meant to be alive. In the heat of battle, with the lives of his teammates on the line, killing had been simple, easy. Now that the immediate threat to the team was ended, he heard the pounding of the man's heart, growing fainter as the distance between them grew. He knew it was time to still that pounding, to slide the trigger back, but Schweitzer found himself listening to that steady rhythm, each beat pushing warm blood through a body that could love and age and hurt and die.

Crack.

The man pitched sideways and collapsed. The heartbeat fluttered once, stopped. Schweitzer looked up. Reeves was kneeling, rock steady despite being soaking wet in the freezing weather, still sighting in through the smoke wafting up from his carbine. 'He's down,' he said, looked up at the confusion in Schweitzer's eyes. *What's wrong with you?* that gaze said. *Why didn't you take the shot?*

Schweitzer didn't have an answer. He only knew that he felt a pang of regret, of something lost with the stilling of that heart. It was unpardonable. The lack of focus would cost him, cost the team. There was only one life he needed to save, Patrick's. He would stop the Cell, make the Director pay, and then . . . and then what? He would worry about that later; for now, he had shivering people on the shore. He jogged toward them.

The plane had finally broken up on the rocks, the halves dragged by the undertow, tumbling out to sea. The front was a crumpled ruin. The pilots were not on shore, and Schweitzer didn't see how they could have survived. Most of the gear was gone. The team had managed to salvage their weapons and a few of the pelican cases. Nalren had one open at her feet, was distributing warming packs to the rest of them. 'Stuff them into your gloves and boots,' she managed through chattering teeth.

'The pilots . . .' Schweitzer began.

Nalren raised her pistol. 'Back off. Not one step closer.'

'Stand down, Master Corporal!' Desmarais said.

'No, sir,' Nalren said. 'I don't know what the hell is going on here, but our dear friend Jack has a buzz saw for a hand and I just saw him jump a hundred feet in the air without a running start while making a fifty-yard pistol shot. Now, either Jack is going to tell me what's going on or your CIA buddy is, but I will take a court-martial before I go one more step.'

'Damn it,' Desmarais began, 'we don't have time for . . .'

But Schweitzer was already pushing the hood back, lifting his goggles, looking at Nalren with the burning silver of his eyes. To her credit, the Master Corporal met his gaze unflinchingly, a slight increase in her heartbeat the only indicator of fear.

'Magic is real,' Schweitzer said. 'I'm dead, and so are the bad guys.'

Nalren blinked, exchanged a glance with Montclair,

looked back to Schweitzer. She gestured at the cooling corpses along the shore. 'Those guys looked pretty alive to me.'

'That's the B team,' Schweitzer said. 'I guess they were hoping to shoot us down, kill us in the crash, and not have to commit their A team. But it's not going to take them long to figure out that didn't work out as planned. The A team is inbound, and they move every bit as fast as I do.'

'What do we do?' Nalren asked.

Schweitzer scanned the terrain. It was flat, windswept, and bare. He looked back at the team. They were all freezing, huddled in their sopping winter gear. He could feel the body heat draining from them, their core temperatures plummeting.

'We can't run. Not now. We need to get inside, get you warmed up. Preferably a fixed position, something we can defend.'

'That's the town,' Desmarais said. 'Come on.'

The Canadians led the way, putting up a good show of being alert and focused, but Schweitzer could hear their breathing, see the tremors in their steps. If the enemy came on them now, Schweitzer would be their only defense. The Americans were far worse, barely able to make even a show of doing anything more than freezing to death on their feet. Ice rimed their eyebrows, their beards, the fur edging of their hoods.

Schweitzer set out at a fast jog, careful to keep the pace brisk enough for the team to warm themselves in their effort to keep up. He heard their heartbeats rise a bit, their body temperatures cooling more slowly, but it still wasn't enough. They needed to get inside.

Fort Resolution materialized out of the white horizon, a scattering of plastic-sided shacks and trailers, dotted here and there with more solid construction that spoke of a municipal building, a church, a storehouse.

It didn't take Schweitzer's augmented senses to know that something was wrong. Black smoke rose in a column from the center of the town, thick and greasy.

'Oil fire,' Nalren said. 'Burned out, mostly.'

'I wonder if anyone's still alive,' Desmarais said.

'They're still alive.' Schweitzer could hear the faint crunching of boots on snow, voices calling to one another. 'I can hear them.'

Nalren caught her breath, and he heard her heartbeat speed up, but she gave no outward sign. 'How do you know it isn't the enemy?'

'The Cell's trained operators. They'd be quieter. Whoever's making all this racket is untrained, to put it charitably.'

'Well' – Reeves's teeth were chattering so badly he could barely get the words out – 'at least that fire'll thaw us out.'

They kept up a brisk jog, and the town grew before them. It looked to Schweitzer like any of a dozen New England fishing villages he'd visited with Sarah, right down to the cedar-sided boathouses, complete with sagging roofs and peeling creosote. Log rafts lined with old tires were stacked alongside prefabricated metal shacks. Of course, no New England town had ever been in the grip of such a winter, and the layer of ice made the town a museum exhibit, a place dipped in preservative plastic.

The streets were deserted. The ground was crisscrossed with tracks, military boot treads among others. 'The bad guys were here,' Schweitzer said.

'No shit.' Nalren jerked her chin in the direction of the column of smoke, its source screened by a low line of buildings.

'Can' we jus' go in one of these?' Cort slurred, trying the door on one of the boathouses. The metal latch banged against the wood frame; it was locked.

'We need to keep going.' Schweitzer was troubled by the slurred speech. 'These aren't heated. Probably almost as cold inside as out here.'

'Can't get it open,' Cort said, pulling on the door. His teeth weren't chattering; he didn't even appear to be shivering.

'He's got it bad,' Nalren said, taking Cort by the elbow and leading him away from the door. 'He needs inside now.'

'Follow me.' Schweitzer ran on toward the voices, toward the column of smoke, heedless now of the ground or the pace or the cover, knowing only that he had to get his team to warmth before he lost them. He could hear their heartbeats slowing under the onslaught of the cold. So many heartbeats had ceased since he'd become able to hear them. If it was in his power to keep a few more beating, he would. Compassion was the last inch of humanity, and he clung to it.

The team was stumbling now. Schweitzer could hear their shuffling steps, their labored breathing. It was insane to approach like this, with no cover, with no idea what they were rolling into, but the sound of those slowing heartbeats drove him on. The least he could do was soak up fire if someone got the drop on them.

The first round whined off the hood of a Bobcat, its bucket filled with snow it had been plowing when it was abandoned. Schweitzer knew right away that the shooter wasn't from the Cell. The shot was far too wide of the mark. A trained sniper would have missed closer, if they'd missed at all.

'Friendlies!' he shouted, raising his hands, realizing too late that one of them was a jagged-toothed saw. 'Don't shoot!'

He could see the shooter now, an obese woman with more gray hair on her chin than her head. She was perched behind the bed of a burned-out truck, far from the engine block that could actually stop a bullet. She wore a threadbare pink sweater hanging open to reveal a T-shirt advertising a tractor company. She was sweating despite the cold. 'Fuck you, zombie!' she shouted. 'You're one of them things!' She sighted in again, and Schweitzer could tell from the wavering muzzle that he needn't worry about it.

'I'm a good thing,' Schweitzer said, keeping his hands high. 'I'm not going to hurt you.'

'Fuck you!' the woman shouted again, and Schweitzer saw two more heads appear, both blinking at him in shock. They held guns but at least had the sense not to point them at him. She fired, the bullet breaking high and passing two feet over his head. He heard a distant *thunk* as it drilled through some unfortunate building's second story.

'Jesus Christ, lady,' Schweitzer said. 'Have any of the monsters talked to you before? Put their hands up? These people behind me are Canadian Army and they're soaking wet. I need to get them inside before they freeze to death. We're here to help you if you'll stop shooting at me for five minutes.'

Another woman appeared beside the shooter. Her wide face was placid, her eyes alert. A high-powered Alaskan hung across her chest, her finger properly indexed along the receiver, the muzzle pointed at the deck. She pushed the barrel of the other woman's rifle down. 'Come off it, Laura. He ain't tryin' to fight nobody.'

The woman turned to Schweitzer. 'What do you want?'

'To get my people inside where it's warm and into dry clothes.'

'You guys are Army?'

'That's right,' Desmarais said. 'I'm Colonel Desmarais, from Northern Headquarters. We're here to assist you with your defense. Are you Sheriff Plante?'

The people behind a barricade had a hushed conversation before the woman with the Alaskan shouted at them to pipe down. 'That's me. You guys got a defibrillator?'

'We do,' Nalren said, raising one of the pelican cases. 'Small portable one in the trauma kit. Why do you need it?'

The sheriff looked at Nalren like she was an idiot. 'Why the hell does anybody want a defibrillator? On account of someone's heart stopping.'

'Well, here it is,' Nalren said, stamping her feet.

'All right,' the sheriff said. 'Come on in, but I'm warnin' you, if this is some kind of a false flag, you're gonna be sorry.'

'It's not a false flag,' Schweitzer muttered, jogging toward the line of burned-out trucks.

He cleared the barricade to find a clot of people, all armed with a patchwork of hunting rifles and high-caliber pistols. Each one of them carried a hatchet or a long knife slung in easy reach. Which surely meant they had faced the Golds. There was no other reason Schweitzer could imagine folks like these bringing knives to a gunfight. They clutched their inadequate weapons firmly, giving him a wide berth, nervous eyes locked on him, ignoring the living members of the team as they came stumbling in. They were all of them past shivering now, their eyes glazed, jaws slack.

The hard-eyed woman tapped the woman with the rifle on the shoulder. 'Laura, get these folks inside and warm 'em up.' She turned to Nalren. 'Gimme that defib.'

Nalren half handed, half dropped the pelican case as

she stumbled into the small, scorched building that Schweitzer could only guess was the town's police station. It was well fortified, the walls blackened and pocked with bullet holes. Brown smears that could only be old blood still darkened the frozen ground near the charred husks of trucks hastily assembled into a barricade.

'Ollie!' the woman shouted. 'Got a defib comin' in! Get it on Joe right now!'

'Oh, thank God,' came an older man's voice, labored, the breath coming out at a steady rhythm, one every second and a half. Chest compressions. CPR. 'My arms are 'bout to fall off.'

Schweitzer made to follow and the sheriff raised the Alaskan, pointing it at his knee rather than his face. She definitely had some experience fighting Golds, then. 'Not you,' she said. 'You stay where I can keep an eye on you.'

'I promise you, I'm not going to hurt anyone,' Schweitzer said. 'You know what we can do. If I wanted to take you down, I'd have done it already.'

'Well, maybe you would and maybe you wouldn't, but you sure as hell don't need to be warmin' up in my office, and I bet you'd jus' pass on a mug of coffee, so you can stay out here 'til I know what's what.'

'Sure,' Schweitzer said, taking a few steps backward to ease her mind. 'No problem. Cold just keeps me preserved.'

'You're an *?eyune*? I thought that only worked with animals.'

Schweitzer gave her as much of a smile as his steel-and-corpse-flesh face would allow. 'I thought it only worked with people. Nice to meet you, Sheriff Plante.'

'People call me Mankiller.'

'That's . . . kind of badass, actually.'

'Yeah, well. Mom named me after the first lady chief of the Cherokee. She was the real badass.'

'Your mom or this chief?'

'Both.' Mankiller smiled. 'Mom never got into politics or anything, but she once shot a chargin' grizzly without even tryin' to get out of the way.'

'My name's James Schweitzer. People call me Jim.'

'Didn't know *?eyune* had names.'

'Well, this one does. Dying didn't change it.'

'Okay, Jim. Good to meetcha. Sorry you died.'

'Thanks. I'm kind of over it.'

Mankiller smiled, said nothing.

'Well, anyway, I guess I am a . . . whatever you said. I heard your granddad makes things like us.'

Mankiller nodded. 'He says it only works with animals, and it has to be *bedáyíné*. Like, for *sélat'in*.'

'I have no idea what the heck you're saying. I only speak English.'

''S all right,' Mankiller said. 'Anyway, I never met a *?eyune* that could talk. The ones that've been comin' here may look like people, but they're more animals than the ones Grampy makes.'

'Honestly? I'm amazed you survived. I just watched a few of those things take out most of a team of hardened operators. I wouldn't think you could stand up to them. No disrespect,' he hastily added.

'None taken.' Mankiller finally lowered her rifle. 'I was in the Army. EOD. Afghanistan.'

'So, how many have you taken down?'

'Three, though one took itself down. Blew up one of the trucks while it was standin' next to it.'

'They're not too bright.'

'Animals.' She shrugged.

'The other two?'

'Well, I figured it out. You can't jus' put a hole in their heads, on account of 'em bein' dead already. I guess you just gotta chop 'em up fine.' She paused. 'Yeah, real fine.'

'Or you can burn them.' Schweitzer indicated the black smear by the burned-out truck.

'Yup.' She nodded. 'So, don' try nothin' stupid.' But she was smiling now, warm and open. The silence stretched.

'So, Mankiller, huh?'

'Yup.'

'You ever kill a man?'

'A few. Nobody who didn' need it.'

'Look, can we please go inside now? I want to see if . . .'

'We got a pulse, Sheriff!' came the man's voice from inside the station. Mankiller immediately turned, leaping over the splintered remains of a tiny staircase and up into the station. Schweitzer followed, figuring he was off the hook.

'Joe!' Mankiller was kneeling beside a small folding table, sagging under the weight of an enormous man with a shock of wet black hair. His skin was gray and his eyes had the shadowed look of a corpse. His soaked parka was thrown open and his shirt cut through, the defibrillator leads still attached to his chest. An old man squatted beside him, tall and thin, with tears running down his face. 'He made it,' he said. 'Praise Jesus, Sheriff, he made it.'

Mankiller swallowed, her eyes misting, but not so badly that she showed tears. A leader, then, maintaining her self-control in front of her people. 'Well, that's jus' fine, Ollie,' she whispered.

The old man looked up at Schweitzer, reached for his gun.

'It's all right, Ollie,' Mankiller said. 'He's a good guy. I think.'

The old man stayed crouched, frozen.

'What about her?' Schweitzer asked. Beside the folding

table was a military cot. A woman lay on it, her face gray and drawn. A bloodstained blanket was thrown over her mid-section.

'Gutshot,' Mankiller said. 'We couldn't get her medevac'd. Ollie, recharge the—'

Schweitzer shook his head. 'She's gone.'

'The fuck can you know that?' The old man was on his knees, recharging the defibrillator. 'She could be comatose.'

'I can hear heartbeats, breathing,' Schweitzer said. 'She's gone. I'm sorry.'

'I ain't givin' up,' the old man said, hiking up the woman's shirt and clearing her chest to attach the leads.

Schweitzer left him to it. Mad hope was better than none at all.

The American and Canadian teams were slumped on the floor, huddled together, shivering again now, which was a good sign. Schweitzer could hear their heartbeats, steady now, could feel the warming temperature of their blood. 'Everybody okay?' he asked. 'We can feel all our fingers and toes?'

Each member of the team nodded, and Ghaznavi stripped off her glove and wiggled her fingers. Her skin was unnaturally white, but she would be okay. 'Gonna start to burn once you warm up,' Schweitzer said. 'Get ready.'

'Yes, thanks,' Reeves said. 'We remember cold-weather training.'

Mankiller had her hand on the big man's forehead. She was breathing evenly, but the emotion in her face pulled on Schweitzer's heartstrings.

'Was he . . .'

'He was my deputy . . . is my deputy, damn it; he's alive, praise God. His name's Joe Yakecan.'

Ollie shouted, 'Clear,' and the small machine

administered its shock. The dead woman's muscles clenched slightly, her head lolling to one side, but it made no difference, as Schweitzer had known. Ollie cursed and set the defibrillator to charge again.

Schweitzer's heart went out to the old man, but there was nothing he could do. Ollie would have to find out on his own that she was gone, decide for himself that he had done everything he could.

Schweitzer turned back to the big man on the folding table. He could see that the man was alive, but he could also see that his heart had been stopped for a very long time. 'How long was he down?'

'Jesus,' the man Mankiller called Ollie whispered after the second electric shock failed to revive the dead woman. He cursed, threw the paddles down. Then looked up at Schweitzer. 'Didn't think you could talk.'

'Looks like you can talk too,' Schweitzer said. 'Except maybe when it comes to answering questions.' Among operators, rough gibes were the best way to get a man past grief and shock.

It didn't work with Ollie; his face darkened, and Schweitzer leaned in before he could retort. 'You did everything you could for her, Ollie. Not your fault. Now we need to focus on the guy who's alive. Just tell me how long you were doing CPR on him.'

'I dunno,' the older man said. 'A few minutes. Maybe ten? Fifteen?'

Schweitzer could see the dark bruising that indicated Yakecan's ribs had been broken. On the one hand, it meant the CPR had been done right; on the other hand, it meant it had been done for too long. The brain damage had to be severe.

Mankiller seemed to have the same idea; she bent over Yakecan, pried open his eyelids.

'Now, Sheriff, you don't have to go . . .' Ollie began.

Mankiller looked up, and her eyes stopped him mid-sentence.

She looked back down at Yakecan, pulled a small taclight from her pocket. She thumbed the base, shined the beam directly into his eye.

Nothing. His body remained completely still, the pupils precisely the same size. Mankiller cursed, stripped off a glove, revealing thick fingers, the nails a little long. 'Sorry, Joe,' she said, reached out with a pinky, and tapped the white of his eye.

Yakecan showed no reaction at all. His chest rose and fell steadily, but his eyes stared as sightlessly as if he were dead. Mankiller took a long, shuddering breath and stood. 'He's gone.'

'He ain't gone,' Ollie said. 'He's breathin', for Christ's sake.'

'Still gone,' Mankiller said. 'His body just ain't figured it out yet. It will in a couple of weeks. I've seen it before. Went too long without oxygen to his brain. He's a vegetable.'

'He'll get better,' Ollie said.

'No, Ollie. He won't,' Mankiller said, her eyes flashing, 'and talkin' that kinda shit isn't going to make anyone feel better 'cept maybe yourself. If we're gonna have hope here, it's going to be the *real* kind and not Hallmark-card bullshit, you hear me?'

'I hear you, Sheriff,' Ollie said, straightening.

Schweitzer put a hand on Mankiller's shoulder. 'Sorry about your man, Sheriff. How'd it happen?'

Mankiller looked at Schweitzer's hand but made no move to remove it. 'They got our VHF jammed. Joe figured he could squirt, get far enough outside the range that he could make a call and get us help. They chased him, and I guess he didn' get far enough. Came back frozen half to death. Musta fallen through ice somewhere.'

'Sounds like he went down fighting,' Schweitzer said.

'Yeah,' Mankiller said. 'Guess so.'

'Help came.' Desmarais gestured to the huddled team members just beginning to test their thawing fingers.

'With all due respect, sir,' Mankiller said, 'I don' think you're gonna be all that much help.'

'I will be.' Schweitzer remembered the words he'd said to Patrick back in the Virginia woods. *There are different kinds of monsters, sweetheart. Some are good monsters, and some are bad monsters. Daddy is one of the good ones.* 'You've got your own monster now. But all the same' – he turned to Desmarais – 'I think it's time to make that call we talked about earlier. They got the jump on us. We're cut off out here and clearly outgunned and half-frozen. I understand the need for secrecy, but I suggest you put a call into Yellowknife and let the QRF know you're in need of their services.'

Desmarais looked to Ghaznavi, and the SAD Director opened her mouth to reply.

'You ain't makin' no calls,' Mankiller said.

'What?' Desmarais asked.

'Go ahead, check out your comms gear.'

Desmarais pulled a satellite phone from his cargo pocket and punched buttons on its face, cursing. He then switched to his personal cell phone, shook his head. 'Damn it.'

'Got us jammed. No calls in or out. Guess we'll just have to make do.'

'Well, there's more of the good guys now, at least,' Schweitzer said, 'and we're trained. That's something.'

'Thanks,' Mankiller said. 'Mind if we chat in my office for a sec?'

'Certainly,' Desmarais said. 'Is it back here—'

'Wasn' talkin' to you, sir.' Mankiller kept her eyes on Schweitzer.

'Sheriff. This is my expedition—'

'Good for you. This is my town.' She waved a hand toward a lopsided doorway, one of the two leading out of the room, looked at Schweitzer, inclining her head.

'It's all right, Colonel,' Schweitzer said. 'I promise to say good things about you.'

'You too, Ollie,' Mankiller said, walking into her office.

Schweitzer and Ollie followed, the old man closing the door behind him. Mankiller's office was tiny, the space dominated by an old steel desk piled high with papers. Schweitzer noted the absence of a computer. The walls were hung with plaques and pictures, including a framed discharge certificate from the Canadian Army. There were a couple of law enforcement awards, but the vast majority were native community honors. Best Volunteer, second place in a tournament of a game called 'snow snake', and another for 'hand games'. There was a picture of a much younger Mankiller in a group of people playing shallow, tambourine-shaped drums on a small stage.

'Close the door, Ollie,' she said without turning.

'Already done, boss,' he said.

Mankiller slumped into a creaking wooden swivel chair. 'Jim, this here's Ollie Calmut. He's been my other deputy after Joe.'

'I don't do much deputyin', honestly,' Calmut said. 'Mostly, I dispatch and talk to folks. You may have noticed that Boss can be a little short.'

'She's okay,' Schweitzer said.

'Anyway' – Mankiller slapped her palm on the desk – 'Ollie here can absolutely be trusted. So, you should speak freely in front of either one of us.'

'What did you want me to speak freely about?'

'Why you're here.'

'The Colonel said. We're here to—'

'Christ as my witness, do not screw with me, Jim.' Mankiller slapped the desk again. 'The Army didn' just show up without Joe gettin' through to get a message to 'em. And I can tell from the accents that half of you are Americans. And there's you, the good monster. They jus' thought they oughta bring you along? I think I know why you're here, but I wanna hear it from you.'

'Why me? Ask the Colonel.'

'Hell, no. You think the *ní ghâ k'áldher* gives a fuck about any *dene dédliné*? I don' trust those fuckers any farther'n I can throw 'em.'

'But you trust me?'

'You're *Bescho Dené*. Also, you're dead.'

'Not sure that makes a difference.'

'Tell me why you're here, Jim. I don' know when the enemy is goin' ta come again, but I doubt it'll be long. Can't sit here wastin' time.'

Schweitzer sighed. She was right, of course, and as little as he knew of her, he had to admit he liked her. In her gruff directness he saw the same kind of fearlessness he'd known in the teams. In Perretto. In Chang. He felt a stab of grief at the thought of his best friend, pushed it aside.

You wanted to be a human, he said to himself. *She's treating you like one.*

'We're here for your grandfather. Hard to find a solitary guy out here. We were hoping you'd take us to him.'

She nodded, unsurprised. 'I figured. What do you want with him?'

'It's not what we want with him. It's what the bad guys want with him.'

Mankiller twirled her wrist. *Go on.*

'They're led by a man . . . well, not a man . . .'

'A *?eyune*,' Mankiller finished for him. 'Like you.'

'Yes. We call him "The Director".'

'I think I met him. He's smart like you, talks. Mean as a hungry wolf, though.'

'That's probably him. I'm surprised you survived.'

'I gotta tub under a tarp just outside the station. Been brewing TATP in it since we first got hit. Got a few jars with fuses stuck in 'em. Crude but enough to make him think twice 'bout comin' in.'

'Right on top of the station? Jesus, Sheriff, that thing so much as gets jostled and you'll kill everyone in here.'

'I know that. But if I don't have it close to hand, we're all jus' as dead. Anyway, the temperature helps a bit with that.'

'Didn't know they taught you EOD types to make TATP.'

'Can't go unmakin' bombs if you don' know how to make 'em first. TATP is what the bad guys use.'

'Not these bad guys. They're better equipped than any army in the world.'

'Well, we done okay so far. What does the *ní ghâ k'áldher* and the—'

'Sheriff, English. Please.'

Mankiller smiled. 'Why is a combined mission of Canadians and Americans lookin' for my Grampy? To protect him against what?'

'This Director, he thinks your grandfather can put his spirit in a living body. We figure he wants to get into someone important.'

'Why?'

'To rule. You may have noticed he's not particularly charismatic right now.'

'Well, he's outta luck. Grampy can only do it with animals.'

'With all due respect, Sheriff, we're not willing to

chance that. The Director is awful good at persuading people. He runs a government organization that is dedicated to plumbing the depths of what this magic can do. If anyone can figure out how to make your grandfather do it, he can.'

'How do I know you won' jus' try to get him to do it for you?'

'We absolutely will, but we're the good guys.'

'Not from where I'm sittin',' Mankiller said. 'We Dene believed in *inkoze* since long before any white folks came this far north. Now you're jus' gettin' caught up. White folks treat every new thing the same way.'

'What way?'

'Like *?así bet'á hat'î*, "resources". Somethin' you can mine and use up. My Grampy ain't a forest to be logged or coal to be burned.'

'I get it,' Schweitzer said, 'but standing on principle here isn't going to help, Sheriff. You can either let us protect your grandfather, or you can sit back while the Director finds him and does whatever he needs to to ensure his cooperation. We'll be nicer than the Director. That's the most I can promise.'

Mankiller didn't show the anger in her face, but Schweitzer could hear it in her voice. 'I can also turn your whole team out and let you take your chances with the bad guys.'

'Don't be stupid. I've got six hardened operators with military-grade gear warming up just outside this door. That's the kind of bump that can keep you in the fight, and that's not even counting me.'

'You work for your government.'

'Wrong again. I work for me. I promised to lay down my life in the service of my country, and I've done that. My contract is fulfilled.'

Mankiller looked at him and said nothing.

'Look, I'm playing it to you straight,' Schweitzer went on. 'Do you honestly think that after all of this shakes out, your grandfather will just be left in peace? That you will? This is an advance team, Sheriff. If we fail, they'll send another, and then another, and they will never stop until they get what they're after. I wish it were different, but it isn't.' He thought of his own son, who had nothing to do with any of this. It had made no difference for him.

He wasn't sure how he expected Mankiller to react. It wouldn't have surprised him if even one as coolheaded as she flew into a rage at the threat against her family, but she only stared, blinked once, slowly. 'And if he helps, then what?'

'I don't know,' Schweitzer said. 'I don't exactly run things. Maybe they'll let him be, reach out to him when they need his help. Keep watch from a distance. It would make sense to do that with a cooperative asset.'

'But not with a noncooperative one.'

'You were in the Army, Sheriff. You know how these things go.'

'Yeah,' she said. 'I guess I do.'

In the awkward silence that followed, Schweitzer caught Calmut staring at him. 'Can I help you?'

The old man swallowed, looked down at his feet, back up again from the cover of his brow. The glance was so childlike that Schweitzer almost laughed.

'So, you're dead, huh?' Calmut asked.

'Yeah,' Schweitzer answered. 'Last time I checked.'

'It hurt?' Calmut asked.

'Getting killed? I honestly don't remember. It happened kind of fast.'

'What about being dead all the time?'

'Nah,' Schweitzer said. 'I mean, I wouldn't recommend it.'

Calmut smiled, and Schweitzer could hear his heart rate slow. 'So, you're a spirit in there?'

'I have no idea what I am,' Schweitzer answered. 'I've got a lot to do, and so far, I'm able to keep doing it.'

Calmut looked pensive as he nodded. 'Well, if you're a spirit, and this Director is looking to have boss's Grampy put him in a living body . . . might be he could do the same for you.'

Schweitzer felt his spiritual stomach turn over. It was a thought he'd avoided facing, because it was so enormous he couldn't wrap his head around it. What if he could be alive again? Would he even want to, now that everything he loved in the world had been taken away? What kind of life would he have? Would the government give him a job? Would he meet another woman? Raise his son? The questions swirled, as loud and confused as the soul storm itself. Each one led to another hundred. At last, Schweitzer threw up his mental hands. 'I try not to get my hopes up with stuff like that. I'll see what happens.'

Mankiller read his thoughts. 'Would you want to be alive? If you could? If you can do what those other things can, that's not a thing you give up easy.'

'I don't know,' Schweitzer answered honestly. 'I really don't.'

Mankiller grunted, accepting the answer. 'Okay, Ollie, you can open the door now.'

'What are we doin', Sheriff?' Calmut paused with his hand on the knob.

'We're gonna take Jim to see Grampy. The rest of the team'll stay here and help us hold down the fort.'

'The Colonel won't like that, Sheriff.'

'Not his call,' Mankiller said. 'Open the door, Ollie. I'll handle the talkin'.'

Ollie sighed and turned the knob.

The room outside was chaos. The villagers were jumping to their feet, scrambling to take up firing positions inside the ragged remains of the window frame. Reeves had Sharon with him, was making his way to the door, both of them shivering.

'Where are you going?' Schweitzer asked.

'We've got contacts inbound,' Reeves said through chattering teeth. 'Someone's got to cover our flank.'

'You're still hypothermic. You're not ready to go out there.' Ghaznavi scarcely looked better, pale and shivering, her eyes shadowed. 'You're not going to do anybody any good if you get yourself diced up by one of the Gold Operators.'

'Respectfully, ma'am,' Reeves said, 'I'm amazed this place hasn't fallen already. We can't just turtle up here. We get flanked, we're done.'

'I've got you, ma'am,' Cort said, trying to usher Ghaznavi back into Mankiller's office.

'Get the hell off me.' Ghaznavi shook herself free. 'I've got my damn self.'

She turned back to Reeves, but he and Sharon were already out the door and jogging across the snow, carbines at the low ready. Schweitzer prayed they were as stable as they looked. Their heat signatures were already fading as they ran, and Schweitzer didn't have time to see if it was because of the dampening effects of the cold outside the battered station.

Because he had looked out the window and seen what was coming.

All along the sloping ground down to the village, shapes were moving. Schweitzer counted at least three fire teams skirting the edges of the houses, fanning out, covering the approach from all angles. They weren't taking any chances now. They knew that their ambush on the plane had failed, and they were coming to finish the job.

'That's a lot of firepower,' Nalren said, taking a knee. 'Fitzgerald—'

'I've got him, Master Corporal,' Fitzgerald said, tugging on Desmarais' elbow and motioning him toward Mankiller's office.

Desmarais looked at Ghaznavi, back up at Nalren. 'Stand down. We're going to need every hand in the fight.'

'Sir, that's not—' Nalren began.

'Up for discussion,' Desmarais finished for her.

Nalren gritted her teeth. 'Montclair, take the opposite flank. Don't let them get around us.'

Montclair nodded and leapt out through the mangled window, cutting across the front of the building and heading out in the opposite direction to Reeves and Sharon. She looked a bit steadier on her feet, but not by much.

Mankiller knelt at Nalren's side. 'I got bear traps between those two trailers there.' She pointed. 'I had some over there' – she pointed again – 'but they got sprung the last time they came for us.' She gestured toward the track. The snow there was churned, stained black and red. Close to the station, the barricade of trucks was badly holed, the vehicles turned on their sides, burned out and scattered. 'We're open here, you can see.'

'That barricade wouldn't stop them for long,' Nalren said, 'even if it was brand-new.'

'Well, it ain't gonna stop 'em at all right now.' Mankiller sounded irritated. 'I need you to cover me while I get a scrape set up there.'

'Wilma Plante!' A voice echoed through the freezing air. Not the tinny buzz of electronic amplification but the natural yell of a creature with superhuman lungs. Schweitzer could see the skin on Calmut's arms prickle into gooseflesh.

'It doesn't need to be this way!' the Director boomed. 'There's been too much bloodshed already and there'll be more. We don't want to hurt you. We just want to speak with your grandfather, then we'll be on our way. No one else has to die! Just come out, alone and unarmed. Don't be selfish! Do it for your people.'

Calmut's thin hand clamped on Mankiller's forearm, so quick that she flinched, whipping her head toward him. 'You ain't goin' out there, Sheriff. No way.'

'He's right,' Schweitzer answered. 'It'll end worse for everyone. I promise.'

He could see the conflict behind Mankiller's eyes, the love for her people as she looked at them shaking their heads. 'Listen to Ollie,' one of them said.

'You stay right here, boss,' said another.

'Yeah.' Mankiller finally choked out the words, clearly overcome. 'Guess I'll stick.'

'We can put Schweitzer there.' Nalren pointed to the gap in the barricade, her voice trembling only slightly now. 'He's the closest thing we've got to armor out here.'

'Nope,' Schweitzer said, making his way to the door. 'You're just going to have to cover her.'

'Where are you going?' Ghaznavi asked.

'High ground,' Schweitzer said. 'I need to see the battlefield.'

'This is the highest ground there is,' Mankiller said. 'You don't need to see the battlefield. You're in it.' She pointed out the shattered window. 'The enemy is right there.'

'The living enemy, sure,' Schweitzer said. 'The Golds won't be mixed up with them. They usually just go for whatever beating heart is closest, so the Cell will want to make sure it's yours. If the living are coming from there, then I bet the dead are coming from somewhere else.'

'Where?' Mankiller asked.

'I'll let you know when I find out,' Schweitzer said. 'Good luck.'

He turned and went out the door, ignoring Ghaznavi's calls for him to wait. Whatever she thought she knew about the Golds, she wasn't prepared to make the deck plate-level decisions on deploying troops. She would find out what she was up against soon enough.

'At least take a gun!' Ghaznavi shouted after him.

'Got one,' Schweitzer said without turning, holding up Nalren's .45.

'That's mine!' Nalren shouted after him.

'Sue me!' Schweitzer shouted back as he edged through the line of trucks.

He paused, surveying the ground. The station was perched on a slight rise, but the town itself was situated in a small bowl, the frozen ground surrounded by gently sloping hills thickly clustered with scrub pine. The lakeshore was to their rear. The low buildings sprawled, creating a series of broad lanes choked with piled snow and abandoned vehicles. It was a shooting gallery, the worst ground Schweitzer had seen in a long time. If there were time, he would move the people to a more defensible position, but there wasn't. He could see the heat signatures of the Cell's forces spreading out along the town's perimeter, beginning to move into the lanes leading toward the municipal center. Schweitzer didn't have time to get a count, but there were a lot of them.

The Golds. He scanned the second stories of the structures, looking for a hide-site where he could get a view from above. The buildings were disappointingly low. The best candidate was what looked like the town's main government building, which was only barely taller than the town's lone tavern. If only there were a . . .

There was. To his right, Schweitzer could see a blue-trimmed chapel, the steeple shorn of its cross by the winter wind a long time before. Like everything else in Fort Resolution, it was a small affair, but it was taller than the surrounding trees at least, and that was something.

Schweitzer leapt easily up onto the station's roof, ignoring the shouts from the defenders at the sound of his boots striking the shingles. He pushed off, leaping the distance to the second story of the tavern, and then again to a house nearby. Two more jumps got him onto the chapel's steeply sloping roof, so slick with frost that he scrambled for a moment before finally pushing off again and grabbing hold of the gutter below the spire. He let his momentum carry him through the wooden slats that covered the window. The resulting crash was louder than he liked, but there was nothing for it. Hopefully, the human operators were too far and too focused to pay much attention, but it might alert any Golds nearby.

He saw them as soon as he righted himself and turned to look out the hole he had made.

There were five, spread out in a delta like a flock of migrating geese. They loped along the gentle slope that made its way up to the lakeshore, a stumbling half run that was doubtless faster than it looked. They were uniformly naked, as all Golds were, the only interruption in the bleached color of their skin made by the purple of stitched scars and the flashes of metal where their reinforcing cables breached the skin. Schweitzer almost let his eyes pass over them, trying to pick out the path they would take through the buildings to reach the station. It amazed him to think that the sight of magically animated corpses could have become mundane, but . . .

Something different.

At the delta's apex, the leading Gold was black.

Schweitzer tightened his hands on the shattered remnants of the sill, leaned forward, focused.

Not black. The figure was clothed. A cheap black suit. Its head was partially covered in a filthy white hood ripped across the face.

As Schweitzer watched, the leader's leg twitched and it stumbled. Something was wrong with its hip. That wasn't remarkable for a Gold that had seen some service. Schweitzer himself had put more than a few dings in them himself. But what was remarkable was that the rest of the creatures stopped with it, slowed their pace to keep formation to its rear.

Golds, subordinating themselves to something other than bloodlust. They were still functioning like animals, but now they appeared to be *pack* animals. That Gold out front must be impressive, indeed. This had to be the famous Director. The one Eldredge had warned him of, the one Mankiller had spoken to. The undead thing that seemed to have conquered its animal lusts every bit as much as Schweitzer had.

Later. Focus. It was a simple-enough plan of attack: occupy the defenders with the living troops making their frontal assault, and run the real threat right up their backside. If they were going to hold out for even a short time, Schweitzer would have to stop the Gold force here.

Fortunately, the Director's ostentation had given him a target. If the Golds were playing follow-the-leader, then he would simply have to stop that leader.

Schweitzer sighted in the .45, bracing it in the crook of his elbow. He targeted the Director's flexing knee, rising and falling as he ran.

The Director was inhumanly fast, and his lurching gait made it difficult to lead the shot, predict where the round would fall once Schweitzer pulled the trigger. The Director turned and the delta turned with him, making their way up a narrowing track between a pair of winterized trailers. The Director slowed as he drew close to the junction, no doubt careful of whatever traps Mankiller and her people might have laid for him.

The leg rose and fell more slowly now. It wasn't going to get any better than this.

Schweitzer drilled his focus down, shutting out all else, the wind and the cold and the shadowed closeness of the steeple's interior, until the world was reduced to the pinpoint of the pistol's front sight post, hovering over the distant blurred dot that Schweitzer hoped was the Director's knee.

The Director stepped forward, and Schweitzer pulled the trigger.

Bang.

Schweitzer knew the shot was perfect before the round even left the barrel. It was a feat of marksmanship he would never have achieved in life and would likely never equal even in death. He had accounted for everything, the tremor of the muzzle, the strength of the wind, the arcing velocity attenuating as the round sped toward the target. By all rights, it should have drilled a half-inch hole through the Director's knee, hopefully crippling him, at least until he could get to a technician for repairs.

But it didn't.

As soon as the shot broke, the Director leapt, a long, lunging step that brought the target up and out of the way at the perfect instant. His half-hooded head snapped in the direction of the steeple, and Schweitzer saw the ragged mouth spread in a grimace. The cheek had been flayed open, showing mandible and rows of yellow teeth.

'Jim!' The Director shouted, turned, leapt.

It was a jump of astonishing power, even for a Gold.

The Director cleared the trailer and the building beyond it, pausing only to push off the roof hard enough to carry him in a soaring arc up and over the road toward the chapel where Schweitzer crouched.

The rest of the Golds, released from their master's thrall, held position, confused by the sudden absence of their leader. The Director had clearly been trying to impress some semblance of organization on them, and if he was willing to let it lapse, it could only be because he didn't expect to be gone for long.

Schweitzer would have to prove him wrong.

He sighted in and fired again, this time aiming for the center of the shredded hood. Again, the Director dodged the shot, ducking his head, sending his body spinning. He fell earthward, and for a moment, Schweitzer thought he would miss the chapel entirely, faceplant in the snow-covered parking lanes beneath it.

But the Director had planned his trajectory perfectly and, at the last moment, snaked out a long-fingered hand to grasp the gutter at the edge of the chapel roof. The force of his descent ripped it away from the building, sent it sliding down to the ground, but not before it gave the Director the leverage he needed to throw himself upward. He landed below the steeple, his feet touching down on the frozen, steeply angled shingles. His body shuddered as it found its center of gravity.

At last, he slowly straightened. 'Hello, Jim.'

The voice was crooning, the hiss-whisper that Schweitzer had come to associate with the dead's attempts at speech. But it was hauntingly familiar all the same.

'Get off my roof,' Schweitzer said. 'This is a church, for Christ's sake.'

'You're the one who broke the window. Jim, this is going to end very, very badly for you. For Patrick, too. I hate to sound like the villain in a science-fiction film, but you're far better off working with me than against me.'

'No, thanks. You're fucking ugly.'

'So are you. We're precisely the same brand of ugly, in fact. Why the hell would you help these people?' He waved an arm in the direction of the station. 'That's over for you, Jim. Surely you know that.'

'Call me an idealist.'

'You know what your problem is? You haven't been dead long enough. You're still clinging to the trappings of life. I was the same way at first. You let it go after a while.'

'Then why are you trying so hard to get in a living body? You must miss it something fierce.'

'Not even a little bit. Dying is the best thing that ever happened to me. You, too.'

'You're not going to think it's so great after I rip your fucking arms off.'

'Last chance, Jim. My eyes are as silver as yours. We're not like the Golds. Magic made them to hunger and kill. It made us to rule.'

'Jesus. Can you be a little more dramatic? Why don't you just clench a fist and say, "Jim, I am your father"?'

'I'll do even better.' The Director reached up, tugged the filthy, shredded remnants of his hood away. 'Jim, I am your brother.'

Chapter Thirteen
All in the Family

The world vanished. Schweitzer's vision shrank to a tunnel every bit as tight as when he'd finally reached the end of the rose-petal road, found his wife alive and well and awaiting him.

Except now it wasn't his wife, it was his brother, and he wasn't alive.

Whatever had killed Peter had mangled his face badly. The gray skin had been sewn back together, a jigsaw puzzle of thin black stitching that couldn't quite reconstruct his old features. The stretched skin helped the scars a bit but not enough to hide the fact that Peter had been badly burned as well. *Oh, God, Pete. You must have died horribly.*

But it was his brother. There could be no mistake. Peter's misaligned eyes burned solid silver.

Schweitzer's training screamed at him to stop talking, stop posturing, to get into the fight and get it over. His enemy was downhill from him, balanced precariously on an icy roof ledge. He wouldn't get better ground than this.

But Schweitzer the SEAL was bludgeoned into silence by Schweitzer the kid brother, looking at Peter for the first time since he'd seen the scrolling banner across his television screen: FOUR SEALS CAUGHT IN FIREFIGHT. SURROUNDED BY INSURGENTS.

Schweitzer could imagine the Cell's finders combing through the battlefield, carting off the bodies or maybe spiriting them out of the morgue. More grist for the magical mill. They worked exclusively with dead special operators, so of course they would have wanted Peter.

'Sorry you had to find out this way, little brother,' Peter said. 'There was a while there where I thought about coming to find you. But I quickly learned that was useless. Because I was in the next phase already. I was beyond the SEALs, and I figured if you had what it took to join me here, then it would happen in its own time.'

Attack, Schweitzer's mind screamed. *Enough talking. Get on him.*

But his mouth moved of its own accord. 'Your eyes are silver. You're supposed to be good.'

Peter laughed, a short, barking sound. 'I am good. I'm the best there is. Haven't you figured it out yet? It just means that you won, that your soul was stronger than the one they paired you with. That kind of strength is almost singular. I thought it was unique to me before you came along. I guess it runs in the family, eh?'

'Why . . . why didn't you come to me . . . Even when I was in the Cell . . .'

'Oh, I watched you, little brother. Believe me, I watched you. There were more than a few times that I almost considered reaching out to you, but I needed to be sure that you had the stuff to hang in there. I didn't want to invest the time and energy in another Gold.'

The thought kindled anger and grief in equal measure. His brother, the man whose example had pulled him into the SEALs. Peter had always believed in him. That Peter would think he would become a Gold . . . but he nearly had become a Gold. He remembered his own body shrinking in his vision as Ninip's corrupting influence struck down a child and simultaneously pushed Schweitzer out to tumble through the void.

But he had clawed his way back. Tooth and nail, inch by inch, until he had won. For Sarah. For Patrick.

'By the time you did win out, you were already on the run,' Peter said. 'I was glad, of course, but you know that line from the movies. "There can be only one". I'm not going to compete with you to run my organization.'

'Jesus, Pete. I wouldn't have competed with you.'

'No, I suppose not, but neither would you have allowed me to expand it to the extent I must. The age of the living is over, Jim. Welcome to the dawn of the dead. There's a place in it for you if you want it.'

'Why?' Schweitzer asked. 'Christ, Pete. There's nothing for us. We can't eat; we can't love. All we can do is protect the things that used to matter to us.'

Peter shook his head. 'You never got it, little brother, not like you needed to. It was never about the pin. It was never about the brotherhood. It was about being the best. It was about fulfilling our warrior legacy, Jim. That's the thing you never understood. You bought the package they sold you in basic. God, country, family. Very pretty stuff, the same brand of BS they've carted out since the beginning of history to entice men to go to war.'

'It meant something to me, Pete. I thought it meant something to you, too.'

'Oh, cut the crap, Jim. If that's why you did it, then why be a SEAL? You could have been a corpsman or a boatswain's mate or an aircraft mechanic and still got your fill of God, country, and family. God doesn't exist, Jim. Maybe dying and coming back to life underscored that for you? The SEALs are the elite. You don't suck sand and bleed salt for as long as we did for ideals, Jim. You do it because it is the pinnacle.

'And what happens when you reach the pinnacle? How do you rise higher? I was a motherfucking god of war, little brother. There wasn't a man alive who could beat me.'

'Christ, Pete. Someone did beat you. They fucking killed you.'

'No!' In an instant, Schweitzer's brother vanished, and he was the Director, a Gold in every fiber of his being save the silver flames burning in his eye sockets. His body tensed, poised to strike. His rent cheek curled back, showing the gray flexion of his mandible. 'A fucking RPG killed me, fired by a coward from cover while I was pinned down by an overwhelming force. Alexander the Great was almost killed at Granicus! It was a matter of a quarter inch. Any man can die, Jim. It doesn't mean you lost. Look at me! Do you think it's a coincidence that even death couldn't stop me? Do you think it's random that I'm standing here now?'

Shots. Ranging fire from the station. If Schweitzer was going to help them, he needed to stop talking and get in the fight. But he couldn't move; he was transfixed by the tunnel-focus, pushing out everything but his brother's face, gray and ragged, and still the thing he had longed to see for all these years.

'You said you didn't believe in ideals, in metaphysical bullshit,' Schweitzer said. 'Listen to you now. Of course it's random. You were a SEAL and the Cell uses SEALs. You were just the body they found. If you'd died farther afield or at a different time, you'd just be worm food.'

Peter barked, an animal snarl. His jaw flexed, his tongue swelling. His ragged suit rippled as his bone spines poked through his skin. 'You don't get it. That shit is not random. It is destiny. I could have died in a pit in Chicago and this would still have found me. I don't expect you to understand it, and I don't expect to know exactly how it happened in this lifetime, but the truth is this: I knew from the day I was born that I was going to be the greatest warrior-king the world had ever known. I knew it from my first fight in school. I knew it when I enlisted, and I knew it when I graduated BUD/S. I didn't know how it would happen, but I still knew it. And now that it has happened, I—'

Schweitzer struck.

He exploded out of the ragged window frame, his shoulders ripping fresh splinters from the wood. He plummeted down, spinning saw extended, trying to ignore the fact that the target was his brother, that after all these years of dreaming of their reunion, he would cut it short. *No. Peter is dead. This is a crazy, dead thing standing in his place.* Schweitzer aimed the saw for his brother's left thigh. He'd have to immobilize him first, then maybe . . .

Peter moved with almost-plastic elasticity and astonishing speed, even for one of his kind. He kicked his leg high, and Schweitzer's saw cut air. Peter brought his heel down on the back of Schweitzer's head. The blow hammered Schweitzer into the roof shingles hard enough to jar his bones, and then he was hurtling face-first over empty air.

'An A for effort, at least,' Peter said as Schweitzer fell.

The ground rushed up to meet him, and Schweitzer realized he'd been baited. The ranting, trembling anger had been a feint to draw him out of his superior position. Schweitzer had lost the bubble, the professional sangfroid that had carried him through countless battles. He extended an arm to catch his fall, send himself into a roll that would bring him to his feet. He reached out for the calm, for the distance, for the tunnel that shut out distraction.

The Golds were still in their delta, awaiting their master's return. They crouched forward, taking little scurrying steps before casting worried glances at the chapel, like dogs commanded to stay when food is near.

Schweitzer got to his feet, spun, raising the buzz saw for the attack he knew must be coming. There was nothing, only the chapel's whitewashed wall, the remnants of the torn gutter hanging from it like a corpse-limb.

He heard the impact of Peter's feet behind him an instant later, and was turning to face his brother when the blow landed. Peter had been aiming for his back, but the kick caught Schweitzer's side. He went flying, feeling his ribs flexing, sailing through the air until he smashed into the chapel's side hard enough to splinter the wood. He slid to the ground, got to his feet, buzz saw spinning in front of him.

Peter glanced at the crouching Golds. 'I trained them a little too well,' he mused. Gunfire was chattering in the distance now. 'I got obedience but sapped all initiative. I'll fix it in post, I guess. I have the opposite problem with you. You going to heel, little brother? Or are you going to join Sarah in the great beyond? I suppose you'd be happier that way, souls mingling and all that foolishness.'

Schweitzer lunged, a diagonal slash with the saw that would have unseamed his brother from shoulder to crotch. But before he even completed the motion, he knew it was telegraphed, that distraction made him clumsy. Peter stepped into the blow, effortlessly catching Schweitzer's mechanical arm at shoulder and elbow, yanking it down as he brought his knee up. The limb groaned, creaked, and finally splintered, sparking as the piezoelectric leads snapped. The saw went askew in its forks, tines whining against the adjacent metal, spinning slowly down.

'I must say,' Peter said, releasing the arm and pushing Schweitzer back. 'You have a tough time hanging on to your right arm.'

Schweitzer staggered backward, broken arm hanging from his shoulder, little more than a dragging weight now, the saw canted and still in its housing. Peter took a step toward him. His shredded cheek made his grin lopsided and impossibly wide. 'I get that you don't buy the whole destiny argument, but you have to admit that this is playing out like a movie. Maybe "destiny" is just a word we plaster over events to give them more meaning. I get it. But this is just too . . . dramatic to be coincidence. Maybe dying has made me superstitious.'

The dull *whump* of an explosion sounded in the distance, and Peter glanced toward the station before looking back to Schweitzer. 'Well, that can't be good. Guess I'd better finish this and get in the fight. So long, little brother.'

He darted forward so quickly that Schweitzer barely had time to raise an arm before Peter struck. But it was the broken arm, and Peter slapped it aside with enough force to turn Schweitzer away from him. Peter followed the movement with fluid grace, throwing a shoulder into Schweitzer's back, slamming him into the chapel wall.

Schweitzer lashed out with his good arm, aiming his elbow at Peter's face. Peter caught the blow easily, yanking Schweitzer's arm down, pinning it behind his back. He grabbed Schweitzer's good arm and his shoulder, pulling back so hard that Schweitzer's chest bowed. Schweitzer strained against his brother's grip, feeling the pressure gather in his ribs and spine. He felt his dead muscles clench, a low groan rising in his throat as he fought against Peter's grip. It was useless. His brother's strength was terrible, as great compared to Schweitzer's as Schweitzer's was to a living man's. 'In death as in life,' Peter whispered over Schweitzer's shoulder, 'always just a little bit ahead.'

Peter slammed his knee into the base of Schweitzer's spine. The blow was perfectly targeted, focused on the gap between the vertebrae. Schweitzer felt his spine flex, the first tiny cracks opening in the magically reinforced bone. Schweitzer tried to twist toward his brother, but Peter's knee was already coming up again and again. Schweitzer's spine shuddered, and he knew that it would only take another blow or two to sever it. He kicked out, planted his feet on the wall, walked upward.

Pete laughed. 'Nice! Good initiative! Bad judgment, though.' He brought his knee up another time, and Schweitzer realized his error. The new position left his spine as flat as a table, a perfect ninety-degree angle from his brother's knee.

He felt his spine shear as the blow impacted. The lumbar vertebrae exploded, tearing away from one another, the fragments migrating a few inches through the surrounding flesh before coming to rest. Schweitzer felt his legs go slack as the stability imparted by his upper torso was ripped away.

But his brother didn't stop; the knee came up again and again into the weakened spine, and each blow shivered more bone, the column coming apart, the soft flesh insufficient to the task of keeping it together. Pete grunted in satisfaction and stepped backward, dropping Schweitzer's arms at last.

Schweitzer tried to keep his feet beneath him, to stay upright, to turn and face the threat. Instead, he pooled like a discarded sheet, folding over backward on himself. His shoulders rested on his heels, his body literally broken in half. Still he fought, struggling to get his arms underneath him, to push himself upright. But his back was a piece of loose rubber, the network of muscles without anchor. Even his magically enhanced strength was useless as he flailed like an astronaut in zero gravity, just as likely to slide in the wrong direction as the right one.

Peter put a foot on Schweitzer's shoulder, pinning it in place. Schweitzer could see the pack of Golds clustering about him, waiting for their master's command. 'Stop wriggling,' Peter said. 'This is enough work as it is.'

But Schweitzer didn't stop struggling. Ghaznavi and Desmarais and Mankiller might not be his son, but they were decent people, striving toward the same goal, to rid the world of the threat of the Cell. Between his brother and the Golds, he couldn't see them standing much of a chance. Six operators, no matter how skilled, were still just living people.

Peter increased the pressure on Schweitzer's shoulder, reached down, gripping his chin. 'I've spent a lot of time trying to figure out the threshold at which the body is destroyed enough to free the soul to return to the storm. It's difficult to proceed scientifically, since the Golds aren't exactly open to being interviewed and my Summoners are needed for other tasks. You cost me Dadou, Jim. I wouldn't even be in this godforsaken wilderness if it weren't for you. Did you ever think of that?'

Schweitzer's only answer was a strained groan.

'I've been working on a theory that it has something to do with the eyes. They're the only visible evidence, you know? The only thing about us that's immediately and evidently magic. I'd been planning to experiment on Golds, you know, crushing their heads, but they've been too precious to let go lately. So, let's start with you. One last service you can perform. Eh, little brother? For family.'

He moved his hands to Schweitzer's temples, began to squeeze. Schweitzer clamped his hand on his brother's wrist, desperately attempting to pry it away, but without the anchor of his spine, it was so much slack rope. His brother's muscle was as unyielding as iron. The world began to bow and he felt his skull flex.

A sharp bang sounded, followed by a roaring whoosh. Schweitzer heard the pattering of feet on snow, and the pressure on his skull suddenly eased.

He tried to roll over onto his back, but his newly jellied back refused to support the motion, and he merely succeeded in shifting his torso far enough to one side to enable him to see the open ground. Two of the Golds were twitching ruins, bodies excavated as if they'd swallowed dynamite. The remaining three had been blown clear by the blast, were scrambling to their feet. Schweitzer caught a whiff of burned peroxide, the molten smell of fused glass. He caught a glance of dark boots, thick snow pants, the dangling muzzle of a high-powered Alaskan rifle.

Peter snarled. 'You brave little shit.' He spun, lunged for Schweitzer's rescuer.

'You all fuck off back home,' Mankiller said. Schweitzer heard liquid sloshing against glass as she threw another of her homemade TATP bombs. The Director dove aside, and the remaining Golds followed suit, desperate to be beside their leader and smart enough to know that there would be nothing gained by charging into the explosion.

The unstable explosive detonated barely after it left Mankiller's hand, and Schweitzer could see the shock wave blow her hood back, send the skin on her face rippling, forcing her mouth into a flapping grin. Powdered glass sprayed her face, embedding in her parka, her gloves, her skin.

Mankiller didn't flinch. She did nothing more than squint, as if high-brisance explosions were something she experienced every day. She swept a hand up, pointed a slender black tube at Peter. Schweitzer could smell the gasoline, saw the flashing silver of the tank over her shoulder. He didn't even bother to roll aside. He was as flat to the ground as he could get.

Mankiller thumbed the trigger and the tube spat fire. Peter rolled aside, but he was moving against the momentum of his last dodge, and the fire washed over him, the jellied gasoline adhering to the fabric of his cheap suit, to the pale surface of his exposed skin. He went up like a torch, howling and beating at himself.

Satisfied, Mankiller transitioned to the Alaskan, dropping the flamethrower nozzle and raising the rifle to her shoulder. She pulled the trigger and worked the bolt with the rapid precision of a competition target shooter, sending round after round into Peter's burning silhouette. Bullets were of scarce use against the undead, but each high-powered round drove Schweitzer's brother back a step, opened the distance between them a little wider.

Peter screamed, a high, plaintive mewling like a cat with a broken tail. At last, Mankiller finished the rounds in the magazine tube, and the moment's respite allowed Peter to turn, free from the pounding hail of bullets, and crouch to charge his enemy. Mankiller seemed to have anticipated the move, and she dropped the Alaskan to hang in its sling, picking up the flamethrower again. 'Come on, *yedáísåine*. I can do this all day.'

Peter swatted tentatively at the flames, but he had to know the jellied emulsifier would never permit them to be extinguished that way. As Schweitzer watched, the decision hung on a knife's edge. He could see the fabric of his brother's ragged suit quickly vanishing into greasy smoke, the skin beneath already beginning to blister. Peter's silver eyes still blazed, clearly visible through the surrounding peaks of orange flame. Mankiller raised the flamethrower's nozzle and his brother flinched away. He might be able to extinguish the current burning, but if he gambled a second dousing and lost, there wouldn't be enough of him left to fill a coffee can.

Schweitzer watched his brother's eyes, and Mankiller leveled the flamethrower's nozzle, unwilling to risk a shot at this range, waiting for her target to close. 'Come on,' she whispered.

But Peter didn't come on. He turned, and he ran, and the last of the Golds followed him, flying across the packed snow of the trail churned to gray slush by the force of their exertions. Schweitzer watched them until they turned the corner of a building and vanished from sight.

Mankiller moved forward until she was standing astride Schweitzer, the muzzle of the flamethrower hovering over his head. He could smell the emulsifier, see the blue pilot light in the recesses of the metal tip. 'Don't drip any of that shit on me.'

Mankiller laughed. 'That sure don' sound like a thank-you.'

Schweitzer bit back anger. How could she laugh now? How could she smile and banter when his own brother had risen from the dead to snap him in half? Sarah's betrayal with Steve had stung, but it was blunted by the knowledge that she had only done it because she had believed Schweitzer to be dead. But Peter . . . *He's the Director*, Schweitzer thought, clamping down on the hollow, sick feeling in his spiritual stomach. *He calls the shots. He called your recovery, your creation, your oversight. He might even have been the one who ordered you taken down in the first place*. The thought made Schweitzer want to weep. That Peter, his idol, his aspiration, his friend, could have known all that Schweitzer had, all that he was, and killed him anyway. *Not just you*. Peter was ultimately responsible for Steve, and for Sarah. Rage warred with grief and confusion, and here was Mankiller, laughing and joking.

No. She didn't know. It wasn't her fault. She had saved him. Schweitzer swallowed his anger, forced himself to respond. 'Thanks, but the damage is already done. You're better off leaving me here. I can't move. I sure as hell can't fight anymore.' What was the point of going on, anyway? Steve had slept with Sarah, Sarah had looked at him with disgust, and now his own brother . . . *Lock it up. Stop feeling sorry for yourself. You have to carry on to save Patrick.*

Mankiller was oblivious to the war raging inside Schweitzer. 'Think I killed him?'

'I don't know' – Schweitzer forced the grief and rage down, spoke evenly – 'but I doubt it. That's the toughest sonofabitch I've ever tangled with, and I've tangled with a few. How's the fight going on your end?'

'We've reached somethin' of an understandin'. One of your Canadian pals is gutshot. I don' think he's gonna make it.'

She looked down at him, frowned. 'Christ, you're folded in half like a towel. That don' hurt?'

'Not really.'

'You sure do look funny.'

'At least I got snapped in half. What's your excuse?'

Mankiller laughed again, a short sound that quickly faded into a pensive look. 'We can't hold out, Jim. We've been real lucky so far, but they're gonna overrun us if they keep at it much longer.'

'I know. We need help and we need it soon.'

She grunted, scanning the horizon where Peter and the Golds had fled. 'They're gonna go get that fire out and then figure out a new angle. Let's get you back to the blockhouse and we'll come up with a plan.'

She began scrounging in the snow, kicking with the steel toes of her boots. She grunted again as she bent over, pulling on something.

'What are you doing?' Schweitzer asked.

'Stick.' Mankiller stood, brandishing a frozen length of branch. 'They're all over. Feels like I spend half my life takin' 'em away from kids in the summertime.'

'You're building a pyre? I don't think there's time.'

Mankiller looked at him like he was mad. 'A travois. Even broken in half, you're still too damn heavy for an old woman to carry. I'll have it put together in a sec.' She began stripping off her parka.

'Did you miss the part where I can't move? I'm no good to you now, Sheriff. I'll just slow you down. Leave me here. Get your ass back to the station. Your people need you.' *And I don't want to keep going. I don't want to exist in a world where everyone I care about betrays me. I just want it to stop. I've done my time, living and dead; let me go.*

But Mankiller was lashing her parka across two frozen branches, shivering in her base-layer shirt that fit so tightly it framed her flat breasts and powerful shoulders. She paused, looked at Schweitzer, reproach in her eyes. 'I dunno how you did things in the American Navy, but in the Canadian Army, we have a motto: "Leave no man behind".'

'I may have heard that Stateside.'

Mankiller nodded and turned back to the makeshift travois. 'Well, quit with the John Wayne bullshit and grab on to this.'

'Sheriff, it's "Leave no man behind". As in "living man". I'm dead.' His eyes were pleading. A part of him almost told her the truth, that he didn't want to be rescued, that he just wanted to be dead. Truly dead. Gone from this world at last. But there was a splinter in his soul that wouldn't give up, a strand of DNA that simply wasn't made to quit. It was the part of him he had always been most proud of. Now he hated it with every fiber of his being.

'You ain't dead,' Mankiller said, levering the travois under Schweitzer's shoulders. 'Dead people don' talk. I'm takin' you back to the station, and we'll figure out how to get you fixed.'

'Sheriff, my spine is shattered. Unless you've got an auto-body shop and a hospital back at your station, there's no fixing me. Don't be a fool.'

'You know, for a dead guy, you sure do argue a lot,' Mankiller said. 'You're wasting time. Grab hold and let's get you drug back. Sooner we get that done, the sooner I can get my parka back on. I'm freezin' my ass off out here.'

You will have to go on – his thoughts in Sarah's voice – *if only for a little while.*

Schweitzer swore and looped an arm over the taut fabric. His jellied back weakened his grip, but he was able to lock his elbow in place firmly enough to keep him from sliding off. Mankiller grunted, grasped the branches, and pulled. Schweitzer hadn't been light even when he was only flesh. Now much more of him was metal, and he knew he weighed as much as three men his size. Mankiller barely showed the strain, dragging the travois without complaint. Schweitzer could hear her labored breathing, her heart rate rising, but her face remained calm, even placid, her jaw muscles relaxed.

She rounded the corner of the Loon, and the line of burned-out trucks came into view. Schweitzer could see a body face-down in the snow, two others gathered around it. They looked up at the sound of the travois' scraping, raised weapons. Mankiller turned the corner and Schweitzer was turned away from the others, faced backward.

'Jesus, Ollie!' Mankiller shouted. 'It's me; don't shoot, for chrissakes.'

'Sorry, boss,' Calmut's voice came back. 'You okay?'

Mankiller ignored him. 'How is he?'

'He's gone.' Desmarais' voice. 'Bled out a few minutes after you left.'

'Sorry, Colonel,' Mankiller said. There was a pause, and Schweitzer could picture the tightened jaws of the Canadians, swallowing their grief and focusing on the task at hand. Everyone had lost someone; there was no point in making more of it than was necessary.

'Jesus, is that Schweitzer?' Ghaznavi's voice. Feet pounding in the snow. Schweitzer could hear a heavier tread alongside. Reeves, faithfully protecting his boss. 'Christ, Jim. Are you okay?'

Banter, Schweitzer thought. *Their morale is hammered as it is. Don't let them know how turned around you are.* 'I've still got my rapier wit,' Schweitzer answered, releasing the travois and slumping backward into the snow. 'But I would now classify me as "combat-ineffective".'

'Shit,' Reeves said. 'There goes our armor.'

'What happened?' Ghaznavi asked.

'The Director happened,' Schweitzer answered. *My brother happened.* He kept that information to himself. No sense in letting them know until he understood what the information meant. 'Guy's a fucking Cuisinart.'

'Shit,' Ghaznavi said. 'That's not good.'

'Listen to you whine,' Mankiller said. 'He didn' Cuisinart me, and I'm not a superpowered *?eyune* like you.'

'You fought him?' Ghaznavi couldn't keep the disbelief out of her voice.

'Yeah,' Mankiller said. 'Blew up a couple of 'em with TATP, then cooked him with the flamethrower. That oughta take some of the starch out of his collar.'

'It won't,' Schweitzer said. 'He'll be back, and he'll have reinforcements. How'd it go over here?'

'Fitzgerald's gone,' Desmarais said.

'Cort and Sharon haven't come back, but there was heavy fire off our left flank,' Reeves said. 'We were kind of hoping you'd be available to act as a QRF in case they're still pinned down.'

'Yeah,' Schweitzer said. 'That's not gonna happen.'

'We're holding, though,' Ghaznavi said. 'They haven't thrown any Golds at us so far.'

'No, they did,' Schweitzer said. 'There were a bunch of them inbound right on your six. I intercepted.'

Mankiller snorted. 'You got folded over backwards. *I* intercepted.'

'Two are down. The rest bugged out with the Director. They'll be back.'

Ghaznavi cursed. 'We can't hold against that many Golds. Not without your help.'

'Well, I'm not going to be much help,' Schweitzer said.

Ghaznavi and Desmarais looked at one another over Schweitzer's limp body. 'I can call for a QRF from Yellow-knife,' Desmarais finally said. 'It won't be JTF bodies. It'll be straight-up Canadian Special Ops Regiment operators. The 427 pilots who bring them here can be relied on to keep their mouths shut, but I can't vouch for the rest. This will probably leak.'

Ghaznavi swallowed. 'Hodges won't like that.' She looked around, taking in Mankiller and Schweitzer, Reeves kneeling at her side, eyes scanning the horizon. At last, she looked over her shoulder at Calmut and some of the other villagers, who were taking advantage of the lull in the fighting to scarf down granola bars.

'So, it's a good thing Hodges isn't here,' she finished. 'Call your QRF.'

'We can't call anyone,' Mankiller said. 'That's how Joe got killed, remember? It's jammed.'

'Not to speak ill of the dead,' Desmarais said, 'but your deputy was just one guy. A team of JTF operators will get the job done.'

'If there's a way, sir, we'll find it,' Nalren said.

Mankiller's face was stone, but Schweitzer could smell the bitter tang of cortisol and adrenaline pumping into her bloodstream. Desmarais' comment about Yakecan had pissed her off. 'What's your plan? Goin' after the jammer?'

'No,' Desmarais said. 'We just have to get outside its effective range.'

'What's that?' Mankiller asked.

'Tough to say,' Desmarais said. 'Depending on the model, could be a couple of klicks.'

'That's pretty vague,' Ghaznavi said. 'Is there some way to know for sure?'

'Yes, ma'am,' Nalren said. 'You make a call on the satphone. If it goes through, you know you're outside the jammer's effective range.'

'Cute,' Ghaznavi said.

'Ground's pretty damn flat out here,' Desmarais said. 'Any high points?'

'Nearest range is the Mackenzies,' Mankiller said. 'It's practically to the Yukon. You'll be outside jammer range long before you reach the foothills.'

'I don't need a mountain,' Desmarais said. 'Just want to get my ass a little higher off the ground is all. Anything closer?'

'You could climb a tree.' Mankiller smiled.

Nalren shot her a blank look and she snorted laughter. 'There's an old mine down the shore,' Mankiller said. 'Lead and zinc. Nothin' that should mess with a signal. Been shut down since before I was born, anyway.'

'The mine's on a high point?' Desmarais asked.

'No,' Mankiller said, 'but they got all the dirt they took out of it in a big pile, and all the drill cores stacked on top of that. Closest thing you get to hill around here. You should be able to hoof it in around thirty minutes. Less if you take a snowmobile.'

'We'll hoof it,' Nalren said. 'If we make it, it's going to be because we weren't discovered, not because we fought through.'

'You'll have to fight through,' Schweitzer said. 'There's no way they don't have pickets out, snipers on overwatch. The Golds will smell you. Their senses are sharper than a cat's. We can't spare you, anyway. They're going to be coming back.'

'We were doin' okay before you showed up,' Mankiller said. 'I guess we'll do okay until you get back. Besides, you might draw some of 'em off.'

Nalren and Desmarais looked sharply at her at this, and Mankiller smiled. 'Look, if we just hole up here, they'll shave us off by inches. Half a chance is better 'n no chance at all.'

'More like a quarter of a chance,' Ghaznavi said. 'A tenth.'

Mankiller shrugged. 'Is what it is. No sense in standin' around jaw-jackin' about it. We're gonna do this, we'd better get movin'. Sooner out is sooner back.'

'What's this "we" business?' Desmarais asked.

'You thinkin' you're gonna find it yourself?' Mankiller asked. 'I don' have a map handy and the Internet's down, so it's not like we can Google it.'

'Can't you just tell us where it is?' Desmarais asked. 'I don't like the idea of peeling you off this position. These people are counting on you. It'd be bad for morale.'

'Sure, I'll just write directions on the back of a napkin

and count on you not to get lost. Ollie'll do okay. He 'bout ran that damn town when Jake and I were out on collars or doin' escorts. Folks'll do what he tells 'em.'

'What'll he tell them?' Desmarais asked.

'Hole up, shoot at the bad guys. Don't get killed. Ain't rocket science.'

Desmarais glanced at Ghaznavi, who shrugged. 'We better make it count.'

'Okay, I'll send my people. If we're calling a CSOR QRF, we want Canadians on the line.'

Nalren nodded, the ghost of a smile lifting the corner of her mouth. 'I'll grab Montclair.'

Schweitzer watched the hope in their eyes, smelled it in the chemical composition of their blood. These were people with a purpose. They were frightened, but it didn't change the fact that they welcomed the challenge, were grateful for the chance to rise to it, to test themselves against the impossible. They were people anchored to the world, first by life and then by the people they loved. Schweitzer had neither. How he envied them.

'Don't waste time with anything other than ammo,' Desmarais said. 'You wind up overnighting this, and we're all dead anyway. I want you light and fast.'

Nalren's smile widened. 'You're staying here, sir. Let me run my op.'

'It's my op,' Mankiller said, shouldering the Alaskan and heading back toward the station. 'You can wave a flag and make speeches or treaties or whatever, but this is Dene country and always has been.'

'I'm Dene,' Nalren said.

'Good for you,' Mankiller said. 'I also happen to be the sheriff of this municipality and we're not in a declared war, so your army rank means exactly nothin' to me. You come along and bring that radio of yours, but you do what

I say when I say it. Not goin' to have time to argue if we get into a scrape out there, an' we probably will.'

Nalren opened her mouth to respond, shut it, glanced over at Desmarais, who shrugged.

'Good.' Mankiller grinned. 'That's settled. Let's get this show on the road.'

Chapter Fourteen

Signal

Mankiller got a box of .375 ammo out of the locker, dumping the loose bullets into the pockets of her parka before grabbing a radio off the rack in the dispatch room. Nalren gathered her go-bag and a few bottles of water from where she'd unloaded them while she defended the building. 'You got a bedroll? Anything we can use as a windbreak?'

'I thought your boss told you to travel light.'

'Good for him. He's not ground-pounding here; I am.'

'This ain't a campin' trip.'

Nalren shrugged. 'If you need it and don't have it, you'll never need it again.'

Montclair appeared in the doorway. 'Boss said we're going on a field trip?'

Mankiller took a long look at her. 'You look like a *dogrib.*'

'I am.' Montclair shrugged.

'Okay, well I guess the Indians are gonna save the day. We're gonna break out of here and try to get some comms to call for help.'

Montclair nodded. 'Sounds like a hundred-yard fight.'

'I hope not, but you're probably right. You all loaded up?'

Montclair knelt by her pack and began pulling out magazines. 'Nope. I'm shot dry.'

'You shouldn't miss so damn much,' Nalren said.

Montclair gave her the finger. 'Too many to engage properly. I just kept their heads down until they fucked off.'

'Well, they won't fuck off for long,' Mankiller said. 'You ready? Oh, hey. Guess it's all girls, too. Ain't that a thing?'

'Girls' night out.' Nalren smiled.

Mankiller smiled back. The thought cheered her, but she missed Yakecan like an ache in her side. 'Let's go.'

'Go where?' Calmut looked up from the tiny camp stove where he was heating up a can of beans.

'What the hell are you doin'?' Mankiller asked. 'They're gonna catch you stirrin' a pot when they come next.'

Calmut shrugged. 'Gotta eat, Sheriff. Fightin' don' change that.'

'Well, jus' make sure you turn that damn thing off before you get yourself shot,' Mankiller said. 'Nearly had the station burned down as it is.'

'Where you goin', boss?' Calmut repeated.

'Gonna go get us some help. You're in charge 'til I get back.'

Calmut looked pale; his jaw worked. 'Boss . . .'

'Ollie, are you my goddamn deputy, or aren't you?'

'You know I am, boss, it's jus'—'

'No "just". Joe's out of the fight, and somebody's gotta show 'em the way to the old mine so we can hopefully get high up enough to get a signal.'

'I can do it.' Calmut swallowed, the corners of his mouth turned down. He looked scared to death.

'No.' Mankiller shook her head. 'I need you here. Folks trust you and they'll do what you say. I'm better out on the range, anyway.' The truth was that she knew Calmut was no fighter, and didn't trust him to keep his cool if they came across any of those dead things. At least here, he could shelter in place, and maybe she'd get lucky and they'd be back before the enemy regrouped and came at them again.

Calmut made to speak and Mankiller silenced him with a look. 'That's my final word on it, Ollie. We'll be back as quick as we can.'

She signaled to Nalren, and the JTF2 operators followed her out without a second glance at Calmut. The truth was that Mankiller had no idea whether or not he'd be okay, but she'd been a warfighter and a cop long enough to know that hesitation was almost as bad as the wrong move nine times out of ten. She'd made the decision to help these folks get their satphone to the top of the mine, and wavering over that decision wouldn't make Calmut any stronger than he was. Best to get it done as quickly as possible.

She led them out the back of the town, down along the twisting track toward the boathouses that lined the lakeshore. She could see the chapel steeple off to her left, the louvered wooden slats smashed and the roof gutter dangling like a broken limb.

'This is where Schweitzer got his ass kicked,' Nalren said.

'Yeah, a few feet that way. They were fightin' on the roof.'

'Well, didn't you say you torched the Director to get Schweitzer out of there?'

'That's right; he ran off. He was burnin' pretty good, I guess.'

'But Schweitzer said he didn't think you . . . killed him, and he had two Golds with him to boot.'

'You got a point?'

'Why the hell are you leading us right into that? Might be more fight than we want to take on right now.'

Mankiller swallowed her irritation. Nalren wasn't Joe Yakecan, who'd learned to trust her instincts over the years. If she wanted Nalren's trust, she'd have to earn it. Mankiller pointed to the lakeshore in the distance. 'It's wide open. We can pretty much see for miles. If they had any surprises waitin', we'd be wise to 'em by now. We go out of town by the tree line, we could get zapped before we even know they've sighted us. I figure the Director went back to his camp to lick his wounds. I guess I could be wrong, but it's a risk either way. We stick close to the shore for as long as we can, then we sprint for the mine once we're well clear of town. I'm hopin' whatever cordon they got goin' on, they ain't closed it yet. Besides, this is the most direct route.'

Nalren looked like she would protest, and Mankiller turned away before she could speak, setting a good pace along the shoreline. The gentle padding of the soldiers' boots told her they were following. They crouched low, keeping close to the sparse cover, the drifting bergs of ice dappling them with shadow. Still, Mankiller knew how painfully exposed they were, felt as if she were a single black dot on a field of stark white, practically visible from space. Funny. She'd been a fighter all her life and normally painfully conscious of cover, lanes of fire, angles of attack. But not here. Never at home, where she was the law, where she knew everyone by name, where there practically were no secrets. She'd never needed cover in Fort Resolution before, and the effect of suddenly having to worry about it was jarring.

Eventually, Mankiller angled them away from the shore, cutting across the cracked surface of the narrow road and out into the frozen scrub growth beyond. Their footsteps fell louder there, and Mankiller winced with each crackle of breaking ice and branches, but there was nothing for it. This was the way to the mine. She tried to keep her eyes on the horizon, watching for movement. The sound of her own steps and the rising fear in her gut made it impossible to concentrate. The uneven terrain made her head bob with each step, turning every rock into a crouching enemy, every branch into the muzzle of a gun. After a while, she gave up on trying to keep watch and just concentrated on moving forward as quickly and quietly as she could. Nalren and Montclair were the hard operators; they'd keep her covered if it came to a firefight.

At last, the scrub gave way to a slight rise carpeted by frozen gravel. Mankiller spotted the rotted remains of railroad ties alternating with the rusted metal of the cart tracks. She took a knee behind the remains of an ancient collapsed cabin, creosote-stained wood studded with pitted nailheads.

'This is it?' Nalren asked. 'I don't see anything.'

'It's a little ways that way,' Mankiller said, pointing at a sizeable stack of thick metal beams jumbled haphazardly atop a huge pile of frozen dirt. 'See it?'

'That's barely a hill,' Nalren said.

'Best I can do. You don' like it, you can ask for the Army to bring one when you call 'em in.'

Nalren thumbed the button on her phone and shook her head. 'Nothing. Let's hope the extra height makes the difference.'

'What about that?' Montclair asked, pointing at a gray-brown wooden tower leaning threateningly to one side, its cross-braced timbers smashed in some places, dry-rotted in others. At its peak stood a cylindrical water tank with a conical slate roof that was mostly staved in; the shattered tiles were littered all around its base.

'What about it?' Mankiller asked.

'Well, it just looks higher than that hill,' Montclair said.

'I guess it is,' Mankiller said, 'but you're a damn fool if you climb it. That thing loses more pieces of itself every year. I been askin' the fed to come take it down for longer 'n I can remember.'

'Well, desperate times,' Nalren said.

'Look,' Mankiller said, 'I'll be honest with you ladies. I'm damn surprised we ain't got shot full of holes jus' gettin' out here. You try to climb that, and the whole thing comes down, people are gonna hear it for miles.'

Nalren and Montclair exchanged a look that Mankiller didn't like at all.

'How far you say we've gone?' Montclair asked.

Nalren shrugged. 'Two klicks?' Montclair offered. 'Pretty damn far.'

'How come nobody come after us?' Mankiller asked. 'Nobody's shot at us. I can't believe we got out that easy.'

'I can,' Nalren said. 'How big's town? Five hundred square kilometers?'

'Less than that,' Mankiller said.

'But not much less,' Nalren said. 'You'd need a battalion to cordon that completely. They don't have enough people.'

'You don't know how many people they have,' Mankiller said.

'Ever try to hide a battalion?' Nalren asked. 'Well, I have. It's fucking impossible. That many people make too much noise, kick up too much dust. Hell, you'd know something was up just by the smell of that many farts. No, they're understrength. Might be we just slipped through.'

'Well, I guess we're finally catchin' a break,' Mankiller said. 'Let's get this done and get back before our luck changes.'

She was loath to leave the shelter of the ruined cabin, return to the agoraphobic dread of moving across the open ground, but the hill of excavated dirt and piled drill cores beckoned, and with it, a chance that they might actually live through this. Mankiller swallowed and rolled out, leading with the Alaskan's barrel, advancing at a crouch. She heard the crunch of boots on snow that meant the soldiers were falling in behind her.

Then the footsteps abruptly stopped, and Mankiller heard the creaking of Nalren's plastic kneepad as it touched down on the snow. She turned toward the master corporal. 'What's . . .'

But Nalren's eyes were fixed past her on the hill in the distance. Montclair had rolled smoothly back behind the cover of the ruined cabin, was sighting down her carbine over Nalren's shoulder.

Mankiller took a knee at Nalren's side, sighted down the Alaskan's scope. Even magnified and in the daylight, the hill was a mass of crosshatched shadows, the irregular angles of the broken drill cores overlapping with the piled stone, frozen roots, and chunked mud. If there was something up there, she was going to have a hell of a time picking it out. She was painfully conscious of the lack of cover, the sky feeling much too big above her, the plain much too wide. She itched to follow Montclair behind the cabin's ruins, but she forced herself to stay on the rifle scope. Taking cover was useless if you didn't know where the threat was coming from.

Her heart pounded as she squinted into the scope. She'd drawn a bead on bad guys before and by now was well familiar with the changes it wrought in her body – the clenching in her stomach, the sweat on her palms, the dulling of her fine motor skills. Once, after a firefight outside Kabul, it had taken her a full minute to figure out how to get the Humvee door open.

But this was a terror of an entirely different stripe. It might be a person awaiting her atop that hill, someone who breathed and bled like she did, someone who was probably feeling that same clenching, that same sweat, the same pounding heart and shortness of breath. But it also might be something else. Something made of *inkoze*. Something like what her grandfather made, only darker, crueler. Something that crawled out of a grave, its bones lengthened, sharpened.

This new terror eroded her warrior's sangfroid. It made it hard to concentrate, to pick movement out from the jumble of earth and metal that was their objective. That could be a man's shoulder, or maybe it was just a rock . . .

Bang.

Mankiller saw the muzzle flash in her peripheral vision, outside the scope's tunnel, but definitely on the hill. She felt a burning in her thigh, and knew immediately that she was extremely lucky. She'd been shot before, a stray low-powered .22 round from a child's hunting rifle. That had penetrated her abdomen and by some miracle missed all her organs, exiting the other side with so little impact that she'd been able to walk to the doctor under her own steam. She remembered the jarring impact, the spreading cold, the unbearable pain.

This was nothing like that. The bullet had merely striped her, parting her snow pants and base layer, digging a neat furrow in the flesh beneath that only barely grazed the muscle. She couldn't resist clapping a hand to the wound, which took her off the Alaskan's scope. And now she did run for cover, the wound making it more of an exaggerated limp. Nalren was one step ahead of her, diving on her face and eating snow as more rounds came in, sending smoking splinters showering down around them.

'Guess they beat us here,' Montclair said. 'Lemme see if I can get around the other flank.' She duck-walked to the cabin's far side, leaned out, jerked back as a line of rounds stitched the snow before her. 'Nope. That's not gonna work.'

'We better hope they don't have a bigger munition,' Nalren said. 'We can't stay here. This is a big fucking target for an RPG.' She tossed Montclair the satphone. 'Any luck?'

Montclair shook her head. 'No. We need to get higher and farther, and probably both.'

'Fuck,' Nalren said. 'Okay, we're gonna have to shoot our way out.' She rolled out from her corner of the cabin, sighted into her scope, and fired.

Mankiller found a portion of the sloughed roof battered low enough for her to aim over and sighted in again. She could see muzzle flashes now and figures moving, but they were good about moving immediately after they signaled their position with gunfire, making it difficult to pick a target. In Afghanistan, the enemy were rank amateurs, firing and then sitting tight to line up their next shot, blissfully unaware that meant Mankiller was also lining up her shot on them. Not these operators. They were professionals. If she'd had an automatic weapon, she might have considered laying down suppressive fire, but the Alaskan's bolt action made it impossible. She cursed herself for bringing a hunting rifle to a firefight and did her best to draw a bead on likely firing positions in the hope that someone would be kind enough to pop into her field of fire. No one was. To either side of her, she could hear the steady cracking of the soldiers' carbines.

'Boss!' Montclair called. 'Make the call! Getting pinned down here is not an option!'

'I'm thinking!' Nalren called back. 'Just stop fucking

missing and thin out some of this fire for me.'

Montclair cursed. *I should be thinning out some of this fire for them*, Mankiller thought. Something slid into her field of vision and Mankiller pulled the trigger, hoping for a lucky shot. The Alaskan punched her shoulder and she saw a spray of earth through the scope that confirmed the waste of ammunition. She racked another round, feeling useless.

'Shit, fuck this,' Montclair said. 'Moving!'

'What? Wait!' Nalren said, but it was too late. Mankiller could already see Montclair breaking cover from the cabin, raising her carbine to her shoulder.

'We gotta make the call, boss!' she shouted back. 'We gotta get help!'

Montclair slapped the trigger on her carbine, which began to cough bursts of three rounds. Montclair was at a flat-out run, her muzzle dancing wildly. It was a miracle that her rounds were even hitting the hill, much less the people taking cover on it. It was suicidal.

But Montclair advanced, carbine chattering, pausing only to swap magazines. The earth on the mound exploded in showers of ice and dust. Mankiller desperately added her own slow contribution to the volume of fire, hoping she could at least help to keep the enemy's head down. Beside her, she could hear Nalren doing the same, cursing a blue streak under her breath between each slap of the trigger. It was an impressive storm of bullets, but Montclair was exposed, running in a straight line over flat ground, and Mankiller winced with every passing second, thinking that would be the one in which she would see Montclair jerk, spin, and fall, an exit wound blossoming in her back.

But if there was one thing Mankiller's experience downrange had taught her, it was that nothing was more unpredictable than battle. Montclair did not jerk, spin, or fall. She kept running, her carbine barrel smoking, until she had mounted the bottom of the hill and begun to climb.

And then an amazing thing happened. One by one, the enemy began to drift out from behind cover, giving ground against Montclair's constant fire. Mankiller had spent the entire short duration of the fight with no targets. Suddenly, she had five, appearing so quickly that she was nearly as helpless as when she'd had none. They were falling back.

Mankiller sighted in. The Alaskan's scope was set up for taking down exposed targets at extreme range. It was almost too easy. The rifle punched and the first target dropped. Mankiller was able to chamber another round and take down a second enemy before the rest scattered.

Nalren gunned down one more before the other two fled, with two more appearing beside them. They ran in a zigzag pattern, taking cover behind the jumbled fragments of mining equipment and returning fire. Not fleeing, then; retreating. Montclair was still in trouble.

She didn't show it. She scrambled up over the broken slabs of drill core, firing the carbine one-handed now, lifting the satphone to her ear.

'Jesus, that fucking idiot!' Nalren shouted. Mankiller couldn't help but agree. The carbine fire was inaccurate enough with both hands, but now it was all but useless. The retreating enemy swarmed forward, and now Nalren abandoned cover, advancing at a slow walk, her aim steady. She laid down burst fire, not trying to hit anyone, just trying to drive the enemy back.

'Well, shit. Guess we're all gonna die,' Mankiller muttered, breaking from cover herself and advancing, working the bolt on the Alaskan as fast as she could. She had no idea whether or not she was hitting anything, concentrating only on keeping the rifle jumping, on the steady rhythm of pulling the trigger, slapping the bolt up and back, then forward and down. She took a knee, smoothly reloading bullet after bullet into the Alaskan's magazine well, her eyes locked on the chamber, because she knew that if she were to so much as glance at the enemy while she was so exposed, she would surely lose her nerve.

Bullets slammed into the snow around her, kicking up puffs of white dust. They snapped through the air, so close she swore she could feel them brushing her ear, but there were no more stinging sensations, no more hammerblows. If she was hit, she didn't know it, couldn't worry about it now. She slammed the bolt forward, stood, and resumed her firing, advancing in a synchronized dance, squinting through the smoke at the shapes of the enemy.

There were more than four now; others were coming to help. Mankiller didn't even try to count them all. There were too many, and that was all she needed to know. The urge to take cover, to run, to do anything other than advance at a walk and fire, was suffocating. Each step was a battle she felt she was on the verge of losing. *Christ, give me strength.* Nalren was a blur in Mankiller's peripheral vision, crouched, her carbine rock steady, the muzzle flashing orange and yellow.

And then Nalren was pausing, her weapon coming down to the low ready, her eyes wide. Mankiller felt her stomach turn over. If Nalren was hit, she would . . .

But Nalren wasn't hit. The master corporal was staring wide-eyed at Montclair pelting toward them with everything she had, sliding the satphone into the pocket of her cargo pants. 'One bar!' she shouted. 'Almost got through, but the call dropped. Need to get higher!'

Nalren got back on her carbine and started shooting again, backing up this time. 'All right!' she called to Montclair. 'Let's bug out and we'll figure out another way!'

Montclair didn't follow. She veered off to her right, running even faster. 'Got another way!'

'What the fuck is she . . .' Nalren began, but the words died on her lips. Because she saw. Montclair was racing for the tower.

'Oh, fuck,' Nalren said.

'"Fuck" is right,' Mankiller agreed, got her rifle up, and started firing again. There wasn't time to try to convince Montclair of the error of her ways, and she wasn't going to tackle her. The only option was to keep covering her and pray the rickety structure held up under her weight. *Jesus fucking Christ on the cross. Just a week ago, everything was normal. Everything was fine.*

Montclair had reached the tower, launched herself up at the lowest of the cross braces. The whole structure shuddered as she caught hold, creaking as it swayed. The ruined cabin wouldn't give them the field of fire they needed to provide effective cover, and the ground was flat and unadorned everywhere else. Mankiller joined Nalren in sheltering behind one of the tower's thick legs, leaning around to get her shots off.

It was barely concealment and certainly not cover. Even a 9mm round would drill through the wood like it was paper, and Mankiller could tell from the sharp reports of the enemy guns that they were firing high-powered carbines, probably 5.56mm and possibly 7.62mm. As if to remind her of that fact, the wood exploded on the opposite side of the beam from her face, showering her with splinters. The wood hadn't stopped the round, but it had caused it to tumble, ending up on a trajectory that had spared her life. It was the kind of luck that she couldn't rely on.

Montclair was still climbing, the tower shaking like it had palsy. 'If this fucking thing comes down,' Mankiller shouted to Nalren, 'it's coming down on top of us.'

'There's no other cover and I'm not leaving her,' Nalren shouted back as Mankiller stopped to reload.

Slap. Bolt up. Slam. Bolt back. Her fingers yanked the loose rounds from her pockets, walked them from palm to fingertips, and slid them into the magazine well. The metal was burning hot now, the skin over her knuckles complaining. Mankiller winced, dropped the round in the snow. She knew better than to hunt for it, sent her fingers back into her parka pockets for a replacement, her eyes still down, locked on the breach, unable to face the storm that she knew was ahead of her.

Her fingers quested, searched, found nothing. Her heart hammered in her chest, her throat felt dry.

'Nalren,' she shouted. 'Last four rounds! I'm empty!'

Nalren didn't answer, but Mankiller could tell she had switched from burst fire to single shot.

Pat. Pat. The rifle chamber was suddenly wet, red spatters appearing on the copper jacket of the bullet. Mankiller resisted the urge to drop the rifle, run her hands over her body. If she was hit, then she was hit. What mattered now was putting rounds downrange until Montclair was back on the ground and they could run.

She glanced up, deliberately closing her eyes as her field of vision took in the horizon and the enemy. Montclair was still climbing, the tower swaying dangerously, leaning farther and farther out in the direction of her weight. A drop of blood leaked from Montclair's waist, falling from the spreading stain that spanned her shirt and the waistband of her trousers. She was hit. Mankiller couldn't be sure, but the entry wound looked to be below her body armor. If it pained her, she didn't show it; it certainly didn't slow her. Montclair practically leapt up the tower struts, climbing with a single hand. The other held the satphone clamped to her ear. Mankiller could see her shouting into it, but had no idea whether it was frustration, optimism, or actual conversation.

She looked down at her rifle, slammed the bolt home. Hit or not, good comms or not, it made no difference. Mankiller's job was the same no matter what: pour the fire on.

And she did, for four more shots. At last, the bolt slid back and locked to the rear, stubbornly resisting her efforts to slide it home. 'Empty!' she shouted, turned to look to Nalren.

The master corporal had let the empty carbine fall. It hung by its sling, barrel trailing in the snow. She had her pistol in her hands, blazing away. The fire came quickly but not so quickly that she wasn't picking her shots, making each one count. It was untenable. Mankiller was no coward, but they couldn't take on a squad of well-armed enemies with nothing more than a pistol. Montclair or no Montclair, it was time to go.

As if it knew her mind, the tower gave a loud, creaking groan, underscored by the sound of splintering wood and the scream of shearing metal. The tower's shadow length-ened. The beam that saved Mankiller from the bullet suddenly lurched away from her. Montclair's weight had finally gone high enough. It was all coming down.

'Timber!' Mankiller shouted, but Nalren ignored her, staying on her gunsights. The tower's shadow grew over her head. She was unwilling to stop the covering fire, wasn't going to move, and that meant she was going to be crushed.

Mankiller wasn't going to let that happen. She might not be able to save Montclair, but she could do something here. She dropped the Alaskan and dove for Nalren. Her shoulder struck the master corporal at the waist, carried her past the tower's beam and into the clear snow beyond. They tumbled, Nalren's curses lost to the freezing snow that packed Mankiller's ears, her mouth, her nostrils. She felt something hard strike her head, Nalren's pistol butt most likely, as the master corporal tried to throw Mankiller off and return to the aid of her friend.

There was a thundering crash, and Mankiller felt a gust blow over her, sending needles of ice, splinters of wood up under her parka. She coughed, shut her eyes and mouth so tightly that the muscles in her face hurt, did her best to push away from Nalren and roll clear.

Nalren kicked in the opposite direction, and suddenly Mankiller was free of her, the horizon and the ground switching places, gray-white, gray-white, gray, white, gray, white.

Blue.

Mankiller blinked up at the sky. She was lying on her back, coughing the wood dust from her frozen lungs, her rifle tangled between her legs.

The first thing that struck her was the silence. It was near total, as if the explosion of the falling tower had ripped all other sound from the air, so that even the flying bullets would make no impression on her. Had she gone deaf? She raised a fingertip to her ear, examined it. No blood. No clear fluid. She was conscious of some sounds returning. The sighing of the wind, distant calls of alarm from birds, receding as they fled the commotion.

No, her hearing was fine. The shooting had stopped.

Mankiller propped herself up on her elbows.

The first thing she saw was Nalren getting to her hands and knees, fumbling for her pistol, which lay a few feet away, barrel stuck in the snow, helpfully propping the handle toward her grasping fingers.

The tower lay on its side, a jumble of rusted metal and

shattered wood, stretching out across the snow as if someone had painted it there. Mankiller was amazed that
something so substantive could crush down so flat, little
more than two-dimensional. *Well, at least I don't have to
worry about it falling and hurting anybody anymore*, she
thought as she scrambled to her feet, ran her hands over
her body, checking herself for wounds. Her hands came
away dry, and she felt no pain other than from the furrow
in her leg. If there was something to be discovered, she
supposed she'd discover it when the adrenaline wore off.

Nalren was standing now, her pistol coming up to
the low ready, turning toward the tower. 'Montclair!' she
shouted, heedless of what enemy might be around to hear.
'Montclair!'

Mankiller stumbled after her, picking her way through
the wreckage of the tower, trying to find her way to where
she remembered last seeing the leading seaman, her eyes
flicking constantly to the horizon, body tensed with
anticipation of enemy rounds, for the sharp report that
would mean their foes had returned.

It never came. Instead, they found Montclair halfway
up the tower's length.

She was in two pieces, severed neatly by a rusted metal
joining plate. The ropes of her intestines played out in
green and purple loops that wound around the wreckage.
She was smiling, her face as white as the snow behind
her, her mouth working. 'Can't feel my legs,' she said.

Nalren knelt beside her. 'They're fine,' she whispered.
'You're fine.'

The stink of Montclair's innards was worse than an
outhouse baking in the sun.

'Made the call,' Montclair coughed. 'Got through. Gave
them grid coords off the phone. Help's coming.'

'You're a fucking hero,' Nalren said. 'You know that?

Christ, I'm putting you in for the Victoria Cross.'

'You can't do that.' Blood bubbled at the corners of Montclair's mouth. 'Why's the shooting stopped?'

'You scared 'em off,' Nalren said. She was crying now, tears tracking through the dust of the shattered tower coating her face.

In the distance, a long, low howl sounded. *Something scared them off,* Mankiller thought, *but it wasn't us.*

'Nalren,' Mankiller said, standing. 'It's comin'.'

'I know that,' Nalren said. 'You think I don't fucking know that? Just give me a minute.'

The howl again, much closer, rising to a broken wail. 'We don' have a minute.'

'Fuck,' Nalren said, looking around. 'Help me to find some—'

'No.' Mankiller's stomach was doing loops, tears gathering at the corners of her eyes, but she made her voice steel. 'Call is made. We need to go.'

'She's right, boss,' Montclair coughed. She reached a hand up to her tac vest and unclipped one of the small green globes there, hooked a finger through the metal loop at the top. 'You can't fix me, but I can buy you some time. Head out.'

'Fuck,' Nalren said again, 'you don't know that. I just need to find a way to carry you and—' Her words were cut off by the metallic *chink* of Montclair pulling out the pin and tossing it away.

Nalren turned back to her, eyes wide. 'You dumb fuck. What the hell did you do that for?'

'Pin's out, boss. I'm letting go of the spoon in exactly five seconds. You better get moving. You're the best NCO I've ever worked for, and I'll see you in heaven. Thanks for everything.'

'Jesus,' Nalren began, but she was already backing up,

and she didn't resist when Mankiller seized her elbow.

'Five.' Montclair looked away from Nalren and fixed her eyes on the sky. Mankiller could see the Gold now, tearing around the side of the hill and loping toward the shattered tower. Mankiller looked at Montclair's steaming innards, her hot blood soaking into the packed snow.

'You know how these things operate, boss,' Montclair said without looking away from the wide gray-blue expanse above her. 'It'll come straight to me. The mess will bring it. Four.'

And now Nalren did turn and run, and Mankiller turned with her, pelting heedlessly back the way they'd come, letting the fear of the Gold and the grenade both drive them on. Mankiller caught Montclair's faint 'Three' before they moved down a gentle rise that pushed them out toward the rocky shore, cutting off the softer sounds behind them. Mankiller heard the Gold's shriek again, sounding so close that she feared the thing had bypassed Montclair and was right on top of them.

But when she glanced over her shoulder, there was nothing but the unbroken gray-white of the slope, the scrub trees that managed to cling to life despite the sub-arctic cold. A moment later, there was a sharp bang that shook the snow from the branches.

Nalren flinched, tears frozen on her cheeks, turned back toward the sound. 'Can't do that.' Mankiller put her hand on Nalren's elbow. 'Either she blew it up and the living enemy will be coming back, or she didn't and it's after us already. We gotta keep moving.'

Nalren turned and ran, so fast that Mankiller could barely keep up. She could see Nalren's pumping thighs and knew her pace was about more than wanting to escape the enemy. She thought of Yakecan, his staring eyes. *I know exactly how you feel.*

They ran on, not even bothering to seek cover this time, racing across the lakeshore with complete abandon, as if speed alone could protect them from enemy weapons. Mankiller felt too tired, too empty to care much. If there was a sniper out there who had her number, well, he could just punch it and let her get some rest.

But if anyone was able to line up a shot, they didn't take it, and the women ran flat out until the edges of the village cleared the horizon and reared up out of the field of frost.

Chapter Fifteen

Relief

Mankiller was fortunate that Calmut wasn't particularly eager to shoot anyone. She realized that she was running straight toward the station as fast as her exhausted legs would carry her. It would be the most ironic event of her life if she'd survived the trip to the mine, the lopsided firefight, and the Gold, only to be gunned down by one of her own frightened townies.

Mankiller realized the danger only as she cleared the barricade line of parked trucks and leaned panting against the station's blackened wall. She found herself angry. No one had shot at her, which was good, but no one had even challenged her, which was not. 'Jesus . . . Ollie,' she panted. 'Nobody's watchin' . . . the back.'

Calmut appeared around the broken entry stairs. 'Everyone's real tired, boss. Figured if I didn't let 'em get some sleep, they wouldn't be any good, anyway.'

'So you post watches, damn it!' The effort of raising her voice took the last of her breath and brought on a coughing fit that lasted a solid minute. 'You're lucky nobody crawled up your damned ass! What the hell would we have done if we'd got back here and you was overrun?'

'We had an eye on things,' Desmarais said, appearing

beside Calmut. His eyes immediately narrowed. 'Where's Montclair?'

'She was wounded getting signal on the satphone, then stayed behind so we could get out. She went down fighting, sir. I'll write the citation if we ever get out of here.' Nalren's eyes were dry and her voice composed now. There was no trace of the grief she'd shown back at the mine.

Desmarais' face tensed in sadness for an instant, but it was all the grief he showed. 'I'll sign it,' he said. 'Did you get through?'

'We did, sir,' Nalren said. 'Coordinates are at Yellow-knife. They should be scrambling a team now.'

A rifle cracked, and Desmarais' head swiveled toward the station. It was followed by a shotgun blast, which made Mankiller wince. Nobody was close enough for that shot to be effective. It was just wasted ammo. Yakecan would have known that. That old 870 was always his favorite long gun.

She raced up the steps to find Calmut sighting down his rifle, an old .22 target piece, into the distance.

'They comin' again?' Mankiller asked.

'I think they're sounding us out,' Calmut answered. 'Just a couple of fellas sticking their heads up on purpose. I think they want to see if we're payin' attention.'

'I don't see why they don't just blow us up,' Reeves said. He was crouched under the window, so still that between the shadows and the scorched wall, Mankiller had missed him.

'Because then they won't get what they're after,' Ghaznavi said from the doorway to Mankiller's office. Schweitzer lay slumped against the wall beside her.

'Her grandfather,' Schweitzer said. 'He's the reason they're here.'

'Lived-With-The-Wolves.' Calmut shot again, cursed. 'These fuckers are persistent.'

'They want his *inkoze*,' Mankiller said. 'They ain't gonna get it.'

'They might,' Schweitzer said, 'if they have you over a barrel when they ask him.'

The words stopped Mankiller short. She had always just assumed that they hadn't gone after Grampy because they couldn't find him. She had never considered the possibility that they would use her as a bargaining chip. The fear immediately gave way to anger, and she gritted her teeth. 'I ain't so easy to get over a barrel.'

'Well, if they don't want to blow us up,' Reeves said, 'why don't they just send a bunch of those dead things?'

'Two reasons,' Schweitzer answered. 'One, the Golds are like wild dogs. They're not the best tool for the job if you're wanting to capture someone. Two, I think they might be running out.'

'Runnin' out?' Mankiller asked. 'They had a big cage full of 'em.'

'How many have you killed?' Ghaznavi asked.

'You can't kill 'em,' Mankiller said.

Ghaznavi rolled her eyes. 'How many have you destroyed?'

'Dunno,' Mankiller said. 'Haven't been keepin' count.'

'Around five,' Schweitzer said, 'and that's not counting the ones we took down when we hit their facility before coming out here. These things are tough to make. You need the corpse of a special operator just to get started, and then you need a Sorcerer to Bind the spirit in.'

Mankiller stared at him, feeling as if the world was spinning away from underneath her. She had always known that *inkoze* was real, but it had always been confined to the medicine of her grandfather, of the holy men of the Dene, as rare as diamonds. She had never believed that white people could use *inkoze*, let alone . . . formalize it. For her, magic had always been part of the woods and the snows, her people's patrimony out in the wilderness. The thought of it happening in a city, on a military base, in the cold bureaucracy of a government office took something that had always felt like a part of her and ripped it away.

'And the Director's personally banged up, thanks to you,' Schweitzer went on. 'He's going to be cautious from now on, particularly with his most limited asset.'

'It's not like he can get living people anymore, either,' Ghaznavi said. 'Hodges cut off his funding line.'

'All the more reason for him to be careful. We'll have some breathing room now.'

'Well, we got other problems,' Calmut said. 'Ammunition, for one.'

'How're we lookin'?' Mankiller asked.

'Not good,' Calmut said. 'We ain't snipers, boss. People get scared and then they just start unloading. We need resupply or we're gonna run dry halfway through the next attack.'

'Shit,' Mankiller said. 'Grampy's got all that stuff. Enough ammo to stock an army, medical supplies, food, you name it.'

'So, he's the Unabomber,' Schweitzer said.

'He's an old man who lives out in the middle of no-where,' Mankiller said. 'He don' get visitors much and we don' got Wal-Mart out here.'

'We don't need to make it through the next attack,' Desmarais said, stooping through the doorway. 'Yellow-knife is just across the lake. We'll have everything we need soon enough.'

'How soon will they get here?' Mankiller asked.

Nalren appeared beside Desmarais. 'The call went out about an hour ago. If they scrambled right away, it shouldn't take them more than another hour.'

'They won't scramble right away,' Desmarais said. 'They'll go up the chain to find out why the hell we're here. And nobody will know.'

'Why not?' Mankiller asked.

'Because we're in the business of people not knowing what we do,' Ghaznavi said. 'How long will that slow things down?'

'Not long.' Desmarais shrugged. 'Another hour, maybe. I'll catch hell when I get back, but I'll worry about that when I get back.'

'All right.' Reeves stood, dusting himself off. 'Well, ma'am, I hate to leave you here, but we're running short on operators as it is. I'm going to float out and cover our flank until rescue arrives.'

'Yeah, me too,' Nalren said.

'You're sure you don't want . . .' Desmarais began, but he was speaking to her back, and she was already drifting out the door. Mankiller thought about going with her, but she looked around at the frightened faces of the villagers, Calmut chief among them. She was needed here. A familiar face. A Dene face.

She grabbed a rusted folding chair, slid it over to the remains of the window, and slumped into it. As soon as her butt touched the ripped vinyl surface of the cushion, fatigue nearly overwhelmed her. The adrenaline had gone, and even knowing that there were enemy within firing range, all she wanted to do was close her eyes and sleep, if only for a few minutes. 'Ollie, grab me a cup of coffee; everybody else, get some shut-eye. Even if it's just a few minutes, it's something.'

'Sheriff, are you sure—' Calmut began.

'Coffee, Ollie. Right now.'

'Sure thing, boss.'

'You need to sleep,' Schweitzer said.

'I'm not gonna be able to sleep,' Mankiller said.

'You need to at least try. Or look at a wall, something to take the edge off.'

'That's a nice thought,' Mankiller said. 'Don' wanna get jumped.'

'Drag me over to the window. I can see and hear better than you, anyway. They're just trying to sound out your ammo anyway or get you to waste it. I'll sing out when they come on in earnest.'

'Thanks,' Mankiller said, but she didn't move.

'Sheriff,' Schweitzer said. 'I may be dead, but you're not the only veteran here. I know what's going on in your head right now.'

Mankiller turned at that, shrugged. 'Yeah, I guess you're right.' She stood, made her way over to him, paused. 'How do I . . .'

Schweitzer held out a hand. 'Just drag me like a sack of potatoes. I won't break.'

Mankiller smiled and grabbed his wrist. With the travois, it had been relatively easy, but Schweitzer weighed much more than a normal man, and without the even grip and leverage, it proved too much for her. She looked up, embarrassed. 'Guess I'm a little tired.'

'Guess so.' Ghaznavi smiled, grabbed Schweitzer under his armpit, and helped drag him forward.

'There's not a whole lot of dignity going on here,' Schweitzer said as they managed to get him bundled into the folding chair.

'Other duties as assigned, Petty Officer,' Ghaznavi grunted. 'Damn, you're heavy. Putting you on a diet when we get out of this.'

Schweitzer looked ridiculous, more puddle than man, but his head was high enough to see the horizon, and if anyone put a bullet in it, well, Mankiller supposed that would be all the warning they'd need. She turned and went into her office. The rest of them were thoughtful enough to leave her alone, but she could do nothing more than slump in her chair and stare off into space, neither sleeping nor thinking, just existing, conscious only of the steady beat of her heart and the rhythm of her breathing. For now, at least, she still had that.

Everything around her, sound, sight, time itself, faded back, and she drifted in a blissful state of no-thought. She had no idea how long she was in her office, sitting in silence, was only conscious of a vague irritation when Schweitzer's voice pulled her out of her reverie. 'They're coming.'

She knew she should hurry, leap to her feet and race to the window, rally the troops and get in the fight. But she didn't have it in her. She felt like she weighed more than Schweitzer, her arm straining to lever herself out of the chair.

The first gunshots were ringing out by the time she made the door, and she could see Calmut in the window, working the bolt action on the .22 as fast as he could. He'd at least gotten the shotgun away from the idiot who was trying to fire it long-range. It lay propped up against the window beside him.

Cort was the only operator in the station, and he'd taken up position in the doorway, firing single shot by single shot.

'Howdy, Sheriff,' Schweitzer said. He'd dragged himself out of the chair and lay on the floor beside Calmut. 'Looks like the Little Bighorn out there.'

It did. She couldn't see any Golds, but the horizon was boiling with enemy troops darting in and out between the buildings, not even bothering to fire, leapfrogging from cover to cover, drawing down on the station.

'They're gonna rush us,' Mankiller said. She leaned out the window, motioned to the few villagers out at the truck barricade. 'Come on inside.' She tried to keep the panic out of her voice. 'We need to tighten up in here.' It would be close quarters, but defending a small hardpoint against such overwhelming odds would be a hell of a better bet than trying to fight them in the comparatively open ground outside.

She turned to Ghaznavi and Desmarais. 'Call your flankers in,' she said. 'We need to turtle up.'

Ghaznavi tapped the useless radio on her hip. 'And how do you propose I do that? Yell real loud?'

'Shit,' Mankiller said. The jammer prevented their internal comms just as easily as it did their efforts to call for help. Hopefully, they would come back on their own or else find a place to hunker down and snipe at the enemy, maybe draw some of the pressure off.

She brought the Alaskan up and sighted in. The enemy were moving too fast for her to draw a bead without risking a miss. She pushed her hand into her pocket and fumbled around, realized with a start that she was out of ammo. She had no idea how many more boxes of .375 were in the cabinet. Maybe only one. Maybe none at all. She dropped the Alaskan and reached for the 870.

The enemy didn't give her too long to think about it. A moment later, she saw the thick, dark wedge of a crew-served weapon propped up on the hood of a car, two men working frantically on the feed. It was too far for her to be sure, but the barrel looked enormous. A .50 caliber heavy machine gun, maybe. Hopefully, not a minigun, whose 20mm fire would turn the station to splinters in a matter of seconds.

'Big gun's up!' Mankiller shouted. 'Cover!'

She hit the deck as the gun opened up. *Thuka thuka thuka thuka.* It was a .50 cal, all right. The splinters raining around her testified to the heavyweight rounds. The station shuddered, groaned, as if a storm were tearing it off its foundations. In a way, Mankiller supposed, one was. Calmut dove over Schweitzer, trembling there until Mankiller grabbed him by his collar and dragged him off, pushing down on his back until he lay flat on the floor. Fortunately for them, the gunner didn't have a low-enough angle to hit them, and she watched as the rounds made short work of the lintel above her office door. She heard glass shattering beyond and saw her pictures falling to the floor.

She tried to roll onto her hands and knees, thought better of it as the gunner walked his fire down, trying to hit the defenders he correctly assumed were cowering on the floor. 'If they're tryin' to take me alive,' she called to Schweitzer, 'they got a funny way of goin' about it.'

Schweitzer's reply was lost in the storm of fire, the rounds stitching their way down the wall, inching closer. Could the gunner get the angle? If he could, they were dead. She looked around frantically, saw Cort and Desmarais flat on their stomachs in the entryway. Maybe she could crawl over them, find some way to get around the gunner's flank. It would have to be quick and . . .

The shooting stopped. Well, the impact of the rounds stopped, the rain of splinters showering the back of her neck stopped, but the pounding rhythm continued. She paused, listening. No, not the same. Not the *thuka thuka thuka* of the gun. A softer, more distant sound. *Whup whup whup whup.*

Helicopter rotors.

'Airframe coming in!' She jumped to her feet, raising

the 870. It would be one hell of a shot, but if she could get a slug perfectly placed on the tail rotor, she might be able to . . .

She saw them immediately. Two olive-green shapes in the sky, their twin rotors churning the gray sky around them. She'd flown in them more times than she could count, in training at Yellowknife and on missions over the shattered scree of Kunar Province. They were Chinooks, the huge transport helos that moved everything from troops to tanks. Her heart jumped into her throat. If those were reinforcements coming for the enemy . . . But then a gust of wind forced one of the huge green helos to tack, bringing the fuselage into view. Mankiller's knees went weak with relief as she saw the red maple leaf inside the blue circle. The good guys. '*Mársi Sezús*,' she whispered, turned to Calmut. 'Ollie! Cavalry's coming!'

'Pour it on!' Desmarais shouted. He opened up with his pistol, the rounds spitting out so quickly that Mankiller could tell he wasn't bothering to aim. She could hear burst fire coming from off to the station's right. Nalren, most likely, following her boss's lead. It made sense. With help on the way, there was no longer any need to conserve ammunition. The important thing now was to keep the enemy's heads down, distract them so that the helos could touch down safely.

The thought of draining their dwindling supplies of ammunition made Mankiller's stomach clench, but trying to make it stretch was foolish now. If those helos didn't touch down, ammo or no ammo, they wouldn't be able to hold much longer. She crouched, set the 870 in a groove dug in the shattered window frame, and worked the slide as fast as she could, focusing only on keeping the shotgun pointed in the general direction of the enemy. Within moments, all the guns in the station were blazing as the villagers followed their lead and sent rounds downrange as fast as they could. Mankiller could see dark shapes moving between the buildings, but it was impossible to tell if they were doing any damage, or if the enemy even noticed.

A chattering roar rose above the din of the shooting, and Mankiller saw columns of white-orange erupting from the Chinook's sides: the miniguns opening up. She could see the frost churning on the ground below them. One house, she thought it might be Jackie Metcalfe's, who'd always brought a pan of brownies (never cut up) to the station like clockwork every Sunday, collapsed in a shower of dust as the column of fire passed over it, spraying splinters and broken glass. Mankiller instinctively glanced to her left, saw Jackie crouched in a corner, pointing a deer rifle out through a hole in the wall. If she noticed that her house had just been turned into toothpicks, she gave no sign.

Mankiller grunted in satisfaction. Houses could be rebuilt. The people who lived inside them were what mattered. She turned back to her weapon, racked the slide, felt it lock to the rear. 'I'm dry!' she shouted, scrambled back to the cabinet, seeing Calmut take her place out of the corner of her eye.

Someone had had the bright idea to unrig the springs on the doors, and they hung open, the mostly bare shelves making Mankiller's stomach clench all over again. She fumbled through three boxes of 9mm, felt her hand close over the hard plastic tray that held the .375. Twenty rounds. She shuddered and snatched it, upending the tray into her pocket. A bullet snapped past her face, plucking splinters from the doorframe. Maybe a stray, maybe someone drawing a bead on her. It didn't matter. She knelt, ducking behind one of the cabinet's open doors, dropped the 870 and reloaded the Alaskan, stood, and raced to Calmut's side. No sooner had she gotten on the gun sights than she heard the heavy *thuka thuka thuka* of the .50 cal opening up again.

She could see the tracer fire racing upward from the Loon. A building blocked her view of the tavern's narrow balcony, but the gunner had probably set up there. The Chinook pilot was good, and the huge helo danced with an agility that belied its size, but she still saw a few sparks fly from the aft rotor, a thin trail of black smoke rising up. The Chinook shuddered, rocked, held position, the guns opening up, shredding the Loon's roof while the other Chinook descended. As Mankiller watched, the back ramp swung open and fast ropes dropped out. She stared at them, as if her gaze could make her rescuers move faster. 'Come on,' she whispered. 'Come on.'

No figures appeared from the helo. Instead, one appeared on the roof of the house, scrambling up through the wreckage, vaulting over the remnants of the brick chimney, and taking a knee, a long black tube appearing over its shoulder.

Mankiller's throat closed. It was a moment before she could force air through it, screaming as if the helo pilot could hear her. 'RPG!'

In every movie Mankiller had ever seen, RPG rounds flew slowly enough to see, their course almost leisurely compared to the instant impact of a bullet. In real life, RPGs and bullets moved just as quickly. No sooner had the tube sparked than the back of the Chinook detonated, the fast ropes disintegrating in a flash of bright white. The tail rotor spun away, turning sideways and bouncing off the Loon's shattered entrance. The windows along the fuselage exploded, and its guns stopped firing as puffs of orange flame belched out of the gun ports. The helo sagged, the ramp falling off as the tail dropped toward the ground.

Maybe the pilots survived; maybe the blast didn't reach the front end. It was a crazy thought, and proved false a moment later when the cockpit windows shattered, kicked out by a fireball that grew until it consumed the helicopter's entire hundred-foot length. It shuddered for an instant, then exploded with a bang that made Mankiller's ears ring even from this distance, showering the houses below with smoking metal fragments, none of them bigger than a toaster.

A second RPG round streaked past the other helo's nose, and the enemy gunners immediately turned their weapons on it, the lines of tracer fire arcing upward from houses deeper into the village. The helo jerked up as the pilot reacted to the blast, a rookie move that in this case saved it, yanking it out of the path of the .50 cal fire. The helo dipped as the pilot corrected, tried to get back in the fight, but the inbound fire was withering and, without his wingman to draw some of it off, too hot to handle. The remaining Chinook rose higher, and Mankiller's hope died.

Because she knew there was no way it could get through now. It would have to wave off or risk a suicidal touchdown, the troops scrambling off under the enemy guns. She cursed herself for hoping the pilot would risk it. She wanted to live, but not at the cost of condemning all those people to death.

Fortunately, the pilot wasn't crazy. The broadside guns began to sweep left and right, covering fire designed to cool the fight down while the pilot generated the lift they needed to get higher. The helo's nose rose, and then it was banking sharply away, the portside gun going silent as it faced the sky. The guns on the ground gradually stopped firing as the Chinook gained altitude, still trailing smoke from its rear rotor, its aft trembling. It leveled, shrank as it gained altitude and distance, heading back over the still surface of the lake, to Yellowknife and safety.

Mankiller slowly lowered her rifle, staring openmouthed over the wreckage of the town beyond. Nothing moved, the quiet so complete it was as if time had frozen with the helo's departure.

It was Calmut who broke the silence, his voice confused. 'I don't understand, boss. Are they comin' back?'

Mankiller shrugged. Because it didn't matter.

They would undoubtedly be back, and with a force large enough to crush any resistance they encountered, magical or otherwise. But assembling such a force would take time.

And by the time they arrived, it would be far too late.

Chapter Sixteen

The Company of Wolves

Mankiller stared at the drifting ash, the smudge of greasy smoke that had once been her hope of salvation. It seemed to take forever for all the wreckage to tumble out of the sky, bouncing in the steaming gray snow. She could hear the soft patter of debris bouncing off the corrugated metal of the Loon's collapsed awning. Her stomach clenched at the thought that some of that fallout was the remains of her rescuers.

'Boss.' It was Calmut, his voice on the edge of panic. The implications of the downed helo were dawning on him, on everyone. After going on a spending spree with their ammunition, they were suddenly without help. He needed her to say something, something that would give them the strength to rage on against the enemy they now had absolutely no hope of defeating.

But Mankiller was empty. She stared at the shower of wreckage and felt her bones turn to rubber. An exhaustion rose within her, greater than anything she'd thought possible, until the act of keeping her eyelids open seemed to be more than she could manage. It was over. She would sit . . . no, she would *fall* down right where she was and lie there until the monsters out there in the village came to claim her. The tank was empty. She had fought so hard, met with defeat at every turn. It was God's will that they lose. There was nothing more she could do.

'Boss,' Calmut said again, touching her shoulder this time. The need was there in his voice, and Mankiller realized it had always been there, not just for him but for everyone, from Joe to Sally to the mayor to every other resident of Fort Resolution. Always needing her to hold them up, to protect them, to carry them along.

And now, with the burning remains of the helicopter making their way down to the hole in the Loon's roof, when *she* needed to be carried, who would do it?

She knew the answer, and it gave her the strength to speak. "'S all right, Ollie.'

'That was our ammo. Our meds.' Calmut's voice was close to breaking. 'Our troops.'

'We're okay.' Mankiller turned to face him. The effort of keeping her eyes open and her face determined made her knees shake, and she prayed that Calmut couldn't see it. 'That was jus' a recon. It went bad, but that jus' means they'll be chompin' at the bit to get back out here. In case there're survivors.'

Calmut looked at the wreckage. 'Don't think there's any survivors.' He crossed himself.

'Yeah, but they don't know that,' Mankiller said. 'They gotta check, not to mention takin' care of us. They'll be back.'

'We're almost out of ammo,' Calmut said. 'Christ, Sheriff. I ain't goin' back out into town to get food.'

The words bubbled out of Mankiller's mouth before she knew she was going to say them. 'You don't have to. You jus' hole up here and I'll bring it all to you.'

Calmut was so shocked that he only stammered, moving his hands in useless circles.

Ghaznavi appeared from around the corner of

Mankiller's office where she'd been hiding from the storm of fire. 'There's a cache around here?'

'Not a cache,' Mankiller said. 'My Grampy's stores. Got everything we need and then some.'

'Absolutely not,' Desmarais said. 'He's the whole reason we're here, to keep him safe. That's not going to be served by leading the enemy to him.'

'I didn't say nuthin' 'bout leadin' anyone,' Mankiller said.

'But you might do it regardless. I can't allow that.'

Mankiller felt anger boiling in the back of her throat. She welcomed it, if only because it pushed some of the exhaustion aside. 'Maybe you don't read so good,' Mankiller said, stabbing in the direction of the bronze placard outside the bullet-pocked walls of the municipal building. 'This is Treaty 8 country. You don't get to allow or not allow anything.'

Desmarais looked exasperated. 'This isn't a sovereignty issue, damn it. We're in the middle of a military operation and I'm the leading—'

Mankiller turned to Calmut. 'Ollie, did Stewart bring the sledge back?'

'Yeah, boss,' Calmut said. 'It's in the garage. Full o' wood chips, though.'

''S all right,' Mankiller said. 'Harness is out there with it?'

'Far as I know,' Calmut said.

'Okie.' Mankiller turned back to Desmarais, eased around him to the door.

'Where are you going?' Desmarais asked.

'I'm gonna hook up to that sledge, and I'm gonna throw Joe and your boy Schweitzer there on it, and then I'm gonna haul the damn thing in harness up to my Grampy's place.'

'You're not going to . . .'

'No.' Mankiller turned back to him. 'I am, and I wouldn't mind some help.'

'They're coming back.' Desmarais kept his voice level, but Mankiller could tell he was on the brink of an outburst. The fear and exhaustion were taking a toll on all of them. 'We don't have time for you to go mushing out into the bush.'

Mankiller understood that he was trying to protect his position, to stand up for Mankiller's home and people, but it didn't ease the anger rising in her at the thought of yet another white man sauntering into Dene treaty land and acting like he owned the place. She swallowed a retort and turned back toward the exit.

'I'll help,' Ghaznavi said. 'I imagine it'll go faster with two.'

'What?' Desmarais' jaw tensed. 'You're the director of SAD. We can't afford to send you wandering off into the woods!'

Mankiller ignored him, nodded gratefully at Ghaznavi. 'Yeah, it would. Thanks.'

'I'll take point,' Reeves said, shouldering his carbine and casting an apologetic glance at Desmarais.

'No.' Ghaznavi stopped him with a wave. 'We can't afford to draw a shooter off the defenses. I'll go.'

'Ma'am, it's my job—' Reeves began.

'This is ridiculous—' Desmarais talked over them.

'Shut it, both of you.' Ghaznavi's voice was just loud enough to ride over them. 'We don't have time. I'm not a pipe hitter and I'm not doing anything by staying here other than breaking Reeves' concentration. Reeves, if I'm the director, then that means you do what I say, and I say you stay here.'

'You all stay here—' Desmarais said.

'Knock it off,' Ghaznavi interrupted him. 'This isn't just about supplies. If we're going to beat those things, we need things of our own. Our thing' – she waved a hand at the lump of collapsed gray flesh that was Schweitzer – 'is rather limp at the moment.'

'Hey,' Schweitzer said.

'Shut up,' she said. 'If we're to have a chance in hell, we not only need ammunition, food, and medical supplies, we need magic. The whole reason we're in this fight is that there's a source of it back in those woods somewhere.'

'What's he going to do?' Desmarais rolled his eyes. 'All our reporting indicates he only uses the stuff on animals.'

'How the fuck should I know?' Ghaznavi shot back. 'This is magic. Everything is brand-spanking-new here. Maybe your reporting is wrong and he can conjure up a mortar team. Maybe these magic animals can spit 20mm rounds and fart propane. Maybe' – she gestured to Schweitzer – 'he can get this one back on his feet. Any one of those things could change the game.'

'And maybe,' Desmarais said through clenched teeth, 'he can't do any of that, and you just drew off two shooters we desperately need in the fight.'

'Shooting what?' Ghaznavi asked. 'Not sure if you've been paying attention, but we're pretty much out of stuff to shoot.'

'Still doesn't justify the risk of compromising the package.'

'Call the President.' Ghaznavi was already turning to go. 'Or better yet, make yourself useful and ensure they don't track us.'

'I can't let you do this, ma'am—' Reeves began.

'Fuck yourself,' Ghaznavi said. 'That's an order.' She paused. 'Actually, belay that on account of it being disgusting. New orders are for you to stay here and not bother me while I help the good sheriff here haul these fellas into the woods.' She turned to Mankiller. 'Which way are we heading?'

Mankiller pointed vaguely to the northwest. 'We hug the shore again but in the opposite direction from the mine. Cut off into the woods after that. Gonna be a long walk.'

'Okay,' Ghaznavi said. 'Reeves, take Cort and go stir up some shit to the east.'

'Ma'am, there's just two of us and we're low on ammu . . .'

'You think I don't know that? You're the high-speed, low-drag, wind-tunnel-tested hard SAD operator here. Figure it out. Make bombs out of pinecones or something. I spent a lot of money training you. Time to make good on it.'

Mankiller felt her throat close. She'd made a similar call not long before. Her deputy's brain-dead body was a testament to how it had ended. She was grateful Ghaznavi wasn't looking at her. She wasn't sure she could keep the dismay off her face. *Leave it. It's not your call. These are not your people.*

'What if they come back while your boys are out?' Calmut asked.

'Then I guess they better hope you're in a good mood,' Ghaznavi said. 'Otherwise, you might put a hurting on them.'

Mankiller snorted laughter and left. With Ghaznavi at her side, some of the fatigue dropped away. She was determined to go on her own if that's what it took, and she was glad to have someone to split the load. It wasn't just the physical effort; Mankiller had never had a problem with work, no matter how grinding. The truth was that Mankiller's reputation as a loner was unearned. Being quiet wasn't the same as preferring your own company, and between the Army and her career after, Mankiller had ensured she was always surrounded by others. It was the real reason she worked so much. Not dedication to her job but a way to keep her mind from dwelling on the long hours alone in her house, waiting for the dawn.

The sledge was where Calmut had said it was, a half-rotten contraption held together by a few layers of moldering carpet fixed by tenpenny nails. The harness was still attached, only big enough for a single person. A jury-rigged knot of ancient rope was lashed on alongside, stiff and gray-green with mold.

'I'm not touching that rope,' Ghaznavi said. 'I'll get polio.'

'I'll do the rope. You can wear the harness.'

'You sure it'll hold? This whole thing looks ready to come apart.'

'Nope. Not sure we got much choice, though. Snowmobile makes too much noise. Not gonna wind up like Joe.' The mention of Yakecan sent a stab of grief through her. She swallowed it. Now was not the time.

'Don't you have sled dogs out here?'

Mankiller smiled. 'It's not the nineteenth century. We got motors now. Only thing folks use dogs out here is for sports.'

'Well, maybe we could repurpose them.'

'Only kennel nearby was a quarter-klick up the highway, right where the bad guys are. I imagine if there's any repurposin', they already done it. Anyway, dogs make nearly as much noise as a snowmobile.'

Ghaznavi stood patiently while Mankiller slipped the harness over her, and then the sheriff looped the rotting ropes over her own shoulders. The parka provided ample padding, and Mankiller had grown up pulling sledges. She settled into the familiar weight, comforted by the whisper-scrape of the runners over the packed snow. She immediately felt the sledge listing on Ghaznavi's side.

'You gotta pull even with me,' Mankiller said. 'Otherwise, I'm gonna cramp one shoulder.'

'Heavier than I thought,' Ghaznavi grunted, but the sledge righted and they made better progress.

'You'll get used to it,' Mankiller said. 'Havin' the fellas on it'll make it easier.'

'How does adding weight make it easier?'

'Makes it sit down in the snow better. Moves smoother. You don't have to compensate for the drift. You'll see.' Privately, she had begun to worry. If Ghaznavi couldn't keep pace, it would be worse than if Mankiller had gone alone. But the sledge pulled even to the station doorway at least, and Desmarais didn't trouble them any further as they loaded Schweitzer and Yakecan on. Schweitzer's limited use of his arms helped some, as he was able to make sure neither he nor Yakecan would slide off. 'This lacks dignity,' Schweitzer groused.

'Shut up,' Ghaznavi said, handed him a pistol. 'I presume you can still pull a trigger?'

'He broke my spine, not my fingers,' Schweitzer said, taking it.

'Good.' Ghaznavi nodded. 'Cover our six.'

She made a final trip into the station to pillage Calmut's stock of supplies. The old man knew better than to trouble her about it.

When she turned to go, Reeves and Cort were already at the door, Calmut blustering at their shoulder. 'They took all the propane,' he said. 'We're gonna freeze our asses off.'

'Well, that's good,' Mankiller said. 'Might be you freeze solid enough an' the bullets'll bounce off you.'

Reeves and Cort each shouldered cream-colored propane

tanks and trotted off to the east. Mankiller was amazed at how fast Reeves was despite his prosthetic leg. 'Good luck, boss,' Reeves said. 'Hurry back.'

'Leave a light on for us.' Ghaznavi waved.

'That's a bad idea,' Cort called over his shoulder. 'Gives away our position.'

Mankiller and Ghaznavi watched them go, then looked at one another. 'Ready?' Mankiller asked.

'No,' the SAD Director said, but she leaned into the harness anyway.

'Come on, ladies,' Schweitzer said, one arm draped protectively over Yakecan's chest. 'Mush.'

They mushed, and the weighted sled sat down in the snow, smooth and even, the gentle pressure across Mankiller's shoulders making her feel at home, even as home dwindled in the distance.

They had reached the line of boathouses when they heard the first explosion. Mankiller's years in EOD had taught her to identify explosions by sound, from the tinny clap of high-brisance military explosives to the dull *whump* of smokeless powder. This was somewhere in the middle but toward the low end. The propane tanks. Ghaznavi's men stirring shit up as ordered. They paused for a moment, then leaned back into their harness, running the sled along the shore toward the thick tree line farther on.

A staccato string of pops from the direction of the explosions, like fireworks going off. Small-arms fire. 'Looks like Frank and Ernest have attracted some attention,' Schweitzer said.

'Let's hope it's enough,' Ghaznavi said.

The ground rose as they neared the tree line. 'We going to fit in there?' Ghaznavi asked.

'Yeah,' Mankiller said. 'There's a track.'

'How can you tell?' Ghaznavi asked. 'Looks like it's all snow.'

'Grew up here.' Mankiller shrugged.

'Mush,' Schweitzer repeated.

They bent their backs and trudged into the woods. Mankiller felt easier as the trees closed around them, cutting off the open sky and the creeping feeling of exposure. Mankiller felt the muscles in her back relaxing in spite of the sledge's weight. The thick silence of the forest set in, broken only by their grunting breaths and the whispering of the sledge's runners over the snow. The sounds of gunfire grew more distant, the pops farther apart. Mankiller silently prayed it was the sound of the Americans leading the enemy on a merry chase and not the station being overwhelmed. Yakecan's face flashed in her memory, nodding as he accepted the radio, turned to head for the snowmobile. Following her orders.

'Your boys'll be okay,' Mankiller said. The words were directed at Ghaznavi, but she knew she was talking to herself.

'They will or they won't,' Ghaznavi said, shrugging her shoulders to better seat the harness, 'but they signed up to do what they were told, no matter the odds. They can do as they like when they get out or when they die, whichever comes first.'

'I guess,' Mankiller said. She didn't like Ghaznavi's refusal to accept the platitude. The SAD Director's honesty denied Mankiller a chance to make herself feel better.

Ghaznavi misread the tone as disapproval. 'Don't go thinking this is easy for me.'

Mankiller knew she should say something to ease the tension, but as happened so often, she couldn't find the words.

In the end, Schweitzer broke the silence. 'I'd beg to

differ. I've been dead for months and it hasn't stopped me from doing my job.'

Ghaznavi smiled at that, and Mankiller was grateful to put the topic behind them and lose herself in pulling the sledge. The trail hadn't been broken since the last snowfall, and the runners slid easily over the thick crust. But that same snow made the walking nearly impossible, as each step broke through and sank six inches before the footing was firm enough to take the next. Before long, Mankiller was sweating freely in her parka. Ghaznavi moved to take off her hood but stopped at a warning from Mankiller. 'You'll feel good till your sweat freezes, and then you'll be hatin' life. Just let your gear soak it up.'

Twin fears hung over Mankiller's head: that Ghaznavi wouldn't be able to keep up, and that at any moment she would hear the sharp pop of a rifle and feel the burning of a round cutting through her.

But as with most fears, neither came to pass. Mankiller lost herself in the rhythm of the work, each lurching step, the sledge bumping along behind, the feel of the Alaskan thumping against her chest. She'd let off most of the ammunition during the last assault on the station, and there were only three rounds left. The last of the .375 ammunition. If it came to a gunfight, she'd need to make every shot count.

When the light began to fail, Mankiller stopped them in a clearing created by a frozen bog. She remembered catching toads there with Grampy when she was a girl, before he'd realized he had the *inkoze* and withdrew to the cabin where he'd lived ever since. Some of the exposed feeling returned at the sight of the deepening sky, but it was more than mitigated by the safety provided by her childhood memories. She knew it was ridiculous, but she couldn't shake the feeling of sanctuary.

'Reckon we're far enough now,' Mankiller said, easing out of the ropes. 'If they was gonna come, they'd 'a come already.'

Ghaznavi released the harness and sat down where she was, leaning gratefully against the sledge, finally showing her exhaustion.

'Didn' push ya too hard, did I?' Mankiller asked, trying to keep the worry from her voice.

Ghaznavi gave her the finger, eyes closed.

'Pull me up and give me your rifle,' Schweitzer offered. 'I'll keep an eye out while you sleep.'

Mankiller hauled Schweitzer into a sitting position, his broken body propped against the sledge's raised back. She gratefully unslung the Alaskan and handed it to him. 'Only got three rounds, so don' miss.'

'I suck at missing,' Schweitzer said, 'sucked at it even when I was still breathing.'

'Are we far enough out that we can light a fire?' Ghaznavi asked. 'I'm freezing my ass off here.'

'Nope,' Mankiller said, extending a hand to her. 'And it's only gonna get colder. We gotta keep Joe warm and each other. Lemme help you up. Let's go snuggle on the sledge.'

Ghaznavi opened her eyes. 'You're serious.'

''Fraid so. Gonna get real cold once we lose the light.'

'Can't we just drag your guy over here? Or better yet, can't you? I am in favor of any plan that doesn't involve me having to move.'

'Sorry,' Mankiller said. 'Don' wanna lie in the snow. Sledge'll keep us high and dry.'

Ghaznavi groaned, seized her hand, let Mankiller draw her to her feet. 'I can't believe I'm going to snuggle with a corpse.'

'You should be so lucky,' Schweitzer said. 'I'm on

overwatch. You living folks get comfortable.'

Mankiller curled around Yakecan like a lover, putting her head on his broad chest. She was amazed at the strength of his heartbeat, the steady rise and fall of his breathing, half expected him to sit up and ask her what was going on. Ghaznavi tucked herself in alongside, wedged between Schweitzer's leg and Yakecan's, shivering. 'It'll warm up in a minute,' Mankiller said. 'Body heat's gotta build up.'

The trees blocked the worst of the breeze, and within a few minutes, Mankiller felt cozy enough to give the fatigue rein. She drowsed, reassured by Schweitzer's powerful senses and the sight of the Alaskan propped on his knee. The cold and the fear wouldn't let her truly sleep, but the catnapping helped take the edge off her exhaustion. She started awake a few times, her mind translating cracking ice or a frozen branch into distant gunfire or the footfall of an approaching enemy. It was frustrating, but it was a sight better than any rest she'd had since the enemy had shown up outside Fort Resolution, and she was grateful for it.

She wasn't sure when she'd dropped off, only knew that it was full night when Schweitzer spoke, drawing her into consciousness. 'Holy shit.'

There was something in his tone, bemusement and wonder rather than alarm, that kept her at ease. She slowly got to a sitting position, leaning on her elbow, propped on Yakecan's broad chest.

Above them was a shimmering curtain of blue-green light, rippling and dancing across the patch of sky kept open by the bog. Mankiller had grown up seeing the curls of glowing fabric, and had long since stopped wondering at it, but the look on Schweitzer's face, dead and stretched as it was, brought some of the old childhood joy back.

'*Yaka nágÿs*,' Mankiller said. 'You never seen it before?'

'Only in pictures,' Schweitzer answered. 'Before Patrick was born, Sarah and I used to talk about going to one of those resorts in the Yukon where you got a good chance of seeing the aurora.'

Mankiller looked up at the glimmering light curling and sinking toward the horizon. 'Lotta different stories about 'em. Some of the Inuit think it's bad. Grampy always told me it was the spirits of kids who died young, before they got to have any fun. The lights is them dancin'.'

'You believe that?' Ghaznavi asked, sitting up.

Mankiller shrugged. 'Like I said, lotta different stories. That's the one I like best.'

'It's a good story,' Ghaznavi said. 'I'm starving. Got anything to eat?'

Mankiller rummaged in her pocket, slapped a granola bar into Ghaznavi's palm.

The SAD Director looked at it, blinked. 'It's not a roast duck.'

'That's for dessert.'

'If you want meat,' Schweitzer said, 'you can nibble on my thigh. Not like I'm using it.'

Ghaznavi wrinkled her nose and munched in silence. They gazed up at the dancing lights above them, so clear and metallic that Mankiller was continually surprised that she couldn't hear it ringing.

When Ghaznavi had finished eating, she settled back, and Mankiller noticed she wasn't looking at the lights anymore, was staring instead at Schweitzer's rapt face. After a moment he noticed too, met her stare. 'What?'

'I was wondering,' she said. 'Let's say that Mankiller's grandfather does have a way to fix you. Let's say that we do get rescued and beat the bad guys and all that jazz. What's your happily ever after? I go back to DC and get a medal and write a best-selling memoir in my early retirement. What do you do?'

Schweitzer shrugged. 'Not much. I lost everything. I get vengeance, I guess. The Cell did me dirty. It'll feel good to do them back.'

'That's enough?'

'It is for now.'

'Yeah, but after now?'

Schweitzer shrugged again. 'I guess I'll try to find my wife.'

'Ain't she passed?' Mankiller asked.

'Yeah,' Schweitzer said, finally looking away from the aurora, 'but so am I. I don't think it matters anymore.'

They were quiet for a while at that, and Schweitzer at last looked up at Ghaznavi. 'And the Director. I need to settle with him. I'd like to . . . talk to him before I finish it. If I can. It might not work out that way, but I have questions. That'll keep me going for the time being.'

'What questions?'

'I'll let you know when the time comes to get them answered.'

'Come on, Jim,' Ghaznavi said.

'That's all you're getting from me, so don't waste your breath. If you don't like it, kill me.'

Ghaznavi frowned, punched him in the shoulder.

Schweitzer gave a grim glimmer of a smile. 'How about you? Why take the risk? Why not just report Hodges to the President? Why'd you agree to help him?'

'I don't like toeing the line,' Ghaznavi said. 'Never did.'

'That's an odd position to take when you run SAD.'

'You don't seem to be friendly to authority either. Surprising for a guy in the Navy.'

'Different in the SEALs.'

'Different in SAD,' she shot back. 'And you were a white dude.'

'What does that have to do with anything?'

'Try being Persian after 9/11. And a woman. I spent my entire life being told that I would never get a clearance and, once I did, that nobody would ever trust me enough to promote me. I had to do everything twice as well as everyone else. I read it in one of my favorite sci-fi novels – "Be so good that they can't ignore you". Maybe that's the real reason I want to win this.'

'Because it means you're good?'

'Nah,' she said. 'I know I'm good. I just want to give the middle finger to everyone who thinks I'm not.'

Schweitzer laughed, a rasping chuckle that gave Mankiller the chills. 'No wonder you're such a badass.'

'Meh,' Ghaznavi said. 'Just driven. By baggage, like everyone else, I suppose.'

'You ever fail at anything?' Schweitzer asked.

'Marriage,' Ghaznavi said.

'Well, sure,' Schweitzer said, 'but that's pretty much a job requirement in the spy business. Military, too. Other than that?'

Ghaznavi was quiet for a while, thinking. 'No, I can't say I have. I've proved every motherfucker wrong who ever said I wasn't a good American.'

'Does it help?'

Now it was Ghaznavi's turn to laugh. 'No. People may have to do what I tell them, but that's not the same as liking or trusting me. I always feel like I'm . . . separate. Cut off from everyone else, no matter what I do.'

'Try coming back from the dead,' Schweitzer said. 'I'll trade places with you any day of the week.'

Ghaznavi smiled and turned to Mankiller. 'How about you?'

'What about me?' Mankiller knew that Ghaznavi was trying to forge a bond, the esprit de corps that knit fighters together, but she was in no mood. The Canadians and Americans were here, on Dene land, and now she was forced by circumstance to drag them to her grandfather's doorstep. When it was over, she wasn't sure if they would leave, what Grampy's *inkoze* would mean for his future, for the future of her family and her town. There were too many unknowns, and while Mankiller liked Schweitzer and Ghaznavi, she couldn't be certain if they were friends or mere allies.

'Just wondering what your story was,' Ghaznavi said. 'Was wondering what you'll do after we win.'

'*If* we win,' Mankiller said, 'I got a town to rebuild and a lot of folk to bury. Some of 'em got family in Toronto or in the lower forty-eight. Sally's got a sister in London who I gotta track down. Gotta make sure everyone's informed.'

'That won't take more than a few weeks,' Ghaznavi said. 'After that, it'll run itself. What'll you do after that?'

'My job,' Mankiller said. 'If you government types'll let me.'

'You're a government type, Sheriff,' Schweitzer said.

''S different in treaty territory. We mostly take care of things on our own out here.'

'Well' – Schweitzer looked back up at the aurora – 'I don't know if you can ever go back to the way things were.'

'No,' Mankiller sighed. 'I reckon not. That's *inkoze*.'

'*Inkoze?*' Ghaznavi asked.

'Medicine,' Mankiller said. 'Magic. That's the problem with it. Makes a lot of things better, does amazing stuff. But it also changes everything. Permanently. That's the only real guarantee with it, that things'll be different than they were. That's rough on anyone, but Dene people like the old ways most of all. So, it's special rough on us.'

'I promise,' Ghaznavi said with some heat, 'I will do everything I can, and that's a lot, to make it easy on you.'

'Yeah,' Mankiller said. 'Well, thanks. That's appreciated.'

'Bet that still doesn't mean you're going to tell us about yourself, does it?' Ghaznavi asked.

'Nope.' Mankiller smiled, looked back up at the lights dancing overhead. 'Sure don't.'

They sat in silence then, the cold green light playing across their faces, until Schweitzer stiffened, looked to his right. 'Something's coming.'

Ghaznavi moved smoothly off the sledge in the opposite direction, crouching down, easing her pistol up. 'How many?'

'No,' Schweitzer said as Mankiller moved to join her. 'It's an animal.'

Mankiller could hear it now, heavy tread, the sound of branches broken by something huge and careless.

'Sounds like a bear,' Mankiller said. 'Gimme my rifle.'

Schweitzer kept the weapon pointed into the woods. 'It is, and if we're being fully honest, isn't it really *our* rifle?'

The bear loped into the clearing and reared up on its hind legs. It was a brown bear, nearly as tall as the stunted growth around it, paws as big as manhole covers. It roared, waving its arms. Schweitzer braced one fist against the back of the sledge and raised the Alaskan to his shoulder.

'Don't,' Mankiller hissed. 'Look at its eyes.'

The bear's snout was raised in a fresh bellow, but it lowered then, and Mankiller saw the flash of burning gold she'd expected. 'That's one of Grampy's *tháydÿne*. Don't you shoot it.'

'It's a Gold,' Schweitzer said, sighting in. 'It's not safe.'

'No, it's different.' Mankiller was standing now. 'There's an ancestor in there. Someone's great-grandpa.'

She moved around the sledge, hands held out before

her. The bear remained where it was, huge paws waving in the air, narrow chest still twice as thick across as Mankiller's shoulders. It roared again, and Mankiller could feel Ghaznavi flinching on the other side of the sledge.

The bear came down to all fours, still nearly as tall as Mankiller, and sniffed at her. Up close, she could see how skinny it was, knew that the dried blood around its muzzle came from its own mouth. Grampy said that the souls of people were bigger than the souls of animals, and so those he honored with housing *tháydÿne* often had trouble eating, their bodies strained to the limit with the effort of containing the ancestor locked inside them. Sometimes, the strain made them twist; sometimes, it made them bleed. Sometimes, it was too much for them altogether, but Grampy said it was the most honored end a creature could meet.

The bear leaned forward, pressed its nose against her parka, and Mankiller felt a momentary spike of fear. The *tháydÿne* could be unstable, the soul of the ancestor warring with the soul of the beast. A wolf, no matter how frightening, was half her size. This bear weighed more than Mankiller and Ghaznavi combined.

'Thought it was wolves,' Schweitzer said.

'It always was before,' Mankiller said.

She turned back to the bear, careful to speak to it in Denesuline, which Grampy had always said was the language of *inkoze*. 'Hey there, *necácho dléze*. What's goin' on?'

The bear nuzzled her parka, gold eyes level with her gut. She was intensely aware of how close the huge mouth was to her stomach, how easily it could snap its jaws and rip her open if it had half a mind. She swallowed her worry. The *tháydÿne* might forgive her fear, but the bear soul at war with it would not. She closed her eyes, breathed deeply, tried to find her center, slow her pounding heart. 'Did Grampy send you?'

The bear thrust its head forward, rocking Mankiller back on her heels, forcing her to grab the sides of its shaggy head to keep her balance. 'Whoa! Easy, big guy.' The bear stank like an open grave.

With a final snort, the animal turned and trotted back off into the trees.

Mankiller turned, raced back to the sledge. 'Rope up.'

'We're following that thing?' Ghaznavi asked.

'Yup. Reckon it's going to Grampy's.'

'Don't you know the way?'

'Yah, but not in the dark. This'll make things faster.'

'Did he send it to pick us up?'

'You ask a lot of questions. Mush.'

'Mush,' Schweitzer agreed.

'Gimme my rifle,' Mankiller said.

'You know, I've kind of grown fond of it.'

'I'm not playin' with you, dead man,' Mankiller groused as she struggled back into the loops of rope.

'I ask for so little, really. No food, no water. No quality time. All without complaint. I ask for this one little thing.'

'I don' have time for this.' Mankiller was already pulling at the ropes, dragging the sledge sideways while Ghaznavi raced to get the harness buckled up. Mankiller was determined to pull the damned thing herself if she had to, but Ghaznavi had learned much in just one short day's labor, and within moments, they were jogging along the rising ground, following the bear's shrinking back in the darkness.

They navigated mostly by sound. This far into the woods, the trees were close around them, canopies blotting out even the aurora, the darkness almost palpably thick. Schweitzer's augmented vision helped some, and while he would occasionally call 'left' or 'right', the cracking boughs and the spray of pine needles against her face were a far better guide than Schweitzer's commands.

Ghaznavi followed Mankiller's lead, and the sled only had to pull cockeyed for a moment before the SAD Director corrected, grunting with the strain. The bear set a grueling pace, and Mankiller kept worrying that Ghaznavi might stumble and fall, but she kept up, her grunting breaths the only indicator of the strain.

And then the tree line ended. Mankiller burst out into a steeply sloping clearing, the dwarf trees clinging tenaciously to a rare rise in the landscape, creating a natural bowl laid open to the aurora's shimmering glare.

Ghaznavi doubled over, panting, hands on her knees. 'Why . . . why'd we stop?'

'We're here,' Mankiller said.

Grampy had built his shack into the side of the rise, raised the roof out of the earth and tangled roots of the scrub trees. The low wall was wooden, painted with creosote, and patched with corrugated plastic framing around tiny windows. A single metal stovepipe pushed out of one wall like a cowlick. The single door was a patchwork of shipping pallets, covered in metal street signs to give it weight against the grasping winter wind. The structure was tiny, a gray smudge on the white and green hillside, easy to miss if you didn't know what you were looking for. The sight had never failed to fill Mankiller with a deep and abiding calm. She exhaled, the fatigue dropping away. For the first time since she and Yakecan had seen the helicopter dropping off its terrible cargo, she felt that things might be all right.

Slowly, Ghaznavi's breathing evened, and she began to straighten.

Mankiller stopped her with a hand on her back. 'Don't freak out.'

Ghaznavi jerked upright, eyes widening. 'Why would I freak ou . . .'

The answer was immediately apparent. The bear had run up the cabin's sloping sides and stood on the roof, the network of roots and packed earth easily supporting its weight. It stared at them, the twin fires of its golden eyes burning.

It was only one of at least a dozen pairs.

All around the cabin, ranging up the steep slope and clustered about a small, weed-choked bog, were wolves, swiveling their heads to take in the newcomers. All their eyes matched the bear's.

'Shit,' Ghaznavi breathed.

'It's okay,' Mankiller said. 'They won't hurt you.'

'They're fucking Golds,' Schweitzer said.

'They're not the same. They're family.'

'Your family is wolves,' Schweitzer said.

Mankiller ignored his tone and nodded. 'Yeah. Cousins, uncles, and grandparents, and not jus' mine. Folk from all over come to Grampy to bring 'em back.'

'Why not bring them back into people?' Schweitzer said.

'Don' work that way,' Mankiller said as she shrugged off the ropes and sighed gratefully.

'It did for me,' Schweitzer said.

Mankiller shrugged again. 'Talk to Grampy; I'm no expert.'

The wolves were coming closer now, sniffing the air, pointing gray-black muzzles in their direction. Some had the stuttering step Mankiller had come to associate with the *tháydÿne*. Some had their heads cocked at unnatural angles, broken tails, bent legs, and stooped shoulders. More than one bled from their eyes or noses.

'You're sure they won't hurt us?' Ghaznavi asked.

'They never hurt me,' Mankiller said, 'but I'm Dene.

Who knows what they'll do to *Bescho Dené*? Don' try to pet 'em or anythin'.'

'Not funny,' Ghaznavi said as the cabin door swung open.

Charles Plante had been small in his prime. Old age had only made him smaller, scarcely bigger than a boy, bent and dry in a way that reminded Mankiller of a spider's corpse. His white hair was thinner than she remembered, but otherwise he looked exactly the same, from his cracked, leathery skin to his deep-set, smiling eyes.

'Hey, sweetie,' he drawled in Denesuline, 'I had a feeling you'd be up my way. There's coffee on.'

'Does he speak English?' Ghaznavi asked.

'Sure does,' Mankiller said. 'Better 'n me. French, too. Spends most of his days reading.'

'Hey, sir,' Ghaznavi said. 'Nice to meet you.'

'Who is this?' Grampy asked Mankiller, still in the Dene tongue. 'She looks like Dene and sounds like *Bescho Dené*.'

'I thought you said he spoke English,' Ghaznavi asked.

'I do speak English' – Plante switched to English – 'but I'm also older 'n dirt and that means I don't have to do anythin' I don' wanna. Come on in 'fore you freeze. Leave the bodies on the sledge; the *tháydÿne* won't bother 'em.'

'Don't think I count as a body,' Schweitzer said, and Plante stiffened at the words, stepping out into the snow.

Schweitzer shifted on the sledge, looking at the old man, his burning silver eyes shining bright enough to compete with the aurora's ghostly glow.

'What's this?' Grampy asked, coming forward. 'Is he dead? Is he *tháydÿne*?'

'He was,' Mankiller said. 'But it's his body. The *tháydÿne* was another, older spirit, to hear him tell it.'

'His eyes are silver. That only happens when the wolf wins.'

'Huh.' Mankiller knew better than to ask Grampy questions. It irritated him; best to just let the old man know that she was listening, and leave it to him to fill in the blanks himself.

'That never happens,' Plante said. 'The animal always holds on to some extent, but a human soul is stronger, bigger.'

'Well, this was a human and a human,' Mankiller said.

'That's impossible,' Grampy said. 'Who are you?' he asked Schweitzer.

'I'm Jim Schweitzer,' Schweitzer said. 'I was created by the same magic you use on these animals. The people who created me are bad people, and they are here looking for you. I can stop them, but I need your help.'

'That's ridiculous,' Plante said. 'There are no others like me. I am Lived-With-The-Wolves.'

'I'm sorry, Grampy,' Mankiller said, 'but it's true. There are more of 'em. Dead men faster and stronger than any living man I ever seen. In each of 'em, the wolf lost, but they're more wild than any wolf I ever seen. Only one of 'em can think like a living man, and he leads them. It's him that wants you. He wanted me to lead him to you.'

Plante pursed his lips. 'The *tháydÿne* had seen the soldiers searchin' the woods. I wasn' sure what they were looking for.'

'They're lookin' for you, Grampy,' Mankiller said. 'They put the town under siege. Lotta folks dead. Army sent a small force. Some of 'em are killed. Ollie's holed up at the station with the survivors.'

'Jesus,' Plante whispered. 'How's Joe?'

Mankiller gestured at the sledge, and Plante knelt at Yakecan's side, putting one tiny, gnarled hand on his forehead. Yakecan had wet himself during the trip, and Mankiller hadn't had a chance to clean him up. Calmut hadn't had much time to feed him either, and the great walrus bulk of her former deputy was already beginning to waste away.

'What happened?' Plante asked.

'I sent him to get help,' Mankiller said. 'Not sure what happened after that, but he stumbled back into town wet and frozen. Guess the bad guys dunked him in the lake.'

'He's alive,' Plante said. 'He's still in there.'

'Yeah,' Mankiller said. 'Was wonderin' if you could do somethin' about that.'

Plante shook his head. 'I can only call the *tháydÿne* from the next world, sweetheart. This man is alive. Ah, poor Joe. He's a good guy.'

'I figured.' Mankiller swallowed a spasm of grief at the news. 'Had to ask.'

Plante looked up at her, eyes damp. 'What are you gonna do?'

'What can I do, Grampy? I'll keep him alive. He's got a sister in Yellowknife. When all this is over, I'll let her know. I imagine she'll want to take him.'

Plante shook his head. 'Jesus.'

The name was pronounced *Sezús* in Denesuline, but Ghaznavi recognized it. 'Did you say "Jesus"?'

'Yah.' Plante nodded.

'You believe in that? I thought you were some kind of shaman.'

Plante shook his head. 'Ain't too bright, are you? You think I'd pray to the Great Beaver Spirit? Dene been Catholics for two hundred years.'

Mankiller smirked. 'Longer.'

'Anyways, you'll be freezin' your ass off out here,' Plante said. 'I guess everybody should come on in. Be cramped, though.'

Plante made no effort to help, and it was for Mankiller

and Ghaznavi to wrestle Yakecan and Schweitzer's limp forms to the tiny shack.

The wolves formed a tight knot around them. A few tentatively licked Plante's hand or nuzzled Mankiller's hip as Plante led the way inside.

The interior was a jumbled, dirt-floored wedge hacked into the hillside. It was furnished in no discernible style – an old cable spool used as a table, a milk crate beside a folding chair. An ancient mahogany wing chair stood in the corner, upholstered in white with delicate pink flowers. The shack had no electricity, and the cast-iron woodstove did little to warm it, though it did fill the room with a cheery, dancing light that was surprisingly comforting after the alien green cast of the aurora. The hillside that made up the shack's back wall was invisible behind an enormous stack of cordwood, much of it rotting and crawling with beetles. Plante slept on the same old army cot he'd used when he was in the service, said he'd gotten so used to it that he couldn't sleep on anything else. It took up the corner of the shack opposite the wing chair, the olive-green fabric long since gone to gray, threadbare and full of holes.

Every spare surface in the place was covered with the books her Grampy so dearly loved. Moldering green leather-backed classics by ancient Greeks and Romans. Grampy had read to her from them incessantly when she was a girl, but apart from liking the stories about the battles, they never took. Mankiller remembered the names, however: Polybius, Herodotus, Homer, Titus Livius. A stack of Bibles towered closest to the cot. Grampy took pride in claiming to have read the Good Book in Latin, Greek, Hebrew, and Aramaic. Mankiller had no way to verify the claim, but she had her doubts.

Ghaznavi settled Yakecan on Plante's cot at a gesture

from the old man, froze as a shadow uncoiled from behind the wing chair and stepped out into the light.

It was another wolf, rail thin, ribs showing through its sparse, gray-white pelt. Plante had strung a garland of dried mountain avens around its neck, the florets yellowed and bare of petals. Its narrow snout rose defiantly, and then the flickering gold eyes caught Mankiller and it started forward, whining deep in its throat.

Mankiller felt unease mixing with grief as she always did at the sight of the creature. '*Setsoné*.' She knelt and took the narrow head in her hands, gently cradling it to her chest.

'Who's . . .' Ghaznavi began.

'That's my wife,' Plante said. 'Wilma's grandma. She was the first one I called back. That's how I knew I had the *inkoze*.'

The effort of the greeting was clearly all the wolf could manage, and it hobbled quietly to the base of the stove and slumped down before it. Plante quickly retrieved a threadbare gray blanket from behind the chair and draped it over the creature.

'Is she okay?' Ghaznavi asked.

'She's old,' Plante said, sinking into the wing chair, 'and they don' eat so good once they come back. It's a strain to put the soul of a woman inside an animal. 'Specially if it's a big soul, and Mary's soul was as big as they come.'

The wolf whined briefly in response, flicking her eyes toward Plante before closing them and heaving a sigh.

'So, what's goin' on, Wilma?' Plante asked in Denesuline again.

'Hell if I know, Grampy,' she said. 'I told you everythin'. Helicopter showed up with a cage full of things like this one.' She jerked a thumb at Schweitzer. 'Attacked the town, tryin' to get me to roll and give you up.'

'And you came here,' Plante said. 'You shoulda come sooner.'

'I didn't want to risk them followin' me.'

'Why'd you risk it this time?'

Mankiller let her shoulders slump, took a shaking breath, held it for a moment before letting it go, and finally spoke the truth that had been battering at her since she'd first seen that Yakecan had failed in his radio run. 'Because I don't know what else to do. Because I can't protect anyone no more. I'm tapped out, Grampy. I need help.'

Plante nodded. 'What do you need?'

'Bullets, food, medical supplies. As much as we can fit on the sledge. You'll be tight for a bit, but I'll make good on it. The Army sent a flight of helos to help, only one got shot down and the other bugged out, but I know they'll be back. We jus' need help hangin' on 'til they get there.'

'That's what you want from me, Wilma? Supplies?'

'I was hopin' there was somethin' you could do for him.' She gestured to Schweitzer, slumped beside Yakecan against the cot. 'He's the only real weapon we got against them. They're so much stronger than living folk.'

'He's dead, Wilma. If I knew him in life, might be I could put his soul in an animal who'd have him, but what good would that do?'

'Dunno.' Mankiller turned her hands in useless circles. 'You shoulda seen him, Grampy. He could jump high as a building. They can all do that.'

'So, how come he's lyin' there like a sack of beans?'

'The Director, that's the enemy leader. They fought and I guess it got the drop on him.'

Plante was silent, staring at Schweitzer, his tiny, gnarled hands resting in his lap.

'Sir,' Schweitzer said, 'what you can do, it's a known quantity. I was created by someone else who could do it, and I've met others who can do it as well. There has to be a way. There are plenty of dead bodies back in town. Some of them are hard operators; if you could put me into one of—'

'Why?' Plante interrupted him.

'Excuse me, sir?'

'Why do you want to fight? Why do you want to help my granddaughter? The Canadians are nothin' to you, the Dene even less. You're an American, or you were.'

'I still am. The bastards killed my wife. I mean to make them pay for that.'

'That's it? Revenge?' Plante leaned forward, looked deep into the silver flames of Schweitzer's eyes. 'No, I don' think it is.'

'It is, sir. I need your help to do it.'

'*Dëne hél hani*,' Plante said, looking away.

'Sir, I don't understa—'

'He's callin' you a liar,' Mankiller said.

'I been callin' spirits for thirty years,' Plante said. 'I touch each one, and I *know* 'em. Even if I didn't, I'm an old man, and I seen a lot of the world. Man don' get snapped in half and come beggin' for a way to get back in the fight just to punish someone, even if they did kill his wife.'

'What makes you say that?' Schweitzer said, and Mankiller knew he was lying. She'd worked too long in law enforcement not to be able to hear it in the pitch and timbre of a voice.

'When your loved one dies, it's a tragedy,' Plante said, 'but tragedies make a man mourn. They don' make him fight, not like you've got the fight in you. Only one reason a man does that.'

'I don't know what—'

'You still got someone *alive*.' Plante turned back to Schweitzer. 'Someone to protect. Someone you got to get back to. Tell me the truth, son. If there's a way I can help you, I will, but you got to level with me.'

'You said that he killed your wife,' Ghaznavi said slowly. 'You didn't say that he killed your wife and son. That's what we call an anomaly in this business.'

Schweitzer's grinning skull face didn't change, but his burning eyes flicked from Ghaznavi to Mankiller to the old man before glancing down to the dirt floor. 'Patrick's alive.' His voice was heavy, defeated.

Ghaznavi was the only one who showed any reaction, a short intake of breath. 'Where is he?'

Schweitzer raised his head. 'Someplace safe. Someplace you can't find him.'

'Don't be an idiot, Jim,' Ghaznavi said. 'We fucking found bin Laden; we can find your kid.'

'So help me,' Schweitzer growled, 'you find him and I find you.'

Ghaznavi arched an eyebrow. 'You don't need to find me, Jim. I'm sitting right here. And even if I wasn't, what would you do? Drag your spaghetti ass across the country by your knuckles to Langley?'

'If that's what it takes,' Schweitzer said.

Ghaznavi snorted. 'Maybe I'll have Grampy here keep you as you are.'

The anger was sudden in Mankiller's throat; it took her a moment to swallow before she could choke out the words. 'He ain't your Grampy. You call him Mr Plante.'

Ghaznavi met her gaze before shrugging. 'Sure. Fine. Anyway, don't worry, Jim. If we did find him, it would only be to protect him.'

'He's plenty protected as he is.'

'Your problem is that you don't trust your own government. We have a long and storied history of doing the right thing. Competently.'

Schweitzer didn't appear amused, and Ghaznavi gave another snort that turned into a chuckle before she realized the sally had failed.

'Patrick's your boy, I assume?' Grampy asked.

'That's right,' Schweitzer said. 'When I wrap up here, when the Cell is finished, I'm going to find him again.'

'And then what?' Grampy asked. 'How are you gonna raise him? You're dead.'

'So's your wife.' Schweitzer pointed a finger at the wolf curled under the blanket in front of the stove. 'At least you're together.'

Grampy smiled at that, gave a short chuckle of his own. 'Yeah, I guess you got a point.' His face went sad. 'You can't protect him, you know.' His eyes flicked to the starved-looking wolf, ancient and trembling gently under the tattered blanket. 'You can't protect anyone. Not really.'

'No,' Schweitzer said, 'but you have to try.'

Plante looked up at that, his eyes wet. 'You like classics, Mr Schweitzer?'

'I read the *Iliad*, but only because I had to. I have to say I'm surprised to see you're so into them.'

Plante nodded. 'Yeah, I guess it is surprisin'. I jus' wanted to read about a people as old as my own, who weren't my own. I wanted to know how white people were before gunpowder and metal.'

'You didn't go back far enough,' Schweitzer said, gesturing to the heaped books. 'This is all Iron Age.'

Plante spread his hands. 'What can I say? Got sucked in. Anyway, it's full of battles like that. Aemilius against the Ingauni. Alexander the Great against . . . well, everybody. Always hopelessly outnumbered, always finding a way to win.'

'Well, call me Alexander.'

'Self-praise is no praise at all,' Grampy laughed. 'You

know, I never thought Wilma would make it through basic.'

'Yeah, I remember.' Mankiller felt the old flash of anger and pride, a weird mix that translated to love for this old man.

'But you did,' Grampy said. 'Watching you at graduation was the proudest day of my life.'

'Maybe not the proudest.' Mankiller smiled.

'Okay,' Grampy sighed. 'I can definitely load you up with as much stores as you can carry.'

'And him?' Mankiller jerked a thumb toward Schweitzer. 'Is there anything you can do?'

Grampy sighed again. 'I don't want to.'

'I know it,' Schweitzer said, 'but will you?'

'I can't promise I can find him in the beyond,' Grampy said. 'It helps the more you know someone, and I don't know this *Bescho Dené*.'

'Find me in the beyond?' Schweitzer asked.

'I can't retrieve you from a body. I can only retrieve you from the beyond. In order to do that, I have to put you back there.'

'The only way I know how to do that is to destroy this body,' Schweitzer said.

'Not like it's doing you a lot of good as it is,' Mankiller said.

'Absolutely not,' Ghaznavi said. 'What happens if we lose you?'

'You miss out on my dynamic conversation,' Schweitzer said. 'Do you want to win this fight or not? If there's a chance, then there's a chance. If he can put me back into the corpse of one of the operators who fell assaulting the sta—'

'Whoa there,' Grampy said. 'Who said anythin' 'bout corpses? I can't do that.'

'Sir, I know you can; it's the same magic.'

'Do you know?' Grampy said. 'You have the *inkoze* youself?'

'You know I don't, but I know—'

'You don' know anythin'.' Grampy's voice went hard. 'You want my help, you gonna have to trust that I know my own business. I been workin' *inkoze* for years, and I know one thing for sure: I can't put *tháydÿne* in a dead body. Only livin' ones.'

'You can't put me in a wolf, sir. I'm not going to be any help if—'

'I'm not gonna put you in a wolf.' Grampy nodded toward Yakecan's body, still and silent on the cot.

Mankiller's stomach turned over. She wasn't sure what she'd expected in coming here, but it certainly wasn't this. 'No.' The word was out before she knew she'd spoken, welling up from somewhere deep and primal. She liked Schweitzer, but she didn't know him, and the thought of Yakecan's bent and bleeding body, starved and injured like Grampy's wolves, being a vessel for this stranger made her gut clench. 'It's Joe, Grampy. He ain't a wolf.'

Grampy's eyes turned to her, unchanged in their sadness. 'Wilma, Joe ain't comin' back. You know that. He's breathin', but that ain't the same as bein' alive. He'll be more alive with Jim in there. At least then he'd do something more 'n breathin'.'

Mankiller looked at her feet, then up at Grampy, struggling with the tide of grief that threatened to overwhelm her. She knew she didn't want this to happen, even though it made sense, even when it seemed the only way of getting Schweitzer back in the fight. *It's because it means you're giving up on Joe. It means he's gone.*

But Mankiller didn't say that. Instead, she said, 'Will Joe still be in there?'

'If I could even do it,' Grampy said, 'I don't know what it'd be like. Never done it on people before. Not even sure if I can.'

'Will he be like the animals? Having *tháydÿne* in 'em is too much for 'em lots of times.'

'That's because the human soul is too much for the animal body,' Grampy said. 'But in this case, it's both people. No idea what'll happen.'

Ghaznavi took a shuddering breath. 'Guess there's only one way to find out.'

'Can we even make that decision for him?' Schweitzer asked.

'*We* can't,' Mankiller said, 'but *I* can. Joe was my deputy and my friend. Apart from his sister, I'm the closest thing to family he's got, and I guess I know his mind better 'n anyone.'

Grampy smiled, spread his hands. 'And if Joe could talk, what would he tell you to do?'

Mankiller smiled back. 'Aw, hell, Grampy. You know he'd tell me to do it. He'd jump at the chance to help.'

Grampy nodded. 'That's the Joe I know too.'

'How would it work?' Ghaznavi asked.

Grampy shrugged. 'You got to go out if you're gonna come back.'

'The only way to release my soul is to destroy this body totally,' Schweitzer said.

'What if it doesn't work, Jim?' Ghaznavi asked.

'We already went over this.'

'Reckon we can make a bonfire out front,' Plante said. 'Been a while since I had one, and the *tháydÿne* always like it.'

'Nonstarter,' Ghaznavi said. 'I'm not sure what kind of detection equipment they've got. They might even have drones. I don't want to risk lighting up a blaze out here. What if they see it?'

'What if they do?' Grampy smiled. 'I'll be comin' with ya anyhow. Might be good if they wasted time and people draggin' ass all the way up here only to find we're gone.'

'Sir,' Ghaznavi began, 'I can't risk your—'

'Sorry, Grampy,' Mankiller cut her off. 'We got a colonel from the Army down in town, too. They can't decide which of 'em is in charge and can't get it through their heads that it's neither.'

'Listen—' Spots of color appeared on Ghaznavi's cheeks.

'I've done just about enough listenin' to you,' Mankiller said. 'Time for *you* to listen. Grampy wants to come back to town, he comes back to town. You want to jump up and down and cry about it, well, suit yourself.'

Ghaznavi stuttered, shot a pleading glance at Schweitzer. 'What are you looking at me for?' he asked. 'I can barely move and it sounds like I'm about to get incinerated.'

'I'm comin' with,' Grampy said. 'No safer here than with you, maybe less safe since I'm alone. Besides, might be I can do some good.'

'Sir—' Ghaznavi began.

'Yah,' Grampy said, standing up. 'Now, ladies, if you wouldn't mind excusing us, I need to ask you to step outside for a moment. Jim and I need to talk.'

'About what?' Ghaznavi asked, but she stood at least. Mankiller was grateful for that.

'If I'm gonna chase a spirit into the void and bring it back with me, I need some way to find it. I need to *know* him. With the *tháydÿne*, they're people I grown up with, or at least been close to. You' – he pointed at Schweitzer – 'I just met.'

'Okay,' Schweitzer said slowly. 'How do we fix that?'

'You and I are gonna talk, and I'm afraid it's gonna have to be pretty deep, and we don't have time to go slow. That's why I'm puttin' these ladies out in the cold for a spell.'

'C'mon.' Mankiller took Ghaznavi's elbow. 'He knows what he's about. You gotta trust him.'

Ghaznavi sighed, heaved the door open, and winced at the blast of frigid air that swept over them. The *tháydÿne* were gathered outside, sitting in a loose delta, burning eyes fixed on the women emerging into the bitter cold. Ghaznavi stepped out and winced again as Grampy shut the door behind her, leaned against it. 'I know they're family, but they freak me the fuck out.'

'They won't hurt you,' Mankiller said, stepped between the creatures and Ghaznavi. The truth was that they freaked her out too, but she sure as heck wasn't going to tell Ghaznavi that now. Instead, she knelt and held out a hand to one. 'This one's my cousin . . . like twenty times removed, I think.' The wolf sniffed at her fingers tentatively, gave a decidedly un-wolflike twitch of its head, and backed away.

'Your cousin-like-twenty-times-removed seems unfriendly. Anyway, it doesn't matter. We're both going to freeze to death long before anything else can hurt us.'

They stood shivering, staring at the eerily silent wolf pack who sat unblinking and stared back. There was no sign of the bear. Mankiller supposed it might still be on the shack's roof, but she didn't want to break the strange staring contest to look up. The only sounds were the gentle sigh of the wind and the low murmur of Grampy's voice, barely audible through the cabin walls.

At last, the door scraped open and Grampy appeared, dragging Schweitzer by his armpits. 'Jesus, this guy's heavy.'

Mankiller and Ghaznavi rushed to help. 'His bones are mostly metal,' Ghaznavi said.

'Well, that's damn disappointin'.' Grampy gratefully let Schweitzer fall into Mankiller's hands, put a hand to his back, and winced his way over to a low bowl a few feet from the shack, where he proceeded to kick away the snow to reveal patches of black, charred ground covered in a thin rime of ice.

'If you'd be so kind, could I trouble you to run some wood out here?' Grampy asked Ghaznavi. 'We'll take it in shifts.'

Mankiller laid Schweitzer beside the pit and then retrieved Grampy's pickaxe from underneath the frozen tarp where he kept his tools. Unasked, she set to breaking up the ice and clearing away the snow. The wolves silently ringed the pit, sitting at the edge of the clearing, attentive and rigid, like cultists at some religious rite.

And in a way, Mankiller supposed they were. She glanced over at Schweitzer. 'Hope this works. If it does, you gonna have to tell Joe that I'm sorry.'

'Sorry for what?' Schweitzer asked. He was half-buried in snow and chipped ice by now, and looked nothing like the giant thing Mankiller had first met, as if some fundamental part of him was missing.

Mankiller paused, leaned on the pickaxe. 'For sendin' him out. For not thinkin' of a better way. For puttin' him out there where he could get dunked in that lake. For not goin' with him. Heck, tell him I'm sorry for every time I yelled at him. Tell him I'm sorry I made fun of him for Nora. Tell him . . . Just tell him he was the best damn deputy I ever had and a good friend, and I'm real sorry he . . . wound up like this.' Saying the words brought the grief racing up into her throat, and Mankiller was grateful that the cold had made her eyes tear up already. Still, the last few words came out hoarse.

'Sheriff' – Schweitzer's voice was surprisingly gentle – 'I'm not even in his body yet, and I am already one hundred percent certain that he knows all that.'

'Yeah.' Mankiller sniffed, cuffed at her nose. 'Well, you jus' make sure you tell him anyway. Jus' in case.'

'You can tell him yourself,' Schweitzer said. 'Back before I drove Ninip out, we shared my body. Both of us could drive, move the arms, or use the mouth to talk. Kind of like being a Siamese twin, I guess.'

'And that's what it'll be like when you're in there?' Mankiller danced out of the way as Ghaznavi and Grampy showed up, gratefully dumped armloads of wood into the pit, and turned wordlessly back to the house.

'Search me,' Schweitzer said. 'I'm new to this whole dead-reanimated-by-magic thing.'

At last, the fire pit was piled high with wood. Mankiller remembered the last time they'd built one here, the last time they'd held a Stickdance. That had been a time to mourn, but it had also been a time of peace and joy. Doing it now, under the grim shadow of the threat to her home, Mankiller felt her stomach clench.

She nodded to Ghaznavi and stood at Schweitzer's feet. They lifted him between them, swung him back and forth. 'Sorry,' Ghaznavi grunted. 'This isn't terribly dignified.'

'Just get it done,' Schweitzer said. With a final heave, they threw him on top of the wood. There was a brief moment where the insult of rolling down the other side might have been added to the injury of being thrown like a sack of rocks, but Schweitzer was able to stick out his arm and steady himself.

Mankiller stepped back. 'You okay?' she asked.

'Not really,' Schweitzer said. 'I'm dead and broken pretty much in half.'

'Well, we're aimin' to fix that,' Grampy said, dragging out his cot, with Yakecan bouncing along as he went. Once again, Mankiller and Ghaznavi raced to help him, and once again, he gratefully stood aside and let them.

Grandma's *tháydÿne* stood in the doorway, blanket still over her back, watching.

Grampy doused the wood with kerosene next, splashing it out from a jerry can that looked like it was last used in World War II. The acrid fumes tickled Mankiller's nose, and Schweitzer twitched as the liquid splashed across him.

At last, Grampy stood back, grunted in satisfaction, and produced a plastic lighter. He touched the marble-sized flame to a long wooden punk, held it up. 'You ready? Wind's blowin' right through the base, so it'll go up like a torch once I put this in.'

'Hey, Jala,' Schweitzer said.

'Yeah?'

'I hope this works.'

'Me too.'

'So say we all,' Grampy said, knelt, and thrust the burning brand home.

Chapter Seventeen
Brave New World

Schweitzer died for the second time.

His dead nerves reported the pain but without any involuntary reaction, and he was free to ignore it or pay attention as he chose. He ignored the pain, focused instead on the bizarre sensation of his flesh changing state, the glycerol boiling away, the meat of him expanding and bursting and finally drying and shrinking, at long last turning to ash and vapor and blowing away.

The first time he'd died, he had been completely focused on his enemy, on the gun barrel jammed under his chin, on the terrible realization that he had *lost*. Now, he realized with a twinge of doleful humor, there was nothing left to lose. Sarah was dead. Patrick was a world away, and there was no guarantee that he'd even be able to locate Eldredge even if he had a working body to do it.

It was oddly liberating. With nothing left to strive for, Schweitzer had only to let his body go, to will himself skyward as smoke and ash borne on the fire's dancing updraft. There was only the aurora above him, the crisp bite of the freezing air, the high, chemical stink of glycerol and humectants boiling out into gas, and beneath it all, the savory scent of cooking meat, the last of the real James Schweitzer, going up in smoke.

At last, he felt his extremities burning away, the bones of his legs and his remaining arm blackening and turning to ash. The mechanical one had been removed at Ghaznavi's insistence, lay propped against the cabin's side. Even now he felt no different, even as his torso burned up and collapsed, so that he could see his blackened ribs smoking in the freezing air. *What if it doesn't work? What if I'm trapped in whatever charred remains are left?* The thought brought a stab of worry but only briefly. It made no difference. He would be useless either way.

But at last, he felt the flesh around his head consumed by the hungry flames, the metal armature of his skull cooled by the whipping wind. His consciousness came untethered, a pleasant feeling of drifting, loosening. *It's my eyes*, he thought. *That's what's finally burning.* The fire consumed by fire, or at least the flesh that held those fires in place. *So, that's where the soul lives*, he thought, amazed. It was in the eyes. He remembered the passage from the Bible, the gospel of St Matthew: *The lamp of the body is the eye, if, therefore, thine eye may be perfect, all thy body shall be enlightened.* It made him want to laugh. *Fuckers got something right.*

But he couldn't laugh, because the world was fading now, and the aurora was drowning in an inky blackness so complete that it forbade even the thought of light. Schweitzer was caught in a current, an immense undertow reeling him in, faster and farther. Schweitzer didn't fight it, let the current carry him along, floating peacefully, until the blissful darkness was contaminated with a glowing light line, growing larger on the horizon. The first faint screams reached him.

Schweitzer lifted his spiritual head to greet the soul storm sweeping him into its bosom, calling him home. It was a chaos of tortured, tumbling souls, mixing and churning until madness claimed them, until all that was human in them was scoured away. It was as close as he'd ever come to hell, but he greeted it gladly.

Because he knew that Sarah was somewhere in that maelstrom. The scent of her rosewater perfume was suddenly thick in his spiritual nostrils, and he knew in that moment that he would surely be able to find her, that even in the midst of the chaos, he would claw his way to her side. No doubt half the souls in the storm were missing loved ones, but he doubted any of them had such a clear trail to follow. Beside her, he would be close enough to hear her voice above the tumult, close enough for her to hear him, close enough to tell her how sorry he was, and how much she meant to him, and how . . .

Jim.

Schweitzer felt his drifting slow. He was being tugged backward. A gentle but insistent pull.

Jim. You know me. Turn around.

Schweitzer didn't want to turn around. Not when Sarah was so close. He sucked greedily at the scent of her perfume and tried to stay the course. But in spite of himself, he felt his consciousness rotating until he faced back the way he'd come.

A blue road stretched out before him, the stark color ugly in the midst of the quiet black. It stretched off into the distance, arrow-straight as far as his spiritual eyes could see. Schweitzer knew what lay at the other end of it, an old man with leathery skin and kind eyes, sitting beside a bonfire that was taking in what little remained of Schweitzer's old form.

Jim, Plante whispered to him across the strange miles between this world and the one Jim had known. *Come back.*

The screaming grew fainter as Plante pulled harder and the soul storm slowly lost the tug-of-war. The scent of

Sarah's perfume grew weaker, and Schweitzer found himself fighting against Plante's insistent tugging. Schweitzer knew he should let the old man bring him back, that he had something he was supposed to do, though he couldn't remember exactly what it was. All he knew for certain was that Sarah was somewhere behind him. All that Plante could offer was the bitter cold, the biting wind, and the company of strangers.

No. Schweitzer sent the thought down the blue ribbon to the old man at the far end. *I'm staying here.*

What's your rush? Plante's voice was full of warm mirth. *You got all the time in the world to be dead. But first, you should finish up the stuff you need to be alive for.*

Why wait? Schweitzer answered. *Besides, I'm already dead.*

Not for long. Come on back and let me show you.

No. Schweitzer pulled harder. *She's here; I can smell her perfume. I can find her.*

You can find her later. You need to find Patrick now. Patrick is your son. Do you remember him? Do you remember that he needs you to care for him?

Schweitzer said nothing, but neither did he come willingly, pulling against the old man's magic as hard as he could, and succeeding only in staying put.

Do you remember what you told me when we were alone in the cabin, Jim? That dead thing that's running the Cell is your brother. It's Peter, Jim. You can't leave him here. You can't go until he's dealt with.

Schweitzer felt his consciousness jerk at the words, a cold fire growing in his spiritual belly, rising through his chest until it choked him. He remembered now, Peter's words on the chapel roof: *I knew from the day I was born that I was going to be the greatest warrior-king the world had ever known.*

And this above all: *The age of the living is over, Jim. Welcome to the dawn of the dead.*

Yes, Plante said. *He said that, and he meant it. Your brother's aiming high. It's not just Patrick now, Jim. It's all of us. You can delay gratification for a few measly years for that. Souls are eternal. Your wife's not going anywhere. Come back and finish this.*

And Schweitzer felt himself moving now, no longer resisting the old man's pull. The screaming grew fainter and finally silenced, but the scent of rosewater lingered, staying with him all the way down until he felt himself at the very limit of the void and the hard edges of something poised to admit him.

Work with me, Jim, Plante said. *Step inside.*

Schweitzer did. He felt his consciousness slip past the edges and into the dark interior space he had once known. It was the inside of a body, like his own that he had shared with Ninip, but where his corpse had been dark and silent, this place thundered with life. The walls of Schweitzer's new home reverberated with a pounding pulse, hammering in a steady rhythm that he knew could only be a heartbeat. He could feel the searing heat of the living blood; could smell the teeming colonies of bacteria, the bouquet of fields of gut flora; could hear the song of a billion cells dividing and dying, dividing and dying, over and over again. Life was hot and noisy.

Schweitzer was stunned, the jackhammer chorus of Yakecan's living body tossing him like a boat in a storm. He felt the cool peace of the void just outside the edges of Yakecan's body, beckoning him with its placid silence. He could just duck out there for a moment, suck down some more of Sarah's rosewater scent, gather himself for another try.

But he felt Plante's magic ushering him along. He could

scarcely hear the old man's voice through the spiritual din, but he didn't need to. He knew it was warning him, reminding him that if he moved out of Yakecan's inner space and back into the void, he would never return. This was a one-way ticket. He either stayed in the fight or he let the void claim him forever. *Focus*, Schweitzer told himself. *It's about the mission, not you.* If going under the hammer of Yakecan's pulsing heart was what it took to see this through, then that was what he would do.

He gritted his spiritual teeth, reached out for Yakecan. As far as he knew, the magic worked on the pairing of souls. Schweitzer was the only one who occupied his body alone. *No, Peter is the same as you.* The thought shook him nearly as much as the realization that he had no body now. All that remained of him was smoking gristle and ash atop the bonfire. He was a guest in Yakecan's body now, and like all polite guests, he would let the host know that he'd arrived.

Even in the midst of the tumult, Yakecan proved easy to find. When Schweitzer was paired with Ninip, he had pictured the presence as a blackness coiled about him. Sometimes the jinn looked like a slit-eyed serpent, sometimes as he had been in life, armored in bronze, tall, olive complected, his hair in oiled ringlets.

Yakecan also appeared as he had in life, exactly so. The image Schweitzer received when he contacted Yakecan's soul was of the tall, burly man seated cross-legged and naked in a spring field, surrounded by sprays of tiny flowers, grinning placidly into the distance.

Joe Yakecan, Schweitzer said. *I'm Jim Schweitzer. Your boss sent me. I need your help.*

But Schweitzer knew before he spoke that Yakecan wasn't listening. There was a feeling to the presence, to Yakecan's soul. It was resident, clearly tied to the life that thundered all about it, but its spiritual eyes were fixed on the far horizon, on the void that coiled outside the edges of Yakecan's physical being.

Yakecan, Schweitzer said again. *Come on, man. Wake up.*

But Joe Yakecan did not wake up. His soul looked out into the void, the idiot grin fixed on its childlike face, beaming amidst the blanket of flowers. Schweitzer gave him a spiritual nudge, got no response, and turned away. Maybe the shock to the system of Yakecan's near-death experience had untethered his soul somehow. Maybe, like Schweitzer, he was aware of the noise and confusion of his own life now and sought the peace of the void as a refuge. Schweitzer didn't know and probably never would. But he was certain that Yakecan was beyond him. He might share the physical space with Yakecan, but there would be no competition to control it. Assuming that Plante's magic worked.

As if the old man had heard his thoughts, Schweitzer felt a sudden gust pushing him toward Yakecan's soul. The magic shoved them together, and Schweitzer felt the flood of the man's memories washing over him. A gambling game, Yakecan bouncing on his knees to a throbbing drum, flashing hand signals and trading bits of broken twigs to keep score. The aluminum gangway up to an amphibious transport, the dark green camouflage of Canadian soldiers all about him. The backseat of a freezing pickup truck, fumbling for a warm breast and laughing at the shriek evoked by his chilly fingers.

Schweitzer turned away from the memories, gave the man his privacy. Ninip had ravaged Schweitzer's secrets when they'd been paired, and he still remembered the sick feeling of violation, of helplessness. He was not like Ninip. Wasn't like his brother, even. Integrity was the last vestige of his humanity, and he exercised it every chance he got. Schweitzer had been able to push back against Ninip. Yakecan wouldn't communicate with him, was helpless to resist him, but Schweitzer let him be regardless. He embraced the impetus of Plante's magic, let it wrap him more tightly around Yakecan, felt the lines between them blur. The thundering of Yakecan's biology receded into the background a bit. Still painfully loud but not as jarring as it had been before, dialed back enough for Schweitzer to focus on his surroundings.

Where his own internality had been black, Yakecan's was red, a warm closeness that left Schweitzer feeling claustrophobic. The pushing sensation ceased, and Schweitzer reached out, feeling for the same levers he'd always pulled when he'd been back in his old body, the reporting of his dead nerve endings, the corpse-fibers twitching and contracting according to his spiritual commands.

With Ninip, control of his body had been a constant struggle. With Yakecan, the absence of resistance was almost sad, and Schweitzer surged forward, sliding his spiritual limbs into the spaces that drove Yakecan's physical ones, a diver putting on a second skin.

James Schweitzer opened his eyes.

The aurora shimmered above him, green ribbons snaking out into the blackness of the sky. He could hear the popping of the bonfire next to him, feel the heat of it against the side of his face.

'Well, I'll be damned.' Plante's voice, thick with wonder. 'First time I ever did that.'

Mankiller's face appeared over his own, her eyes wet. 'Joe! Joe, can you hear me!?'

'I can hear you.' Schweitzer was used to coaxing air through his corpse's punctured larynx, but Yakecan's working lungs pushed it up effortlessly, and Schweitzer felt a strange queasiness at the sound of his . . . Yakecan's voice sounding in his ears. Speaking forced him to inhale, and the sweetness of breath overwhelmed him.

How long had it been since he died? He had forgotten how amazing it was to simply breathe, to have lungs that expanded and contracted, a stomach that pinched with hunger, a bladder that was dangerously full. The air tasted of charcoal and diesel fumes; the cold had a metallic bite that made his earlobes burn. His foot itched. There was a cramp in the back of his leg. It was a chorus, a litany of smells, sounds, aches, and pains. All had been reported to him secondhand by the magic that kept his corpse animated. Now he was *in* it. He was *feeling* it. A human at last. His heart raced, but the very feeling of it beating was so indescribably wonderful that he pitched forward as he sat up, groaning.

Mankiller wrapped her arms around him. 'Joe! Are you okay?! Say somethin'!'

Schweitzer had never thought about Mankiller romantically, but the mere touch of another human being nearly sent him into spontaneous orgasm. Schweitzer felt blood flooding his crotch, his cock stiffening in his snow pants. *Oh, God*, he thought. *I'm a man again.*

Mankiller was shouting in his ear, barely choking back tears. He managed to flash her a thumbs-up sign, which got her to back off long enough for him to get shakily to his feet. Ghaznavi stared at him openmouthed. 'Your eyes,' she said. 'They're normal.'

Schweitzer raised his fingertip, pulled up his eyelid, tapped the soft-wet surface beneath. He felt the slight pain, the jerking revulsion of his body's involuntary response, reveled in it. All around him, the wolves looked up, the gold fire burning in their still-living sockets. 'Guess it's different,' he offered.

'Why?' Ghaznavi asked.

Schweitzer shrugged, thrilling at the feeling of the parka sliding over his shoulders and back. 'Dunno. Maybe it's because Yakecan was a person.'

'You are Yakecan.' Mankiller sounded devastated.

'I'm sorry, Sheriff,' Schweitzer said. 'I'm Jim Schweitzer. Your deputy is in here with me, but I'm driving right now.'

The look of girlish wonder on Mankiller's face would have been comical if it hadn't been so full of grief and naked need. 'Did you . . . did you tell him what I told you to . . . Can I talk to him, just for a sec?'

Schweitzer put a hand on Mankiller's shoulder, partly to comfort her and partly to drown in the joy of simple human contact. He pulled his face into a small smile, feeling the muscles crease on natural lines, well worn. Joe Yakecan had smiled a lot. 'I did,' he said. 'And he said what I thought he would. You have nothing to be sorry for. You were a good boss and a good friend.' A lie, but a worthy one.

Mankiller struggled with words, clapping a hand over his own. She stammered, and Schweitzer knew she was on the verge of bursting into very un-Mankiller-like tears. He decided to put a stop to it, for all of their sakes, and forged back through Yakecan's memories, looking for something that would cement the truth for Mankiller, that her old friend was still in here. *Sorry, man*, Schweitzer said to Yakecan's smiling, idiot soul. *Just a little something, for her.*

'He says the twenty he owes you is in his locker. It's stuffed into the bottom of his old hip holster. The one he never uses. Or, he says, once this is all over, you can go double or nothing. He's confident he'll win it back.'

And now Mankiller did weep, a short, shuddering cough that made her look nearly as old as her grandfather.

She gave a strangled sound, gritted her teeth, and the spasm was gone as quickly as it had come. She looked up at Schweitzer, swallowed hard, nodded.

Plante beamed at him. 'Can't believe it worked, honestly,' he said. 'That's the first time I ever worked *inkoze* like this.'

'I told you, sir,' Schweitzer said through Yakecan's mouth. 'This thing you call *inkoze*'s got hard edges, and they're nowhere near where you think they are.'

'Can you show me?' Plante asked.

'No.' Schweitzer shook his head. 'But I know somebody who can.'

'We can worry about that once we win this fight,' Ghaznavi said. 'What matters for now is that it works.' She offered Schweitzer a pistol. 'Let's get this sledge loaded with supplies and get our ass back to town. Every second we spend out here is another second for the bad guys to overrun the station.'

Plante nodded, turning back to the cabin. 'All right, Jim. Your first task as a member of the living is to help me get the sledge loaded. Let's see that super strength my granddaughter's been goin' on about.'

Schweitzer chuckled and followed him. His stomach churned, an unpleasant tightening that he only now realized was the sour twinge of anxiety. It was a feeling he'd barely felt when he was alive and certainly not since his death. The unfamiliarity of it was unsettling.

Because the truth was that Schweitzer had awakened in Yakecan's body no stronger than a normal man. The popping of the fire had come through the tinny haze that Schweitzer now knew was normal hearing. His eyes saw the aurora just as anyone else, the infrared and ultraviolet spectrums invisible to him now. His breathing labored under Yakecan's bulk, the bones straining to hold up layers of muscle and fat built by too much beer and not enough exercise. He shivered in the cold, blinked away the brightness as he moved from the darkness outside to the relative light of the cabin.

Plante was kneeling, rolling back a threadbare rug and hauling open a corrugated metal hatch. 'It's all down here.' He looked up at Schweitzer, and his smile looked nervous, so that Schweitzer couldn't help but wonder if he knew.

That Schweitzer had been bound into Yakecan's body, that this miracle had preserved everything that Schweitzer had once been, his memories, his goals, his wants and needs. It had taken all this and bound it within a mortal shell with mortal limits, and had jettisoned everything else. The strength that enabled him to lift a car. The speed that meant he could run faster than a cheetah. The senses that could tell when an enemy was approaching. The steadiness that made his aim as accurate as any laser-guided ordnance.

All gone. Schweitzer was alive, but as he followed Plante down the hatch and thought of the fight that awaited him back at Fort Resolution, he wondered for how long.

Chapter Eighteen
Dead Giveaway

The Director couldn't believe it had come to this. Fort Resolution was a wasteland. Columns of smoke rose from at least three ruined houses. The Loon was a roofless wreck littered with the debris of overturned trucks and the scattered remains of the helicopter.

The wreckage was a reminder of the fact that his tiny force had triumphed over incredible odds, had beaten back the Canadian QRF he was certain would overwhelm them. Schweitzer was broken, the town depopulated and burning, the cavalry turned back before they could save the day. By all rights, he was winning.

Except that he wasn't. The idiot sheriff and the ragged remains of her village were huddled in their makeshift pillbox, ready for his next charge, the one that would surely overwhelm them. Except that he couldn't, because that damned woman was the only leverage he had on her grandfather, and she would clearly rather die than help him. Which meant she had to be taken alive.

If she hadn't gotten away already, that was. The bloody assaults on the town had whittled his platoon down. He couldn't keep a cordon anymore, not nearly as completely as he would have needed in order to ensure that no one got away. The few scouts he'd detailed to search for the old man were a further drain on his precious living man-power. He needed the living more than the dead for once. Living men could capture the sheriff. The Golds weren't interested in taking people alive.

'People of Fort Resolution!' he bellowed, his throat flexing to project his voice farther than the greatest stage actor. 'Why are you doing this? Look at your town! Ruined! Your precious Army tried to save you and failed. Their deaths are on your head. You killed them as surely as if you'd pulled the trigger yourselves. But it doesn't have to be like this. It can all end right now. Send out Sheriff Plante. No one else has to die! We will take her for a little walk, and then she will be returned to you, safe and sound. Surely, you can save your own precious lives for that.' The truth was that he wanted the sheriff for his own uses once she'd brought her grandfather around. A spirit as powerful as hers might pair well with a soul from the void. Maybe she could be the third Silver in the history of the program. Silver or Gold, he'd still have the satisfaction of killing her. After all the trouble she'd caused him, it would be small recompense, but he'd take what he could get.

There was no response from the station, not even a ranging shot at his men, though he knew the sheriff's people could see them. 'They're low on ammunition,' he mused. 'They must have spent their stores when they saw the helicopters coming in.'

'Think it's safe to rush them, sir?' Mark breathed from beside him, elbows propped on an overturned rowboat as she peered through a pair of binoculars. 'You said you wanted to avoid further casualties.'

'No, not yet,' the Director said, instantly regretting the words. He couldn't be letting his subordinates think he was weak, frightened. But he was frightened. Frightened of losing his chance to find another Summoner, frightened of his body being destroyed and his soul condemned to return to that churning horror that he knew awaited him. *Nonsense. What have you to fear?* He was immortal. He didn't need food, water, even air. He could walk out into the waste and hide himself until the threat passed, even if it took years. The only creature on the earth that could have harmed him had proved unequal to the task. He felt a twisting in his spiritual gut at the thought of his brother, but he wasted little time on it. He had given Schweitzer a chance. Even with all the advantages of death, Schweitzer had been too wedded to the trappings of life to take advantage of it. No, the Director would not waste thought on him.

There was nothing to fear. The game was rigged in his favor. Win or lose, he would be fine. So, why did he feel so uneasy?

Mark set the binoculars down and raised her satellite phone to her ear. It worked on a coded channel that the Director had left open for his own people. 'Go for ops.'

The Director heard her heart quicken before he could dial his hearing down to eavesdrop on the call. 'Are you sure?' Mark was saying as he snatched the phone out of her hand.

'Do you know who this is?' he breathed into the receiver.

'Yes, sir.' The man on the other end sounded terrified. 'I don't want to overstate—'

'Just tell me what you were telling her, please.'

'Yes, sir. We've got eyes on a fire, sir. About a quarter-klick out, we think. We're at waypoint Golf, sir.'

'A forest fire?'

'No, sir. Smoke was greasy, and we got a whiff of the chemicals. Could be a cookout or a garbage fire. We're trying to locate it now.'

'Mark' – the Director dipped the receiver away from his mouth – 'do you know of any human habitation within a one-kilometer radius of waypoint Golf?'

'No, sir,' she said, 'but it could be a trapper out on . . .'

The Director ignored the rest of her words. Something deep within him was thrumming, making his spiritual gut tighten. He couldn't be sure it was them. It could be any number of things. But one of those things could be Sheriff Plante's grandfather, and he couldn't shake the suspicion that it was.

'Get eyes on,' he whispered into the phone. 'Call me back the minute you find the source.'

He disconnected and handed the phone back to Mark, busied himself with planning the approach. He did his best to concentrate on the task at hand, to trust his people to do their jobs. But the team out by waypoint Golf was a splinter in his mind, and he found himself counting the minutes. How long did it take to move a quarter-klick, even stealthily? Surely, not this long.

'I am tired of playing with these people,' he said to Mark, alarmed by the edge of anger in his own voice, powerless to stop it. 'I'll go down with your team, and we can make two approaches. I want an LWIR scope, and we're going to count bodies and bulk.'

'Yes, sir.' Mark sounded confused. 'What's the objective?'

'To see if Sheriff Plante has flown the coop. If she's inside, we'll try for a final assault with our regular operators.'

'And if she's not?'

'We turn the Golds loose. All of them.'

'Sir, are you sure that—'

'I said I was done playing with these people! Didn't I? Didn't I say that?' He was barking, growling, his voice easily as loud as when he had called on the station's occupants to surrender. Which meant they could hear his outburst. It was unprofessional, weak, far beneath him. He knew it was the fear driving him, the frustration. He knew he should be beyond those things, that the outburst would degrade the morale of his dwindling, precious living troops. He didn't care. It felt too good to not hold back. He had fought so hard to get here, had planned and shifted with speed and agility when those plans went awry. He would not be beaten by a living woman, no matter how hard-bitten she might be.

'Y . . . yes, sir,' Mark was saying. 'I'll . . .'

But her pocket was buzzing, the satphone inside chiming out its call on the coded channel. The Director struck out, quick as a snake, and plucked it from her pocket, ignoring Mark's wincing flinch as he lunged. He raised the phone to his ear, took a moment to calm himself before answering. 'Yes?'

'Sir.' The man's voice was even more frightened than before. 'It's an old shack, built into a hill. There's a bonfire here, still dying. Burned remains in it.'

The Director barely contained the urge to scream at the man, to tell him to get on with it already. 'And?'

'It's human remains, sir. We can smell cooked glycerol, and there's chromium fragments mixed in with the ash.'

Molybdenum-infused chromium was a rare metal. Heavy, expensive, strong. Its cost meant it had few practical applications. Lock-cutter jaws, race-car crankshafts.

The cables and bone reinforcements in the Cell's undead operators.

Schweitzer.

Chapter Nineteen
Mush

Even piled high with supplies, the sledge wasn't much heavier than it had been with Schweitzer and Yakecan's bulk slung across it, and now Schweitzer, in Yakecan's body, was pulling, straining against a make-shift harness of creosote-soaked rope and bungee cords that Plante had strung together. Plante ambled alongside, surprising Schweitzer with his speed, darting in occasionally to check the straps that cinched the blue plastic tarp over the piled cans of food and cardboard boxes of bullets.

Within moments of setting out, Schweitzer felt the all-too-human effects of his labor. His shoulders burned; his neck felt like a spring wound too tight. He sweated freely, so hot that he would push back his hood only to raise it a moment later, when his sweat froze and left him shivering. He couldn't remember the last time he'd been this miserable, and he wouldn't have traded it for the world.

As weak as this human body was, it was still plenty strong. Even though he had barely eaten over the last few days, Yakecan had a lot of muscle under the fat, and Schweitzer found himself having to slow his stride to avoid pulling out of synch with Mankiller and Ghaznavi. It didn't take long for the three of them to find a rhythm, and the crunching of the snow and whisper of the sledge runners became Schweitzer's whole world. It helped him to forget all he had lost, first his family and then his body and finally his power, and what lay ahead of him at journey's end: the remnants of his brother's army, complete with the remaining Golds, not to mention Peter's terrible strength. Schweitzer hadn't been able to beat him when he had all the power granted by his unlife. What chance would he have now? *Don't think about it. The only way out is through.*

But even if he wasn't thinking about it, others were. 'So, you're sure,' Ghaznavi said eventually. 'No powers at all? I mean, you're pulling the sled awful hard.'

Schweitzer rapped a thick knuckle against one leg, thick as a tree trunk. 'Yakecan was a big boy, and he worked out.'

Mankiller snorted. 'He never did a stitch 'a work in his whole life that he didn't have to. Even if there was a gym in town, he wouldn't 'a gone to it.'

'Well, he's plenty strong, regardless,' Schweitzer said, giving an extra yank on the harness to underscore his point.

'Yeah.' Mankiller sounded wistful. 'I guess he was.'

'Well, doesn't that just take the fucking cake,' Ghaznavi said. 'We haul our asses all the way out here, go through that spooky Beltane Fire ritual . . .'

'That's not the Beltane Fire,' Plante said. 'Beltane's . . .'

'You know what I mean,' Ghaznavi said. 'Anyway, my point is we took all that risk and lugged all this way, and the sum total is we get one more body in the fight. One more regular human body when we need Superman.'

Mankiller stiffened, and Schweitzer knew she was offended at the implication that Yakecan had in any way been regular. 'You watch your mouth.'

'I'm not speaking ill of the dead,' Ghaznavi said,

gesturing to Schweitzer. 'He's up and breathing, Sheriff.'

'Still,' Mankiller grumbled, 'ain't nice.'

'Nice?' Ghaznavi asked. 'Nice isn't going to count for a skinny fuck when we get back to town and have to face those things. We needed Schweitzer as he was – turbocharged.'

Schweitzer supposed she was right, but he was flying too high on the rush of simply being *alive* to let it bother him. He stretched his cheeks in a wide smile, a human smile, a proper smile, unrestrained by the limits of the metal armature that had been a dress mannequin for his corpse-face. He could feel his cheeks rising, his eyes crinkling. *Yakecan's eyes.* But it didn't matter. Yakecan was naked in a field of flowers, smiling beatifically into the middle distance. He wasn't using them, and possession was nine-tenths of the law.

'Still turbocharged,' Schweitzer said. He was getting used to Yakecan's deep bass, starting to think of it as his own. 'I'm a SEAL. That doesn't go away.'

Ghaznavi rolled her eyes. 'We rolled in there with six hard operators out of SAD and JTF2. Hasn't exactly evened the odds. You'll forgive me if I'm not terribly reassured by the addition of a single SEAL trapped in the body of an overweight—' Mankiller shot her a glare and she stopped, raising a hand in defeat. 'Sorry.'

Schweitzer saw her point, but he remembered the last gunshots he'd fired when he was alive. One had arced across five hundred meters of churning ocean to drop a target on the pitching deck of a ship. Another had caught a man's wrist mid-throw from around a doorjamb. There were SEALs and there were SEALs, Schweitzer supposed.

The bear had stayed behind to guard the cabin, but the wolves provided a dark and stumbling escort. Their stiff and jerking strides, coupled with the golden flames of their eyes, were clearly making Ghaznavi nervous.

'Jesus,' she panted, waving to Plante. 'You can't put them in harness? Make a dog team out of 'em? I thought you knew how to do stuff like that out here.'

Plante laughed. 'We do, but do those look like dogs to you?'

Ghaznavi shot a glance at the sleek gray-black shapes of the wolves. 'I mean, kinda.'

'Well, they ain't. They're wolves, which is nothin' like dogs. You and me both got two legs and two arms, but it don't make us the same. I'm Dene and you're *Bescho Dené*, which is why you're pulling the sled and I'm supervisin'. Now mush.'

'Yeah, Jala,' Schweitzer added, grinning fit to split his face. 'Mush.'

'Jesus fucking Christ,' Ghaznavi said. 'We're all gonna die.'

Mankiller insisted they halt about halfway to the town. At least, she said it was halfway to the town. It looked to Schweitzer exactly like the rest of the unending woods and frozen bog that made up the countryside. Ghaznavi was impatient to press on, but Mankiller cut a hand angrily across the ground, ending with a thumb jerked in the direction of her grandfather, who had given up walking and had taken to sitting on the back of the sledge for the last few hours. Schweitzer was surprised to find that he couldn't feel the old man's weight at all.

'Grampy needs a rest,' Mankiller growled. 'And so do I, for that matter. Ain't gonna be no good to nobody, we go stumblin' back there dead on our feet.'

'Fine.' Ghaznavi slumped angrily down against the mound of supplies. 'Instead, we'll go dancing in like ballerinas amidst the burning wreckage and corpses of our people.'

'Ollie's good people,' Mankiller said. 'He'll figure a way to hold 'em.'

'I'm not worried about him.' Ghaznavi shot an accusing glance at Schweitzer shrugging off his makeshift harness and sliding down to join her on the ground.

'Not my fault,' he said, fishing a bottle of water out from under the tarp and unscrewing the cap. 'I thought I'd keep all my powers.'

He tried to keep the humor and joy out of his voice and failed utterly, and Ghaznavi buried her face in her hands in disgust.

They sat like this for a while, the silence broken only by Mankiller's efforts to unpack a small camp stove, then set about preparing a pot of canned beans and franks big enough to feed them twice over. Plante stood with a groan, produced a package of dried fish, which he tossed to the wolves. A few nibbled tentatively at them. Most ignored them entirely.

'She's got a point,' Mankiller said later, when they'd all caught their breath. 'Gonna be a hard fight when we get back.'

'Yeah,' Schweitzer said, 'I guess.'

'We should probably have a plan before we go in.'

'Plan is to hold what we've got and wait for the QRF.'

'Bad guys might feel different.'

'So, we fight 'em. You still got those flamethrowers, right? And you can make more TATP?'

'Yeah' – Mankiller looked at her feet – 'but I don't think the bad guys are gonna hold still for it.'

'Don't need them all to hold still, just one of 'em.'

Ghaznavi looked up. 'They're animals, Jim. You said so yourself. What makes you think they're even going to notice that you killed one of them?'

'Wasn't thinking about them. I was thinking about the

people. Might knock 'em back on their heels to see their magic zombie boss get knocked down a peg. Look, we just have to make them hold off, right? Just get them to think twice. They're not stupid. They know they've got company inbound. They might just give up, try their luck in the woods. They're not concerned about the town. They want the sheriff to give up her grandpa. They might fuck off if they think the Canadian Army is inbound and it's too tough a nut to crack.'

'I don't know about that,' Ghaznavi said. 'They're probably pretty pissed off by now.'

'But they're pros,' Schweitzer said. 'Tell me, if it were you, what would you do?'

Ghaznavi thought about it for a moment. 'I'd have bugged out the minute I thought there was going to be a real fight. Laying siege to a town? I have no idea what the hell they're thinking.'

Schweitzer had an idea, but he said nothing of his brother's gray, leering face, of his burning silver eyes. 'Yeah, well, this is the thing. I fought the Director, and I got a bit of a read on him.'

'How'd you manage that?'

'We talked.'

'What?' Mankiller looked up. 'In the middle of a fight?'

'Just like in the comic books.' Schweitzer grinned.

Mankiller shuddered. 'That's Joe's smile you're wearing. Freaks me the hell out.'

Schweitzer shrugged. 'We're sharing it. It's a good smile.'

Mankiller nodded, stirred their dinner.

'Anyway,' Schweitzer went on, 'he's the problem. He's not feral like the rest of them, but he's also not . . . in control of himself. He's impetuous. I think he's running that outfit based on fear. The Golds I saw kowtowed to him like beta dogs in the presence of an alpha. We take him out, we snap their spine.'

Soft pops in the distance, the faintest echo of a roar carried on the wind. Schweitzer stiffened, glanced at Plante. The sounds were just barely audible to his human ears, but he still knew what they were. 'That your bear?'

'He's his own bear,' Plante said, 'but yeah. Sounds like he got the drop on someone and they're shootin' at him.'

'Enough rest.' Schweitzer got to his feet. 'We need to move.'

'Now, jus' wait a minute,' Plante said. 'Could be hunters. Might even—'

'No, Grampy,' Mankiller cut him off. 'It's the bad guys. Huntin' rounds don't sound like that.'

Ghaznavi was shrugging the harness back on. 'We have to assume they're following the sledge tracks. They'll catch up to us before too long.'

'Well, let's get a move on.' Plante looked tired, but he began digging under the tarp for rope. 'I'll get in harness. I can pull some of the load.'

'No,' Schweitzer said, 'but even if we did put you in harness, we'd still be moving slower than them. We're pulling a loaded sledge.'

'Maybe we can still beat them back to town,' Ghaznavi offered. 'If we start moving now and—'

'No,' Mankiller said. 'No way.'

Ghaznavi cursed, looked at her feet. 'So, we dig in and make our stand here.'

'And if we lose?' Schweitzer asked. 'What then?'

'Then' – Mankiller spoke slowly as Schweitzer's reasoning dawned on her – 'then, they get Grampy.'

'Not if we beat them,' Ghaznavi said.

'We can't take that chance.' Schweitzer turned to

Mankiller. 'How long a walk is it to civilization? Besides Fort Resolution.'

'About a day's walk to Hay River.'

Ghaznavi whistled. 'That's a long walk. Especially for an old man.'

'You'll drop dead long before I stop walking,' Plante said. 'I can hack it.'

'They're going to be looking for a heavy sledge loaded with supplies,' Schweitzer said. 'It'll be tougher without my help.'

'Will be,' Mankiller said, 'I see what you're aimin' at, but we gotta keep Grampy safe. You take 'im and head south. Might be by the time they realize what's up, you'll be someplace safe and the cavalry will have arrived.'

'Me?' Schweitzer asked. 'No, I'll stay with the sledge. You go with your grandpa.'

Mankiller shook her head. 'You know the way back to town?'

'No,' Schweitzer admitted.

'Then, what happens if you win the fight? You gonna just huddle up under the sledge till somebody finds you?'

'We could.'

'You wouldn't make it out here in the open. Not even with all the supplies. You gotta go with Grampy. I'll stay here.'

'But what if they get you?'

Mankiller tapped her pistol. 'They won't. I'll save the last round, just in case.'

'This is ridiculous,' Ghaznavi said. 'Maybe your diversion will work, but it's just as likely they'll catch you out alone, and you'll be fucked.'

'We're fucked already,' Schweitzer said.

'Our first priority is to keep that man' – Ghaznavi stabbed a finger at Plante – 'out of the Director's hands.

Convince me that reducing his guard from three, and eventually dozens, to one, in the middle of a wilderness with no help to hand is the right move.'

'He don't gotta convince you of nothin',' Mankiller said.

'Grampy, are you okay with this?'

Plante nodded. 'I want to see the Fort—'

'Not now, you don't,' Mankiller said.

Plante nodded and continued. 'But I'll swing back around once you get all this wrapped up.'

'I'll go with him,' Ghaznavi said. 'We need Sch—'

'You don't need me,' Schweitzer cut her off. 'I'm just a man now. I'm skilled, to be sure, but so are you. Plenty of folks would be just as happy to have a SAD operator as a SEAL going into a firefight.'

'Grampy's okay with it,' Mankiller said, 'I'm okay with it, Jim's okay with it. You're outvoted.'

'This isn't a vote,' Ghaznavi said through clenched teeth. 'This is a holding action until rescue arrives.'

'Aren't you cute,' Mankiller said, pulling back the tarp and wrestling a backpack out. She dropped to one knee and started packing it full of supplies.

'Now, you—' Ghaznavi began.

Mankiller cut her off with an angry stab of her finger. 'Cavalry's comin', sure, but when? Heck, we might get back there and find everything's cut to pieces. Jim's got the right idea, and you know it.'

'I can't allow you to take a precious asset off in the company of an unknown quantity in the middle of the wilderness in a foreign country!' Ghaznavi seethed.

'So?' Mankiller shrugged. 'Don't allow it.' She stood, handing the backpack to Schweitzer, who worked his arms into the straps. She then turned and waved the sledge harness in Ghaznavi's direction. 'Strap in and mush.'

'Yeah.' Schweitzer grinned. 'Mush.'

Mankiller handed Schweitzer the Alaskan. 'Best gun out here,' she said. 'It'll drop a charging bear.'

Schweitzer took it reverently, slung it over his neck. 'You sure? You'll probably need it more than me.'

Mankiller shook her head, jerked her thumb over her shoulder at Ghaznavi. 'She's right about one thing: keeping Grampy safe is priority one. So, you get the good gun. I got lots more at the station now that we got our pick of the ammo. Oh, and take this, too.' She handed Schweitzer her Glock, which seemed to weigh nothing compared to the Alaskan. He tucked it in his waistband and thanked her. 'Grampy packed plenty o' spares.'

'So, uh . . . how do I cover our tracks in this snow?' he asked. 'You got snowshoes in there, or—'

Mankiller laughed. 'You pray for wind to blow enough snow in 'em that they get covered up, and hope they don't freeze solid. Or you get lucky and some animals foul 'em up or whatever. Unless you can walk on top of the snow without breaking through it, you're gonna have to cut trail.'

Schweitzer smiled. 'Huh, I just thought that—'

Plante laughed. 'That us Indians all know how to pass without a trace? You've been watching too many movies.'

'Good luck, Sheriff,' Schweitzer said. 'Once we reach Hay River, I'll get in touch with Yellowknife and get us linked up again.'

'Maybe we'll get there and find the cavalry's already come,' Mankiller said. 'Which case, they can send a helo to pick you up.'

Schweitzer grunted and turned away. Ghaznavi was pulling on the harness, grumbling under her breath. She made no effort to bid them farewell.

Plante embraced Mankiller. '*Neghânitâ, seyaz beyaz. Nanest'î lasã.*'

Schweitzer couldn't resist running the phrase through Yakecan's memories. The deputy's command of Denesuline was incomplete, but Schweitzer was able to get the gist. *Goodbye, I love you, until we meet again.*

Schweitzer cleared his throat. 'Look, in case we don't see each other again—'

Mankiller stopped him with a wave. 'Don't. Ain't no point in it. I guess whatever we've got to say's been said. Just get movin'.'

Schweitzer smiled and gave her a one-armed hug. 'I'll take care of your Grampy and your buddy,' he said, tapping his own . . . Yakecan's chest. 'Count on it.'

Mankiller nodded and turned back to Ghaznavi, who was staring straight ahead.

Mankiller was still struggling into the ropes at the front of the sledge when Schweitzer finally cleared the horizon and they were gone.

Chapter Twenty
Let Me Help You

They stuck to the woods in the hopes it would be harder to track in the tight confines of the trees. It certainly was for him. Within moments, Schweitzer had lost all sense of direction, but Plante forged ahead unerringly, eyes fixed on some point on the horizon that it seemed only he could see. Most of the wolf pack accompanied them – an absolute boon, Schweitzer thought. He doubted the Cell had any trackers with them expert enough to distinguish the tracks of *tháydÿne* from any other kind of wolf or coyote out here, though their gait was stiff and stumbling.

Schweitzer insisted that Plante go first, though the old man's plodding pace was maddening. 'I've got a bigger footprint,' Schweitzer explained when Plante offered to let him take point. 'I'm making sure I step where you step. Might be they'll assume that it's one guy who broke off, someone a lot bigger than you.' The trees blocked the slight wind, and Schweitzer held out scant hope the blowing snow would fill in their trail. Worse, the sky was clear and bright. No new snowfall threatened.

It took some getting used to, the burning of his muscles, the fatigue. He'd gone so long feeling neither that the intensity was magnified, and it wasn't long before

Schweitzer stopped reveling in the feeling of life and began to simply hate the discomfort.

Plante, on the other hand, was tireless. The old man forged silently ahead, showing endurance that Schweitzer imagined he'd have had difficulty matching even in his twenties.

Neither spoke, and the world receded into an unending landscape of white snow, tightly packed trees, and the gray-blue sky bearing down on them. At last, Plante looked over his shoulder. 'How's Joe doin'?'

Schweitzer swallowed, caught off guard by the question. He glanced inward, saw Yakecan's soul still sitting in silence with the same idiot grin, staring off into the void. 'He's all right.'

Plante chuckled, not breaking stride. 'You're a bad liar, Jim.'

Schweitzer winced. He was far too tired to stonewall the old man. 'How can you tell?'

Plante looked back at him and winked. 'Magic.'

Schweitzer smiled. 'He's in here, but he's . . . spiritually brain-dead too, I guess. He's not responsive. Just staring out into the void.'

'That . . . unusual?'

'Hell if I know,' Schweitzer said. 'This is only the second soul I've been paired with.'

'How was it with the first?'

'Less said about him, the better. Let's just say I wish he'd been spiritually brain-dead.'

Plante chuckled, and they forged on in silence again. The landscape finally changed enough for Schweitzer to get a sense of progress, the ground sloping sharply downward and skirting the edge of a thickly frozen pond. Schweitzer was quiet as he focused on crab-stepping down the slope, marveling at how unsure his footing was now.

At last, he reached the bottom, and they trudged on through the level ground and back into the woods.

'Sir,' Schweitzer began.

'You want to know if I can help you find your wife,' Plante said without looking around.

'Does your magic include mind reading?'

'No, but you don't live as long as I have without learning how to read people. If I was in your shoes, it'd be the thing most on my mind.'

'I just figured if you could put me in a living body, then maybe you could put her—'

'You got a volunteer? Someone also brain-dead?' Plante stopped, turned to face him. 'Or were you planning on just capturing someone and doing it against their will?'

'I'm just thinking out loud, sir.' Schweitzer could feel Yakecan's plump cheeks burning with shame at the accusation.

Plante's face softened. 'I know it. But I also know that men in love do and think crazy things. That's why they're called "crimes of passion". I know what she meant to you, Jim. Hell, it was the first thing I thought when you opened your eyes next to that bonfire and I realized that I could do this.' He shook his head. 'Naw. Bad idea.'

'Why is it a bad idea?'

Plante's eyes narrowed. 'For one thing, I need to truly *know* someone. I was amazed that we were able to make it work based on that little tête-à-tête we had. But I also had you to look at, to talk to, to take the measure of. Been so long for Mary, I realize now that I don't really know who she was anymore. She's faded for me, so much that I can't be confident I could find her again. I'd rather have her as *tháydÿne* nearby than risk sending her back into the beyond, only to lose her forever.'

Schweitzer looked down. 'Then Sarah would be impossible.'

"Fraid so, son. Ask yourself: How well could you describe her to me? Could you make her truly *live* for me? Make me understand who she really was?'

Schweitzer swallowed tears. 'No.'

'You got anythin' of hers I could use to get a sense of her? Pictures? Clothing? A lock of her hair? Her perfume?'

'No.' Schweitzer felt as if he'd been punched in the stomach. 'I lost everything.' All he had left were his memories; the distant fragrance of her rosewater perfume was for his nose alone, he knew. He had nothing.

Plante placed a gentle hand on Schweitzer's shoulder. 'It's okay,' he said. 'Before I had the *inkoze*, I thought that death was it. You never believe the legends, you know? Everyone tells you there's life after death, another world you go to, but you don't believe 'em. But we believe 'em now, don't we? So, it's just waitin', is all. You miss your wife, but all you have to do is wait, and you'll be with her again.'

Schweitzer shook his head, thinking of the whirling chaos of the soul storm. 'That's not how it works, sir.'

'I know how it works,' Plante said. 'Just 'cause somethin's tough don't mean you can't make it happen anyway. You want something, you find a way.'

Schweitzer nodded. 'You should have been a SEAL, sir.'

Plante smiled, clapped Schweitzer on his shoulder, started walking again. 'Balance a ball on my nose? Clap my flippers together? No, thanks. Anyway, you'll have all eternity to be dead. You got a boy still alive, from what I hear; that's where you oughta be lookin', you ask me.'

'Kind of missed the boat there. First I was always deployed, and then I was always dead. Never had a chance to raise him.'

'So?' Plante asked. 'That mean it's impossible? You can't start over? You can't make it right?'

Schweitzer gestured to his body. 'He won't even recognize me now.'

'He dealt with you bein' dead. He can deal with you wearin' Joe Yakecan's skin. Kids always loved Joe. Guy was a natural. Hell, you might be better off.'

Schweitzer felt his smile broaden. 'Way you put it, doesn't seem so bad.'

'All a matter of perspective,' Plante said. 'Joe's . . . Heck, I don't remember how old Joe is. Mid-thirties, tops. You got a lot of life left in that body. Let's focus on gettin' help, and then we can worry about what comes next.'

'Aye aye, sir,' Schweitzer said.

The shot's report sounded a moment after Plante fell.

Chapter Twenty-One
Pump Fake

Without Yakecan . . . or Schweitzer – Mankiller still had a hard time keeping the identity straight – pulling the sledge was twice as hard. Ghaznavi grunted alongside her, not complaining at least but clearly having a tough time with the added weight of the supplies. The sled wiggled and fishtailed as Mankiller tried to increase or decrease her pull to keep steady with Ghaznavi. At last, she could take no more.

She stopped, put her hands on her hips. 'Look, I know you're tired an' all, but you gotta pull even with me.'

Ghaznavi looked at her boots. 'I'm trying.'

Mankiller swallowed her frustration. 'I know it, but . . . just try to match my step, is all. Ain't no time to rest yet, but we're almost to—'

'I know,' Ghaznavi growled. 'Look, I'll try harder to match your pace. Just maybe go a little lighter. Now let's move; we're wasting time here.'

Ghaznavi grumbled under her breath as they started pulling again, but she was more careful now, and they made better progress. Mankiller couldn't blame her for being edgy. She kept straining her hearing, terrified that any minute, gunshots would ring out behind them as the Director's flanking force followed their trail and caught up. She was glad they'd done what they had, but she'd have been lying if she said she wasn't also terrified. If their plan worked, it meant that she'd be bringing the full wrath of the Cell down on her head. She'd do it, and do it without a second thought, but that didn't mean that the idea appealed to her.

She looked over at Ghaznavi, realized with a start that this might be the last living person she got to see before she met her end. She looked at the set of Ghaznavi's jaw and grimaced. 'Hey, thanks,' she offered.

'For what?' Ghaznavi asked without looking up.

'For comin' to help. For pullin' the sledge. I dunno, for everythin', I guess.'

Now the SAD Director did look up, eyes wide with surprise. She stammered, 'Well . . . uh . . . you're welcome.'

They moved on again in awkward silence until Mankiller suddenly stopped short.

Ghaznavi jerked in her harness, stared daggers at Mankiller. 'First you tell me to pull even with you; now what the he—'

Mankiller silenced her with a wave. 'Heard somethin'.'

Ghaznavi froze, squinting into the distance. The trees were thick around them, and the packed snow that passed for a track disappeared over a rise less than twenty feet away. Mankiller struggled out of the ropes and turned back to the tarps.

'What are you doing?' Ghaznavi whispered.

Mankiller didn't answer, feeling around underneath the tarp until her hand closed around the butt of one of her grandfather's hunting rifles, an ancient Winchester Model 70. She fished it out, grabbed the box of .30-06 ammunition beside it, and fumbled out a round. The action was clumsy and rushed, sending much of the box's contents cascading into the snow.

She chambered a round and brought the weapon up to the low ready. The 70 had no magazine, and she didn't have time to go fishing after loose bullets in the snow. She had one shot; she had better make it count.

Ghaznavi whispered something, but Mankiller silenced her with a wave and then motioned for her to get down. She didn't wait to see if the SAD Director complied; she was already tuning out the world, bringing her front sight post into focus, drawing a bead on the top of the rise where'd she'd heard the noise.

She heard it again, rasping breath, crunching footsteps. Whoever was coming wasn't bothering to be quiet about it.

Mankiller took a knee. A hiker running from a bear would sound like that. So would a refugee from Fort Resolution, and so would one of the Cell's operators who'd been ordered to run up the trail to intercept them before they turned off it. She couldn't take any chances. She dialed in her aim and waited.

A figure crested the rise. A man in a parka and boots, a carbine slung across his chest. Not a hiker running from a bear, not with armament like that. Mankiller sighted in and eased the slack out of the trigger.

She should have just shot. Would have been the sensible thing. But the old cop's protocol held her tightly in its grip. Even now, when she was more soldier than cop, when this was more a military evolution than a police one. It might get her killed, but to fail it was a kind of living death, and to be honest, she was dead anyway. Might as well go down being true to herself.

And so, Wilma Mankiller didn't fire. Instead, she shouted, 'Police! Drop your weapon!'

The figure didn't drop his weapon. Instead, he fell on his face in the snow, hacking and gasping as if his heart would burst. Mankiller came off her sights, unfocused her vision.

And recognized him instantly.

'Ollie!' She raced to his side. 'What the hell are you doin' out here?'

Calmut must have been running flat out for a long time, because it took him a solid minute of coughing to get enough breath to speak.

'Sher . . . iff. God. I been runnin' . . . Thought I wouldn'a found you.'

'Ollie, calm down and just breathe. Are you hurt?'

'Got a round . . . in my leg,' he managed, tapping his snow pants.

'You ran all this way with a round in your leg? Have you lost your mind? What if it cuts your femoral, you dumb shit!'

Ghaznavi had taken off her harness and joined them, bringing one of the first aid kits from under the tarp. 'If he's here, that means Fort Resolution has been overrun.'

Mankiller felt her stomach turn over. She put her hands on Calmut's shoulders. 'That true, Ollie? They take the town?'

Calmut shook his head. 'No, ma'am. They came again once more, but we hung on. Lost a couple more. They got Freddie. That Chinese fella who was stayin' with . . .'

'Ollie. We'll deal with the casualties later. If the Fort's holdin' on, what the hell are you doin' out here? Why'd you run all the way with a bullet in your leg? You left all those people holdin' on by themselves? They got an army to hold off and you were the man to help 'em do it!'

'No army,' Calmut spat.

'Whaddya mean, there's no army?' Mankiller's voice went cool.

'That's what I came ta warn ya. They up and left.'

'They up and left?' Ghaznavi asked. 'Maybe they got tired of being repulsed.'

'That ain't it,' Calmut said. 'I saw 'em goin' up out past the lakeshore, same way you went. They musta figured out where your Grampy was at. Came to warn you. Thought for sure they'd have caught you by now.'

'When did they set out, Ollie?' Mankiller stood, panic threatening to rise at the back of her throat.

'Dunno, maybe yesterday? Hard ta think now.'

Mankiller returned to the sledge, started collecting the bullets she'd let tumble in the snow.

'Sheriff, what are you doing?' Ghaznavi asked. 'They're behind us.'

'That's right,' Mankiller said, 'and I'm going to meet them.'

'Why?' Ghaznavi asked. 'We're past them. They're heading to your grandfather's place.'

'They are if they know exactly where it is,' Mankiller said, 'and I pray that they do. 'Cause if they don't, they'll be spreadin' out right where we left Grampy and Jim.'

The sledge tracks might fool a human who was out in the frozen hinterlands of the Northwest Territory for the first time. But she had seen what the Cell's Director could do. If he was out there, then Grampy was as good as caught.

Chapter Twenty-Two

Ancestors

Schweitzer was so used to his augmented hearing dissecting the sound, telling him the precise direction, distance, and caliber of the weapon, that he lost precious seconds frozen, waiting for his human senses to relay the information.

Plante writhed on the ground, hands clamped to his thigh. Schweitzer finally broke his paralysis and rushed to the old man's side, pried his shaking hands apart. Dark blood leaked slowly from the hole in the man's trousers. Not arterial. They had time.

'Pack that with whatever you can reach and stay down,' Schweitzer whispered. There was no time. He had to get off the X before the shooter took him, too.

Another shot sprayed bark from a tree trunk not far from him, and Schweitzer was up and running. He'd figured direction at least and a rough estimate of distance. Whoever it was wasn't a great shot. Schweitzer might lack his magical abilities, but he still had the training of a SEAL, and that training was clear. His instructors at SQT had drilled it into him, referencing a book that would have made old man Plante proud, Arrian's *Campaigns of Alexander*. *To stand still is to cede the advantage to the enemy,* Master Chief Green had said. *Alexander always attacked. When outnumbered. When he doubted the morale or the loyalty of his troops. He always attacked. And so will you.*

Schweitzer brought the Alaskan up, letting his eye drift to the scope, then brought the gun down to the low ready. Weapons had been little more than window dressing since he died, but his training came rushing back to him, his vision broadening to take in the peripheral field, never focusing on anything for long. *Not a threat.* Move. *Not a threat.* Move.

Yakecan's huge body lumbered, and Schweitzer winced at the noise he was making. The first thing he'd be doing if he made it through this was going on a diet. He didn't doubt that he'd be sucking wind and sore by the time the fight was done, but he was willing to pay that price if it kept him alive. He wove from tree to tree, doing his best to keep them between himself and what he guessed was the shooter's position.

He hoped whoever it was, they were dumb enough to take another . . .

Bang. Bark exploded from the trunk in front of him, spraying his face with splinters.

Schweitzer exploded from cover and raced toward the shooter, coming up on his sights and easing the slack out of the trigger. He could see her now, a thick-limbed woman rising to her feet, stumbling backward, trying to get back on her weapon sights. 'I got him, sir!' she was shouting. 'I've got him!'

Schweitzer was tempted to look around, find who she was calling to, but he ignored it. He couldn't focus on the unknown threat when the known one was before him. '*Taking an enemy on the battlefield is like a hawk taking a bird,*' Master Chief Green had quoted from some ancient Japanese text. '*Even though it enters into the midst of a thousand of them, it gives no attention to any bird other than the one it first marked.'*

He slowed his pace, raised the Alaskan, steadying his firing platform as he slid the trigger to the rear. The big hunting rifle was unwieldy, heavy at the muzzle, different from the light carbines he was accustomed to. He relied on the locking muscles in his arms to steady the gun, but without his magically enhanced strength, his limbs trembled. Yakecan hadn't been as strong as Schweitzer in life, and he was unused to the limits of this new body as well as the weight of the unfamiliar trigger pull. There were too many variables, and Schweitzer knew he would miss before the gun went off.

The muzzle jumped and the round snapped against pine-covered boughs in the distance. Schweitzer was already working the action, closing the distance between them. He expected the woman to run, but she stood instead, charged forward. A professional, then.

She punched the quick release on her sling and swung the rifle over her head. Schweitzer punched his own, realized too late that the hunting harness didn't have one, barely succeeded in getting the weapon up to parry the blow. The woman's stock rang off the Alaskan's muzzle, sending plastic fragments flying. Schweitzer kicked out with one of Yakecan's enormous legs. He felt a sharp pain in his hamstring. Yakecan hadn't been any more flexible than he was fit, another limitation Schweitzer would have to get used to. Despite the pain, he managed to commit to the kick, sending his heel into the woman's gut and driving her onto her backside. Schweitzer eased the sling over his head and gripped his gun by the muzzle, lifting it high. The woman threw up her rifle to parry, but Schweitzer had height, leverage, and Yakecan's strength. He'd smash right through her weapon and stave in her skull.

He contracted his shoulders and brought the Alaskan's butt whistling down toward her head.

A crackling of branches, and something collided with his side hard enough to send him flying. His ribs screamed under the sudden pressure, and then he lost all sense of direction, flopping and rolling, his nose and mouth filling with snow. At last, he came to a stop on his back, blinking at the sliver of gray sky visible through the treetops. He could hear the woman shouting something, a man's voice answering, a crooning rasp that made Schweitzer shiver despite the pain in his side.

He heard the crunching of footsteps on snow. 'It is irritating,' Peter said, 'to have to kill the same man twice.'

Schweitzer coughed, rolled onto his stomach. His mind screamed at him not to present his back to his brother, but he knew if he didn't get up, he wouldn't stand a chance. *You don't stand a chance anyway.*

Peter took a light, dancing step and seized the hood on Schweitzer's parka, hauled him upright. 'No, maybe not the same man. Who's in there?'

Schweitzer drove himself forward, trying to break the Director's hold, and when that didn't work, he fumbled with the parka's zipper, tried to wriggle his arms out of the sleeves. The Director laughed, seized Schweitzer's wrist, gripped his chin. Slowly, Schweitzer felt his face rotated until he was forced to turn or else have his neck snapped.

Up close, his brother's face was a gray horror. The rip in his cheek had made his skeleton's smile into a demon leer. At some point, he'd trimmed off the excess flap of skin, and Schweitzer could see the blackened workings of his muscles as he spoke. 'Who's in there, I wonder? They bring you back from the dead?'

Peter hadn't bothered to pin his arms, and Schweitzer delivered a powerful forearm strike to his brother's dead brachial nerve. He knew it wouldn't work, but had no idea what else to do. The Director didn't even notice the blow, strong enough to make Schweitzer's arm sing out in pain.

'Did they put a jinn in you? No. Look at those eyes.'

His brother leaned in closer. 'Who are you, then?'

'I got him, sir!' the woman shouted, running up beside them. Her face was lit, and Schweitzer could tell her breathlessness was from excitement and not exertion. 'I winged him! He's not going anywhere.'

'Damn it, Mark. The man is ancient and decrepit,' the Director snapped. 'He wasn't going anywhere regardless.'

A man's name for a woman. The Cell. Mark looked crestfallen. She stammered a reply, stopped herself. 'So, what you've done is effectively risked the life of the very reason we came to this godforsaken place,' Peter said. 'Go check on him. If he bleeds out, I will be . . . disappointed.'

The woman stammered an apology and raced off.

'He did it, didn't he?' Peter asked, turning Schweitzer's face this way and that. 'He put my baby brother in the body of this walrus. That's wonderful. That's the one piece of good news I've had since I arrived here. It's you, isn't it, Jim? How do you feel? What was it like going in?'

'The name's Joe Yakecan.' Schweitzer managed to bite words out through the Director's viselike grip.

'Oh, I don't think it is,' his brother crooned. 'I think you're a naughty little liar.' He tightened his grip, and Schweitzer felt his jawbone flex painfully.

'Not that it matters,' the Director said. 'You're dead either way. It only remains to be seen how attached the old man is to you. But I can see you like to tell lies with that filthy mouth of yours. So, let me put a stop to that first.'

The pressure on Schweitzer's jaw intensified, the pain focusing behind his lower lip, where the halves of the bone joined. *He's going to snap it in half.*

He fumbled at his waist.

'I was hoping to have the granddaughter for this,' Peter said, 'but a practice run will do me good.'

Schweitzer wrenched his head up and down, desperately tried to shake off that deadly grip. It was useless. The bone screamed, inching its way to failure.

'Boss!' Mark shouted. 'Bleeding's stopped, but I can't wake him up!'

'What?' Peter paused, turning his attention to the woman. 'What do you mean you can't—'

Schweitzer shook the pistol free of Yakecan's waistband, jammed it up under his brother's chin just as a pistol had been jammed under his when he'd still been alive and in his own body.

His brother only had time to saw his head back to Schweitzer before the gun kicked and his head exploded.

The Director's grip on Schweitzer's face slackened just enough for him to slip free, unzipping the parka as he fell, finally shrugging the garment off and running with everything he had. He heard the Director's howl of rage, Mark's semi-coherent shouting. A bullet kicked up snow in front of him, Mark's inexpert marksmanship saving him again. Schweitzer heard snarling, yipping, Mark shouting. The wolves, the *tháydÿne* born of Plante's magic, coming to Schweitzer's aid or Plante's. It didn't matter so long as they kept Mark from drawing a bead on him. Schweitzer thought of their emaciated bodies, their stilted, jerking movement, knew they wouldn't stop Mark for long.

Running was useless and Schweitzer ran anyway, because now that he once again had a living body, the old instincts had returned, the chemical cocktail of adrenaline and blood sugar that sent jittering shocks through his muscles and boiled panic in his gut. He didn't want to die, not now, when he was finally alive again.

'Jim!' his brother gurgled, the sound clotted and wheezing, like a broken bellows straining air through a wet sponge. 'Jim, wha're doin'? You can'd run!'

Schweitzer knew Peter was right, but his legs refused to obey him, and he kept on running, the crunching of the snow suddenly turning hard and brittle, resounding with tinkling cracks under his feet. He glanced down, saw he was pounding across the frozen pond they'd skirted before, the light dusting of snow swirling with each step.

He slowed, conscious of Yakecan's size, of his heavy tread, the ice trembling under him. His mind screamed at him to keep going, that plunging into the icy water was a far better end than whatever Peter had in store for him, but his instincts were confused, his training still adjusting to the shift in his form, to the noise of life all around him. The ice plate shuddered, broke free where it touched the shore. Schweitzer felt the entire plate drop an inch, saw water lapping at the edges.

'Jim.' His brother's voice was close, just a few feet behind him.

Schweitzer slowly turned, wincing at the cracking beneath him.

The bullet had blown the back of Peter's head open like a bomb casing. His scalp bloomed outward, a smoking gray flower, the jagged petals heavy with the shards of his skull. His face had imploded as the structure behind it was torn away, features gone hideously concave. Peter's jaw hung askew by a few threads of muscle, but Schweitzer could tell he was smiling. 'C'mon,' Peter said. 'S's stupid.'

Schweitzer looked left and right, tested his weight. The ice plate rocked, and he pinwheeled his arms, trying to keep upright. Peter shifted his weight seamlessly; Schweitzer knew that his brother's core muscles were locking and unlocking as needed to compensate, effortlessly and with all the magical strength he'd once had. 'Eben now,' Peter said, 'I fogibe you. Eben now, you can come wid me.'

Peter extended a hand. 'I ged you awb dis ice. Come.'

'I've got a better idea,' Schweitzer said. 'I take your hand, and you get me off this ice, and then *I* help *you*.'

Peter laughed, his jaw dancing hideously. 'You heb me how? I don' need yo helb.'

'Yes, you do. Your end isn't an end, Pete. Remember how you used to lionize Alexander the Great? What happened when he conquered the world? He couldn't rule it. He was angry and alone, watching his friends turn on him and everything he'd built slip through his fingers.'

'I'm greader than Alegsander,' Peter said, but Schweitzer could hear the irritation in his voice.

'For all the fucking good it'll do you. This is the problem with greatness for greatness' sake. This is why I bought into the family-God-country stuff. Not because I'm stupid but because it's something to live for.' He thought of his last fight with Sarah, the night the enemy had come for him and his life had changed forever. *Why do you do it, Jim? What do you get out of it? I mean, apart from the adrenaline rush,* she had asked, her cheeks pink with anger, with frustration, with her willingness to lose him.

Oh, God, Sarah. I was such a fool. I made the wrong choice. I'm so sorry.

'This is proof that it works.' Schweitzer gestured to himself. 'It can work for you too.'

'It will wordg bor me,' Peter said. 'Da owd man id alibe.' He pointed a finger at Plante's still form. 'I canb hear his heart.'

'No,' Schweitzer said. 'He'll die first. He doesn't give a fuck about me.'

'Led's test dat,' Peter said, reaching for Schweitzer's

wrist. 'And if nod you, den I find da sheriff. I'll conbince him. I'm good ad conbincing.'

Schweitzer didn't doubt it. 'And then what? Senator Hodges? To what end?'

'Dat's my probrem.'

'It is your problem, and it's a bad one. You think you're going to live again, but you won't. You'll just be a dead man hiding in a living body. Your existence will be just as empty as it was before. You'll be like Alexander: you'll grasp everything and have nothing. You'll be alone.'

'Shuddup.' Peter's voice was dangerously low. He reached for Schweitzer's hand again.

'Sarah's gone,' Schweitzer said. 'Patrick too. I want a family again. We can be that for each other. We'll find another body, the right body, and the old man will put you in it willingly. We can fix this.'

'BS. I fugging made you. You berrong to me.'

Schweitzer felt a gulf open in his stomach, deeper and darker than the void he knew hovered beyond the edges of his consciousness. 'What do you mean?' he whispered. 'You didn't make me.'

'Course I didb,' Peter laughed, nearly losing his dangling jaw. 'I thought youb be sumbting. I thoughtb maybe whatb madbe meb who I am ranb in da family. Thought I was wrong for a bit. But I don' hab ta be. Gib me yourb hand.'

The gulf opened wider, until Schweitzer felt sick, like he was choking on despair. He had lost everything – his career, his wife and child, his very life – all because his dead brother wanted to see if his delusions of grandeur ran in the family. Peter, his brother, his idol. Peter had taken everything for no reason at all. From the moment Peter had died to the moment Schweitzer had joined him, he'd prayed that heaven was real, that there was some paradise beyond the grave where good men like his brother could dwell in peace. Now he just wished the bastard had stayed dead.

'You fucker.' Rage blotted out his senses, dark and sonorous, nearly as intense as what he had felt when he was still paired with Ninip. It choked Schweitzer's professionalism, sent the SEAL packing, replaced him with a violent animal. Schweitzer made no effort to fight it. He was a human with no magic ability to speak of, going up against a magically-powered immortal. Schweitzer didn't stand a chance whether he ran or fought, and being angry felt so much better than being afraid.

Peter lunged for Schweitzer, and though a tiny part of him knew it was useless, hopeless, Schweitzer stepped into the grip, let his brother's dead hands fasten on his wrists. He brought Joe Yakecan's beefy knee up and drove it hard into his brother's hip, right where he'd seen the joint wobble from his vantage point in the church steeple. It gave a satisfying *pop*, and he felt Peter topple sideways, grunting. Schweitzer jerked his wrist back and punched his brother's broken face with everything he had.

Rage gave way to reality. Where a metal bullet had torn through like hurricane, Yakecan's fist crumbled on impact against the metal-reinforced bone of Peter's ruined face. Schweitzer grunted as he felt the small bones of the hand shiver and burst, the fragments shearing through the blood vessels and supporting tendons. Schweitzer drew back his – Joe's – fist, which looked more like a dripping red bag than a hand. If it had been useless whole, it was certainly no help now.

He yanked on the other wrist, but Peter's grip on him was as strong as death itself, and he felt the bones beneath the skin grinding together as his brother held on. Schweitzer let himself fall forward then, his body weight unbalancing

Peter, who cursed and let go. 'Stob, Jim. You canb getb awayb.'

Schweitzer's wrist ached, but it was nothing compared to the flaring agony of his pulped right hand. Peter reached for his wrist again. 'Stob being an idiob and combon.'

Schweitzer let his brother take his right wrist. The broken hand screamed in agony as the pressure of his brother's grip made it balloon, the purple skin going taut.

But it left his other hand, with its working fingers, free.

Schweitzer remembered the Bible passage he'd thought of as he'd laid on the pyre outside Grandpa Plante's shack, feeling his old body burn away. *The lamp of the body is the eye, if, therefore, thine eye may be perfect, all thy body shall be enlightened.* It was the eyes. When his eyes had gone, so had he.

He made a forked V with his first two fingers and thrust them forward, into the silver flames that still burned in his brother's shattered skull.

There was no heat, no pain, only pins and needles . . . strangeness, as the flesh passed through the fire and rebounded off the bone behind.

Peter howled, released Schweitzer's wrist. Could it actually be working? Schweitzer grunted, pushed his fingers harder, hooking them down, knuckling them in, doing his best to fill the cavities of his brother's eye sockets so that no flame could possibly burn there.

Peter went rigid, fingers clenching and unclenching. Schweitzer felt hope blossom in his gut. He was winning. He pushed harder. 'When you get back out there,' he said, 'stay the fuck away from my wife.'

A sharp *crack* sounded and Schweitzer felt a hammer-blow on his chest. Agony flared in his shoulder, and he struggled to draw breath. He spun, fell, hearing Mark's exultant shout of 'Got him!' Her feet pounding toward them.

'No, you fuggin' foo!' Peter was already recovering, the silver flames of his eyes burning brightly again.

Another *crack* sounded and Mark toppled sideways, dropping her rifle. Schweitzer could see a dark shape racing toward them, weapon at the low ready, and then he struck the ice, head rebounding hard enough to make him see stars.

The sudden impact was too much; the ice plate groaned, cracked, and gave way, the icy water reaching up to admit him. Schweitzer forgot his pain as the frigid liquid soaked into his clothing, his limbs crying out and going numb almost instantly. Yakecan's bulk sank like a stone.

Peter danced nimbly off the shattering ice, balanced easily on the extreme edge of the shore, shooting out a hand to grab the back of Schweitzer's shirt. He held his head above the water. 'See? You got sum steelb inb youb. Youb canb be moreb dan dis. Lass chandce, Jim,' he said. 'Do I sabe you or led you go down?'

The figure was closing, but Schweitzer knew that Peter's magical reflexes were agile enough to handle the threat as soon as it came in range. Schweitzer looked up into the lopsided pits of his brother's eyes, stared in wonder at the flickering silver flames there.

Snarling, two heavy shapes landed on Peter's back, sending him toppling forward.

Schweitzer saw two of the *tháydÿne* latched to his brother, jaws tearing at the remains of his shattered head. A second later, they were joined by a third, then a fourth, until it seemed his brother wore a coat of writhing wolves. Peter released Schweitzer's shirt, turned to tear at the wolves, but the water seized him as hungrily as it did Schweitzer, and all of them sank below the surface in an instant.

Schweitzer saw his brother's shadow flailing against the

wolves, sinking deeper into darkness. The cold wrapped itself around Schweitzer and the light faded. He looked up at the rippling surface above, graying. *It's refreezing*, he thought. *It's gone to slush already.*

A thin trail of blood wormed its way up from his chest, reminding him of the rosewater trail he'd followed to his wife. *At least I'll have a chance to find you again, Sarah*, he thought, and then the cold and the darkness swallowed him whole.

Chapter Twenty-Three
Cavalry Arrives

It had been so long since Schweitzer had last slept, or passed out, or known anything other than the long, waking hours of his unlife, that at first he had no idea what had happened. The leaden feeling of his body, the dull, wet ache in his chest, the blackness and lost time. It took several moments to realize that he was awake and alive, that the darkness around him was nothing more than the inside of his eyelids.

He opened them.

Light flooded in, and Schweitzer blinked away tears. The water haloed the world, refracted the light into a spray of rainbows around the edges of some low pine boughs and wisps of cloud in a steel-gray sky. A face looked down at him, silhouetted and wavering. Callused fingers stroked his head, pushing the hair out of his eyes. 'Saved you this time.' The voice was hard, but warm.

'Thanks, Sheriff,' Schweitzer croaked. The effort made his chest contract painfully. 'Joe's grateful.'

'Shut up.' Mankiller smiled. A tear slipped off the side of her nose and pattered on Schweitzer's cheek. 'Grampy told me, you fuckin' liar. Jus' let me indulge my fantasy for a minute.'

'He's alive?'

Mankiller nodded. 'Yeah. And I'm glad you are too, both of you in there.'

'Thanks.' Schweitzer began to sit up, but Mankiller's hand on his shoulder pushed him back down.

'Don't. It's pretty bad.'

Schweitzer pushed against her hand. 'Don't feel that—'

Mankiller pushed harder. 'I got the hole plugged, but there was a lot of air comin' out 'fore I sealed it. As it stands, you'll get sepsis unless we pump you full of antibiotics.'

'Lung's flattened?'

'Probably. How's your chest feel?'

'Like it's full of water.'

'Well, there ya go. If you die after I froze my fuckin' ass off gettin' you out of the drink, I'm gonna be pissed.'

'What about the bad guy?'

'He didn't come up,' Mankiller said. 'I'm guessing he's a frozen brick at the bottom by now.'

'Are you sure? He could still—'

'Relax, Jim.' Mankiller patted his shoulder. 'If he was comin' up, he'd 'a done it by now. You were free-floatin'. He had a whole pack 'a wolves on 'im. You sit tight. Medevac's on the way.'

Schweitzer could already hear the distant patter of rotors penetrating the tree cover. 'Cavalry came.'

'Finally,' Mankiller said. 'Wasn't a lot left of the enemy, but they're runnin' the rest down.'

'We did that much damage?'

'Yeah.' Mankiller smiled. 'I guess we did. Not bad for a town fulla fishermen and trappers. They fucked with the wrong Indians, I guess.'

'I'm not an Indian,' Schweitzer said.

Mankiller smiled down at him. 'Well, you sure look like one, so I guess I'll make an exception.'

'Holy shit,' Schweitzer said. 'We won.'

'Yeah.' Mankiller looked up as the rotors grew louder. 'I guess we did.'

Schweitzer sat on the edge of his bed, stared at the broad instep of Joe Yakecan's foot.

'Well?' Desmarais asked, stirring in his chair.

'What a fucking production.' Ghaznavi shook her head.

'Look, this is a new body, and it's pretty banged up,' Schweitzer said. 'After all I've done for you ungrateful punks, I think I'm entitled to an extra five minutes.'

'Take your time.' Desmarais smiled.

'No,' Ghaznavi said. 'Do not take your time. I've already lost fifteen minutes of my life that I will never get back.'

Schweitzer took his time, but in the end, his shaking legs supported him. He grinned, taking a deep breath, feeling the wounded lung expand painfully and hold. His broken hand didn't hurt at all, but he knew better than to try and wiggle his fingers.

'Well?' Desmarais said again.

'Everything seems to be in order,' Schweitzer said. 'At least, I'm not going to fall over and die.'

'That's a relief.' Ghaznavi didn't sound relieved at all.

'Outstanding,' Desmarais said, grinning. 'Glad you pulled through, Deputy Yakecan.' They'd taken to calling him Joe Yakecan even in private now, to get them all used to it. Far better to say that Mankiller's deputy had never been killed than admit what lived under his skin now. Schweitzer was still getting used to answering to it.

'Thanks.' Schweitzer seated himself back on the infirmary bed, blinked at the sunshine streaming in through the window. 'That's where you've got him?' He stared at the JTF2 building across the flight line, the low Quonset hut where the team had loaded out squatted alongside.

Desmarais nodded. 'We're building a better facility. For now, we've got him in the kitchen freezer.'

'Seriously?'

Desmarais nodded. 'We filled it with water and put it on its coldest setting. It's keeping him frozen solid. Like I said, it's not ideal, but it'll do until we get something purpose-built.'

'You better hope he doesn't thaw out.'

'We're not too worried.' Desmarais smiled. 'After all, you're back on your feet now.'

Schweitzer snorted. 'Fat lot of good that'll do you. I'm just a regular Joe now.'

He chuckled at his own joke.

'Well, we're going to need your help anyway,' Desmarais said. 'You're the closest thing we've got to an expert on the topic.'

'You've got Grandpa Plante.'

'He's the Summoner. You're the . . . Summoned, I guess.'

'My team's en route as we speak,' Ghaznavi said. 'It'll be a joint op, right here. Welcome to the Aquila Cell.'

'I'm not sure calling anything a "cell" is the best plan after what we've just been through.'

Ghaznavi rolled her eyes. 'Inside joke, between us.'

'Uh-huh,' Schweitzer said. 'And what's the government calling it?'

'They're not calling it anything, because they don't know about it. Unfortunately, the cat is sort of out of the bag as far as magic goes.'

'The Gemini Cell facility in Colchester . . .'

'It went down,' Ghaznavi said, 'but it went down hard. Some folks got hurt. Some things made the press. The President isn't pleased.'

'That can't be good for Hodges.'

'He's a trooper,' Ghaznavi said. 'For now, he's acting as liaison to an Army outfit they're calling the Supernatural Operations Corps. They're running it out of MacDill. Supposed to be in charge of all things magic.'

'Are there enough . . . things to merit that kind of a public stance?'

Ghaznavi shrugged. 'President seems to think there are. Anyway, we're only concerned with one magic thing, and that's you, and we've got work to do.'

'You're moving awful quick, aren't you? Making a lot of assumptions?'

'Joe,' Ghaznavi said. 'You wanted in on the op. You're in on it. Are you having second thoughts?'

'Hell, no,' Schweitzer said. 'I'm in with bells on. I want to see where all this goes more 'n anyone. It's just that I have certain demands.'

Desmarais blinked. 'Demands?'

'That's right. You want my help? Fine. I want yours.'

'Patrick,' Ghaznavi said. 'We're already on that. We've been on it since before you even admitted he was alive.'

'Yeah, but you don't know what I know.'

'Jesus Christ, Joe,' Ghaznavi said. 'What the hell do you know?'

'Well, I'll tell you.' Schweitzer smiled. 'On the condition that I be put in charge of the team that acts on the information.'

Desmarais and Ghaznavi exchanged looks. 'I could just have it tortured out of him,' she said.

'That shit never works,' Schweitzer said.

'Fine,' Ghaznavi sighed. 'The hunt for your son is all yours. Supervised, of course. Now, what do you know?'

Schweitzer nodded. 'You fuck me on this, and I will never cooperate with you again. You'll have to kill me.'

'What do you know?' she asked again.

'Patrick is in the care of the Cell's old lead scientist. I

gave them instructions to make for the West Coast. They should be there now.'

'They should, but they're not.' Ghaznavi said.

Schweitzer's stomach turned over. 'You knew?'

'Your government's not totally incompetent,' Ghaznavi said. 'Eldredge made contact with one of your shipmates, trying to set up a place for Patrick. Fortunately for everyone involved, that shipmate is a loyal citizen of the United States.'

'He told you.'

'He told his chain of command, which is what he's supposed to do.'

'And you bungled it.'

'Eldredge had help. Major help.'

'Who?'

'We're not sure. All we know is that Eldredge is in the wind and likely with Patrick. We've been searching since before we came north. No joy so far.'

'You just told me the government wasn't completely incompetent.'

'Well, no doubt things will go much better once you're on the scene.'

'They might.'

'We'll see.'

'You're really going to let him go?' Desmarais asked. 'He's needed here.'

'You shouldn't deny your people when you need them,' Schweitzer said. 'It's kind of Officer 101.'

'Officer 101 is getting the job done,' Desmarais said. 'And I'd be in a better position to know, since I'm actually an officer.'

'If you labor under the delusion that officers actually do anything, then you haven't had very good noncommissioned officers guiding you.'

'I've had just about enough—'

'So have I,' Ghaznavi cut him off. 'Joe, step outside and let me talk to the Colonel for a minute. Someone's here to see you.'

Schweitzer took a shaking step toward the door, slowly easing his weight onto the leg, ensuring it was steady before lifting his foot to take another step.

'Any day now, Mr Yakecan,' Ghaznavi said.

Schweitzer moved more quickly and was overjoyed to find he could do it. He threw the door wide and let the fresh air of the waiting room wash over him. He hadn't realized how musty his sickbed had smelled until he stepped outside.

''Lo, Joe.' Mankiller was leaning her chair against the wall, balanced precariously on its back legs. 'How's the lung?'

'Reinflated.' Schweitzer smiled at the sight of her. He hadn't realized how much he'd missed her worn, easygoing style. 'Hurts when I breathe.'

'Pain means you're alive. Count your blessin's.'

'Trying to, boss.'

'Aw, hell.' Mankiller rocked her chair forward, letting it *thunk* onto all four legs, stood. 'I ain't your boss no more, Joe. Not now.'

'How's Grampy?'

'He's not real happy to be here. Don' like small towns, let alone a city like Yellowknife, but he's no fool. He knows what he's into.'

'Yeah. I guess he does. Once I get cleaned up and dressed, maybe I can go see him?'

'I think he'd like that. He's jus' been readin' and cookin' to pass the time, so maybe he'd scare us up a meal.'

'Sure. What's your plan?'

'Once they let Grampy go? Guess I'll head back to town and work. Rebuildin's gonna take some time.'

'They're not going to let Grampy go, Sheriff. Probably not you, either. Not sure they'll ever rebuild the town.'

Mankiller smiled. 'White folks spend a lot of time tellin' me how it's gonna be. They're pretty much always wrong.'

Schweitzer smiled. 'Seems like it.'

'So, you're gonna keep me company 'til I convince 'em?'

'Actually, I need to be getting on, Sheriff.'

'Your boy,' Mankiller said.

Schweitzer nodded. 'They tried to tell me how it was going to be, too. They were wrong.'

Mankiller laughed. 'Good luck, Joe. I'd go with you if I didn't have Grampy to tend to.'

'You don't mind?'

'Heck, why would I mind?'

'Because' – Schweitzer gestured at his chest – 'because of who I am.'

'People die,' Mankiller said. 'That's the way of things. At least I got to pull you out of the drink and breathe life into you. At least I get to see Joe's face and remember. You're all right, you know? I suppose if someone else had ta be Joe, I'm glad it's you.'

'Thanks,' Schweitzer said. The word caught in his throat.

'Don' mention it. Why don' you get scrubbed up and we'll see what Grampy's got on the stove?'

Schweitzer turned away and moved down the hallway toward the showers. It took him a long time, and he had to stop more than once, leaning against the wall and pausing to catch his breath. A doorway stood opposite him, opening onto a nurse's station. An empty desk stood beyond with a computer atop it, bright screen still not yet gone into sleep mode.

Schweitzer looked over his shoulder, limped the few steps to the chair, and slumped into it. Bringing up a browser using only his left hand took some doing, but he managed. The machine was online, the Internet at his fingertips. He realized with a start that he hadn't so much as accessed the Internet since this all had started. It was one of an ocean of things, from eating to sleeping, that had simply faded into the background. He hadn't known how much he'd missed them until Joe Yakecan's body had made it possible for him to experience them again.

But as much as he wanted to indulge in the simple pleasure of surfing the web, catching up on the news he had missed while he'd been . . . gone, there was only one thing he urgently needed to see.

He punched in the address for Craigslist and began to search the personals. He tried a few cities over a few dates before giving up. There was simply too much noise to find what he was after. What was it Eldredge had said he would post? *I'm more Mark Twain than Bettie Page.*

Either one of those names alone might have yielded quite a few responses, but not both together. Schweitzer searched on those terms. Nothing. He went back a week, then two. Still nothing. He was considering standing up, moving on to the showers before the nurse came back, but he figured he may as well be exhaustive. He didn't know when he'd get the chance to look again. Eldredge might have been captured or killed for all he knew, and his son with him. Eldredge had said he'd post weekly, after all.

Schweitzer opened the parameters to a month and searched again.

And gasped.

And now he did stand up but only after he closed the browser window. There was no reason to let the nurse know where the Cell's lead scientist had fled to, where he had taken Patrick.

Schweitzer no longer wanted a shower. He no longer

wanted food. All he wanted now was to return to his room where Ghaznavi and Desmarais still stood, to give them the news, to get the mission started.

The hallway seemed to stretch on for miles, and as he inched his way down it, he thought of how much farther it would be to Mexico and the search for his son.

It would be a long road, to be sure. He was used to long roads and the hardship of moving down them.

But it would be worth it.

Because when he found his boy, he could fold his child's head into his warm arms, hold it to his chest, against his beating heart.

Glossary of Military Acronyms and Slang

ABC's – Airway, breathing, circulation. First responders check these vital signs to ensure a patient's vitality. Direct-action teams check them to ensure that a target has been neutralized.

Bird – Aviation asset such as a helicopter or fixed-wing aircraft.

Bleed out – Death via blood loss.

BMF – Boat maintenance facility.

BSD – Berkley Systems Distribution. A variant of the UNIX computer operating system.

BUD/S – Basic Underwater Demolition/SEAL training. The six-month training course that all sailors must graduate to become US Navy SEALs. BUD/S alone does not make one a SEAL, and additional training is required. BUD/S is intensely grueling, with an 80 percent attrition rate.

Carbine – A long gun with a shorter barrel than a rifle. Carbines are better suited to combat in close quarters than their longer cousins.

CAS – Close air support. Action taken by fixed- or rotary-wing platforms to assist ground troops.

CDC – Centers for Disease Control.

CGIS – Coast Guard Investigative Service. A unit of the United States Coast Guard that investigates crimes in which the Coast Guard may have an interest.

Chemlight – Also known as 'glow sticks'. A short plastic tube filled with chemical compounds in separate compartments. When the stick is bent, the barrier between the compartments breaks, allowing the compounds to mix. The resultant chemical reaction causes the tube to emit a strong colored glow.

CIA – Central Intelligence Agency.

Cleared hot – Authorized to open fire.

CO – Commanding officer.

Condition Black – A state of paralysis brought on by sudden, unanticipated violence.

Condition Yellow – A state of hypervigilance where a person is constantly anticipating sudden violence.

CONEX – A type of intermodal shipping container.

'Coords' – Coordinates.

COP – Combat outpost.

Corpsman – Job title for United States Navy personnel assigned to field medical duties.

CQB – Close-quarters battle. Refers to the tactics of breaching and clearing confined spaces such as a building or ship.

CSIS – Canadian Security Intelligence Service. Comparable to the CIA in the United States.

Danger close – Indicates a friendly force in close proximity to a target of fire, usually from artillery or close air support.

DFAC – Dining facility.

Dust off – Evacuation via helicopter.

Dynamic – An operational state wherein the enemy is aware of the assault team's presence, rendering stealth unnecessary.

Embed – Embedded or one who is embedded.

EMT – Emergency Medical Technician.

'Eyes on' – Indicates the speaker is observing the subject of the sentence. 'I have eyes on the door'.

Fire team – The smallest operational military unit, usually composed of four to five members.

FLIR – Forward-looking infrared.

FNG – Fucking new guy/girl. A person who is newly assigned to a military unit. This friendly pejorative is meant to indicate the likelihood that the described will make mistakes.

GAU-19 – A .50 caliber, electrically powered Gatling gun.

GROM – Grupa Reagowania Operacyjno-Manewrowego. Poland's elite counterterrorism unit.

Hawk – Armed aviation asset such as a helicopter or fixed-wing aircraft.

Hazmat – Hazardous materials.

HVAC – Heating, ventilation, and air conditioning.

'In the wind' – Whereabouts unknown.

JSOC – Joint Special Operations Command.

JTF – Joint Task Force.

K-9 – Canine. A unit that employs working dogs for law enforcement or military operations. The term is also used to refer to the dogs themselves.

KC – Kill-Capture. A direct-action mission wherein the team's first goal is to capture a human target. If the team is unable to capture the target without risking harm to their own number, they will kill him/her. A successful KC must conclude with the target either captured or dead.

'Keep it dark' – Keep it secret.

Klick – Slang for a kilometer.

LNO – Liaison Officer.

LWIR – Longwave infrared.

MAM – Military-aged male.

MANPAD – Man-portable air-defense system. A shoulder-mounted missile launcher.

MASINT – Measurement and Signature Intelligence. Intelligence gathered from scientific instruments such as undersea acoustic sensors to detect submarines, or radiation sensors for nuclear detonations.

MCE – Mapping and Charting Establishment. Comparable to the National Reconnaissance Office and National Geospatial Intelligence Agency in the United States, the MCE provides mapping and imagery intelligence support to Canadian intelligence services and the armed forces.

MCPO – Master Chief Petty Officer.

Medevac – Medical evacuation. An emergency retrieval and removal of a casualty from a crisis zone. The patient is stabilized and transferred as quickly as possible to a medical facility where adequate care can be provided.

MGRS – Military Grid Reference System.

'Mikes' – Minutes.

MOA – Minute of angle. A measurement of the accuracy of a shot taking the distance it was fired from into consideration.

MWR – Morale, Welfare, and Recreation center.

NCS – National Clandestine Service (formerly the Directorate of Operations or DO). The branch of the CIA responsible for intelligence collection.

NGA – National Geospatial Intelligence Agency. The US intelligence agency primarily responsible for geospatial intelligence, also known as GEOINT. Formerly known as the National Imagery and Mapping Agency or NIMA.

NOC – Non-official Cover. The government denies all association with NOC persons and organizations, even in the event of a compromise.

NODs – Night optical devices. Mechanical devices that permit the user to see in the dark.

'Off to see the wizard' – Slang used to indicate a visit to a mental-health professional.

Op – Operation. Refers to any military undertaking with a discrete beginning and end.

Open-Source – Intelligence derived from publicly available sources.

Operator – Members of special forces elements who engage in special operations. Term connotes members of direct-action elements whose primary tasking is breaching hardened targets and neutralizing a dug-in enemy.

OPLAN – Operational plan.

PA – Public address system.

PAX – Passenger or passengers.

Pipe hitter – A fighter. A person whose principal occupation is the use of force.

PJ – Pararescue jumpers, also known as pararescuemen. A special operations element within the United States Air Force.

Platoon – A military organizational unit consisting of twenty-eight to sixty-four members.

PMO – Paramilitary officer. CIA special-skills officers specializing in military operations. Usually drawn from the military special operations community.

PTSD – Post-traumatic stress disorder.

'Push a button' – Assassinate.

'Push a button on someone' – Assassinate someone.

'Put a siren on it' – Exhortation to perform a given task very quickly.

QRF – Quick Reaction Force. A standby troop of warfighters positioned to respond rapidly to an emergency.

R and R – Rest and relaxation.

RCMP – Royal Canadian Mounted Police.

'Read on/Read in' – The act of authorizing an individual for access to a compartment of classified information. Such an individual is said to be read onto or read into the program.

ROE – Rules of engagement.

SAD – Special Activities Division. A division within the CIA in charge of covert activities.

Seabees – CBs, the construction battalions of the United States Navy.

SEAL – 'Sea, Air, and Land'. A special operations force of the United States Navy.

SITREP – Situation report.

SO2 – Special Warfare Operator 2nd Class.

SOAR – Special Operations Aviation Regiment. A special operations force of the United States Army that provides both general and specialized aviation support.

SOC – Supernatural Operations Corps.

SOCOM – Special Operations Command.

SOF – Special Operations Forces. Also referred to as 'SF', as an acronym for 'Special Forces'.

SOG – Special Operations Group. A division within SAD responsible for tactical paramilitary operations.

Spectre – A flying gunship.

SQT – SEAL Qualification Training.

Squirters – A colloquial term for those enemy who flee a targeted location.

SSCI – Senate Select Committee on Intelligence. The senatorial committee charged with overseeing federal intelligence operations.

SSG – Special Services Group. Pakistan's Special Operations forces.

SSO – Special Security Officer. An individual charged with the oversight of the security clearances of personnel and the proper storage, handling, and disposal of classified information. SSO is also the acronym for 'Special Skills Officer', a federal government title usually used for various functions within the CIA.

SST – Special Security Team. An elite counterterrorism unit in the Japanese Coast Guard.

Stick – A group of operators. Named for the long, narrow formation when they stack on entryways.

TATP – Triacetone triperoxide. A homemade explosive popular in improvised explosive devices. Easily made from household chemicals, it is highly unstable and extremely susceptible to heat, shock, or friction. It is extremely risky to employ TATP as ordnance, as it is just as likely to harm the user as it is the target.

TCCC – Tactical combat casualty care. First-responder medical training given to operators. It is designed to allow nonmedical personnel to engage in triage under fire and to stabilize casualties for medevac.

TIC – Troops in contact. Indicates that the speaker is engaged and fighting with the enemy.

'Tin your way out' – Referring to the silver color of a police officer's badge, tinning your way out refers to using any kind of government credential to evade consequences. Likewise, a government agent can also 'tin their way in' to restricted access facilities.

TL;DR – 'Too long; didn't read.'

430

VAX – Virtual Address Extension. An antiquated computer operating system.

VTC – Video teleconference.

WIA – Wounded in action.

YN1 – Yeoman First Class. A senior enlisted member of the US Navy or Coast Guard specializing in administration.

Acknowledgments

Just a few short years ago, I was an aspirant who never thought he'd publish a novel. This book in your hands is my sixth out with a major publisher, and I currently have three more under contract. What's more, by the time this book prints, I'll have been on a major prime-time TV show, signed my first deal to write history, and announced a board game based on my Shadow Ops novels.

My point (apart from bragging) is this: I never, ever, ever thought any of these things would happen. And they weren't happening, until suddenly, they were. You have your span of years on this earth, and while I can't promise you'll hit the marks you set, I do think you may as well keep aiming for them. Don't give up. I'm so unspeakably glad I didn't.

Of course, none of it would be possible without you, the readers and fans. It's impossible to thank each of you individually, but those of you who've caught up to me at cons have hopefully gotten at least a handshake, a signature, and a brief chance to chat. I also owe thanks to all the people who believed in me and gave me my shot: Anne Sowards and the staff of Ace/Roc, Joshua Bilmes and the folks at JABberwocky Literary Agency, Laura Fuest Silva and her crew at Endemol Shine, Glenn Geller and his people at CBS, Anji Cornette and the brilliant actors and engineers at GraphicAudio, and Deputy Commissioner Jessica Tisch and her command at the NYPD. And this doesn't even cover the legions of friends, family, fellow

432

authors, and gamers, my endless nerd tribe. To thank you all properly would be a book in itself.

But I do want to single out Peter V. Brett, as I have done for six books running now, because he is both Aaron and Hur to my Moses, holding my arms up until the battle is won. Thanks.

Control Point

Myke Cole

All over the world people are 'coming up latent' – developing new and terrifying abilities. Untrained and panicked, they are summoning storms, raising the dead, and setting everything they touch ablaze.

US Army Lieutenant Oscar Britton has always done his duty, even when it means working alongside the feared Supernatural Operations Corps, hunting down and taking out those with newfound magical talents. But when he manifests a rare, startling power of his own and finds himself a marked man, all bets are off.

On the run from his former colleagues, Britton is driven into an underground shadow world, where he is about to learn that magic has changed all the rules he's ever known . . . and that his life isn't the only thing he's fighting for.

'Realism is tightly interwoven throughout Cole's writing, giving the book such power . . . A nonstop thrill ride that's almost impossible to put down' *Fantasy Faction*

'A great book' Patrick Rothfuss, *New York Times* bestselling author of *The Wise Man's Fear*

'Hands down, the best military fantasy I've ever read' Ann Aguirre, *USA Today* bestselling author of *Perdition*

978 0 7553 9397 8

HEADLINE

Fortress Frontier

Myke Cole

The Great Reawakening did not come quietly. Suddenly people from all corners of the globe began to develop terrifying powers – summoning fire, manipulating earth, opening portals and decimating flesh. Overnight the rules had changed . . . but not for everyone.

Alan Bookbinder might be a Colonel in the US Army, but in his heart he knows he's just a desk jockey, a clerk with a silver eagle on his jacket. But one morning he is woken by a terrible nightmare and overcome by an ominous drowning sensation. Something is very, very wrong.

Forced into working for the Supernatural Operations Corps in a new and dangerous world, Bookbinder's only hope of finding a way back to his family will mean teaming up with former SOC operator and public enemy number one: Oscar Britton. They will have to put everything on the line if they are to save thousands of soldiers trapped inside a frontier fortress on the brink of destruction, and show the people back home the stark realities of a war that threatens to wipe out everything they're trying to protect.

'Propulsive . . . Highly entertaining . . . Reads like an intense game of Dungeons & Dragons' *Kirkus Reviews*

'There are some truly surprising twists and turns . . .' Tor.com

978 0 7553 9399 2

HEADLINE

Breach Zone

Myke Cole

The Great Reawakening has left Latent people with a stark choice: either use their newfound magical powers in the service of the goverment, or choose the path of the Selfer, and be hunted down and killed by the Supernatural Operations Corps.

For Lieutenant Colonel Jan Thorsson, the SOC is the closest thing to family he's ever known. But when his efforts to save thousands of soldiers leads to the impeachment of the President, he's suddenly cut off from the military and in the same position as his rival Oscar Britton, an outcast criminal who is leading the fight for Latent equality.

This latest schism is perfect for the walking weapon known as Scylla, who is slowly but surely building a vast and terrible army. The Selfers and the SOC will have to learn to work together if they are to have any chance of preventing a massacre. Because this time, Scylla is bringing the fight to the streets of New York.

'*Breach Zone* is filled to the flanks with action, intrigue, and simply all-out mayhem . . . A book that you simply shouldn't miss' *Fantasy Book Critic*

'Pulse-hammering action . . . Myke Cole has outdone himself' *52 Book Reviews*

978 0 7553 9401 2

HEADLINE

Gemini Cell

Myke Cole

US Navy SEAL Jim Schweitzer is a fierce warrior and consummate professional. When he sees something he shouldn't on a covert mission gone wrong, he finds himself – and his family – in the crosshairs.

The enemy bring the battle straight to Jim's front door, taking him down together with his wife and son. It should be the end for Jim, but his story is just beginning . . .

Raised from the dead and left to wrestle with new powers he doesn't understand, Jim is called to duty as the ultimate warrior for top-secret unit known as the Gemini Cell. But he will soon realise his new superiors are determined to keep him in the dark on everything – including about the true fate of his wife and son . . .

'His best work to date . . .' Tor.com

'Myke Cole's *Gemini Cell* is military fantasy at its best!' *Fantasy Hot List*

'A powerful and engaging novel . . . Highly, highly recommended' *SFF World*

978 1 4722 1189 7

HEADLINE

Javelin Rain

Myke Cole

Javelin: the loss of a national security asset with strategic impact.
Rain: a crisis of existential proporations.

Javelin Rain incidents must be resolved immediately, by any means necessary, no matter the cost . . .

Being a US Navy SEAL was Jim Schweitzer's life until the day he was killed.

Now, his escape from the government that brought him back from the dead has been coded 'Javelin Rain'. Schweitzer and his family are on the run from his unit and, while he may be immortal, his wife and son are not.

It's up to Jim to keep his family safe and free from the clutches of his former masters, whose plans could spell disaster not only for him, but for the entire nation . . .

'Military fantasy like you've never seen it before' Peter V. Brett

'Character rich and action driven – a Molotov cocktail of human weaknesses and superhuman abilities' Robin Hobb

978 1 4722 1191 0

HEADLINE